Over The Hills Of Green

by E.V. Svetova

Over The Hills Of Green

a novel

E.V. Svetova

Over The Hills Of Green
Published by Ananke Press

Interior and cover design by Ananke Press
Photography by Alex AG © 2019

ISBN: 978-0-9849040-6-8 (paperback)
ISBN: 978-0-9849040-8-2 (hardcover)
ISBN: 978-0-9849040-7-5 (kindle)
ISBN: 978-0-9849040-9-9 (ebook)

Ananke Press
178 Columbus Avenue, #230137, New York, NY 10023
anankepress.com
info@anankepress.com

For my kin.

Contents

SEEMING

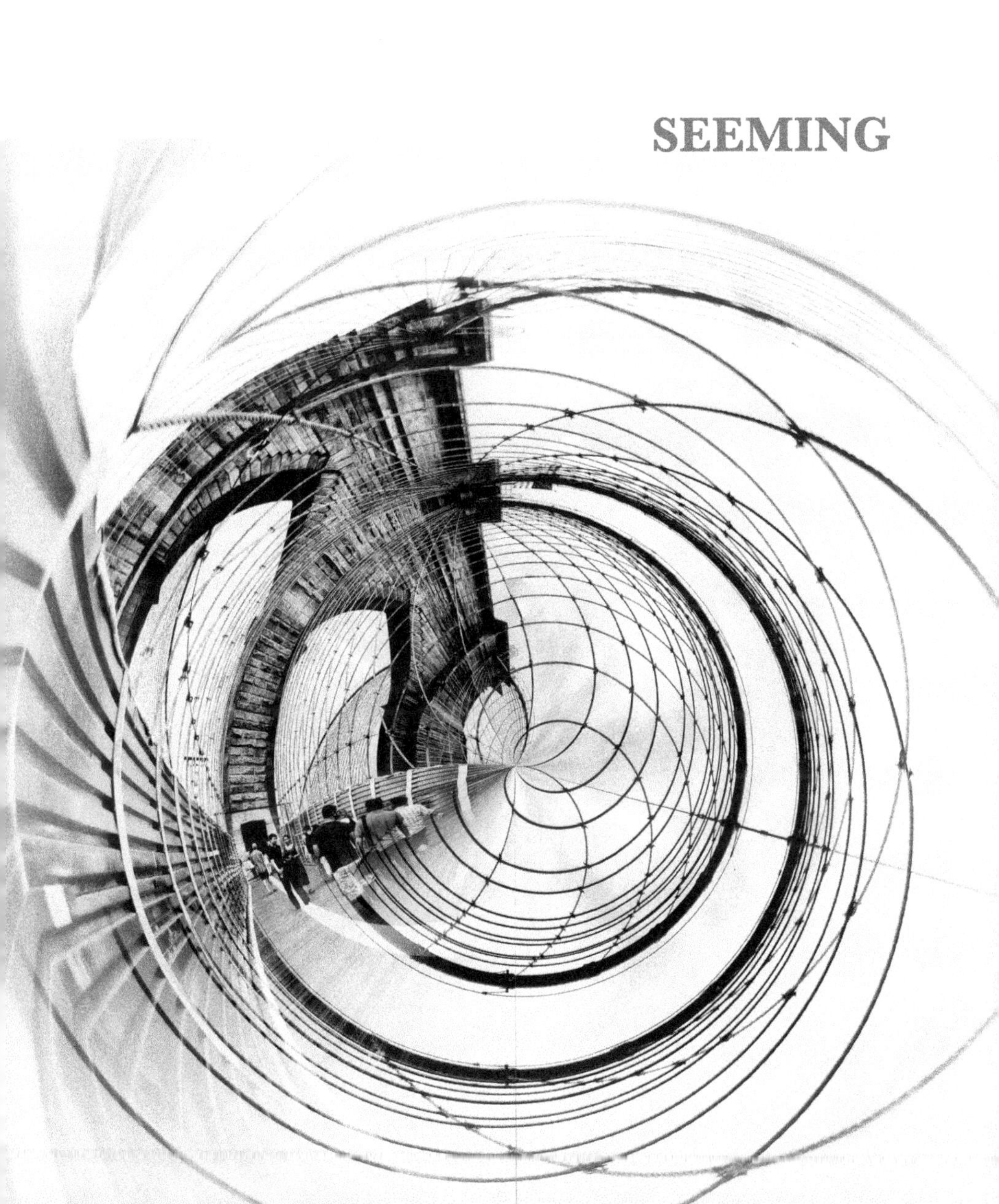

Thursday, November 27

The gods who still believe in us raise their voices, and he can no longer pretend to ignore them. *Up! Up! Up!* they sing in an excruciating harmony, so he gathers himself and comes out into the cold light. He is afraid of heights but obeys the voices. Up it is.

Above Broadway at Seventy-Seventh the sky is crowded with grotesque floating shapes. Deformed animals and bloated clowns are jerked about by strong gusts of wind. He approaches the parade. To calm his nerves, he considers asking for change—usually the revelers are eager almsgivers—but the voices in his head shriek in protest. He is relieved because now *Up!* should be understood as *North!*

He shuffles his aching feet up Broadway, stopping by diners until somebody hands him a piece of sugary food and a hot drink. By the time his body awakens, the sun is high. He doesn't need to see it in the overcast sky, he remembers it. Remembering is what he has. Against his best self-interest, he remembers snow. Snow is like that, he has to remember it. The day he forgets, it will never snow again. People on the inside don't know it. They don't have what he has, and they're better off for it. It's best not to know what you can't have.

His trek terminates in Riverside Park above One Hundredth. It's early afternoon, but beneath the trees eternal twilight reigns. He stumbles off the path onto the crispy ground. At once, he is overcome with nausea, which means he's close. There is always a shift when worlds collide. Then, he sees the light behind the trunks. There it is. Brighter than the sun, like they all are.

The body lies face down on the ground, covered with the silver silk of its hair, only the sharp shoulder blades poking through. Underneath the shroud of hair is bare skin. It glows. He has never seen anything more beautiful.

He doesn't dare touch it with his hands, instead kicks it a little. The hair spills onto the ground. It is time to perform his task. He weeps, but obeys. Its slippery luminosity wrapped around his fist, he cuts the hair off. A quick slice, without stirring the body. Let it lie. Nothing else he can do, except maybe throw some leaves over it.

The gods reward him with a song of true love. He shudders in ecstasy, his gratitude habitually infused with self-loathing. It hurts to know love you can't have.

He pulls a rubber band off his wrist and ties the severed hair where the ends gather into a soft thick brush. Cradling the precious ponytail under the many layers of his overclothes he climbs up the slope back to the path. Farther on, he notices a jogger, but the jogger looks through him, because people on the inside are unable see the ones on the outside, and choose not see the ones on the edge.

Friday, November 28

The monsters, Anna told herself, *aren't real.* She took a deep, practiced breath and felt her feet. The knot of anxiety in the pit of her stomach coiled one last nauseating loop and came to a stop.

She wasn't even supposed to have been there, her ER rotation was Wednesdays. She was heading upstairs to the clinic and stopped by to drop off a diagnostic manual she'd borrowed, when she heard a commotion. A male nurse hit the floor, nearly knocking her off her feet. A large man blocked the corridor, roaring, rolling his wild, desperate eyes. Everybody pressed their backs against the wall.

The wild-eyed man was a repeat patient, his name was Willis, his diagnosis—paranoid schizophrenia. This time he'd been delivered to Bellevue psych ER after breaking down on a subway platform, freaked out by invisible monsters. He was being uncuffed when he tore himself away, slamming into the intake nurse. Out of nowhere, he pulled a pair of scissors and waved it violently, barely missing the young transit police officer who'd brought him in.

"Drop 'em, Sir!" barked the cop. No recognition in the man's eyes. With the look of a cornered animal, he jerked the open scissors up to his throat. The fluorescent light struck the blade, and Anna saw the pulsing vein where the metal bit into his skin.

A patient at the other end of the corridor wailed, startling her. Willis didn't flinch. A disconnect. A broken line. *He can't hear*, realized Anna with dream-like clarity.

"Didn't you search him?" the nurse, still on his haunches, hissed to the hospital guard.

"I didn't *strip*-search him." The guard cursed under his breath. "He's a frequent flyer, never been violent. . ."

Willis stared in their direction, cocking his head dog-like. His breathing was labored, with an asthmatic wheeze. And just like that, Anna knew what to do. Ignoring the guard's warning hand, she pushed away from the wall and stepped forward.

With a lurch, the world slowed down and came in focus: each hair of the man's stubble reflected in the dull mirror of the scissor blade; the sharp note of hospital disinfectant cut through the cloying stink of unwashed flesh; the rubber soles shuffled on linoleum across the corridor; the metal against the skin—all pulsing in time to the beat of blood pumping in her temples.

She opened her arms and spoke in a barely audible whisper, "Mr. Willis? Can you hear me?" Inside, she felt the knot loosening. She visualized a silvery glowing thread stretching outward. On an exhale, she tossed the line.

"I hear you, but nobody hears me." Willis shifted to face her. Their eyes connected, locked. The line caught. "They're real, the monsters. Nobody believes me."

"I believe you." For a split-second she feared she'd said too much. Inside, she tugged, reeling in. "I want to help you. Will you let me?"

"Yeah." His Adam's apple twitched against the blade. "I . . . need help. I need meds."

"I'll get you some. Promise. But will you please do something for me?" She took another step. "Please?" She was within an arm's reach now—the line between them sang, stretched to its limit. "May I have the scissors?"

Willis pointed the blade at her, and back at himself. His hand trembled, went flaccid, dropped. Gently she pulled the scissors from his fingers, and slackened the line.

Everything sped back to normal: a blur of white coats and blue uniforms, arms around her shoulders pulling her to the side, away from Willis who was being tackled by the guards. Anna was patted on the back and asked if she were okay, over and over. She assured everyone she was fine. The psychiatrist on duty praised her call identifying a hearing impairment stemming from schizophrenia and comorbid asthma as "exceptionally intuitive for a non-clinician." Only when the young transit cop, blushing, reached to shake her hand did Anna notice she still had the blade clenched in her fist. She stared at a red line fading across her palm. *Didn't hurt a bit.*

Afterwards, in the bathroom, she scrubbed her hands till they went numb. The antibacterial foam smelled like a mix of alcohol and flowers—*a lilac schnapps*—but the metallic taste permeated her, lingering on her tongue. She rinsed her mouth with cold water, breathed slowly, in and out. The coolness was comforting.

It had been a while since she'd had an episode. The anxiety self-help protocol had been working. She'd been in control for years. She was in control now. Holding on to that thought, Anna headed to the morning conference.

"And how was your Thanksgiving?" Anna's counseling workshop partner, Michael Campbell, propped the conference room door with his shoulder: armed and loaded, a brown glazed coffee mug like an organic extension of his hand.

"Just a dinner with family. Yours?"

"Chinese and a movie."

With a belated sense of guilt, Anna realized she could have invited him to her parents' home for dinner—like most interns in her group, he was a transplant living in the dorms. *No need getting too familiar*, she reminded herself: their internship was ending in a few months, and it was time to brace for the loss. She didn't want to miss him.

"But never mind me," Michael continued brightly. "You're the talk of the town. Preventing a suicide by a violent paranoid schizophrenic before your first cup of coffee. Impressive."

"Come on, it wasn't like that. I just took scissors away from a mildly agitated man."

"How does it make you feel?"

She shot him a mock-warning glare.

The medical doctor on call reported on the previous night's events: the adolescent on suicide watch slept through the night, the sleepwalker tried to exit the observation unit and was promptly returned, the paranoid ex-con responded well to medication, and the early morning incident in the ER was efficiently resolved due to the quick thinking of their own Anna Reilly. The staff and the other interns looked at her, and there was a small buzz of approval around the room. Anna squirmed in her seat. Not that she was a stranger to spotlight—having been a serious Nordic skier all through her teens, she was accustomed to standing on the top tier of the podium—yet, ever since she was a kid, conditional approval always triggered her resentment. Being loved for her worth had always felt to her as worthless as not being loved at all. But, catching Michael's professionally keen gaze, she readjusted, making sure her imposing frame projected confident composure.

"Seriously, how are you?" whispered Michael.

"Seriously, I'm fine."

"Now, for last night's admissions," announced the psychiatrist on duty, Dr. Cohen.

Two of Anna's four cases had been closed a week before, so she was up for a fresh one. Thomas, the medical intern, glanced at her and turned to his notes. Just great. The last thing she needed today was his attitude. In the complex and subtle hospital hierarchy, all the student interns shared the bottom of the totem pole, but true to Sayre's law, the lower the stakes, the more bitter the rivalry: medical students found a reason to look down on psych grad students, psychiatrists saw themselves above clinical psychologists, who, in turn, entertained notions of a mild superiority over cognitive psychologists, like Anna. She had to be impeccable just to keep up.

Anna didn't mind. She'd always run her best races in the worst weather.

"An elderly female presenting with depression." Dr. Cohen leafed through his notes. "A repeat hospitalization."

Next to Anna, Michael's hand flew up. Seeing the older man squint at his ID tag, Michael offered: "Campbell."

Typical Michael, so cognizant of the subtle signs, so accommodating. Selflessly volunteering for a decidedly dreary case. Anna, a cognitive psych grad, was lucky to have been paired with a clinical psych postgrad. She'd learned more from watching Michael lead a group than from any course book. He was a natural.

"Next," said Dr. Cohen, "A homeless male with what presents like—huh, what do you know, a retrograde amnesia. Voluntary, compliant, had a comprehensive medical and, due to the nature of his hospitalization, an MRI."

"I'll take him." Thomas half-raised his hand.

"Looks like Dr. Stevens has already assigned him to . . . Anna Reilly?"

Anna bit the inside of her cheek to hide a triumphant grin. Before taking off for the Thanksgiving weekend, her supervisor—who happened to be the head of inpatient psychology—had left her a thoughtful and generous gift. Clear-cut cases fitting Anna's academic research were hard to come by, and a full-fledged amnesiac was a rare treat indeed. Handing such a juicy morsel to an intern was a genuine gesture of support, even if it made Anna look like a teacher's pet.

"What should I prioritize," she asked, ignoring Thomas's scowl. "Establishing his identity or gaining diagnostic clarity?"

"Begin with a mental status exam," said Dr. Cohen. "The diagnostic investigation itself can have a therapeutic effect. If his episode doesn't clear within seventy-two hours, and he is admitted, he'll undergo a standard battery of tests. In the meantime, it's your call. Next!"

Current cases updated and new cases assigned, the meeting broke up, and the staff went off to start their day. Anna and Michael walked out together.

"Congrats on a curious case." Michael carefully clanked his glazed mug against her stainless steel thermos. "You don't seem too enthused about it, though."

"I am. Here's my happy dance." She rolled her head in a little slide, her shoulders relaxing.

He laughed as if she'd made the wittiest joke. She would miss him.

"So, you think you could use the amnesiac for your paper?"

"Won't know until after the interview. His memory impairment could be due to substance abuse or a head injury or a psychiatric condition, all of which would put him outside of my measurement model. See, what I need is a person who copes with trauma by generating a delusion while remaining psychiatrically sound otherwise. It's a pretty narrow human subject pool."

"Or, a pretty wide one." Michael winked.

"Yeah, as in the whole of New York City."

"Why settle? The whole of the humanity. We all cope with the trauma of everyday life, some more elaborately than others, and memory—well, memory is notoriously subjective. But, say you establish evidence of false memories accompanying a psychogenic amnesia and take him on. How do you get an informed consent form signed by a man who can't remember if he is capable of informed consent?"

"Odds are he recovers his memory by the time I'm done with the initial round of interviews."

"Here's your opportunity to practice your psychoanalytic skills. I keep telling you, they're better than you—"

"I won't get to be his treating therapist," Anna said quickly. "It's unethical for a researcher to get this close to a subject. I mean, one on one with patients is not my thing, anyway."

"I don't get it," said Michael. "I know you must have jumped through hoops to get this internship. Here's your chance to work with live people, intimately. You do get excellent results. The PTSD vet last month? And the strung out girl last week—you did great with her. Your mirroring was effective. Yet you do anything to avoid one on one."

Maybe because I don't like what I see in the mirror.

"I'm a cognitive scientist, not a counselor. Intimacy isn't in my required skill set."

Michael nodded, looked about, and spoke with a quiet urgency, "Listen, about this morning, it might not feel like a big deal now, but you're talking to someone about it, right?"

"I have a nine o'clock supervision session with Dr. Stevens on Wednesday."

"I mean, your personal therapist," said Michael. Clearly, to him, a clinician coming from trauma counseling, it was inconceivable that she wouldn't have a personal therapist. Anna's slight embarrassment mixed with momentary irritation, the two cancelling each other out.

Since her face didn't give anything away, and Michael kept looking at her with genuine concern, Anna bent her neck to give him one of those upward, soft glances that are meant to convey silent, noncommittal gratitude. She was a good head taller than him, and the back of her neck echoed with a dull ache, a reminder that some expressions of emotion were psychically challenging for a woman like her.

A fast-eyed nurse was waiting at the ward to introduce Anna to the new case. According to the police report, the mid-twenties Caucasian male had been discovered the night before in a pile of leaves in Riverside Park, nude. The jogger who called him in initially reported a corpse, but when the police arrived they were surprised to find the young man deeply asleep. Once shaken awake, he appeared disoriented and failed to identify himself. Eventually, he communicated that he had no memory of his identity or past. He was photographed, fingerprinted, and dropped off at Bellevue, where he underwent a standard medical examination. He consented to all the tests.

He had scrapes on his face and hands, but no damage to his head or sexual trauma. His blood work came back negative for STDs, HIV, drugs, and alcohol. Although naked in the November cold, he showed no hypothermia. In fact, his body temperature was slightly elevated as if he had been running a low fever. Despite appearing slightly malnourished, he had been deemed exceptionally fit and healthy—"For a man in his circumstances," added the nurse, rolling her eyes.

Anna leafed through the examination report: the man's body hair had been removed, probably by electrolysis. *Kinky*. Her smirk faded when she saw a snapshot of round, pale pink scars in an oddly regular pattern—like holes on a flute—along his forearms: healed cigarette burns. *Self-harm?* The round scars also ran along his spine. *More likely, torture.*

She shut the folder. This new case excited and disturbed her in equal measure.

"The officer who brought him in said he must have been engaged in the sex trade." The nurse made a face. "No wonder, with his looks . . ."

"What about his looks?"

Without answering, the nurse pushed open the door to the interview room, a small square space painted in institutional beige with a desk in the middle and an empty chair to one side. Across the desk, a young man lounged in his hard chair with an out-of-place air of serenity. His bandaged hands, resting on the table, made him look like a prizefighter—or, rather, an East Village boutique mannequin displaying a prizefighter Halloween costume. His hair, cropped unevenly above his shoulders, was so blond it looked synthetic. A raw graze marred the smooth skin over his cheekbone. The oversized hospital-issued pajamas hung off his shoulders as if off a rack. Yet none of this could hide the obvious: the young man was strikingly handsome. His exquisite, almost feminine beauty felt ostentatious in the bare room of a mental ward. As Anna entered, he lifted his face: wide-set gray eyes flashed, dark eyebrows furrowed, finely cut mouth tightened. Anna could've sworn she'd seen this face before, but it was impossible. *That* she would have remembered.

"Good morning." She made sure her voice projected warm authority. "I am—"

"Ahn-nah," exhaled the young man, then threw back his head and burst into wild, hysterical laughter.

Anna and the nurse exchanged glances.

The young man stopped laughing as abruptly as he'd started, and fixed his attentive gaze on her. His clear eyes were rimmed with long eyelashes, thick and black, as if painted with mascara.

"You know him?" asked the nurse under her breath.

"'Course not! He must have read my badge." Anna straightened the ID card on her chest.

"I'll stay."

"No, it's all right." This case was hers and hers only.

"The security guard is down the corridor," whispered the nurse and left, half-closing the door behind her.

Slowly, Anna pulled out the empty chair and sat, facing the man. His stare was making her self-conscious. Her casual pencil skirt squeezed her thighs, her turtleneck choked her throat, and she regretted not wearing the protective armor of a lab coat. The standard protocol of the mental status examination she'd performed countless times, in supervised training and with actual patients, evaporated from her memory. *Are you suicidal? Homicidal? Do you hear voices? See things?* What was she going to say—

He kept staring at her. She stared back. He had a curious double curve to his upper lip, a shadow of a smile lurking in the corners of his tight mouth.

"Your hair is long," he finally pronounced. His voice was low, smooth, melodic, and unambiguously masculine.

Mechanically Anna touched her hair, pulled back lacquer tight in a low ponytail. His inane statement hit a sore spot. What's next, his commenting on how tall she is? She'd heard it before— height is perceived as intimidating, long hair as unapproachable. A surge of anger cut through unease and helped her focus. She may not have been a natural, but she'd been well trained. By focusing on a physical feature he'd served her an opening, and she used it:

"How long have you been growing yours?"

"It hasn't been this short since I was a child." Mirroring her, he ran his fingers through his disheveled hair. The gauze bandage caught in the tangled strands. He pulled out a dry leaf.

Appearance, Anna wrote, and paused, giving him another look. She couldn't in her right mind put "gorgeous" on an MSE report, so she wrote, *youthful, fragile, ~~sexually ambiguous~~, unkempt, consistent with being found outdoors.*

"It should fall below my waist, that much I know," he added, twirling the leaf in his fingers.

"Why isn't it?"

"Someone must have cut it off."

"Why would anyone do such a thing?"

He shrugged one shoulder, tilting his head to the side. In contrast with his measured speech, his movement possessed an exaggerated, theatrical grace—no wonder the cops took him for a gay hooker.

"When I woke up without my long hair, I asked myself the same." He sounded bemused. "When they brought me here, a woman requested some of my piss. I found it odd, but did as bid. Next they wanted some of my blood. Clearly, your people have an unnatural fascination with bodily fluids. Makes me wonder what else they may ask for. This is a strange and terrible world you live in, Ahn-nah." He pronounced it with oddly open vowels and doubled consonants, making her plain name sound exotic and grand.

"If you call me by my name, wouldn't it be fair for me to call you by yours?"

"Why don't you?"

"Because I don't know it."

"But you must." He leaned across the table, making Anna want to lean back. She stayed in her place. Contrary to what she expected, the man didn't have body odor. Instead, there was a distinct freshness about him, like he had come from a glacier—a high, indefinable scent of snow.

"I don't know your name," Anna repeated firmly. "Would you please tell me?"

His angular face expressed disappointment. "So, you don't know me. When you walked in, I had a feeling—" He let out a soft groan, the way large dogs do. "I had a hope you would know me. See, I cannot honestly say that I know myself. My memory must be clouded by the hardship of my journey. I cannot even recall my name, although the men who brought me here called me John Doe."

"May I call you John?"

"John is as good a name as any."

Rapport: cooperative, wrote Anna.

"So, John, you mentioned a journey. What was it?"

"Why, my having traveled through space and time, of course."

Anna lowered her face to hide a smile. Despite the diversity of delusions, a human mind could concoct only a finite number of unique self-created narratives. A systematic methodology allowed them to be classified, and, hopefully, demystified, which she'd always found reassuring. Only so many stories in the world.

"Do you mind if I tape you?"

"I certainly do." His dark eyebrows came together. "Why should you bind me? I am here willingly. For now."

Anna put her phone on the table. Last month James, her gadget-freak stepdad, bought her a discreet microphone that turned her smartphone into a digital recorder: sensitive yet subtle enough not to alert the suspect, he'd said—*ever a cop*, she thought with tenderness.

"I'm asking if you don't mind me recording our conversation for later."

"With this?" John cocked his head. "I have never seen one of those."

"It's a new model. One, two, three."

When the recorder played Anna's voice back, John's eyebrows arched.

"Ah, how clever. Yes, you may record our conversation." He rolled his *r*s ever so slightly.

Speech: archaic, formal, slight accent, otherwise highly expressive.

"All right. For the record, do you know your age?"

He sighed. "No, I do not. But I feel as if I have lived through hundreds of winters."

"You don't look that old." She caught herself feeling uneasy commenting on the patient's appearance, as if his arresting beauty was a kind of unmentionable deformity.

"If you say so." He pursed his lips. "Truth be told, I feel I have lived and died."

"Those marks on your arms. Do they have anything to do with those feelings?"

He pushed up the sleeve of his hospital pajamas and caressed the inside of his forearm; so sensual was his gesture that fine hairs stood up on Anna's arms. She wanted to look away but forced herself to keep her eyes on the small, round scars along his radius. A good reminder that the attractive person in front of her was a trauma victim, someone in need of professional help.

"No," he said with conviction, finally looking back at her. "This is not a mark of death. Rather, a mark of another life. I understand, it sounds unlikely, but you must believe what I say to you."

"Tell me about that other life in which you . . . died?" asked Anna, scribbling, *Perception: experiential anomaly*.

Suddenly John hugged himself, like he was freezing, and began to rock back and forth with a little whimper.

"What is it?" Anna instinctively pressed against the back of her chair.

"I don't know who I am!" Tears filled his eyes. "I cannot recall! I sense the memory locked inside, yet lost to me. Pray you never know the torment of such a loss."

"It's all right, John, we'll skip it for now," said Anna quickly, and wrote, *Cognition: severely impaired memory, loss of identity.* "How far back can you remember?"

"Stars and snow were falling from the sky. On a hilltop I knelt, praying to be welcomed into my father's house . . . and snow covered me . . . and ages flowed by like a dream. Then, a door opened and I went through."

"What kind of door?"

"I have no words to explain!"

"Where did this door lead?"

"Nowhere— no, where and when, it led through time and space. I cannot—"

"We can talk about it later, when you remember. But one more question now: why did you come through the door?"

He drew a ragged breath.

"I followed my desire." His sharp teeth raked over his bottom lip. It glistened. "Why are you asking me these questions?"

"Because I want to help you." For a split-second Anna worried if her voice came out overly heartfelt, but her words seemed to have an immediate soothing effect. John exhaled with relief and stopped swaying.

Wide emotional range, high affect intensity, she wrote.

"I was right to put my trust in you." He tucked a strand of blond hair behind his ear. "When my story comes back to me, you shall be the first to hear it. You have my word." And he gave her a smile.

A smile can illuminate a plain face and can turn a pretty face ugly. John Doe's smile reassembled his sharp features like shards of glass in a kaleidoscope to create an image that was simply dazzling.

At that moment, Anna realized what felt odd about his appearance: the delicately shaped ears were longer than usual, and stuck out quite a bit.

Together with the clear, almond-shaped eyes, his ears made him appear somewhat feral. But this smile of his, which could easily turn into a wild grin, was so genuine, so guileless…

"Let's talk about something you do recall. What is your most recent memory?"

"I was awakened by a stranger, in a foreign place. I had no possessions, no clothes. These are not mine." He tugged at the collar of his hospital pajamas like it suffocated him. "I was awake and aware, but my life was a forgotten dream. Do you know this feeling, this bitter taste under your tongue left by loss and longing?"

As much as she disliked his turning the conversation to her, his poetic way of describing his disorientation struck a chord. Unfortunate that a man capable of such self-awareness was so lost. Anna knew exactly what John Doe was talking about. He was describing derealization, an altered perception resulting in the external world appearing alien, the real feeling unreal. She felt a sharp pang of empathy for this waiflike man.

Thought process: logical, reasonable. Thought content: delusional ideation as rationalization of anomalous experience. Derealization? She circled the latter. The tips of her fingers tingled.

"At first, my senses were numb," he continued pensively. "The world began whispering to me, first vaguely, and then more clearly. I began to seek things familiar: simple things, like the smell of the leaves, the roughness of a stone, the bark of a dog. I reckoned that the only sensations I recognized were those that time cannot change, and it comforted me, because at this moment I understood my predicament and submitted to it. I allowed strangers to handle me. And you came." John leaned back in his chair, a picture of stoic contentment, as if his hysterical outburst of a few minutes ago had never happened.

"Wait, you stated you understood your predicament. What did you understand?"

"That I have traversed time and space on a quest for the worthiest prize."

"Which is?"

"I am not entirely sure yet," John lowered his eyelids, suddenly demure, "But I expect it has to do with true love."

The words *true love* falling from his lovely lips made Anna gag a little.

"And how is your quest going so far?" she asked, and immediately regretted the sarcasm spilling into her voice.

"So far, so good." John looked up.

Meeting his earnest gaze made her uncomfortable. Something was wrong, beyond the usual wrong you'd expect at the Bellevue psych ward. This man did appear submissive, but it seemed that with each acquiescence he claimed a new degree of intimacy from her. To ask him an upsetting question felt like injustice, not to return his smile felt plain evil. But she was supposed to elicit a reaction from him, not the other way around! Anna chewed the tip of her pen.

"Let's approach this from the other end. Wouldn't it be more reasonable to assume that everything seems strange because you are experiencing a kind of internal breakdown?"

"Such an assumption feels wrong, so it is wrong. I trust my heart. I may not remember my past, but I am aware of the present. When I grew accustomed to the speech, I asked where I was, and was told this is New York. A new York, imagine!" John laughed softly. "Would I know of an old York? Obviously, time has passed. Everything looks—how shall I put it—overbuilt. I must have lived in a place simpler than this, a place with trees, open fields. And animals! When the sheriff's dog licked my fingers, I nearly wept, so dear was the sensation."

Anna suppressed a skeptical snicker at the mention of the K-9 unit dog licking a civilian's hand.

"So, you are familiar with a rural environment. Did you live on a farm?"

"A farm?"

"Are you accustomed to farm work? Did you care for animals, I don't know, drive a tractor?"

"Animals care for themselves. Attractor, who is he?"

"*It* is an agricultural machine."

"Oh, yes, the machines. This world is full of the most sophisticated contraptions with purposes I cannot conceive of. And the magnificence of stone buildings! Impressive." He nodded with lordly approval, as if complimenting Anna's personal achievement. "It appears humanity has advanced quite a bit in the study of mechanics, masonry, and magic."

Here it comes. "What do you mean by magic?"

"The power to reorder the creation." John set his elbows on the table, placing his sharp chin on locked fingers. Looking at his hands, Anna decided that those nails—the shape and luster of peeled almonds—could not have belonged to a farm laborer. Even bandaged, his hands looked like they'd never picked up anything heavier than a flute of champagne.

"John," she spoke as amiably as she could. "Magic is not real,"

"I beg to differ."

"Why?"

"Because I feel so, which means it must be the truth."

"Very well. Do you have magic powers?"

John studied his palms. "I'm afraid not. Not here, not now."

"Then what makes you think magic is real?"

He smirked with gentle condescension. "You do not think magic, you feel it."

Anna rubbed the bridge of her nose. John Doe's life philosophy seemed to be "I feel, therefore I am." Descartes would be spinning in his grave.

"John, there is no such thing as magic."

"How else would I be able to travel through time and space if not by a mighty magic?" He batted his smoky eyelashes.

Anna took a deep breath. John Doe was going in circles, and she was getting nowhere. She needed to snap him out of his loop, but carefully, without damaging an already fragile psyche. She wished she were better at this, more intuitive instead of having to rely on protocol. What would Michael have done? Anna mentally shuffled through her inventory of techniques. The patient was highly sensitive. A guided imagery visualization could be a fitting tool to gently pry open the locked vault of his mind.

"All right, John. Let's try something else. Please close your eyes and try to imagine what I'm describing. Humor me."

With an expression of mild amusement, he shut his eyes.

The Green Hills walk was Anna's favorite visualization routine—she had come up with it as an undergrad. Her Green Hills was a place of infinite beauty, where luminous planes of landscape overlaid each other all the way to the horizon, all in a promise of endless possibility. She had no idea where it came from, probably from an idyllic countryside, Ireland or Tuscany or some other lovely unpeopled terrain computer companies use for screensavers—certainly, not a place she'd even been to or was going to any time soon.

"Imagine yourself standing on top of a hill. The gentle wind is warm against your skin. You are at peace. In front of you is a path. You begin walking downhill. You come into a valley, following the path. Tell me about the path."

John's eyelids quivered. "Nooo," he exhaled. "There is no path in the hills."

Anna made a mark in her notes. The patient was not pretending. In his own mind he was literally lost.

"Now, you see someone." She led him to the next stage. "Describe this person."

"There is no one here. Wait, I do see someone, a youth with cropped hair. He looks young but strong—no, wait, he is a she."

Danke schön, Herr Jung. The imagery generated by John Doe's psyche was textbook archetypal. Without a doubt, the female figure in his vision represented his Anima, the feminine aspect of his own psyche.

"What is your relationship to this woman?"

"We are . . . together." His eyelids trembled. "And yet we are apart."

So, John Doe's personal femininity was represented by a tomboyish girl. An archetype of the Maiden: an innocent, an eternal juvenile, arrogant but ultimately needy, assertive but ultimately vulnerable, full of potential for both success and failure—all the qualities he must have adored and despised in himself.

"The woman is giving you something. What is it?"

"She holds her hand to me, but her hand is empty. Nothing for me in that world."

The patient readily acknowledging the discord within his own subconscious—a good sign.

"You return to the top of the hill. The gentle wind is warm against your skin. You take a deep breath, and you open your eyes."

John opened his eyes and rubbed them with his fists like a child.

"How did it feel?"

"As a walk in the hills would."

"Would you describe the hills?"

"There are grassy green hills as far as the eye can see, veils behind veils suspended in the air all the way to infinity beneath the sunless pearly sky."

Anna felt a touch of unease. In her imagination, the sky was indeed sunless. Pearly-gray, when she thought about it. John was inexplicably specific about something he had no way of knowing. It was an intriguing angle worth exploring, but it would have taken her away from her primary line of inquiry, so she shrugged off cold tickle between her shoulder blades.

"I know and love this place well. I believe I always have." John's pale face was slightly flushed. "Thank you for reminding me."

An hour later the orderly came to escort the patient back to the observation unit, and Anna was no closer to solving John Doe's mystery than she'd been when she started. In essence, the man had lost himself. He had no idea of his identity. He could only recollect emotions, not facts. But Anna gathered that he had grown up in a rural setting, possibly an isolated compound with no access to modern conveniences (he was sincerely impressed with the ward's indoor plumbing). His memory of life prior to being found in the park was fuzzy, and every attempt at recollection threw him into fits of despair. However, here the aberrations stopped.

John Doe was lucid. He expressed common sense. He showed no signs of a thought disorder. Other than suggesting he'd traveled through time and space, he appeared reasonable and aware of his surroundings. Although he came off a bit affected, he didn't check out for histrionic personality. He didn't exhibit psychopathic or antisocial tendencies either. His manner of addressing Anna bore no trace of flirtation or sexual manipulation. Overall, he came through as a sincere and intelligent, if eccentric, individual suffering from memory loss due to an unspecified trauma. Someone coping with trauma by generating a delusion while remaining psychiatrically sound otherwise. Her dissertation's definition of the perfect subject, verbatim. Anna chewed her lip to suppress a nervous grin.

Just as the orderly came over, John leaned across the table and said pleadingly: "I am suffocating here. The smells and sounds are horrid. I need air and sunlight." He covered her hand with his narrow palm. Even through the bandage, it felt hot and hard. The sensation gave her an adrenaline jolt, like she'd misstepped down an uneven staircase. She pulled her hand away.

The orderly tensed up, and she motioned for him to take it easy.

"No, John, you'll have to spend the night here."

"Am I jailed?" He jerked up his chin and folded his arms across his chest. The contrast between his defiant posture and the fragility of his body pierced Anna's heart. What kind of trauma was he trying to forget? What kind of reality made him want to escape into a fantasy?

"You're not jailed, but I want you to stay overnight." She stood up.

"What is that you want from me, Ahn-nah?" John rose too. He was taller than she expected, in fact, they were the same height, eye to eye.

"I want to know your story."

He let out a deep sigh and fixed her with his Siberian husky stare.

"If I give you my story, will you free me?"

"I will," she blurted out, and blushed, because at that moment she was not the coolheaded, detached mental health professional, but the little girl who simply had to rescue the puppy from the pound.

"I have your word." He exhaled, as if bracing himself, and nodded to the orderly, "Lead the way, my good man."

The report Anna filed before leaving for the day stated that John Doe was deemed to present no immediate danger to himself or others. However, the subject was gravely disabled due to identity/memory loss, rendering him unable to provide for his own basic personal needs such as food, clothing, and shelter. While the police worked to establish his identity through their channels, Anna recommended that John Doe be kept in the seventy-two-hour holding facility, starting at the time of his arrival, for extended observation to gain diagnostic clarity.

That Friday night, Anna's mother and stepfather were going out—undoubtedly, following the "How to keep your fire going" advice from *Woman's Day* or any of the other magazines that littered the coffee table at her parent's place. As always on her parents' date night, Anna stayed home with Jack. Jack, who preferred to think of it as his own rightful date with his sister rather than babysitting, was disappointed when she showed up with her boyfriend—*correction, fiancé.*

Anna had been dating Ted for nearly a year. They had met during her second year of graduate school, at a conference where he, a recently board certified pediatric psychiatrist with his own brand new practice, was giving a presentation. She hadn't dated in high school, and while she had made a concerted effort to catch up in college, the random hookups at the dorm parties rarely went beyond a one-nighter. Of course, there was Genie, but what Anna had with Genie was not dating.

A few weeks before Thanksgiving, they talked about the future, and by the end of the conversation it came up that getting married was the next logical step in their relationship. Ted expected that they'd announce it at Thanksgiving dinner, but Anna suggested they wait to tell her family. This was primarily because of Jack, who was as much her baby as her half-brother— possessive of her, perhaps inappropriately, but nevertheless. Anna was grateful that Ted didn't openly express any resentment. His appreciation of her boundaries was one of the qualities she found most attractive.

In his usual constructive manner, he offered to spend more quality time with Jack. Sooner or later, the eleven-year-old would have to start getting used to his sister's boyfriend—*yes, fiancé*—being a part of the family. The initial discomfort was natural but would eventually be overcome, he said, and Anna agreed. Still, as she now watched Jack follow Ted with eyes full of jealousy and mistrust, she couldn't help but feel torn.

"*Pokémon*?" Ted picked up a deck of brightly colored trading cards.

"It's *Yu-Gi-Oh!*" Jack glared. "I'm not into Pokémon. Pokémon's for losers."

A shadow of embarrassment passed over Ted's kind face. He prided himself on following popular cartoons and toys, always striving to establish common ground with his young clients. Adolescents comprised a good portion of his private practice, which, as he himself complained, had lately become less about handing out Ritalin prescriptions and more about treating opioid withdrawal.

"Do you still watch *Naruto*?" asked Anna to change the subject.

"Nah. I read the manga now. It's much further ahead than the animation."

"Wow, you're hardcore. So, what's up with Naruto?"

As Jack launched into an enthusiastic and detailed account of the complicated social life of a demon-possessed ninja boy, Anna's mind wandered to John Doe.

"You're not listening!" Jack nudged her shoulder.

"I'm sorry, buddy. It's just . . . I keep thinking about this patient with amnesia . . ." Anna stopped short, catching Ted's warning glance. Ted believed that even casually mentioning a case to civilians violated the therapist's integrity.

"In this one episode, Pikachu gets amnesia and joins Team Rocket, then he and Ash Ketchum fall in the river, and then they almost drown, and then he remembers the times they had together, and then his memory comes back," declared Jack with authority.

"I thought you're not into Pokémon." Ted squinted.

Jack shrugged, doing his best to be nonchalant. His eyes darted around the room. "Hey, you know what? I got a bunch of super-rares and some ultra-rares since we played last time. And Egyptian Expansion." He grabbed his Yu-Gi-Oh! card deck. "Wanna play, Annie?"

Feeling guilty for neglecting her brother, Anna threw herself into the game. From the many times they'd played together, she knew the rules and could hold her own, but Ted kept getting beaten by Jack, who showed no mercy after Ted's Pokémon jab. Things got brutal. Soon—but not soon enough for Ted—it was Jack's bedtime. Anna cuddled up next to him, and he was out cold before she finished a chapter from his favorite book de jour, another dystopian young adult fantasy. For a boy who still loved being read to, Jack always insisted on books above his grade.

Mom and James returned soon after that.

"Your mother kept smiling at me," said Ted as they walked to the subway stop.

"She always smiles at you."

"She was smiling *knowingly*. Did you tell her about our engagement?"

"I told Mom. She wants me to tell James personally, and I will. He's treated me as his own since the day we met, I owe him that. He is sensitive. Tough guys often are."

"And sensitive guys are often pragmatic." Ted smiled. "About that: I was looking at two-bedrooms in our price range and found some interesting offers in the upper Eighties, around York. Oh, and of course I was looking only at elevator buildings."

He didn't have to say that. Anna knew he'd rather they spend the night at his place than at hers. Her studio was at the top of a four-story walk-up in the Garment District, right off Sixth Avenue, only the skylight between her and the starless Manhattan skies. The narrow brownstone had only four apartments, one per floor, all semi-legal residential spaces above a barbershop, its red and blue neon swirl like a beacon at night, when the colorful windows of wholesale fabric shops disappeared behind graffiti-painted eyelids of metal shutters, and the bustling commercial neighborhood turned into a graveyard. Anna loved her funky neighborhood and her peculiar little apartment, which was taller than it was wide. It would be a shame to give it up.

A homeless man in a green tarp parka was shuffling down the sidewalk, asking for change. He stopped in front of them, twitching and mumbling.

"Come on, kiddo, you got to—" He stared directly at her. In the cool streetlight his green irises looked unnaturally radiant, out of place in his weathered face.

"Uh?"

"Change!" the beggar exhaled into her face. Instinctively, Anna held her breath, but man didn't smell foul. He didn't smell at all.

"Easy now," warned Ted, shifting his weight. He wasn't athletic—even climbing the stairs to Anna's fourth floor got him winded—but his size alone was imposing.

"It's okay." Anna dug through her purse. Usually she had cards with a list of local homeless services in her wallet, but today she was all out, so she pulled out a dollar bill. "Here you go."

"Don't gimme that!" The man huffed, ignoring her outstretched hand. "None of it is real! Damn, kiddo! Change!" He shot a disappointed glare at her and continued his unsteady trek, muttering, "Change, anyone, change?"

Anna chuckled. "I once interviewed a person who didn't believe paper money was real, transferred his paycheck into dollar coins monthly. A neat man, quite intelligent, had a wonderfully logical, deeply paranoid narrative about the conspiracy within the world financial system."

"And you think it's cute?" The palpable disgust in Ted's voice took her aback.

"I didn't say that."

"Sometimes the way you speak about delusional patients makes it sound like you think their illness is some sort of art project."

"Well, a delusional mind can be very creative. To acknowledge it is a question of ethics, and yeah, aesthetics, too. Besides, isn't psychotherapy just two people playing together?"

"You don't have to quote Winnicott to me, Ann. I'm surprised you're so flippant about this. It's not a game. The ethical thing to do is not to indulge the illness and chat it up, but to treat it by medical means."

"Chat it up. . . I'm not a therapist, Ted, I don't have a horse in the race. I'm just a humble researcher with my nose buried in statistical data, trying to devise more ways to dig up more data."

"Precisely why I'd expect you to take a more scientific view."

"Well, neuroscience proves that the human eye receives only raw sensory data, light and shadow, planes and edges. It's the brain that processes it into what we distinguish as objects and backgrounds. In that sense, we all live inside our minds, each of us constantly perceiving and simultaneously creating reality."

"Forgive me if I keep getting the impression that you romanticize the phenomenon."

"I'm only suggesting that eliminating the symptoms prematurely may prevent insight into the origins of the condition. You know, the psyche exploring itself through the illness . . ."

He responded with a passion she didn't expect from him: "When they bring me a little girl weak from sleep deprivation because monsters under her bed keep her up, or a boy whose reliance on an imaginary friend turns him into an outcast at school, or a teen who self-mutilates because she believes she's a dragon—should I tell their parents to tough it out because it's the psyche exploring itself through the illness? No, Ann, I don't think so. If a medication can eliminate these symptoms, I'd make sure the patient receives it. The sooner the better."

"You would, you drug pusher, you," Anna muttered through a grin. She wanted to sound playful, but it came out mean-spirited, so she threaded her hand under Ted's thick arm and rested her cheek on his shoulder. She didn't feel particularly tender toward him at that moment, but continuing the argument was even less enticing.

As soon as they entered her apartment, Anna dropped her phone into the speaker dock on her tempered glass computer desk, and let the syncopated melody of Jethro Tull's "Living in The Past" fill the room, its gentle whimsy preempting further conversation. Another quality of Ted's that Anna appreciated was his indifference to music, which she took as an indulgence to her 70s progressive rock addiction—something most boys had found decidedly uncool.

Anna's studio doubled as an office where she sometimes conducted interviews, so she kept it uncluttered and impersonal. The only sentimental object on her desk was a glass vase with a tall, dry, gorgeously fractal maple branch trimmed with a collection of tchotchkes she'd accumulated over the years.

She flicked the crystal pendant that hung between an antique Christmas ornament and a small dream catcher, sending it into motion. She was a kid when she made this trinket with a leather cord, some wire, and a pointed crystal shard. She'd used to pretend it was magical, had this secret game where she'd put it on and count the monsters she saw out the subway car window. What New York teen doesn't cope with anxiety? Some girls binged and purged, others cut. She'd counted monsters in the subway tunnels—yet another thing never to speak about. *Do you hear voices? See things?* No and no.

Later, as Anna brushed her teeth in front of the bathroom mirror, she calculated the odds of Ted's interpreting her disinterest in sex as punishment for disagreeing with him. Withholding intimacy would make her look petty, but she wasn't in the mood. When Ted reached out to hold her in bed, she hesitated.

"That tired, huh?" Ted knew better than to sound disappointed, and Anna knew better than to think he wasn't. He'd spent the evening with her family. She owed him. She mirthlessly grinned to herself: look at them, two mental health professionals, not even married yet, but already keeping careful score of positive and negative coupons. She turned toward him, pressing against his soft body.

"Never that tired."

"How did I get so lucky to net such a hot babe?"

"Yeah, and here I thought you loved me for my brains."

Anna had never considered herself hot. Growing up, she had valued her lung capacity above her looks, because back in Michigan one wasn't made captain of a middle school Nordic team for being cute. At her new high school in Manhattan, it was her top ranking on the track and field team, not her freckled face, that made her popular. During her freshman year at NYU her gangly frame had filled out, and she'd begun to turn heads, however, by then the inventory of her assets and insecurities had been assembled, and her body image placed low on both lists. As they said in her social psychology classes, her identity has been already informed by other things.

And then Genie burst into her life, supernova-hot, with kohl eyes and vermillion lips. They'd met at a party first-year drama undergrads were throwing at the dorms. Anna, a psych undergrad, had been still living at home with her mom and stepdad the cop; the wild life outside of parental supervision had been new and exotic to her. Eugenia Sokolova, or Genie, as everyone called her, was as exotic as they came. A foreign student whose father, a Russian oligarch—*A small-time oligarch*, she'd say with a sneer, *not even in the top ten,*—financed his daughter's thespian habit along with all the other habits inherent to a theater student in New York City. All Anna remembered about that night was winning a drinking contest. Genie was the prize. Anna had had her share of girl locker room makeouts, but this was a whole new ballgame.

Tall, dark-haired, reserved Anna and petite, foxy-red, exuberant Genie were the two girls least likely to bond. Besides, Anna, whose class sensitivity had been honed by her years as an athletic scholarship student at an upscale Manhattan high school, was wary of the rich kids. And yet, they hit it off like crazy. When the next semester came, Anna moved out of her parents' apartment and in with Genie into a two-bedroom down in the West Village. Rented from some family connection for a symbolic fee, it was cheap enough for Anna to afford her half and her pride. Their apartment became something of a bohemian salon for the next three years, a never-ending party; it was a miracle (by the grace of Adderal) that Anna got any school work done. But what made Genie so irresistible to Anna wasn't the dubious advantage of befriending someone worldly and generous, if unhinged. After all, her new friend didn't make Anna do anything she didn't want to.

The real reason was that Genie loved her for no reason at all.

But as all things free, Genie's love was not subject to the rules of exclusive ownership. Soon after she realized that, Anna began having sex with men. She discovered she liked it: physical fullness, esthetic validation, social capital—the usual. She mostly liked that it allowed her to expose herself without having to talk. About the dead father, who'd moved from mostly absent to forever gone, leaving her no chance to figure out if she even missed him. About the delicate mother who hadn't missed the dead husband enough, remarrying indecently quickly and happily. About the baby brother who'd needed her more than she needed her teenage freedom, and just wouldn't let go. About the old friends who'd let go too easily, and the new best friend who was content remaining just that, albeit with benefits. About herself for foolishly wanting the things she couldn't have.

It was good to feel wanted instead. Almost boyish despite her shapely butt and thighs—it took a while to stop referring to them as *glutes* and *quads*—Anna retained the physique of an athlete even after quitting sports. She was surprised to learn how her height, her long black hair, and her sarcastic demeanor could not only intimidate, but excite. She began to relish the expression of disbelief in the face of a next target when he realized he'd been chosen. She always kept them at arm's length, even if they wanted more. Especially when they wanted more. She'd rather be cool than hot.

A year after Genie left for a graduate program in London, Anna met Ted. When he formally asked her out, Anna thought, *this I can have*. Ted was solid, inside and out. He was ahead of her on the same professional path. He was taller than her, unlike most guys, and she liked that. She liked that he paid attention to things other than the tight curve of her behind or her ability to hold her liquor—her academic ambition, or how well adjusted she was for someone who'd suffered the death of a parent as a child. If she were to be loved for a reason, it might as well have been the right one.

Sex with Ted had been an improvement over casual hookups, as she always reminded herself when, afterwards, they'd kiss and roll to opposite sides. Dozing off, Anna focused on the positive feeling.

"Sweet dreams," whispered Ted.

The words gave her a little prick, but Anna bit her tongue. Ted had no way of knowing, because she'd never told him.

Of all the things Anna Reilly didn't talk about, this one was as embarrassing as it was ironic: she didn't dream. To be scientifically accurate, she suspected she did experience normal brain activity during her REM sleep stage, yet every morning as soon as her eyes opened to the world, a curtain would fall over her mind and she'd wake up with a taste of loss under her tongue.

She remembered when it happened. She was fourteen. The winter she moved to New York, she had a nightmare of which she mostly recalled the sense of relief that it ended. Then, abruptly, no more dreams, like someone flipped a switch. Around the same time, the anxiety attacks began.

Later, as a psych undergrad, she had tried everything legally possible to glimpse her own unconscious mind, from setting an alarm at odd times to breathing exercises and guided imagery visualization. She'd tried some of the illegal stuff as well. Still, the most she could recall upon waking was a feeling—an echo of being in love, a shadow of fear, a sense of release, emotions presumably related to the dreams that had inspired them. She hated this helplessness as much as she hated losing control during her anxiety attacks, but not as much as she loathed being found out as a pathetic imposter: a psychologist locked out of her own mind.

She had a close call when her inability to fill up a required dream journal put her in danger of failing her Jungian dream analysis class. "The cobbler's children are always the worst-shod," joked her professor, and explained that loss of dream recall wasn't indicative of anything in particular—especially, not of mental illness—unless it caused emotional distress, which must be addressed in personal therapy. "An issue of personal hygiene," he said.

She remembered being surprised by how much inner resistance his words had made her feel. Back then, she'd secured her professor's permission to analyze her roommate's dreams. Genie's subconscious had always been a fertile field, and Anna had earned her A.

Now she lay next to her future husband, so alone that even having someone to blame would have been a relief. But there was no one to blame, just as there was no mystery to why she'd felt that way. Besides, she had no use for either blame or mystery. No longer was she an insecure, anxious teen clutching in her fist a tacky trinket to ward off the imaginary monsters. She stood on the other side of the barricades now, armed with science and reason, fighting the real monsters lurking in the shadowed crevices of the human psyche. She held onto that thought as she drifted into sleep.

Saturday, November 29

Saturday morning found Anna on the crosstown M23 bus, her notebook on her lap, earbuds in her ears, going over her first interview with John Doe. She was curious to listen to his voice without the distraction of his face. It was, however, no less mesmerizing. Even when saying insignificant things, John spoke as if reciting poetry. At times his voice had a heartfelt urgency, at other times a playful sing-song lilt. He retained a slight trace of an accent, not a stereotypical British though. Some regional dialect? He did roll his *r*s, but softly, on an exhale. Perhaps, not a foreign accent at all, but a unique personal quirk. Maybe all his immediate family rolled their *r*s. Maybe he'd grown up in an isolated community, the kind without indoor plumbing, a cult compound. Maybe he was on the run from the cultists, left for dead after some horrific ritual he desperately wished to forget . . .

Slow down, she told herself. It's good to have an open mind, but inventing narratives is a bad practice.

He could also be a charismatic con artist, a narcissistic compulsive liar with a need for self-reinvention. But why the time traveling story? Why would a clever con man volunteer such an elaborate and unrealistic lie? No, it would be more reasonable to accept the patient's motivation at face value, as all Anna's training and instincts told her to do. If anything, the young man was making a valiant, if misguided, effort to understand himself. By presuming John Doe had indeed lost his memory, she could focus on finding a solution to his problem.

Several conditions caused retrograde amnesia, all pointing at trauma, physical or emotional. Confabulation due to brain damage could have explained the spontaneous production of false memories—as commonplace as petting a dog or as fantastical as passing through a magic portal. Or it could have been the dissociative fugue with a temporary loss of personal identity and aimless wandering—all fitting John Doe's case. Most likely, though, it was something mundane, such as childhood trauma. *He must have been adorable as a child, a molester's dream,* thought Anna with aching sympathy. That would explain his infantilism and sexually ambiguous mannerisms. It could also explain the eagerness with which he fixated on her as if she had some important role in his life, his savior.

Typical transference, Anna's voice of reason reminded her: a patient redirects his feelings toward significant figures in his earlier life onto his therapist, replaying his own subconscious patterns. Anna was taught that transference could be a great tool, pointing to unhealed wounds and deeper issues. It's the countertransference she was warned against: the dreaded emotional entanglement that corrupts therapeutic relationship with the client and leads the therapist into temptation.

And yet, Anna couldn't help but be moved by John's willingness to connect. Having this beautiful, brittle man reach out for her was like feeding a unicorn from the palm of her hand.

At the morning conference Anna kept her report professional.

"Doe may indeed be in a fugue state," commented Dr. Cohen. "Identity confusion is consistent with physical transience. I assume he is not suicidal or homicidal, so he can't be kept against his will past the standard seventy-two hours. He came in the day before yesterday, so unless he checks himself out against medical advice, two more days of observation should be plenty. Hold off on psychotropics for now."

After the meeting, Anna lingered by the nurses' station.

"The amnesiac, how did he do overnight?"

The night nurse's impenetrable features, weathered by years of facing human suffering, softened.

"Johnny's been a good boy."

"Still no recall, huh?"

The nurse shook her head. "For his sake, I hope he remembers who he is before his time runs out."

"And if he doesn't?"

"Next, his picture gets sent to the local TV channel—"

"Wait, what if the people who respond are the ones he is trying to forget? Or random deviants coming out of the woodwork to take advantage of a handsome young man."

The nurse drew back her chin, like she'd heard a dirty joke at a church meeting.

"Sad scrawny kid is more like it, but no accounting for taste, I suppose," she said. "Anyways, if no one responds, with no ID, no money and no insurance, he becomes the ward of the court. You know how it goes."

She did. As a mentally disabled adult unable to care for himself, John Doe would be gobbled up by the system. Anna didn't harbor any illusions about how well it would turn out for him. If she truly hoped to help him, she had less than forty-eight hours to solve his riddle.

Anna had always thought of herself as someone better at designing riddles than solving them. That something as intangible as the human psyche could be quantified and qualified by sifting language through the grid of a questionnaire fascinated and comforted her. She loved constructing labyrinths filled with semantic traps to catch inconsistencies and lies. She liked to think of it as meeting another person at the center of the labyrinth where the prize awaiting them both was the inner truth—the ultimate act of intimacy with the Other. Devising protocols and validity scales was the most gratifying part of her graduate work. The most frustrating was running them on real people. Cases were never clean cut, practice never as neat as theory. No such thing as a perfect subject.

Unless John Doe was it.

At the core of Anna's PhD thesis sat an original multi-axis scale methodology analyzing psychotic traits in subjects with negative psychotic symptomatology—or, like Michael teased her, "test for when sane people believe crazy shit." Trying her custom-built test battery on someone like John was a dream come true.

To kill prescribed time before the interviews, she checked on Willis. According to his chart, the acute episode had been managed with antipsychotic medication, and his asthma with a nonsteroid inhaler. He was responding well to both and would likely be released to his mother in Queens by the following week.

As Anna went through the tasks of the day, she registered a shadow of guilt for her impatience to get to Doe: the same commitment was supposed to be offered to each patient, not only the curious cases. *Well, another reason why my place is at the lab rather than in a therapist's chair*, she said to herself. From where she stood, becoming an outstanding psychotherapist, this holy grail of most young psychology students, was as far out of her reach as Olympic gold in skiing.

She called the radiology department, praying they had the results of yesterday's MRI scan. The specialist on duty was a young resident she'd met during orientation.

"Oh yeah, John Doe with the Spock ears. Quite a comedian that one, kept cracking me up. Let's see. No signs of structural damage, no organic abnormalities."

"Off the record," said Anna, fighting a momentary rush of dizziness. "Is there anything not abnormal per se, but not entirely normal either?"

"Well, the limbic structures are well pronounced. And so is the corpus callosum."

"What are you saying?"

"In essence, the limbic system contains the older, primordial structures of the brain responsible for emotions, motivation for learning, pleasure center, sexual arousal, all the fun stuff that makes you high."

"Ramon, I know what the limbic system is. What do you mean by *pronounced*?"

"With people in a drug-induced euphoria, this area lights up. His was on like the Rockefeller Center Christmas tree. Are you sure he was clean?"

"All the tests came negative. And the other thing?"

"Well, as you know," he continued, play-mocking her, "corpus callosum is the bunch of neurofiber connecting the hemispheres. It helps the right and left brains communicate more efficiently, in your John Doe's case, keeping it in a permanently heightened state of function. In other words, if his brain were a car, it would be a super-tricked-out race car. What's the diagnosis, anyway?"

"I don't know yet. Thanks, Ramon, I owe you lunch!"

Puzzled, Anna looked through the results of the previous day's medical exam. The patient's pallor and low weight, together with a low red blood cell count, signaled anemia. Yet, his muscle development was that of a professional athlete or dancer. Medically, he was cleared, which was a relief: had the exam shown any organic irregularities, the patient would automatically fall out of her hands and become the charge of medical doctors. As she pored over John Doe's file, Anna felt she was being selfish—she was happy about the patient's good health more for her own sake than his. She couldn't bear the thought of losing his case. Her sudden possessiveness surprised her, but she didn't have time to reflect on it. She needed to establish his psychological and medical history, and fast.

A phone call to the precinct wasn't encouraging: John Doe's fingerprints weren't in the system. A check against the digitally aged images of missing children over the last decade yielded nothing. Nobody was missing this man.

"I would appreciate it if you called me directly, if there is anything pertinent," Anna told the police officer. "Anything that would shed a light on his identity, any odd reports from the area where he was found, maybe something on the street population—"

"There're always odd reports on the street population." The cop sounded amused. "Don't know if it's pertinent, but a report came in from the same night and location of a homeless individual attempting to sell a horse tail," he added after a moment's hesitation.

"A horse tail?"

"Yes ma'am, two feet worth of white hair."

Anna considered asking John about this odd coincidence, but decided against it: she knew better than to indulge a patient's delusion. Despite what Ted thought.

Anna's second interview with John Doe would take place after lunch. While waiting in the interview room, Anna studied the observation report. Apparently, the patient hadn't found the hospital food to his liking. All he'd eaten was a single apple. It was a bad sign: in case of an eating disorder, the patient risked being force-fed. Anna imagined John strapped to a gurney with a nasogastric tube disfiguring his face, formula being pumped up his nose and down his throat. She shuddered.

"I hear you are not eating well," she said to him as a greeting. He looked paler than the day before. The antiseptic fluorescent light cast hard shadows, making his face look gaunt and sickly. His breathing was uneven, and his fine nostrils quivered as he drew in air.

"I tried, but I cannot eat here." He sounded apologetic. "I cannot sleep here either. I lay with my eyes closed, but sleep won't come."

Low appetite and insomnia qualified as physiological distress and obligated Anna to turn him over to the medics. The thought of Thomas getting his paws on her John Doe made Anna cringe. He'd be only too happy to write the poor man off as a psychotic and stuff him with meds until he turned into a zombie. She felt a strong urge to tell John he was free to leave at any moment, sign himself out against medical advice, and walk out of the hospital and out of her life. More than an urge, it was the ethical thing to do. *I'll tell him he's free to go*, she decided. *After collecting some data. Not like he has someplace to go anyway. It's for his own good.*

Against her high hopes, the testing wasn't going well, in fact, was going nowhere. She had to quit the psychological assessment after the patient failed to answer *yes* or *no* to a standard statement, such as "I feel involved watching TV soap operas," because he had no idea of what a TV or a soap opera was. The test designed to assess psychopathology, the trusty Minnesota Multiphasic Personality Inventory, didn't apply for the same reason: half of the questions he didn't understand, the other half he couldn't answer because he didn't remember who he was.

Even the standard IQ test was useless. Not only did he not know who wrote *Tom Sawyer*, or who the current president of the United States was, he also seemed unaware of his own ignorance.

On a whim, Anna paused the interview and ran into her office to pick up a test that wasn't part of the standard battery. The Culture Fair Intelligence Test was composed mostly of graphic images, specifically designed to assess logical reasoning in the absence of any cultural bias. John seemed mildly irritated by the tests she'd given him so far, commenting on the pointlessness of questions and concepts he found absurd, but the brightly colored graphics of the CFIT cheered him up—clearly, he enjoyed solving puzzles. Anna decided not to time him, but as she observed him, she realized that John Doe was breezing through the most complex logical puzzles much faster than she expected. Despite his inexplicable cultural and social retardation, John Doe's overall level of intelligence was significantly above average.

"These games are amusing, but for how much longer do you wish to play them?" John interrupted her train of thought.

"Are you not feeling well?"

"How can I when there is nothing good to feel?" A hysterical note crept into his measured voice. "I am surrounded by unhealthy people, life being drained out of me. The smell of misery permeates this place."

"What smell is that?"

"The same I smelled on you when you walked in today. You didn't have a good night either, did you?" He patted her hand. There was nothing flirtatious about this gesture, but she hurried to pull her hand away.

"What about you, have you been able to remember more?"

He shook his head. "Today I learned I like apples and not bananas, as a child who discovers his tastes for the first time, except instead of enjoying the thrill of newness I am exasperated."

"Perhaps, rather than trying to remember, you could try to imagine something. . . pleasant. What is your perfect day?"

He lowered his eyelids and tilted his head, as if listening to himself. "A perfect day is made of perfect moments, and you know a perfect moment only after it passes, not before. But you are aware of this."

Anna fussed with her glasses.

It had been the first spring she'd shared the apartment with Genie—must have had been, because she'd taken the modern novel class during her second semester as an undergrad. They'd been dissecting Mrs. Dalloway and had just analyzed the part where the middle-aged heroine contemplates her sexual attraction to women and recalls a kiss from a girlfriend at school as the happiest moment of her life.

In high school, between cramming for tests, track and field meets, and helping with baby Jack, Anna hadn't had much time to read for pleasure. She had signed up for the modern novel class with a goal of developing a taste for high literature. It was a conscious effort, something she did because it had to be done, like taking Statistics, or losing her virginity to a boy a few months earlier. Statistics turned out to be something she excelled at, the same way sex turned out to be satisfying in more ways than she could have thought.

She hadn't expected the story of an upper-class English housewife to resonate with her either, but losing her literary virginity to Virginia Woolf was tremendous—sexual intercourse with another freshman paled in comparison. The very mechanics of her own thinking and perception, her sensuality and emotion were revealed to her with mesmerizing clarity, like popping the back cover of a watch case and seeing the movement for the first time. Navigating those streams of consciousness made her, for the first time, want to become a psychotherapist. She was high on self-discovery, the elusive meaning of life seemed within her grasp, and for an instant she thought she could have it all.

Yes, it must have been spring, because the sun was cutting through the curtains just so. It was the day after a party that had ended with Genie in Anna's bed, because someone else was sleeping in hers. It hadn't been the first time.

The whitewater ride of the night had eased into a slow-flowing delta of a sunlit morning. Her head still swimming, she drove her fingers into the red hair of the head nested into the soft hollow of her stomach, right between the hip and the rib bone. She watched the short red hair catch on fire in a beam of sunshine, revealing dirty-blond roots; it rose and resettled under her touch, like rich fur. She remembered thinking, *Russian mink*, and then, that it was the happiest moment of her life, possibly the perfect moment. She must have muttered something to that effect, because Genie unglued her cheek from Anna's belly, lifted her heart-shaped face, and said with her little lopsided grin, "You're not going all Mrs. Dalloway on me, are you?"

"What do you mean?"

"I mean, you will have many . . . " Genie yawned. "Moments. Many perfect moments. Whole days of them."

"With you?"

"Me, others, all kinds." Genie shrugged. Or maybe she was stretching.

They got up, got dressed, and went to class to discuss how Clarissa Dalloway's identity falls under class and gender constructs marginalizing her femininity in the framework of the bourgeois marriage, and how Virginia Woolf's sexuality and mental illness informed her literary discourse.

In the years to follow, Anna had been moved often: by her brother's adoration, her parents' approval, a sense of her own accomplishments. Sometimes it was something small—the slant of a shadow on a wall when sun cuts through the curtains just so. She was careful to call it happiness, as if by calling it out she was opening a competition for the perfect moment, and she knew it was a losing battle.

By then, she'd accepted what Mick Jagger had rasped decades before her birth: you can't always get what you want.

"When will I leave this place?" John's low voice brought her back.

"Well, not before we figure out a little more about you. Someone must know you and care for you."

"There is no one but you." He spoke plainly, and yet it came off as provocative.

"Besides me," she replied a bit terser than she'd liked.

He glanced at her sideways. She couldn't help but feel she was disappointing him. It hurt.

"Do you remember having a family?"

"No."

"Ever been married?"

"I should hope not!"

He sounded offended, and for a split second Anna registered a guilty pleasure of hurting him back. Perhaps his sexuality provided the key to his personality after all. John seemed too fluid to fit a category, whether clinical or cultural. He likely resented labels. She certainly did—badly enough to get called a traitor once or twice. But her private fear of being pegged had no place influencing her line of inquiry.

"John, if I may ask you." She licked her lips. "Are you gay?"

"Today you seem intent on asking most inapt questions. Naturally, I am gay at times, as any man," he replied with dignity. "However, since I am under duress right now, I see little reason for gaiety."

She took off her glasses and rubbed her temples. He could have a form of high-functioning autism forcing him to take language literally. Asperger's syndrome? True, his linguistic patterns were a bit formal and archaic, yet his whole bearing was expressive, even theatrical, with confidence and grace in each gesture. Despite the obvious eccentricity, he wasn't socially awkward. He didn't avoid eye contact. He was consistent and comfortable in his persona. No, it had to be something else.

Unfortunately, Anna's time was up. She had to keep reminding herself that the mystery man was not her only patient. She had two routine assessments to perform, the afternoon inpatient substance abuse group she shared with Michael, plus mountains of paper work.

Before leaving for the day, she swung by the common room of the observation unit. The patients were watching TV, huddling together. Only John sat apart, staring through the wire mesh of the safety glass window at the night sky outside. His effortlessly graceful carriage seemed to have created a space around him, making him look formidable and vulnerable at once, and very much alone. She didn't plan to talk to him, but as she walked up to the door he turned in her direction, as if he could see her though the one-way glass. She felt grasped and held in his gaze. His eyes begged—no, demanded. He wanted her to take him away from this place. He wanted . . . It didn't matter what he wanted. He was a patient in a mental institution, gravely impaired, with no place to go. The hospital was the best place for him.

She turned on her heels and walked away, feeling like a traitor.

With her mind on her case, Anna had all but forgotten she and Ted were meeting their friends for dinner after work. *Ted's friends* was more like it—Genie went to London for her postgraduate program before Anna met Ted, and over the year she'd been with Ted, most of her single friends had drifted out of her orbit. They were meeting Helen—she and Ted had been active in the Greek life back at Duke and stayed friends in New York—and Helen's boyfriend, whose name Anna could never remember. By the time she arrived at the Italian restaurant in the Village, they were well into a bottle of wine.

"Tough day?" whispered Ted as she sat down. "Would you like to talk about it?" It was a private joke between them.

"Don't shrink the shrink." The punch line didn't come out right. Anna felt as sour as the white wine Ted ordered for her. Wine went with the meal, but as she sipped from her glass, she thought she'd have preferred a beer.

"You're preoccupied, Ann. Something on your mind?" Helen's politeness seemed genuine, but Anna felt a disconnect. Why should she bother trying to win the acceptance of this former sorority queen? They were aliens to each other.

"I have this patient." Ignoring Ted's frown, she downed her glass and gestured the waiter for another. "A young homeless person suffering from amnesia. The loneliest man in the world."

"Sounds like a soap opera character," chimed in Helen's boyfriend.

"Bellevue Hospital, an award-winning daytime television drama starring yours truly," said Anna with a crooked grin. As everyone laughed, Anna realized she couldn't discuss John, neither with the civilians, nor with Ted. Not because of the professional integrity, but because it felt like cheating. *Cheating on whom with whom?* inquired the voice of reason, and she took a quick gulp of wine to hush it.

Matter-of-factly, Ted informed the other couple that he and Anna were now engaged, and their cheers, though appropriate to the occasion, felt a little restrained. *Perhaps the news touched a sore spot*, mused Anna, because you never know with cohabitating unmarried couples. To her relief, the conversation smoothly shifted to Manhattan real estate, and, as she listened to Ted explain the difference between coops and condos to Will (that was it, his name, Will), Anna thought that she had indeed succeeded in not making a big deal out of the whole affair. *Still need to tell James about the engagement*, she noted between the third and the fourth glass of wine.

After the couples had wished each other good night and headed for their respective subway stations, Anna said, "I should go home," before Ted had a chance to speak. "I'm beat."

"You seem stressed out lately. Ann, I'm here for you. I remember how overwhelming grad school can be."

"You know how it is, when a promising case is going nowhere, you keep running in circles, doubting yourself, questioning your whole methodology—"

"You're still talking about the amnesiac."

"You never miss anything, do you?"

"This is why they pay me the big bucks. Tell me about your case."

"It seemed custom tailored for my paper, but now I'm not sure I can use it at all. I feel I'm slipping. The review board is in less than two months, and I still have no centerpiece."

"Look." Ted caught Anna by the shoulders. "Push comes to shove, I can give you one of mine. I have an adolescent who fits your subject. I'm confident I'll get parental consent."

"What's his chief complaint?"

"Her. She has a persistent delusion of being a dragon in human disguise, complete with phantom limbs and false memories."

"Any red flags for abuse?"

"None at the present. Stable family, excellent school. Overall, a well-adjusted teenage girl, except she is convinced that if she jumps out of the window, she'll take flight."

"None at the present . . . wait, such depersonalization could have been caused by developmental trauma. What's her history?"

Ted gave her an approving smile.

"Adopted from a Chinese orphanage as an infant. Unconfirmed, but pretty much guaranteed early childhood trauma. Perfect for you. See, we can make it work."

He hugged her, and she buried her face in his puffy jacket, searching within herself for gratitude. When Ted leaned in to kiss her mouth, she offered her cheek. Perhaps she'd had a glass too many of the sour wine: instead of a pleasant buzz she felt exhaustion, and instead of gratitude, a burden. She said good night and promised to call him the next day.

As she stretched across her own bed, she wished for her usual dreamless sleep. But as soon as her eyes shut, she was surrounded by the hills of green under pearlescent, sunless sky. The rolling grassy hills were strewn with tree groves. A mirror lake sparkled in the distance. The horizon drowned in a blue haze. There was a boy she was in love with, a boy who loved everything, but couldn't love her. It hurt, but pleasantly. With a clarity only possible in a dream, she recognized the hills and the love. She'd dreamed this before. It was a place of absolute possibility, where you could live out any fantasy at all or all the fantasies at once, as long as you loved.

She knew she wouldn't recall it in the morning, and her heart began to tighten with the familiar anticipation of loss. But this time, something was different: a sound, a voice speaking to her in a language she couldn't understand. The voice belonged to someone important, but also frightening. She heard laughter. Silver bells were pealing in his laughter, ringing, ringing, demanding and intrusive like the fake vintage ringtone of her cell phone.

Anna rubbed her eyes open. The clock read 5:00 a.m. Her cell phone was buzzing, hopping on the nightstand like an angry frog. The call was from the chief nurse, Gloria Salazar. Gloria was an ally.

"There's a problem with your John Doe."

Sunday, November 30

Apparently, Sunday had begun with a violent incident: another patient in the observation hold, the paranoid ex-con, had attempted to sexually assault John Doe in the shower. Not only had John resisted, but he'd prevailed over the much larger man. Still naked, he'd punched out the would-be rapist and left him unconscious on the bathroom floor to be apprehended by the security guards.

"What's his status?"

"Sedated. Took a double dose, big guy."

"No, I mean John Doe!"

"He's in seclusion in the medical unit."

"I'm on my way."

Cursing under her breath, Anna put her bare feet on the cold floor and scrambled into the bathroom. As her thoughts vacillated between coveting a pair of sheepskin slippers and regretting that fourth glass of wine, she splashed some water on her dry face and got dressed. She grabbed her purse from the computer chair and swiped her phone into the bag, together with the tangle of wires and her notebook. Her clumsy morning hustle knocked over the pencil holder and unsettled the vase, making the old crystal necklace drop from the dry branch to the desk. Mechanically, she threw it into the bag. *For good luck.* Today, she needed some. The story John Doe had pulled her in was becoming more and more twisted, spiraling away from a reasonable resolution with each turn.

It was still dark when she ran through the hospital doors, flashing her ID at a sleepy security guard. She nearly broke a nail pressing the elevator button. Gloria met her at the nurses' station.

"Was John Doe restrained or sedated?"

"No need for that. He was a perfect angel."

"Angel? He's beat up a man!"

"He was defending himself. Danny witnessed the whole thing and alerted security. He's in the TV room right now." She pointed out a young patient who was biting his nails, absorbed in the antics of the weatherman on the TV screen. The weatherman flailed his arms wildly, as if trying to push away the arctic front threatening the city with a heavy snowfall.

"What did you see, Danny?" Anna pulled out her notebook.

"So, at dinner Big Boy is like, that skinny guy gives me snake eyes, disrespecting, I don't take no disrespect, I did time 'cause I don't take no disrespect. So, he's all in the new guy's face, like, yo, what you looking at, Barbie? And the new guy keeps staring with those blue blinkers. And Big Boy is all, this fag's ass is mine. Yeah." The young man giggled. "Anyways, at night, when the new guy goes in the showers, Big Boy goes too. And I go to check out the action, you know, nothing like a free show. Then there's a bang, and I'm, like, what's that? So, there's the skinny guy standing over Big Boy, naked, yo! Naked and wet! He's all pretty, like a girl, but also, I dunno, nasty, like . . . like an insect. So, Big Boy's out cold on the floor with his pants down, his face one bloody mess. You know what Barbie does? He takes his hands and wipes blood across his own chest, like war paint or something! Telling you, he's nasty!"

It appeared the dainty John Doe had brutally battered a violent ex-con twice his size, not only without exhibiting any fear, but without remorse either. Such callous aggression was a textbook sign of psychopathy, but quite despite herself, Anna was impressed. The regulations, however, required a patient involved in an altercation to be specifically assessed for violent tendencies. With a heavy heart, she picked up a new batch of assessment forms and marched to the medical emergency wing of the ward, wracking her brains to figure out a new angle for her interview.

Solving the mystery of John Doe's identity would have to wait: he might have been a danger to himself and others after all. Anna shuddered at the thought she could have missed something as big as this. She'd been careless.

Just because the puppy is adorable doesn't mean it won't bite.

Since the seclusion room of the psych ward had been occupied by the losing party of the midnight match, John Doe, as the more compliant one, has been transferred to the medical wing. After the psychiatric floor with its secure doors and guards at each juncture, Anna found the atmosphere of the medical wing relaxed, even upbeat. Passing by the reception area with the bright thank you cards from grateful patients to staff, she chuckled quietly—indeed, she had chosen a thankless profession.

Outside John Doe's room the orderly was keeping watch: a man in his late twenties, filling the extra-large blue scrubs with his muscular body.

"I've got to be present during the interview for your safety." He sounded almost apologetic.

"Did he give you any trouble?"

The orderly shook his head. "He seems like a mellow guy. Did he beat up a man for real?"

"I can't talk about it. As a matter of fact, the interview must be conducted in private."

"But the regulations—"

"I'll call you if I need you," said Anna firmly, pushing her way by the orderly. "Everything is under control."

John Doe was sitting in the hospital bed, bandaged hands resting serenely on his lap. He was a surreal sight: in an eerie symmetry to yesterday's red scrape, he had a blue bruise on the other cheek and a split lower lip. His slick straight hair, in contrast, gleamed with pale gold—he must have washed it right before he was attacked. With his long neck and sharp clavicles showing in the opening of the hospital gown, he truly looked like an angel who had taken a rough tumble from heaven, losing his wings in the process but not his grace. As Anna poked her head through the door, John fixed his wide-set eyes on her.

"Ahn-nah! I knew it was you. I can feel when you come." He stretched his broken lips in a smile, winced, but kept grinning, touching his fingers to his mouth. "One of the few things I feel."

Anna squirmed in her clothes. John Doe managed to fluster her even with an innocent greeting. She pulled the chair away from the bed, putting some distance between them.

"You are going to take me away from here, aren't you," continued John in his precise voice. "High time, Anna. I will not miss this place at all."

Anna sat straight, striking the most assertive pose she could muster. She wouldn't let the patient highjack the interview. Stick to business. First, the violence assessment. Second, establishing diagnostic clarity. Depending on the results, John Doe would either be released to roam in the streets of New York, or admitted into the system and put on antipsychotic meds. Then, he wouldn't be of any use to her. More importantly, she could do nothing for him.

"Are you in much pain?"

"Not enough to feel anything." He half-winced, half-grinned again.

Lost in the big hospital bed, bandaged and bruised, he looked fragile, so unlike someone who could beat another man into a pulp. How could a man of such a refined appearance harbor such a ferocious side? Anna cringed at the ugly traces of violence marring his face. Oh, she was taking it all too personally again.

"John, I have to ask you more questions."

"I fear I cannot offer any more than before. My memory is still foggy, and having my head hit against the walls doesn't help in the least."

"Let's talk about it. How many fights have you been in lately? Say, over the last year?"

"I am unable to see this far into my past, but I assure you, I don't seek out a fight. It was low of that man to attack me. Naturally, I fought back. This place is not safe, Anna."

As an androgynous man, perhaps gay or bi, he must be used to being a target, thought Anna, watching his lips move. The witness' testimony supported the self-defense theory. The degree of his response was consistent with a reaction to a sexual assault, violent but not psychotic.

"Have you ever possessed a firearm?" She continued with the standard line of questioning.

"A fire arm? I think we've established that I'm presently incapable of magic."

"Have you ever kicked an animal?"

"If an animal attacked me, I would kick it. Wouldn't you?"

"Would you strike a woman?"

"I'd rather not strike anyone, man or woman or animal." He sighed. "I didn't enjoy having to fight that man. I hope he recovers soon."

Anna bit the tip of her pen. It would have been so much easier if he was without empathy and remorse, the classical symptoms of Antisocial Personality Disorder. Was that where she'd made a mistake? She'd been entertaining exotic theories about John's condition, all the while neglecting the most obvious. Post-Traumatic Stress Disorder would explain his readiness for aggression, his inability to tolerate perceived danger. If John Doe suffered from PTSD, he could become confused to the point of memory lapses, and a radical avoidance of the traumatic memories could manifest itself as partial amnesia.

"John, have you ever considered taking your own life?" Suicidal ideation was a sign of PTSD, and it could give her a reason to keep him for a longer observation. Anna chewed the inside of her cheek, waiting for a *yes*.

Instead, he asked, "Where?"

"Pardon?"

"Taking my life—where?"

"Ending it. As in suicide."

John cocked his head, listening to himself. "I do not believe it's in my nature," he said after a pause. "I'd much rather see this riddle through." He looked her in the eyes.

Under his direct gaze, Anna became self-conscious again. He said nothing overtly flirtatious, yet she couldn't shake a sense of being prodded, as if the patient kept sending her secret signals she was failing to recognize.

She tapped her pen against her notebook. A violence assessment was no good if the patient didn't know his own character. No, recovering his identity had to be a priority. If she could demonstrate to the patient the inner workings of his own mind, she might loosen the memory block.

"Sometimes," she said affably, "when we are unable to deal with something disturbing, we may tell ourselves a story to make sense of it. We tell it to others, and if it's told enough times, we believe it."

John's dark eyebrows arched. "This is not merely forgetting you speak of, but of lying, to yourself no less."

Did she hear judgment in his voice?

"Memories may be suppressed out of self-preservation," Anna tried not to sound defensive. "If an experience is so incomprehensible it makes one think she's losing her mind, sometimes the only way to go on living is to dismiss the traumatic event like it never happened. Could this have happened to you?"

"Could this have happened to you?" He mimicked her intonation perfectly, as if mocking.

She bit her lip: for the first time since they met, the mild and deferential patient was behaving in a confrontational manner. She must have made a wrong turn somewhere.

"We aren't talking about me now," she replied as calmly as possible.

"We aren't? You described lying to yourself with such insight, one may presume you spoke from experience."

A vague impression of the previous night's dream swayed in the back of her mind, making her stomach lurch again. Yes, the fourth glass had been excessive.

"One doesn't have to have a personal experience to recognize these conditions," she said, wiping her palms against her skirt. "But there's no reason to be ashamed if it happens, either."

"Then why are you ashamed? Is it because you forgot your dream?" John's tone was polite, concerned in a friendly way, but his question hit her in the gut, leaving her out of breath. *How the hell does he know . . . what does he know? What is there to know?*

Her throat achingly dry, she reached for a bottle of water inside her purse but dropped her notebook, and knocked the bag over, spilling its contents. As she clumsily raked together the files, the cellphone wires, and her makeup bag from the floor, her fingers touched the leather string of her old necklace, which had found its way into her purse that morning. Some good luck charm. Today was anything but lucky.

"What is this?"

"What?" Anna looked up, blushing. Did he just look down her shirt?

"What is this?" he repeated impatiently. His eyes were fixed on the crystal pendant that hung from her fist, reflecting the artificial daylight with a myriad of faint little rainbows.

"Oh, this." Awkwardly, she held it against her clavicles. "It's just a necklace." As the cold crystal pendant swung against her skin, she got dizzy, as if the air around her shifted: she must have sat up too quickly.

John threw off the blanket, dropped his bare feet on the floor, and stood up in front of Anna. The one-size-fits-all hospital gown wrapped twice around his narrow hips in the manner of a medieval tunic. It opened on his chest, revealing pale smooth skin. His stance was wide, his body taut. Contrary to Anna's initial impression, he wasn't emaciated but lean and supple, battle-ready. *No wonder he kicks ass: he's cut like Bruce Lee*, thought Anna, unable to look away from John's wiry arms. His legs, too, were strong, slender, and hairless like the legs of a prepubescent boy.

His eyes still fixed on the pendant, he put a hand to his naked chest and rubbed it, as if to soothe an ache, but in a disturbingly sensual fashion. His other hand slowly rose, half-pointing, half-reaching toward Anna, and she vividly imagined his fingers touching her between her breasts. Without thinking, she handed the pendant to John. He grabbed it and pressed the crystal chard to his bleeding mouth in some kind of religious ecstasy; his hair floated up around his head, charged with static. Before Anna had a chance to utter a word, he shuddered as if tasered, and crashed to the floor. Powerful convulsions ripped through his body, but his fingers kept clutching the crystal. It all happened so quickly, Anna didn't even have a chance to scream. John stopped shaking and curled up on the linoleum floor. She squatted next to him.

Blood pounding in her ears jumbled her thoughts. *Feel his pulse? Secure his head? Wrangle the damn necklace from him?* Instead, following some uncanny impulse, she leaned over and sniffed his hair. It smelled like ozone, saturating the whole room with the ionized freshness of a lightning storm.

"The hell am I doing? I'm in over my head," she said out loud and shouted for the orderly.

John's eyes snapped open. Seemingly surprised to find himself on the floor, he sat up straight, then bounced to his feet. For several excruciating seconds he towered over her, staring down at her with wide, wild eyes, then helped her up. As he sat her in her chair, he dropped the crystal necklace around her neck. His fingers brushed over her shoulders, giving her a shiver. He hopped back on his bed, and leaned on the pillows with a sigh of relief.

Not only had he fully recovered from his seizure, but it appeared to have caused a mysterious transformation. In shock, Anna observed John rip off the bloody gauze and rub his hands at first in amazement, then with a kind of feminine tenderness. Free of bandages, his hands appeared perfectly intact, even his nails glinted as if polished. He ran both hands through his hair: the crudely chopped hair moved, shifted, poured between his fingers, and suddenly was longer, shinier, more even. With a little moan of pleasure, John stroked his forehead and cheeks with his palms. When he turned his face to Anna it was clear of bruises and scrapes, all traces of violence wiped off his face like stage makeup.

Before the heavy steps of the orderly reached the door, John was lounging comfortably in his bed, reclining on his elbow with dignified grace. A touch of color had returned to his cheeks and lips, his hair cascaded over his shoulder, his eyes sparkled. The blanket draped around him in majestic folds. He looked out of this world.

"Oh, Ahn-nah." He frowned, biting back a smile in some kind of rapturous agony—sunshine against thunderclouds. "You have found me after all."

"Is there a problem?" The orderly filled the door frame with his six-foot figure.

Before Anna opened her mouth, John snapped his fingers, pointed at the orderly and hissed: "Out!"

Anna's jaw dropped at such extreme insolence. The patient had just treated a member of the hospital staff like an intrusive pet. But the fact that John was brazen enough to overreach wasn't as surprising as the orderly's reaction: he took on a blank stare, like he had forgotten what he'd come for, and left, shutting the door behind him.

"What did you just do?" Anna mumbled, unsure whether she meant John's inexplicable arrogance or his impossibly rapid healing.

"I did nothing but trust you, and you did not fail. Ah, precious!" His voice rang with joy. He rolled his head from side to side, pulled out his hand, clenched and unclenched his fist. "I can feel again! Oh, I feel much better!"

"You look . . . much better."

"Doesn't everything?" He gestured as if pushing away an invisible curtain. Obediently, Anna surveyed the windowless hospital room, with its off-white walls, a bed with a nightstand and a chair, all bathed in the antiseptic fluorescent light that made the angles sharp and shadows deep. The air was acrid with the smell of disinfectant detergent. She didn't remember it being so strong—not offensive, rather stimulating. *Lilac.*

The space must have been saturated with the synthetic lilac molecules. Here they were, microscopic bubbles of iridescent matter dancing in the cool light, vibrating in front of her eyes with a thin buzz. It must have been the bright light that agitated them, light so sharp you could prick a finger with it.

Her water bottle rolled on the floor as Anna swatted at the dancing dots, her hand leaving spectral tracers in the air. The light sliced her skin, and her fingers tingled with the pleasant ache of a healing paper cut. A sweet pain surged through her joints. As she shook her head, the walls and the ceiling moved apart, expanding the space. Why hadn't she noticed its magnificence before? It was a spectacular hall, with translucent white walls reflecting the vibrant light. Each hue sang with a different note, and although the harmony was peculiar, it was glorious. She had an urge to share her vision with someone. There was a glowing silhouette across from her, apart from her yet a part of her at the same time. It was craving a connection. Anna leaned forward, devouring the wondrous sight.

The lustrous body belonged to a man who yearned for her as no one ever had or could, his desire radiating from him, his pupilless eyes fixed on her. His gaze penetrated her chest, got a hold on her heart and pulled, tugged at her pounding, pounding heart, pounding and hurting so hard her chest was about to explode and it was so good she could die—no, no, this couldn't be good, this shouldn't be, this was the synapses in her brain misfiring, sending her adrenaline level through the roof . . . *this must stop!*

Overwhelmed, Anna gasped for air, tugging at the necklace around her neck. The worn-out leather cord snapped and the crystal pendant fell on her lap. The world shifted again. Anna shook her head: the colors were fading back to normal, and the ringing in her ears subsided.

"I can't believe this is happening," she muttered, rubbing her neck. "I know this . . ."

"What do you know, Anna?" His voice was heavy with passion. "Say the words!"

"Nothing. I don't . . . I don't want . . ."

"Perhaps you don't." John's bright smile faded to a pout of disappointment. He looked away from her, hugging his knees like a sulking child.

Anna felt queasy—not unpleasantly—as if she'd witnessed, or worse, participated in something deliciously obscene, better not mentioned in polite company. *Why did it have to return now? I haven't had an episode since I was a teen . . . Stop, find your feet, breathe. You've experienced an anxiety attack, probably triggered by the chemicals in the detergent or the fluorescent light. Yesterday's hangover has contributed. What you see is not real. It's all in your mind.* The self-talk calmed her as it always had.

If a rational explanation existed for her altered state, there must have been some rational explanation for John's altered appearance, even if she was too confused to see it.

"Excuse me, I'll be right back." She slid out into the corridor. The orderly still stood by the door with the same dreamy expression on his face.

"Quick question," said Anna, and the man blinked at her, as if waking from a spell. "Why did you leave?"

"'Cause everything is under control, you said so yourself."

"Right. Did you notice anything odd about this patient just now?"

"Like what?"

"Like, that he was bruised this morning, and now he's all right?"

"So, he's a fast healer."

"And his hair, it doesn't look different to you, does it?"

"Look, ma'am," the orderly seemed to be losing patience. "There are a lot of people on this floor. I don't know about each patient's hair, okay?"

Anna returned to the room, closing the door behind her carefully, picked up her water bottle and took a big gulp. It was disturbing to admit she'd had a psychotic episode originating in the course of a severe anxiety attack, but she took comfort in confirmation that the altered reality was contained inside her head. As long as she remembered her vision wasn't real, she was in control.

"All right," she did her best to sound casual. "Do you mind if we talk about the morning's incident?"

"Nothing to talk about." John's voice was cool. "I am fully recovered."

He pursed his lips and looked away, signaling his frustration, but Anna was determined not to give in. She was in control.

"So, do you know who you are?"

"I do, indeed." Still pouting, he tucked a strand of hair behind his long ear.

"And before, when you said you had memory loss, were you telling the truth?"

"Why would I pretend to suffer from such a disgraceful affliction?"

"I'm not accusing you. I hope you wouldn't lie to me."

"I never lie, not to you, not to anyone."

"Good. For the record, what is your name?"

"My family name is Fairfax."

"And the first name?"

He tightened his mouth, shooting her a reproachful glare.

"May I continue calling you John?"

He sighed and shrugged. She chose to interpret it as an agreement.

"Are there any family members you'd like me to contact?"

"They all died ages ago."

"And what is your current age?"

"Twenty-seven years."

Only a year older than me, thought Anna, allowing the soothing sensation of normalcy to saturate her. She would break this case after all.

"All right, Mr. Fairfax, where you were born?"

"I was born in my family homestead, in the village of Lynton, by the Roman wall."

"Lynton. Romanwall. Great. What state is it in?"

A smirk twisted his mouth. "It must be in a rather decrepit state, I'm sure, considering that over thirteen hundred years have passed."

All air of normalcy dissipated as a violent wind of the otherworldly ripped through the space. Anna felt chills.

"You promised me I'll be the first to hear your story." She heard herself sound like a whiny child. "You gave me your word!"

"I have, indeed, made such a promise." He leaned on the pillow. "But not a soul in this whole world has heard it yet, so as long as I keep it this way, I'm honoring my word, aren't I?"

Where was the sincere, amenable patient who was so eager to help her solve his own tragic mystery? Where had the vulnerable and sweet boy gone? Before her was an unpredictable man, who playfully broke through all the structures she'd so carefully constructed. Now he lounged in his bed, twirling his hair, flashing an arrogant grin, so full of himself, so sure he had beaten her.

"I don't think you understand the seriousness of your situation, Mr. Fairfax." Anna's formal tone barely concealed her anger. "Let me sum it up for you. You were brought into a psychiatric hospital by the police. You have no identification, no money or clothes—"

He broke her off with a huff. "These are such trifles! What matters is I know who I am. Can you in all honesty say the same about yourself?"

She wanted to scream, "I know who I am!" but that would be admitting defeat. She pushed on, as if against the wind. "Before your fight, you could have walked out freely, but now the hospital won't release you unless you have a permanent address and assurance of supervision."

"Let me understand this: you could have told me I was free to go at any time, yet you chose to detain me here, to solve riddles for your pleasure. Ah, you do care after all!" He threw back his head and burst into a wild, triumphant laughter.

It was bad enough she'd succumbed to a panic attack, hallucinated to a point where she couldn't distinguish illusion from reality. Now he mocked her authority.

"We are done here." Anna rose and headed for the door. "I'm afraid I can no longer help you."

He stopped laughing as abruptly as he had started and sat straight on the edge of the bed, dropping his feet as if he were about to run after her.

"Anna, I have wasted enough time." His voice now rang with a dire sincerity. Her plan to scare him straight had worked. "You were the only one I knew even when I didn't know myself. You gave meaning to my being here. Please allow me to tell you my story."

"Please get dressed, Mr. Fairfax," she said quickly, looking away from his neat ankles. "It's almost eight o'clock, time for breakfast. The nurse is about to bring your meal. You must eat, you have a long day ahead."

She expected him to plead or bargain or at least inquire if she was coming back for him, but he only bowed his head. In the doorway she couldn't help it and glanced over her shoulder: he was looking at her with a docile yet cheery expression, the same way a large, powerful dog grovels only for the sake of being playful.

Anna knew it was her duty to report the unexplained seizure that had taken place during the violence assessment. Yet, even before she entered the group room for the morning conference and sat in her chair, she had decided to lie about it—*correction, omit it.*

The fight had been bad enough. It meant she'd missed something about John when she'd initially assessed him. Bringing up the seizure meant revealing it was her necklace that had triggered it. She would have to describe John's inexplicable transformation, which had no rational explanation besides that she'd been tripping balls. She knew exactly what it looked like: the spontaneous visual distortions she experienced resembled the psychedelic effects of an LSD high. But the few times she had she had dropped acid—out of scientific curiosity, of course—she'd gotten so anxious that Genie had had to spend hours talking her down. This time she felt strangely energized.

But to go before the staff psychiatrists and announce that she had come to work hungover, and experienced a severe anxiety attack involving a psychedelic hallucination while interviewing a patient who'd gone violent on her watch . . . no, she simply could not bring herself to do so. Why did it have to happen with Dr. Stevens away? Screwing up meant not only a personal disgrace, but also failing her supervisor who had gone out of her way to be supportive, even given her, a lowly intern, a case custom-tailored for her dissertation. And as to the ethics of omitting information pertinent to a patient's health and security—well, John looked mighty healthy and secure when she left him.

"A violent altercation between the paranoid ex-con and the amnesiac Doe. The first patient is mine. As of 6:30 a.m. he is admitted and being treated for physical injuries. Anna, would you like to report on the amnesiac case? Anna? Anna Reilly!"

The voice of Thomas, the medical intern, knocked her out of her panicked thought loop. Then she heard calm and confident words coming out of her mouth, as if she were reading a prepared text off a page.

"A twenty-seven-year-old homeless Caucasian male with no criminal record has been brought in by the police after being found unconscious and naked in the park. The initial MSE revealed no pathology besides the memory loss due to an unspecified trauma. While in observation, he defended himself against a sexual assault by another male patient, but otherwise exhibited no violent tendencies—on the contrary, has demonstrated a consistently compliant attitude. In the follow-up interview he was able to recall his last name, Fairfax, as well as other details of his life. While he refused to divulge any more personal information, Mr. Fairfax appears lucid and reasonable. He is in excellent physical health, with no signs of substance abuse. Considering that he's been voluntary, and the seventy-two-hour observation period is ending, I recommend discharging Mr. Fairfax into a temporary housing facility with a follow-up interview scheduled in a week."

"Does anyone have anything to add?" asked Dr. Cohen without looking up from his notes. Silence was the answer. "Very well. I concur with the discharge. Next case!"

As she walked back to her office, Anna marveled at the power of language. She told a story, and it was like magic: spelling out the mystery of John Fairfax in clear and positive terms made everything look clear and positive. Yes, she would discharge him to a shelter, do the follow-up, then get him as her research participant, signed consent forms and all. She'd make sure he was properly compensated. It would be good for him. It would be good for them both.

Now, all she had to do was to find Mr. Fairfax a free and safe shelter. In New York City. On a Sunday. *Pull off a magic trick, why don't ya?* No problem, she can do it. His case will make her academic career.

"Or break it," she said out loud and laughed, and stopped abruptly, realizing her laughter sounded as wild as John's.

The Bellevue live-in rehab was her first choice. John qualified: a homeless male with no history of substance abuse, he was eligible for a six-month stay. Not surprisingly, though, the rehab was full. Her next choice was Saint Francis Residences, where Bellevue and the on-site teams worked together, and she would have direct access to John. But she only succeeded in placing him on the waiting list for Tuesday. Anna kept calling shelters and rehabs in the directory, and with each rejection her heart sunk lower. She couldn't tell what was worse: the possibility that John Fairfax would end up lost in the cold winter streets of New York, or the thought that she would never get to solve his mystery. Trained to analyze her own inner motions, Anna readily admitted professional ambition to be not her sole motivation. Somehow, this man disturbed some deep layer of her psyche, a part she couldn't access on her own. The anxiety attack he triggered in her was nothing short of a psychotic episode complete with severe derealization, the worst she'd ever had. She should have been concerned, and yet she felt stimulated, almost thrilled with the promise of discovery—better yet, self-discovery. Now, this was a mystery worthy of investigation. It reminded her of one of her professor's words: "All grand pronouncements aside, the most noble reason to go into the mental health profession is to better understand oneself."

So what if she was being a little selfish? Her motivation was good. She was in a position to help someone else. Was it so bad if she helped herself in the process?

The only place with an immediate vacancy was a homeless shelter located all the way across town, near the Lincoln Tunnel. Anna knew the neighborhood. It wasn't far from her own stomping grounds, the Garment District, in the gloomier and more industrial area near the bus terminal. The municipal facility wasn't Anna's first choice, but it was better than nothing. The social worker she talked to on the phone promised a bed for at least one night—sufficient to discharge the patient legally. She didn't want to think about what would happen the day after tomorrow. *We'll cross that bridge when we come to it*, she said to herself and began filling the discharge papers for John Fairfax, formerly John Doe.

Time flew by, and she all but forgot to call Ted and take a rain check on their usual Sunday evening dinner. She told him she had to work late because of an emergency. It was almost the truth.

"The patient is waiting in the lobby. Someone has to take him to the discharge location to make sure he's signed in." The nurse sounded irritated, preempting Anna's potential discontent. "And the social worker is gone for the day. Oh, yeah, and it's snowing."

Anna looked at her wristwatch: it was seven o'clock. "I'll have to deliver him myself, I suppose." She allowed just enough reluctance to leak into her voice to conceal her glee.

The nurse looked at her like she had volunteered to donate her kidney, and Anna felt an immediate pang of shame.

"Has he eaten?" Business-like, she shoved Mr. Fairfax's file into her handbag. It was too late to turn back.

"He was served dinner at six. Oh, and I've got him a winter coat from the Coat Drive bin." The nurse's tone had switched to that of concern. Anna chuckled: now they sounded like amicably divorced parents making arrangements for a child's sleepover.

"Thanks for the coat! See you on Wednesday."

Anna's shift included the weekend, with Monday and Tuesday off. This gave her plenty of rest before Wednesday, which was her ER rotation. It was a harsh way to start the work week. "A bit masochistic, maybe?" Ted had commented when she showed him her internship schedule. "Comes with the territory," she had answered, shielding herself behind self-deprecation. The truth was, Anna welcomed the challenge. She had long ago reconciled with the fact that she enjoyed the extreme pressure, indeed, thrived under it. She loved the tough cases, the mystery, the chase, the high stakes, and ultimately, the happy exhaustion washing over her upon completion of a case—just like competitive sports, but with higher stakes, because in intellectual pursuits the only true competition is yourself.

John Fairfax was not in the lobby. Panicked, she ran outside, into the hospital garden. Anna's heart was pounding, hot bitter tears burned her throat. How could he bail on her now, after she'd put so much work into helping him? It served her right for making exceptions.

"Ahn-nah!" called the familiar voice. She turned around. Bareheaded, John stood under the trees, seemingly undisturbed by the snow. He wore a long wool coat, one of those ridiculous vintage pseudo-military coats with big shoulders and elaborate trim. White tennis shoes on his feet completed the absurd picture. In the back of her mind, Anna registered that the falling snow obscured the shabbiness of his secondhand garb, so to a casual observer he might have looked quite dashing, like a fashion-forward young New Yorker with a penchant for ironic apparel.

"You can't just—" She felt like kicking him. "—leave me!"

He blinked. "I would never! Unless you command me."

The bluish streetlight cast sharp shadows on his hollow cheeks, making him look frail and fragile, much more like a regular patient than the supreme being from her hallucination. He had snowflakes in his hair. Anna was ashamed for yelling at this willowy young man in a silly overcoat. The opulence of his features made her forget he was in need: of shelter, clothes, human connection. Too wound up to talk, she silently motioned for him to follow, and strode out of the hospital gates.

Puffy snow clusters floated on the air, dissipating before they touched the ground. As Anna inhaled the cold damp air, she wondered if her pace was too brisk for John, who'd been in his sick bed only this morning.

"I hope you're up for a hike in the snow." She tried not to sound overly apologetic.

"I like snow," replied John, turning his face toward the dark sky speckled with white flakes.

"We'll head for the cross-town bus. I could try to catch a cab, but . . ." Just as Anna contemplated the proposition of being stuck in a tight backseat with John, he said with a sweet smile, "I'd rather walk. I like walking."

The homeless shelter was all the way across town, in a neighborhood dominated by the Port Authority Bus Terminal, a massive utilitarian construction without much pretense at aesthetics, surrounded by speakeasies and strip clubs welcoming the weary traveler as he stepped off the bus. The exhaust from the idling buses mixed with an occasional whiff of pot. Busy with commuters during the work week, on Sunday evening the neighborhood had a distinctly desolate feel. The few people in the street seemed to be passing through, couldn't get away fast enough. It was hard to believe that the glamorous Theater District and Anna's own blue-collar Garment District were only a couple of blocks away.

Anna watched John furtively, trying to gauge his reaction to the city he claimed was so alien. The first couple of times he heard the scream of a siren or the screech of brakes he flinched, but got a hold of himself right away. He sniffed the air and scanned the buildings, cars, and crowds, watching businessmen and the homeless with the same reserved curiosity, but if he had any impressions, he kept them to himself. Every once in a while he would catch Anna's eye and his face would light up. Anna would look away.

The promised safe harbor amid the sea of chaos was located in an old warehouse-like brownstone. Anna pressed the doorbell till her thumb went numb. The metal door finally opened, revealing a night attendant. He looked like he could have been a resident: an overweight man, a life of hard times spelled out on his ruddy face.

"I have an appointment," announced Anna, flashing her Bellevue ID. The heavy door shut behind them, and they followed the attendant down the corridor to the social worker's office.

"Ah, smells like a dozen broken men and one angry woman," declared John with some kind of idiotic amusement. The red-faced attendant gave him a look-over and produced a grin that, Anna could have sworn, qualified as salacious. Suddenly, she was about to throw up. She couldn't leave the sensitive, vulnerable John in this place. He would get into trouble in no time. But what else could she do? It's not like she could bring him home . . .

"I called from Bellevue. Here, the patient's discharge papers." She placed John's file on the desk. The social worker reluctantly looked up.

"To be admitted you've got to register before four thirty. It's quarter to eight. The curfew is at eight," she replied in a monotone.

Anna could physically sense her authority evaporate under the stony gaze of the tired-looking older woman.

"I made arrangements over the phone around noon today."

"I have no record of it."

"He's a patient right from the psychiatric emergency unit, he needs a bed for a single night in order to be discharged . . ."

"He should have registered before four thirty."

"But I was promised a bed by the person I talked to . . ."

"You didn't talk to me."

"Look, I can't leave the man in the street. It's snowing!"

"And this is why the facility is maxed out."

"Come on, what do you want me to do with him?"

"Miss, he's your problem."

Anna knew the system well enough to see that persistence was futile. Pressing John's file against her chest, she stepped out of the office and leaned against the wall, trying to hold back angry tears. John, who was waiting in the company of the red-faced attendant, gave her a concerned look.

Anna cursed under her breath and took off her glasses to rub her eyes. A tactful cough reminded her of the source of her troubles. John was hovering over her, propping himself against the wall on his arm, as if trying to shield her from the inhospitable world.

"There's a complication," muttered Anna, too demoralized to care about his overwhelming closeness.

"What would you have me do?" His voice rang with resolve and, unexpectedly, kindness. With no trace of the earlier arrogance, he was back to the gentle and compliant boy she'd met seventy-two hours ago.

"Well, you can't spend the night here."

"No, I can't." He wearily leaned against the wall next to her. For a moment they stood shoulder to shoulder, a parody of comrades in arms, the two of them against the world. Anna noticed that John was slowly sliding down.

"Hey, hey, Mr. Fairfax." She grabbed him by the forearm, pulling him up to his feet. His coat opened, and she was hit with a wave of heat radiating from him: he was running a fever. "Are you all right?"

"This stench . . . of misery. I need fresh air." With a wince, he leaned against her.

When Anna was little, she got a Pet Rock as a joke gift—a plain smooth stone in a cardboard box, a fad that came and went before her time. The joke backfired when she cried with inconsolable tears of a deceived child: what she really wanted was a puppy. To make it up to her, her mom replaced the box with her cosmetics bag, a drawstring purse made of lush Chinese silk that little Anna coveted. The heavy hard rock through the thick slippery fabric fascinated her senses, she couldn't stop touching it. This is how John felt: rock wrapped in silk.

Furiously blushing, with her handbag under one arm and John clinging to the other, Anna saw herself out. The cold sooty air with a tinge of garbage had never felt so refreshing. John appeared to have recovered from his fainting spell, but still looked feeble—the recent trauma must finally have caught up with him. Looking into his drawn face, Anna flushed with guilt. She'd had no right to discharge him in his current state. She'd ripped this man out of the only place he was safe, and now she bore direct responsibility for him.

She needed to think, to come up with an alternate plan. A diner across the street seemed like a perfect spot to regroup.

"What would you like to eat?" she asked, watching John lodge his narrow body in the corner of the pleather-covered booth seat.

"I can't eat here," he muttered, hugging himself.

"Two coffees, please," said Anna to the waitress.

"Both for you?" The waitress sounded perplexed.

"Why, one for me and one for him." Anna nodded at John across the table.

For a moment, the waitress stared at her blankly, until John stirred in his spot. She turned to him and nearly dropped her notepad.

"Ah! Didn't see you there." She was too startled to apologize. "Be right back with your coffees."

"That was odd," said Anna, bemused.

John twitched his shoulder dismissively.

"I was effecting obscurity." Responding to her raised eyebrows, he explained, "It's a way of making people pay you no mind until you want them to."

"Why would you do that?"

"For safety."

"You don't feel safe with me?"

He managed a small smile. "No offense, dear, I know you mean well. However, my current state is precarious."

Before Anna could ask him about how exactly one effects obscurity, someone turned up the volume on the TV above the counter.

"Continuing with the weather report," announced the talking head on the screen. "The National Weather Service has issued a blizzard warning for New York City and Long Island northeastward along the southern Connecticut coast to the Providence and Boston metro areas. Winds of up to ninety-one miles per hour and accumulations between sixteen and twenty inches are forecast, with heavier snow expected in some areas. Looks like we should expect a regular nor'easter, which is—ha-ha—quite irregular this early in the season."

"You don't want to be out in the streets tonight," commented the waitress, placing two coffee mugs on the table.

In the warm incandescent light of the diner, John's pallor had acquired a creepily sallow tint. Next to his sunken cheeks, his ears stuck out more than usual, animal-like. His sleek eyebrows had been drawn into a permanent frown of concentration, as if he were making an inhuman effort to hold himself together. Slowly, he twirled his mug on the table, leaving the coffee untouched.

"How long ago did you find me?" His mug made a full circle.

"You were brought into the hospital a little over three days ago."

"This means I haven't slept for three nights." He rubbed his face as if to hide the expression of panic Anna could clearly read in his darkened eyes. "If I don't rest properly, I . . . won't live long. You see, my kind . . . we dream to live. Without sleep there is no dreaming, and without dreaming life will not be sustained."

It's hard for him to admit to weakness, thought Anna, listening to his labored speech. He resorted to poetic metaphors every time he found facing reality difficult, as if manifesting an enchanted armor to protect his soft skin.

“You mentioned it in the interview, but I didn’t realize you are in such discomfort.” She mumbled, crushed by unbearable shame. The fiasco at the shelter was her fault, and now the vulnerable man had no place to spend the night.

“Neither did I, but what dreams may come at a filthy place like that prison house? I need a clean place. A place where I am want— welcomed.”

His smooth voice, with a subtle rumble, sounded urgent. Without a doubt, in his mind he was facing a real danger, and it terrified him.

“You may spend the night at my place.”

The words rolled off Anna’s tongue, and a heavy burden fell off her shoulders. It was a solution, an unconventional, borderline unethical solution, but quite possibly the only humane one. John would spend the next two nights at her apartment—*no, it sounds wrong, rephrase*: the patient would be temporarily accommodated at her office while waiting for the bed at Saint Francis, available on Tuesday. She wasn’t back to the hospital till Wednesday anyway. She could monitor him for thirty-six hours and still get some rest. *Yeah, this is it!* Anna smiled.

John responded with a look she interpreted as grateful.

The snow flurry was over. Only single specks danced in the glowing columns underneath the street lamps, like tiny moths drawn to the light. The glorious city reveled in its holiday fuss. In shop and restaurant windows Christmas reds and greens had begun to phase out the Thanksgiving browns. They walked down Eighth Avenue past the ever-bustling Penn Station, through the festive crowd gathering for some event at Madison Square Garden, crossed Seventh Avenue, and entered the heart of the Garment District. It was right before nine when Anna opened the door to her apartment.

She flipped the light switch, suddenly feeling exposed as her small studio lay in front of the two of them. Seeing John hesitate at the threshold, she muttered, “Welcome,” as she let him pass. John stepped right into the center of the room and looked at the skylight, his sharp chin up, his blond hair spilling over his shoulders.

“This is home, then.” His tone was half-affirming, half-questioning.

Anna expected a comment to follow his remark, either a compliment or a condescending observation, but he said no more, leaving her to wonder. She followed his gaze as he surveyed the space, rotating clockwise, trying to see it through his eyes. A work desk to the right from the door, next to it a futon couch and a coffee table with an armchair across, the bed in the window corner walled off by bookshelves, an open kitchenette at the opposite wall and another door leading to the bathroom. Her studio was pretty bare: anything personal she kept at her parents' place, and anything work-related at her office at Bellevue.

"More like a workplace," she replied dryly and waved her hand at the futon, inviting him to sit. He plopped down without taking off his coat.

So, the patient ended up on my couch after all, she thought, watching John assume a languorous pose. Even in his current poor shape he managed to exude elegance, making Anna's humble space grander and brighter.

"It's generous of you to share your bed with me." He caressed the futon cushion with the tips of his fingers.

"This is not my bed."

She went behind the bookcase separating her private space from the office, where her actual bed stood in an alcove by the window, and returned with an extra pillow.

"Here. Grab the throw if you get cold." She picked up her laptop from the desk and checked the locked drawers. It was smart not to keep anything valuable here. Of course, leaving a stranger alone at her place was a risk, but how much damage could one exhausted man do?

"There's bottled water in the fridge, some cheese, bread, cold cuts. If you get hungry, feel free to make yourself a sandwich. Have a good night, and I'll see you tomorrow morning."

"Where are you going?" inquired John, observing her manipulations with a deepening scowl.

"I'm spending the night at my f . . . friend's home." She caught herself right in time before saying *fiancé*. She didn't need to surrender that bit of personal information.

"Leaving me here?"

"It's only overnight, until long-term housing becomes available," said Anna, annoyed by his lack of appreciation. She was showing him a lot of trust, and he sounded as if she was dumping him in the gutter.

"Alone?"

"Yes."

"Don't go." His eyebrows quivered. "I . . . won't sleep alone."

"And I won't sleep with you . . . er . . . I mean, under one roof with you!"

"We don't have to sleep," offered John hurriedly. "We could spend the night talking. I'll give you my story. Isn't it what you want?"

The trauma was finally manifesting: perhaps his fear of abandonment rendered him willing to offer disclosure in exchange for company. She could work with that.

"Didn't you say you'd die if you don't get some sleep?"

"I have been welcomed in, so my demise is no longer imminent." With a lopsided grin, he shrugged out of his coat and kicked off his shoes. Anna exhaled. She was breaking his walls after all.

"How are you feeling?"

"Deeply." He scratched behind his long ear and swallowed a yawn.

She hung up both their coats, moved aside the little dish with jellybeans to make room for the phone and the notebook, and sat in the armchair across from John. "Are you ready to tell me who you are?"

"Yes." He propped himself with a pillow.

"Give me your story, Mr. Fairfax, as you promised."

"Like any story without end, mine has no beginning."

"Begin as far as back as you can recall."

He leaned back, put his narrow palms flat on his lap, took a deep breath, and spoke in his low, melodic voice: "Their hair was the color of straw, and that's how the Fairfax forefathers earned their name."

AWAKENING

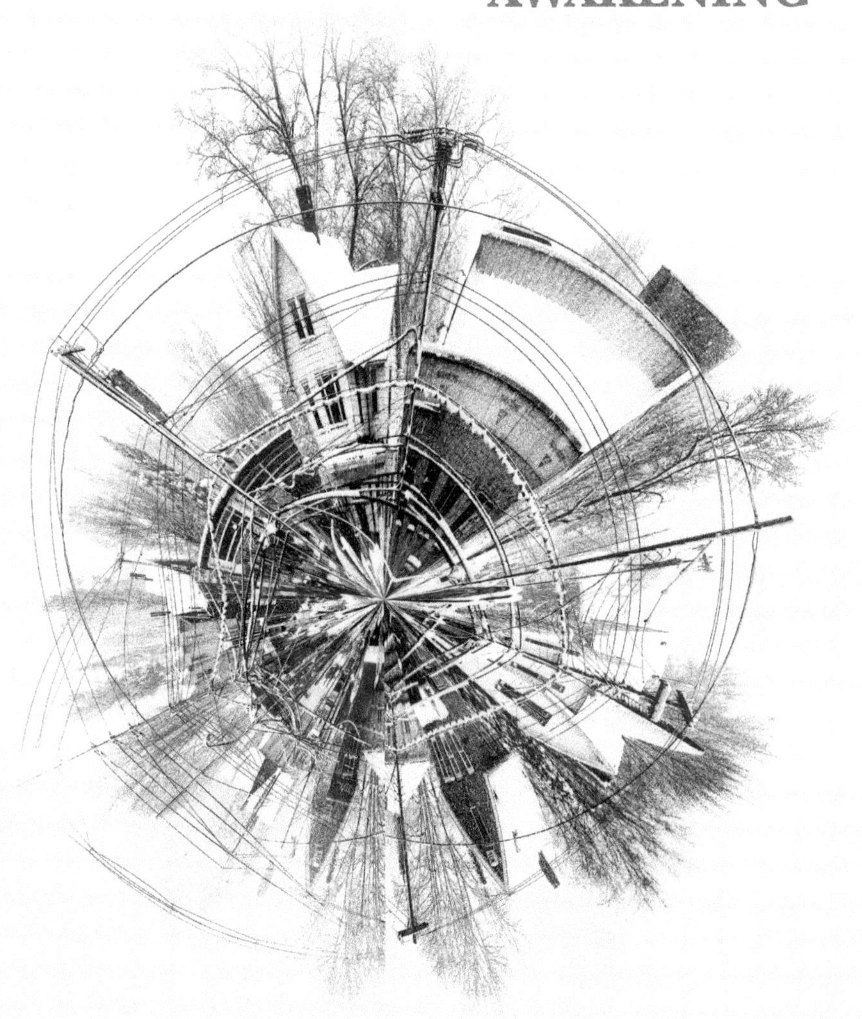

Monday, December 1

The light becomes darkness, the darkness fades, and everything is clear, and everything is bright. Snow rushes in her face. She is a girl again, back in Michigan, running a ski relay with her school's Nordic team. Accompanied by the strong drumbeat of her heart, her young body sings a high, triumphant chord. Arrow-like she flies along the track, high on the frozen air. But each powerful stroke, each deep breath fills her with a certainty: she is her fourteen-year-old self in present day New York. *This never happened*, thinks the real Anna. This must be a dream. Suddenly, her twenty-six-year-old self stands on the top of a hill, still wearing her old ski boots and jacket, except the snow and her skis have vanished. Green grass is everywhere the eye can see. The still air is warm against her skin. A sunless sky. Pearlescent light floods everything.

The boy of her dream is here. She's sure of it, even though she can't see him clearly. His silhouette fades in the bright haze, and every time she looks, he shifts out of sight.

What happened? she asks, and a man's voice behind her answers, *The binding is broken.*

She wakes up.

At first she kept her eyes shut, relishing the perfect recollection. Then came fear of loss. A moment passed, and another, but the memory of the dream lingered—crisp like winter air, fragrant like a summer breeze, enticing like the voice that had spoken to her. She knew this soft, low voice, she'd been listening to it all night long. It belonged to . . . damn.

Trying not to stir in her armchair, Anna opened her eyes and took stock of herself. Her shoulders were stiff, legs had fallen asleep. A plaid throw had been tucked around her. *I don't recall putting on a blanket*, she noted with a hollowness in her chest like when barreling down a steep hill. She'd fallen asleep in front of a patient. No, worse: she'd spent the night with a man she'd dragged home from the Bellevue psych ward. Panicked, she looked around, doing her best not to make a sound.

The ghostly glow from the skylight illuminated the figure across from her, a face in a halo of white hair belonging to a man curled into a cozy ball in the corner of her couch, his head resting on his folded arm. Side lit, his angular features appeared deceptively plain, sculpted by the unfaltering hand of a minimalist artist. Almost too fine to be attractive, the same way an essential oil is too intense to be pleasant. Yet, a distinct sense of power radiated from his face and body, as if he were a master model of which everyone else, including her, was a scale cast. No wonder strangers seemed drawn in by his mystique, each in a way revealing their own character, some compelled to protect him, others to possess.

What draws me? The thought made her sigh.

His eyes snapped open, he sat upright and batted his eyelashes at her.

With a moan, Anna threw off the blanket, unfolded her tingling legs, and wobbled out of the chair. She flipped the light switch on and squinted, her eyes adjusting to the light. The coffee table was littered with candy wrappers. A pile of papers on the floor. Her phone, dead.

"I'm so sorry, I must have dozed off."

"No, I beg forgiveness for wearing you out. Twenty-seven years in a single night. . ." He slicked back his ruffled hair with his fingers. "I trust you enjoyed your dream?"

She frowned, taking off her glasses to rub her eyes. "What time is it?"

"Sun will rise any minute," he replied with a little yawn. His voice was raspy from sleep, but he seemed much healthier than the day before; in fact, he looked as good as right after his mysterious transformation at the hospital. His pale skin gleamed, his gray eyes shone bright and clear. Even his hair seemed glossy.

Anna made a mindless circle around the room, picking up strewn sheets of paper and candy wrappers, folding the blanket—anything to bide her time and collect her thoughts. She knew he was following her with his eyes. He seemed relaxed, perfectly at home, like lounging on her couch was his usual thing. It was strange how normal it felt, considering his recent disclosure. But then again, in her own notes from last night the words *unreliable narrator* were underlined twice, so everything he'd told her was to be taken with a bucketful of salt.

"So." She took a deep breath. "You are an elf."

He winced. "It is Alva. The Firstborn. The Fair Folk, Brighter Than The Sun. In any case, I am half-human."

"Right. Half-man, half-Alva. And you are over thirteen hundred years old."

"No, I'm still twenty-seven years old. I haven't aged since I was taken to the Otherworld."

"Right. And before you . . . were taken, you lived in North Umbria?"

"Northumbria. In the north of Britain, by Hadrian's Wall."

"And what year were you born?"

"The year of Christ Six Hundred and Fifty. Anna, did you pay any attention, or do I have to tell you everything over again?"

He didn't have to. Even without checking her extensive notes, she could easily recollect his story, which was as vivid as it was fantastic.

According to John Fairfax, he'd been born in mid-seventh-century Britain to a teenage girl and an unknown male *elf*—a term he deemed derogatory. The boy, who was named Yaret, had never met his supernatural father, and his mother died a week after childbirth. His mother's grieving twin brother, Alric, became a devout Christian, entering the priesthood and forcing a religious education on his nephew as well. The Church upbringing didn't prevent young Yaret from developing supernatural abilities, like forecasting weather and healing minor ailments. He seemed eager to please others, but socially awkward: Anna gathered he was a profoundly empathic child, but with no clue how to interpret the emotions he observed in others. Among other otherworldly gifts, he claimed, was his inability to lie, which she found ironic.

Despite being the only heir of a family with a high social standing, he'd been starved for affection. He had no friends his age. His only living relatives, grandmother and uncle, seemed wary of him. One day, as the nine-year-old boy was wandering the woods on his own, a drifter tried to rape him. He claimed to have killed the man "without even soiling his blade." Anna was horrified when she heard this, but after he elaborated, she became convinced that, while the attempted rape could have been real (giving a context to the recent incident at Bellevue), the killing was likely the fruit of the child's imagination—after all, he insisted he had "turned the man inside out" by the means of elf magic.

Whether the retaliation had taken place or not, the trauma had been real for the boy, because after the incident he had run off into the woods, half out of his mind, only to be rescued by a woman named Caireann, who was, in his own words, a "wild witch."

For the next six years the witch Caireann took young Yaret on as an apprentice. The way he spoke, or rather gently avoided speaking about her, showed an affection so deep and tender that Anna felt relief: a textbook sociopath would have been devoid of loving attachments. According to him, by the age of fifteen he went from student to suitor, but before their relationship was consummated some accident occurred, which he described vaguely. To escape the consequences, his uncle, the priest, had to whisk him away on a pilgrimage to Rome.

Anna had never been to Italy, but the way he described the Eternal City's sights, sounds, and smells had a gritty authenticity she couldn't help but trust. Apparently, at first the sixteen-year-old Yaret hated the city, showing his resentment by drinking heavily and participating in underground cage fights (the latter, again, explaining the practiced brutality with which he'd dispatched the ex-con at Bellevue). To bring him into the fold, his Christian hosts assigned him a companion, Valerian, a novice monk of his age. Again, Anna could sense genuine love in the way he described Valerian, but he became elusive again, leaving Anna with a distinct feeling that his concept of love contradicted Valerian's. So, young Yaret found himself crushed and alone once more.

Sometime around the Roman part of his adventure, her phone had run out of memory. By then, she was struggling to keep her eyes open, so the rest of his story was a blur.

At twenty, Yaret returned to England where he led the quiet life of a gentleman farmer, interrupted only by an occasional plague or Viking invasion. Martha, a mute teenage girl he bought at a slave market (Anna shuddered re-reading those lines) became his companion for the next seven years, though (as she was relieved to confirm) the relationship never turned physical.

And then Anna fell asleep.

And had a dream.

And remembered it—the first dream she was aware of in over a decade.

And he was in it.

Right now, all she wanted was to sit quietly and contemplate her personal breakthrough. But another person shared her couch, someone so damaged he wasn't even able to address his past without dressing it in a fancy medieval garment. Her inability to access her dream life seemed insignificant next to his inability to access anything but.

Her training dictated that the patient comes first. *He is not my patient,* Anna snapped back mentally, but, nevertheless, forced herself to file her dream away and focus on John. He might not be her patient formally, but even in her capacity as researcher she was already engaged in a therapeutic relationship with this man, and he was in desperate need of professional help.

Anna was well versed in translating the archetypal imagery into medical language. Mr. Fairfax's magical Dark Ages fantasy revealed real-life issues. An identity confusion. Problems with authority. An indication of trauma: possibly physical and emotional, probably sexual. Definitely, a history of romantic dysfunction: he had admitted to romancing a much older woman, a heterosexual man, and an underage employee. Whoever those people truly were, or whatever the metaphors of *witch*, *monk*, and *slave* signified in his narrative, to her it was clear as day: in all of his life this man had never had an adult relationship. For all his developed intellect, sensibility, and physique, psychologically he remained very much a boy.

So, he came up with this alternate persona of Yaret the half-elf, reasoned Anna. His elaborate fantasy must have started as a way to cope with trauma and became the core of his personality, in effect making his false memories the only memories he had. He'd created a whole universe inside his mind, equipped with a unique personal mythology of elves, whom he reimagined not as the magical fairies of legend but rather as an otherworldly alien race, erroneously deified and even more falsely demonized by our primitive human ancestors.

His delusion was as spectacular as it was profound. Whether she took him on as a research participant or as a client, any kind of inquiry would have to address the real circumstances behind his fantasy, the actual trauma he sought to escape. Although Anna never fancied herself an intuitive therapist, she knew that the very process of her inquiry could mitigate the patient's pain, ease his descent to reality. He needed her.

But she needed him just as much. In her wildest dreams, she couldn't have found a better illustration for her paper. John was a psychiatrically sound person who was coping with trauma by generating a delusion—her perfect research subject. All the years of trying to put together a puzzle of statistical data, case studies, and her own insights, all her hard work could gloriously culminate in this final piece.

To help him, she had to have his trust within his own internal frame of reference. The only way to establish effective communication was to speak the language of his delusion without indulging it.

She had to enter his reality. Share his world while staying anchored in the real.

Anna looked at her watch: quarter to six on Monday morning. If Saint Francis took him in as she hoped, she had two free days ahead before her next shift at the hospital.

Should be enough to figure out the right course. She felt resolved and hopeful, for the first time in a long time.

Seeing her smile, John said brightly:

"Well, on with my tale. In the year of Christ Six Hundred and Seventy-Seven winter came early, first snow fell by the end of *Blōtmonaþ*. On one such snowy night, the burden of my heart grew too heavy to bear. I ascended to the top of the hill fort and prayed to be accepted into my father's house. The snow purified me until the earthly life left me, the falling stars streaked the skies, and the Alva welcomed me. In my father's world—of which I shall not speak—I lived for many centuries, until . . ."

"Stop!" cried Anna, dropping her notebook on the desk. "I can't absorb any more. I need coffee. I need food. Real food, not jelly beans. You must be hungry too."

"Like I haven't eaten in a thousand years."

She opened the fridge. "Let's see what I've got here. Do you eat eggs?"

"I don't like eggs."

"Tater tots?"

"What is it made of?"

"Potato."

"What is that?"

"Oh, never mind. Pasta?"

"Pasta?"

"All right, Dark Ages Europe had no potatoes. But how could you have lived in Rome and never eaten boiled noodles?"

"Those were baked. I don't mind those. I like bread too."

"Cheese?"

"I only eat cow cheese."

"Fish?"

"If I catch it myself."

"Meat?"

"Depends on how fresh."

"Riiight . . . What do you like?"

"I like apples, berries, nuts, and honey."

"Well, aren't you granola."

John pursed his lips and lowered his eyes. "You're well aware I don't know what it means. You talk to me as though I am a child or a savage. It behooves you to remember, I am neither younger than you, nor less cultured."

She bit her tongue. Her sarcasm was out of line, unprofessional.

"I was only complimenting your food choices," she mumbled, trying to avoid a direct apology.

He rose, stretched his wiry limbs, and stood before of the full-length mirror by the front door, looking himself over with a visible displeasure.

"No wonder you talk down to me," he said testily. "I look disgraceful. I must cleanse myself with water. And these clothes are tainted with the stench of unhealth. I'd rather go naked than wear these." He tugged at his hospital shirt.

"That won't be necessary," squeaked Anna and hopped to her closet. "I'm sure I can spare some clothes."

She handed John a fresh towel, and, after brief consideration, a pair of clean sweatpants and a T-shirt. He was wider in the shoulders and narrower in the hips than her, but she was sure he wouldn't have a problem fitting into her clothes—they were nearly the same size. She demonstrated how to operate the capricious mixer shower, which hadn't been replaced since the 1930s, then told him to put his hospital garb in a plastic bag and leave it outside the bathroom door. As he reached for the elastic band of his hospital pants, she hurried to exit the bathroom. Soon a pale hand poked from behind the bathroom door, dropping the plastic bag. Anna grabbed it and ran out of the apartment, down the four flights of stairs, to the street.

The chilly wind cooled her cheeks. At first she thought of dropping John's clothes off at the 24-hour Laundromat around the corner. Instead, obeying some unexpected squeamishness, she dumped the whole bag into the trash. In the dark winter air, a faint fog rose from the rotting trash, like the smoke of burning bridges. The trash can lid slammed with a bang, and Anna was struck by the irrevocability of her action. She was like the hero of the fairy tales she used to read to Jack, the dimwit who destroys an enchanted creature's old skin and by this impulsive gesture invites all kinds of trouble.

What the hell? inquired her voice of reason. *How's it going to look tomorrow when he shows up at the shelter wearing your clothes?* The answer was simple: John, of course, was going to look gorgeous, and she was going to look like a creep. *Hey, it's not what it seems*, she said to herself. *All I'm doing is building trust. I'll get him some new clothes before I take him to the shelter. But right now, it would be inhumane not to feed and clothe the man.*

She stopped at the corner deli to get him a toothbrush and also grabbed a carton of orange juice, a two-pound sack of apples, a tin of mixed nuts, and a jar of honey. After a little hesitation, she bought a quart of expensive organic blueberries. This man was already costing her more than she could afford.

She looked up: the lights going on and off in her apartment, John playing with the light switch. He was consistent in his persona of a time traveler curious about modern technology, and she found it oddly comforting. As she climbed the stairs, she registered that leaving this stranger alone in her home didn't bother her in the least.

He was standing by the bookshelf, his freshly washed hair lustrous in the electric light. Barefoot, he was the same height as Anna in her shoes, but his slender build and elongated proportions of an art deco figurine made him seem taller. Her purple NYU T-shirt stretched tightly over his straight shoulders, and her gray drawstring pants slung low on his hips, offering a revealing view of a long narrow torso. He was slight, but all muscle—even, smooth, rolling muscles of a wild animal. The grace of his body was matched by the radiance of his face. Involuntarily, Anna licked her lips.

He caught her appraising glance, and his fine mouth curved in a grimace of disappointment.

"Child, savage, or stud. What will it be, Anna?"

"I don't mean to offend you by staring." Trying not to giggle at his choice of words, she unloaded her purchases on the kitchen counter. In the back of her mind, she was glad he resented being objectified—a man of such sensitivity was less likely to be a sexual predator. *Still could turn out to be a high functioning sociopath*, chimed in the voice of reason, but she shushed it and continued out loud: "It's just that I've never met anyone like you . . . I mean, who claims to be nonhuman."

He huffed.

"Because the difference is not evident," continued Anna. How much prodding could he take before he buckled? "By simply looking at you, I couldn't tell you are . . . half . . ."

"Alva."

"Right. The Alva. Extra-terrestrial humanoids."

He made another soft noise, this time more like a derisive snort.

"It's more fitting to refer to humans as *terrestrial alvanoids*, since the Alva is the progenitor race, but your confusion is understandable—indeed, an Alvan male's outward appearance is quite similar to a human male's."

"How are you different?"

"For one, I'm taller than most Alva. My ears are not as. . ."

"I mean, different from a human."

"If I tell you I perceive the world around me incomparably more clearly than any man, or that I am capable of sensations and feelings incomparably deeper than any man's, it wouldn't satisfy you, would it? I suppose you want palpable proof?"

"It's not that I don't believe you, but all the things you mention are subjective."

He thought for a moment. "I've never had lice."

Anna laughed. "So? Neither have I."

"You do not understand. I've never been bitten by a gnat, a tick, or a flea. Insects do not feed on Alvan blood."

Anna rubbed the back of her neck. A Dark Ages native would be crawling with parasites, anything to the contrary would have been extraordinary. He was consistent in his complex delusion down to the smallest detail.

"I've seen your blood test. You blood is perfectly normal. A bit low on iron, but otherwise—"

"Pure Alvan blood contains no iron. In fact, iron can be poisonous for the Alva. Being half-human, I can tolerate iron, although not as well as a full-blooded man."

"Or you would be anemic. Any other special features?"

"My ears." He pushed away a blond strand, revealing an elongated ear, lobeless, with a slightly pointed tip.

"Well, some people have uniquely shaped ears. What else?"

"You be the judge," he said with a weary shrug. Dressed in her clothes, barefoot, his hair still wet, he stood before her with his arms open slightly—a picture of sincerity.

Feeling like an evil scientist performing a vivisection on a unicorn, Anna picked up his slack hand and studied it. It was a normal man's hand, narrow but sturdy; a faint net of blue blood vessels showed through the pale skin like water through ice; the elongated nails were trimmed short, fingertips soft and pink. She lifted his forearm, stretching the translucent skin between her fingers. The scars from the cigarette burns she dreaded to see were barely visible, as if they'd dissolved overnight.

"You skin looks human," she said. "Though very smooth."

"The Alva grow neither body nor facial hair."

He sounded testy, like she'd touched a sore spot. According to his initial physical exam, his body hair had been removed by electrolysis or some other procedure. It must have been agonizing, not to mention humiliating.

Could be an integral part of his trauma and subsequent delusion, thought Anna, and said as amiably as she could, "Some men have little body hair."

He rolled his eyes and pulled at the string of his pants, baring the bottom of his flat stomach and the side of his pelvis. Below the sloping roll of the hip muscle, the top of his pubis was completely smooth. Anna stared at the delicate vein that ran along the sharp hip bone. His skin looked pristine, never exposed to the elements, like the stretch of skin under her own breast.

"Neither body nor facial," he repeated, straightening his clothes.

Anna looked up at his face, and, unable to resist the impulse, lightly drew her thumb against his cheek. His skin was slippery-smooth and unnaturally warm.

For a moment, his eyes went vacant as if from pain, but he didn't flinch.

She could tell, he was getting peeved. Poking a man like an inanimate object was rude at best and improper at worst, but she couldn't stop herself. His insistence on his inhumanity had triggered something visceral in her, as though dismantling his delusion could mean much more than a professional triumph—a deep affirmation of the most profound kind, an intoxicating promise.

"What else?" She demanded, stifling a giggle. John's proximity made her giddy, as if his fresh, slightly metallic smell carried some kind of mirth-inducing drug.

"I have a greater command over the members of my body." He narrowed his eyes.

"This is not unusual. You're pretty fit, but—"

"Beyond that," he cut her off. His expression was vague. Shame or mischief? She couldn't tell. "Observe."

He cupped her hand and pushed it over his crotch; her palm felt his soft warm flesh under the thin fabric.

Anna sobered up at once. Her first urge was to pull her hand away, but his fingers locked like a wolftrap around her wrist. "Hold it," he ordered, looking down with a queer little smirk. She gasped, because the flesh under her palm tightened and bulged, becoming rock-hard and filling her hand. He let go of her wrist at once, and she jerked back her hand like she'd touched a venomous snake. The last thing she expected from this delicate man was an instantaneous erection. Her cheeks burned and she averted her eyes, but John said, "Pay attention." She glanced at his dispassionate face, and turned her eyes down to his crotch. The erection was gone.

Anna stood dumbfounded, nursing her hand like it'd been burned.

He bared his teeth in a wide grin, no longer bothering to conceal his vindictive amusement. "Palpable enough for you?"

Her hand was tingling. For a second she became aware of a strong desire to smell her palm. She rubbed her hands to get rid of the sensation.

"If you're in such control of your body," her voice came out hoarse, "can you stop your heart?"

John furrowed his brow. "Well, yes, it's a part of the Alvan warrior training, but is this the best use for my ability you can think of?" His smile faded to a pout. "You can be awfully crass at times, dear Anna."

He'd just forced her to fondle him, made it look like it was her idea, and now she was crass! *Son of a bitch,* thought Anna with reluctant admiration. Her voice of reason kept silent, buried underneath the rubble of the ethical boundaries she'd crashed.

It's not like she didn't understand the importance of boundaries. Like fences, they are meant to separate the therapist and patient for their own good, to exclude the possibility of mutual exploitation. A therapist is expected to build a sense of shared reality with the patient, but how personal could such a relationship become before it stops being healing and becomes abusive? Touching, no matter how seemingly innocent, personal disclosure, sharing a meal—those were all steps down a slippery slope leading to the ultimate crime, sex with a patient. This was what Anna had been taught, and this she believed, as a professional and as a woman.

The lectures on the ethical code in psychology were fresh in her mind. As an undergrad, she had been appalled by the notorious affair between Carl Jung and his patient cum student cum mistress, Sabina Spielrein. Her heart had ached for all the vulnerable women who had been seduced by their male therapists. She had felt righteous when her ethics professor suggested that feminization of the profession offers a reprieve from the pattern, since female practitioners are statistically less likely to enter illicit affairs with patients. "Despite what Ingrid Bergman did in Spellbound," she quipped.

The ethics which Anna had studied in grad school were more focused on appropriate incentives and fair compensation for the research participants, yet still addressed the same power dynamic: the dangers always lurked whenever a subject fell into a dependency relationship with the researcher.

It didn't matter that she was a grad student and an intern, that she wasn't John Fairfax's caseworker or personal therapist. She was employed at a hospital he'd entered as a patient. He depended on her for his well-being, and she had an obligation to treat him as a client even if he wasn't formally one. But the boundaries, set in place to protect them from each other, had already been crossed back and forth more often than the Brooklyn Bridge on a given day.

This man had slept under her roof. He was wearing her clothes. She had ogled him, worse, touched him in a way she shouldn't have. Now, they were about to share a meal. She had gone against everything she'd been taught.

Was there any chance to restore even a flimsy facade of propriety?

"Look," she said firmly. "Before we continue, it's imperative we establish certain rules to ensure the success of our . . . relationship."

"Relaaationship," he drawled, tasting the word on his tongue. "What is our relationship?"

"First, let's make it clear: you are not my patient, and I am not your counselor."

He tightened his mouth. Again, she couldn't tell if it was a grimace of discontent or a suppressed grin.

"At the same time, I am in the position to help you get better adjusted to . . . um . . . modern life. I do want to help you. While doing it, I would hope to get to know you better, to understand you."

"To what end?" He still sounded testy.

"I hope that by studying you I can come one step closer to an ultimate truth about human nature," she said in a single breath. While she was being perfectly honest, the choice of lofty—for John's sake—language made it hard to keep a straight face. "I propose you and I work as a team."

"I appreciate my current predicament and don't have illusions of being seen as your equal. Saying you and I could work as a team is like saying a hunter and a hound could work as a team." He paused and added in a softer tone, "Which is not entirely false, I suppose. So, what would you have me do in exchange for the accommodation?"

Anna blinked fast and hurriedly said: "You mustn't feel obligated. I'll get you a bed in a shelter whether you agree to cooperate or not. You have shared your life story with me. All I want you to do is to continue talking to me. You would never have to reveal anything you're uncomfortable with, and you are free to stop at any moment. Does this sound fair?"

He gave her a level gaze. She held it.

"It is fair," he said finally. "You have my consent."

She produced a standard voluntary consent form, made sure he read and comprehended it, and offered him a pen. He gave the pen a quick examination by poking the tip with his finger, then put it to the page, and wrote what Anna presumed to be his full name in a neat, rounded Latin script without much flourish.

"Ga . . . Gare . . . what's this letter?"

He waved his finger in unnerving proximity to her nose. "The first letter is *gar*, like so." He traced a symbol in the air, remotely resembling a hand-drawn capital G. "Then *aaa*, *errr*, and *eeeh*," he drawled and rolled, while his long, pink-tipped finger danced in front of her face. "Ends with *eth*." He drew the last figure and crossed the invisible line in a precise motion. "In runes—*gyfu, ac, rad, eh, thorn*. Would you rather I write it out in runes for formality's sake?"

"No, the script is okay, thank you. And it's pronounced *Yaret*?"

"The Alvan language is spoken both on inhale and exhale. My name properly spoken would sound like this: *Iaaah* . . ." he quietly gasped in mock astonishment, held his breath for a second, and exhaled. "*Rethhh*," he rolled the *r* almost like an *l*. A silver bell rang in this sound.

"Ya-ret," Anna breathed in and out. The sharp inhale gave her a momentary high. She thought she saw a hint of a smile in the corners of his mouth.

For a split second, a doubt stirred: the name he signed belonged to an imaginary persona, which undermined the legitimacy of the contract. *But John Doe hadn't been legally declared lacking "capacity to contract," so, as long as he persisted in his delusion, Yaret Fairfax was in effect his real name*, she reasoned. *Not like I want him to stay delusional, of course not, if—no, when—he has a breakthrough I'll be the first to address this, but for now the compromise is necessary for me to proceed.*

"So, to answer your earlier question," she said firmly. "Let's consider our relationship a working partnership based on mutual respect."

"I trust your good intentions." His gaze was sincere, no more traces of bitterness in his voice. "Likewise, you mustn't expect any disrespect from me."

Anna looked into his face and once again marveled at his bright beauty. It was easy to believe his every promise. She twitched her shoulders to shake off the spell.

"We begin working in earnest when you settle in your new residence. Since you are staying in my house until then—which is somewhat irregular—I expect you to comply with my rules and wishes."

His left eyebrow arched. "And if your wishes come into contradiction with your rules?"

"To avoid a possible misunderstanding, I'd suggest you follow direct verbal instructions rather than perceived intentions."

"In other words, submit to your commands," he stated wryly.

She opened her mouth to rephrase, but he raised his hand.

"I shall submit." His lips folded into a little smirk. "It will be my pleasure."

"Excellent!" She forced a smile. "So, no more inappropriate behavior, I mean hugging, intimate touching, and such. For example, what you did just now, with your demonstration. Do you understand?"

"I do."

She expected an apology to follow, but it did not, so she continued: "If there is anything else you want me to offer in this regard, I would love to hear it."

He bit his lower lip, looking at her with narrowed eyes. She waited.

"Please refrain from touching my face unless you mean it," he finally said.

"Mean it—what do you mean?"

"My face is sensitive in a . . . ah, most intimate way. In light of all your rules of propriety, it's only fair that you don't touch it carelessly, since I promise not to endeavor anything that might remotely arouse you," he rolled his *r*s with a mocking clarity.

So, making me grab his crotch was revenge for stroking his cheek, thought Anna with amazement. *There may be more physical dysfunction than meets the eye.*

"Just a common courtesy," he continued, responding to her hesitation. "It's not like I'm asking you to always say what you mean, now that would be too much for you, people, wouldn't it?"

"You, people? What kind of question is this?"

"You, humans. And it is a question of a rhetorical kind. But you have my word. Do I have yours?"

She gave him her word, noting the sheer number of sworn oaths passing back and forth. John saw right through her: it was true, all her limits were of a sexual nature, and it was she, not him, who seemed eager to violate them. He'd been nothing but respectful—moreover, and cooperative. He'd never attempted to lay a finger on her, never cast a lascivious glance. And the whole crotch-grabbing incident was nothing but his reacting to her relentless, dehumanizing prodding. For all she knew, he might well have been gay—mischievous and provocative, but sexually nonthreatening.

She, on the other hand, had behaved like a complete degenerate, no better than a pervy doctor groping a young female patient under the pretense of scientific research. John's pure beauty and infantile precociousness made her want to take care of him, but also to take him over. Besides awaking her nurturing side, he'd stirred something monstrous inside of her.

This ends now, she told herself and focused on the most nurturing of activities, serving food.

She made an egg sandwich for herself and sliced two apples for John. She was still chewing her first bite when he inhaled the apple slices. It was uncanny how he could eat so fast with his hands while maintaining poise. As he looked at her with the eyes of a hungry puppy, Anna got up to serve him the rest of the apples.

"Don't bother cutting," said John and proceeded to chomp down apple after apple. He devoured them whole—core, pips, and all. After he was finished with the last apple, he licked his fingers and turned to the blueberries. Mesmerized, Anna watched him throw his head back and pour a handful of blueberries into his mouth, moaning with pleasure as he chewed; he pulled out his long, blue-stained tongue, and looked at it crossed-eyed, laughed, and turned his merry gaze to her.

"Ah, what a delight! Allow me to repay your hospitality by preparing a meal for you tonight." The sharp contrast between his clowning and his formal speech was disconcerting.

"I didn't realize you liked to cook."

"I don't. I believe cooking food is a waste of both time and food," he replied with a pleasant smile. "But I would gladly cook for you."

"No need," she said a bit more curtly than was polite. "I don't want . . ."

"Oh, but you do." John seemed unscathed by her tone. Clearly, apples and berries had put him in a jolly mood. "Sharing a meal is a way of knowing one another. You said it yourself, you want to know me—" he wiped his mouth with the back of his hand. "—and my magic."

"I want to understand you," corrected Anna, momentarily anxious whether he meant knowing in a biblical sense. "I admit, you have some unusual . . . um, characteristics. Which doesn't mean you have supernatural powers. Perhaps you could show me something—a magic trick?"

"I don't think you realize how discourteous this request is. I am no traveling conjurer."

"I am holding you to your promise of complete disclosure," said Anna, and suddenly, overcome by some childish impulse, she blurted out, "Show me your magic!"

"Very well." His eyes darted around the room until they fell on a dry plant withering on the windowsill, a housewarming gift from a year ago. Anna had long given up on it, and only laziness prevented her from throwing it out. She held her breath, thrilled: was John about to revive the plant with a touch, like ET? But he just poked the dry dirt with his finger and demanded: "Fetch me a cup of water!"

A little disappointed, she filled a glass from the tap and gave it to him. He held it between his palms for a while, as if trying to warm it up, and carefully watered the dead plant. She stared at the plant wide-eyed, and for a split second her heart skipped a beat in a childish anticipation of a miracle. But nothing happened. Did she expect the dead plant sprout in time-lapse? She felt foolish.

"And?"

"And what did you expect?"

"Weren't you trying to revive the plant?"

"You are perceptive."

"Shouldn't it, I don't know, grow in front of my eyes?"

"Only in fairy tales. Magic doesn't work this way."

"You know what, you're hilarious," said Anna. *And I am an idiot*, she thought.

"Don't doubt me, Anna," he replied softly. "Or yourself."

"I don't doubt you see yourself as different, possessing unique perception, but so does everybody. Everybody thinks they are special, deeper than the rest, that their emotions are the most profound. Everybody believes in their own fairy tale. None of it means magic is real."

He sighed. "What do you think magic is?"

"I remember your saying that magic is the power to control the world."

"I said reorder, not control. But what is the path to this power?"

"I wouldn't know . . . knowledge?"

He shook his head. "Before you know, you believe. When you know, you love. Love is the source of power. What of it if I can bend others to my will with a word, or rearrange particles of air to float crystal orbs. Those tricks are nothing compared to living each moment in love. For the one who's mastered this magic, power is everywhere. But it is subtle and reveals itself only in the presence of faith."

John stepped aside, exposing the plant on the windowsill. Its dry leaves had blackened and fallen off, giving way to a thick bright-green sprout. It wasn't spectacular, but life was blooming where it hadn't been a moment ago.

Outside the window, the first rays of sunrise painted long ribbons of gold and crimson against the dark winter sky. The world was awakening.

Sucking on his pricked finger, John sauntered to the couch and dropped down. He took his finger out of his mouth only to say in a comically smarmy voice: "I hope I was sufficiently entertaining, because now it's your turn."

Anna swallowed hard: what kind of reciprocation could he have in mind? Whatever he was about to ask her was going to reveal the true level of her control over the situation and his commitment to the process. She squared her shoulders and took in a deep breath.

"What would you want me to do?"

"Teach me about this place."

Her stomach unclenched. "Don't Alva keep up with the world news?"

"It's been a long time since Alvaheim cared about the affairs of mankind. Anyway, human nature is well known. It's not the strategy I require help with, but the tactics. I need to know how this land of yours is governed, who it is at war with, who the allies are. What are the current customs, mores, fashions. What is most desirable to your people, and what is most frightening. What's the fastest way to get killed, and what's the straightest path toward wealth and power."

Anna was jarred by the military talk and blatant pragmatism. She didn't expect the ethereal and eccentric John to care about how to acquire wealth and power. Then, again, according to his story, he was accustomed to the life of a warrior and an aristocrat. Why stop now?

But where to start? It was ludicrous, as if she were a character in a sci fi B-movie interrogated about planet Earth by the advancing forces of an alien invasion. And then, she had an idea.

"I think the best way to get acquainted with the modern culture is to watch a movie. Do you like movies?" It was a trick question, so she wasn't surprised when John announced that he had no familiarity with the concept. She explained it was similar to theater.

"Theater?" John stretched his neck to look over her shoulder as she shuffled through her DVDs. Anna's meager film library consisted mostly of the Miyazaki animated classics she watched when Jack came over and a few socially conscious documentaries Ted had left at her place. "I love it when people sing."

"Well, musical it is!" The only musical she had, besides cartoons, was Hair, and that was what she put on.

John looked determined to keep his cool. However, when the moving image came on the screen, his lips parted and his eyes widened. With the first sound of the title-sequence music, he asked, cocking his head dog-like.

"What is this instrument?"

"Which one?"

"The one which sounds *wah waowww.*"

"You mean the electric guitar?"

"I like electric guitar," he muttered, peering into the screen.

Mentally, Anna congratulated herself on her cleverness: assessing one's reactions to a classic film was as good as doing the picture-based Thematic Apperception Test for personality assessment. She sat on the futon next to him, ready to diligently record his reactions to the imagery on the screen.

When the "Age of Aquarius" was over, he turned to her. "I fear, this story won't be a happy one," he said, his long dark eyelashes suspiciously slick.

Those were the last words John uttered for a while, because for the rest of the film he never spoke, but alternatively laughed out loud, like he was tickled silly, or wept without bothering to check the flow of tears. It had been a while since Anna had seen a grown man cry, and she'd never seen a man remain pretty while at it. She'd long ago stopped paying attention to her notes, watching John instead: it was particularly surreal because his reactions were seemingly arbitrary. She was so mesmerized that she barely registered how explicit some of the lyrics were; in any case, John reacted to the notorious "Sodomy" song with no more than mild amusement.

When the final musical sequence began, with the doomed recruits marching into the belly of the airplane to be swallowed by the death's maw, John was sniffling. When the piercing chorus cried out in a minor key, "Let the sunshine in!" he collapsed in silent sobs but kept his eyes on the screen with some kind of masochistic persistence. The sight of the triumphant antiwar protesters made him chuckle through the tears, and an idiotic smile of catharsis remained on his face through the final credits. She saw his lips move in synch to the "Hair" song, like he'd already learned the lyrics by heart from the scene earlier in the film. When the screen went dark, he sat still for a moment, then reached out and squeezed her hand.

"Thank you! This was truly moving. Now I understand why it's called a movie."

Anna snatched away her hand to write in her notebook.

"If I may ask, what did you gather from the story?"

"Oh, the story is trivial: hair represents free thought, love defeats obstacles, war breeds sorrow, and to transcend oneself one must face death. It isn't the story but the harmony of music, images, and sentiment—all splendid." He wiped his face with his fingers slowly, as if relishing his tears.

"Is this why you cried?" she asked carefully.

"Does my expression of feeling offend you?"

"No, I'm impressed that you express your feelings with no inhibition."

"Well, isn't the purpose of art to elicit feeling? Isn't this why you're showing me these works of art, to glimpse my soul as it gleams in their reflection?"

Not expecting an answer, he stood up and walked to the window. Grateful for a pause, Anna continued scribbling in her notebook.

"The story we watched took place in this very city, didn't it? I'd love to see more of it. Can we take a stroll while the sun is still high? I treasure your hospitality, but I must have some fresh air."

Anna looked up from her notes. She wanted to do more work, but she could sense her charge growing restless. Her room was becoming too small to contain the energy he radiated. She glanced at her watch: it was half past ten, she had a whole day to kill before dropping him off at Saint Francis. But what to do with a man who is neither friend nor stranger? All of a sudden, the bright idea to keep John Fairfax at her place seemed not so bright.

We'll take it one step at a time, thought Anna and said out loud, "You can't walk around dressed like this. Let's get you some clothes."

Since she'd so carelessly discarded the overcoat John had gotten from Bellevue, she had to give him something to wear over the skimpy NYU T-shirt. She rummaged through her closet, until way in the back her fingers felt the rough leather of her old motorcycle jacket—a flea market find she wore as a teen for her prepschool rebel-slut look. John's eyes flashed at the sight of the leather, and he sniffed the sleeves as he eagerly put it on.

"One more thing." She pulled the hospital discharge sheet from John's file, quarter-folded it, placed it deep inside the top pocket of his jacket, and snapped the flap securely. "Here. You've got to have an ID in this city. This will do for now." She patted the pocket. John's chest rose in response to the touch of her palm, and she quickly withdrew her hand.

Despite the air of inner-city shabbiness and constant street noise, living in the middle of the Garment District had certain advantages. Anna's block alone hosted at least three clothing boutiques dealing in trendy swag at discount prices; while being officially wholesale, they weren't beneath selling to a retail customer, especially if the customer could pass for a fashion industry professional. When they walked down the street, Anna thought that platinum-blond, rail-thin John, ridiculously elegant in his gray sweatpants, white canvas tennis shoes, and black biker jacket, could easily pass for another student from Fashion Institute of Technology, a wannabe designer moonlighting as a model to supplement his tuition. What did she look like next to this exotic creature: a handler, a business associate, a groupie? Could they look like a couple, like Superman and Lois Lane, the kind of couple making people wonder *what does he see in her*? Like she'd always suspected people had wondered about her and Genie. She shuddered.

The first store they walked into carried nothing but beaded prom gowns. "Rich!" John commented with either irony or admiration, or both. They didn't linger. The next store, however, had a more casual inventory. The Middle Eastern salesman with the face of a somnolent angel sized them up from behind the counter.

"He needs a pair of pants, something dark and simple," Anna declared in a businesslike manner. "And we're on a budget."

"Prêt-à-porter in the back," replied the salesman, losing interest.

"You must know, I have no money," John said.

"I've got it," she muttered under her breath.

"I will repay your expenses," replied John with a sidewise look.

"It's no big deal. Consider it a part of the therapy. Shopping therapy."

Seeing him frown gave her a moment of wicked satisfaction, as if by paying for John she claimed a degree of control over him. *This is wrong on so many levels!* screamed the voice of reason. But wasn't acknowledging one's weakness the sign of an ethical practitioner? *Besides, this could fall under the category of providing incentive to a human research participant,* she thought. Perfectly within the boundaries.

In front of the denim rack she stopped. "Try some of these."

With several pairs of jeans in his arms, John obediently marched to the dressing room. While waiting for him, Anna checked her phone, hoping for a message from Saint Francis confirming their arrangement. No message. Instead, a missed call from her mother. She must have wanted to talk about the engagement. The thought made Anna's jaw ache.

After John was gone for some time, she went into the back of the store to check on him and found him chatting with someone who looked out of place among racks of knockoffs: an impeccably groomed middle-aged woman, her cashmere overcoat exuding understated luxury. As Anna approached, the woman scanned her with the unseeing gaze of a Bergdorf Goodman's patron glancing in a Walmart window.

"...If you're so inclined," she finished what she was saying to John, handing him a business card, and departed, the heels of her red-soled booties clicking on the linoleum floor.

"This woman was eager to help me choose the right size," explained John. The pair of tight ink-blue jeans looked indecently good on him. "She introduced herself as a scout, I'm sure in jest. Ah, Anna, she said you ought to buy me some briefs."

"Oh, boy . . ." Anna let out a quiet moan, realizing she must have dumped his hospital-issued underwear with the rest of his old clothes. "Did she do or say anything . . . inappropriate?"

John gave her a sly glance. "I refuse to be responsible for her intentions."

"What did you talk about, exactly?" A treacherous blush stained Anna's cheek—despite herself, she felt a prick of jealousy.

"She said, although I may be vertically challenged for the runway, she can see me doing editorial. I won't pretend to know what it means."

"I believe a model scout has offered you a job." Answering his confused frown, she added, "Models are people who are paid to be photographed wearing clothes."

"Paid to wear clothes? Why?"

"So the manufacturers can sell more clothes. Factory makes more clothes, employs more people, more people get paid, more clothes get bought. Circle of life of the consumer society." Seeing John wrinkle his nose as if he smelled something foul, Anna added less sardonically, "Modeling can be lucrative, much more so than working in a factory."

"There must be more dignified ways to acquire wealth," he declared with a huff.

"You can always try your hand at the stock market," muttered Anna. His act, whether real or pretend, suddenly felt annoying. To add to her vexation, the boutique didn't sell underwear. She paid for the jeans, wishing she could take him straight to the shelter, ready or not.

They walked out of the store and crossed Broadway. John was babbling, making little observations about the buildings along the street, clearly enjoying himself. At first, Anna avoided eye contact. He kept trying to look her in the face; finally, giving up on subtlety, he stepped in front of her, and walked backwards facing her, navigating the dense crowd with an uncanny agility. Against her will, she grinned.

In the middle of Herald Square, the Midtown traffic roaring all around them, John stopped, his curiosity piqued by the stone monument with bronze statues in a niche and the clock at the top. They circled it. Anna must have passed this spot a million times without ever having bothered to look at it. To hide her embarrassment, she began reading the inscription out loud.

"Owls!" interrupted John, pointing up. Indeed, perched on either side of the James Gordon Bennett monument's upper tier sat a bronze owl. She'd never noticed them before.

"I love owls." He tapped the round medallion etched into the access door at the side of the monument. It depicted another owl sitting on the pointy chin of an anthropomorphic new moon. "What an excellent door, " he muttered, running his fingers over the relief.

"If I remember correctly, the owl is an attribute of the Roman goddess Minerva," said Anna. She wasn't much into mythology—not beyond her Jungian studies—but she used to read to Jack, and Jack adored classical myth as much as his comics. Now, she was glad some of it had rubbed off on her. At least it gave her a chance to redeem herself as a tour guide.

"Indeed, it is. There was a small round Minervium on the other side of the river from the Saxon Quarters," replied John casually. "But I was too young and ignorant, too bogged down in my own shallow depths to care about ancient treasures."

He shook his head with his little smirk, and Anna had the distinct feeling that this gesture of self-deprecation was for her sake.

"Perhaps someday you'll visit Rome and see all the familiar sights," she offered, curious for his reaction.

"*Dìs es tòn autòn potamòn ouk àn embaíēs*, dear."

"What?"

"A bit of old wisdom. One cannot step twice into the same river."

"Is it Latin?"

"It's Koine."

"Does it mean you don't believe in revisiting the past?"

He tipped his face.

"It means I believe in the present. Show me more! Take me someplace high. I must see this city from the top of a tower."

In the meantime, the wind had picked up the uneven rhythm of strong gusts, sprinkling a thin powder of snow flurries with each blow. The snowflakes dissolved without touching the asphalt, yet the heads of the bronze statues were dusted with white.

"I don't know how much you'll see through this fog," Anna grumbled, lifting her face toward the foreboding sky. A snow cloud was slowly descending on Manhattan, swallowing the city one rooftop at a time, but only a block away the Empire State Building was still defiantly piercing the clouds with its silver spire.

She still had the rest of the day to kill. Might as well do the touristy thing. After all, her student ticket discounts had to be good for something.

As much as she hated to admit, Anna enjoyed the ambiguity of her relationship with this charming eccentric. So far she seemed to have gotten away with bending the rules, but entering him into the system meant the end of the fairy tale. She would see him only in a formal environment. No more movies, no more shared meals, and no more moments of dangerous intimacy. The trip to the top of the Empire State Building would be the last indulgence she allowed.

After a surprisingly short wait in the ticket line and a predictably ear-popping elevator ride, they were herded together with the other visitors into the observation deck's glass enclosure, and suddenly they were on top of the world.

It was as if the laws of nature were suspended here, between earth and sky. The fog, which from the ground looked thick enough to shroud the spire, in close proximity turned into a fine, see-through mist. The city panorama was in full view, watercolor soft. It stretched without an end in sight, dripping off with soft gradients of gray and brown. The southern tip of the island faded into the snow clouds above the Upper Bay, dissolving into the ocean. Beneath lay the gritty three-dimensional mosaic of Manhattan roofs, powdered with fresh snow.

It had been a while since Anna had seen the glorious city from above—a jaded New Yorker, she took the famous sights for granted. Now she wondered, what John was seeing. He seemed transfixed by the view, grasping the railing so tightly his knuckles turned white.

"What do you think?" she asked, realizing he could stare forever.

"Thank you for this," he uttered breathlessly. Without turning his eyes from the view, he locked his fingers around her wrist. She expected his hand to be ice-cold after holding the metal railing, so its penetrating warmth took her by surprise. John lifted her hand, wrist up, and touched his lips to the bare skin between her sleeve and her glove. His touch was chaste, nothing but an expression of gratitude in his mind, Anna was sure, because for a split second she knew and understood him better than she had ever understood herself. Her head spun. The warmth of his touch spread through her veins like a shot of hard liquor. Her own ideas of propriety felt as small and insignificant as the people and cars crawling on the streets far beneath them.

"You are welcome." She wrestled back her hand. Out of his grip, her skin was slashed by the cold, and right then she felt guilty for the pleasure, foolish for letting him force it on her in public. What if someone saw them together? What if Ted saw them?

"Hi, Ann." Ted's voice came from behind her. She spun around, only to see an unfamiliar man taking a picture of his kid against the backdrop of the city panorama. "I said, hold on, one more!" repeated the man.

Great, now I'm hearing things, she thought, glancing back at John.

The habitual nauseating fear stirred inside of her, awakened by the drumbeat of her heart: the signs of an approaching panic attack. Her skin was flushed with prickly pain, like she was caught naked in a blizzard. She felt everyone stare at her, accusing, judging.

What was she doing here, on the top of the Empire State Building, with this man? Taking a mental patient around like a casual friend was the worst kind of madness. With each new small act of intimacy, she was hoisting herself higher and higher on the gallows of her own making, and now she was dangling helplessly high up in the air above Manhattan, choking, her feet unable to touch the ground.

Salvation came with the bells of her old-fashioned ringtone. The call was from Father Joseph of Saint Francis Residences, informing her they were ready to receive her client at noon on Tuesday.

"Thank God for monks," she muttered as she hung up. Her heart was settling.

"Monks?" John shoved his hands deep in the pockets of his jeans, suddenly looking brittle in his short biker jacket and rubber-soled tennis shoes.

"Tomorrow you are going to a permanent place of residence. It's an excellent facility run by Catholic monks."

"I've lived with monks, and this's precisely why I am disinclined to stay at a monastery."

"It's more of a hostel than a monastery. It's one of the best in the city, the safest. They will help you with identification papers and job placement. You want this!"

"I want what you want, as per our covenant." He frowned. "I know no one in the world but you, and no one knows me. You welcomed me in your home yesterday. What has changed?"

"Nothing!" She raised her voice. "Spending the night together at my place was wrong yesterday, and it's still wrong today."

"Why? Did my presence disturb your sleep?"

"It's not that!"

"Perhaps a dream was too vivid for your liking?"

Their animated conversation began to draw attention from the tourists on the observation deck. Some pretended to ignore them, others smiled awkwardly at what seemed to be a lovers' spat.

"I don't know where you're getting these notions about my dreams, which, by the way, have nothing to do with you, that much I remember."

"The only reason you remember is because you slept next to me."

Anna gasped, infuriated more with herself than with John's insinuation. This was precisely why falling asleep in front of a patient was against the rules. She must have mumbled in her sleep, her inadvertent disclosure handing him a trump for his mind games.

"This has gone far enough!"

"The trouble is, it hasn't." By now John was shivering, as if the early December chill had finally gotten to him. "We are still as far from the truth as when we first met."

Annoying as he was, if there was one right thing he could have said, that was it: she did need to know the truth about him in order to legitimately build his case, just as he needed to acknowledge the truth in order to heal. By simply asking the right questions she had been able to help him remember his name. If she could help this man reenter reality, his recovery would justify the infractions of ethical rules she'd committed so far.

She could still solve the case.

But there was something else, much less selfless. It had been years since she could recall a dream. Just as her necklace had made John recover his past, his story triggered something in her mind, his very presence opening some long-locked door to her own personal truth. She wasn't only helping a person in need—she might be facing a chance to gain deep insight into her own subconscious while at it.

I'm still capable of fostering a therapeutic engagement. If only I could trust him.

"Trust is a choice," John lowered his voice. "I've made mine. What good was concluding our agreement with all the rules of conduct if you don't believe us capable of holding true to our own commitments? If you trust in me as I trust in you, you will trust in yourself as well."

It was as if he were answering her thoughts. Despite the presumptuous "we" and "us" he kept throwing around, Anna had to admit he had a point.

"I want us to find out the truth together," she said, choosing the words that would resonate with him. "But please be aware: our time together is not indefinite."

"I am aware," replied John. "Sorely."

"All the more reason to use it constructively," she said as casually as she could. "Let's go home and do some tests."

“First, let’s stop at a market and pick up some food.” He mimicked her offhand manner as naturally as if they’d been roommates for years.

At the grocery store he asked how much money she was willing to spend. She was taken aback by the question, so she told him the first number that came to mind: twenty dollars.

She expected him to play up his amazement over the abundance and variety of products at the store, which would have been consistent with his time traveler’s persona. However, he showed nothing but methodical attention. He went straight to the butcher’s case, drawing his palm over the meats behind the glass. Evidently dissatisfied, he had a short exchange with the butcher, who then disappeared in the back and returned with a neatly wrapped package.

“All butchers are the same, no matter what century,” John explained, answering Anna’s quizzical look. “He had a private stash.”

“So, you commanded him to give you the piece he reserved for himself, and he complied. You ordered the hospital worker out, and he complied. How do you do it?”

“As long as my request is righteous, it cannot be refused,” he spoke with some reluctance. “Alvan birthright, inherent magic, if you will.”

“And how do you decide what’s righteous and what isn’t?”

“All I did was inform him I wished to buy the best piece of lamb he had.” John looked away, avoiding a direct answer. “He was glad to serve me the best he could. You may pay him now, by the way.”

“We pay at the checkout. Wait, what if you asked for the stuff and didn’t offer to pay? Would he still be able to refuse you?”

He shook his head. “Stealing things and forcing beings is not the Alvan way.”

“Right, except in all the fairy tales where elves play tricks on the village folk, steal babies and . . .” Anna was tempted to say “and knock up teenage girls” but caught herself in time.

“Don’t trust fairy tales,” replied John. He was making his way down the produce aisle, sniffing vegetables like a regular housewife, dropping into the shopping basket some misshapen yellow carrots and overgrown radishes and bunches of large green leaves she didn’t recognize. She checked the labels: parsnips, turnips, kale. Dark Ages indeed. Anna wasn’t much of a cook beyond the simple meals she used to throw together for

Jack, who, like many finicky eaters, only consented to food he could easily identify on the plate.

"Trusting fairy tales told by humankind," continued John, "is the same as trusting fish to tell about birds." It occurred to Anna that some fish could tell a lot about some birds, especially if the latter were of the fish-eating kind.

"If you must know," he droned on distractedly, "Reciprocation is a basic law of practical magic. In the Otherworld, nothing is taken for granted. Anna, tell me you're paying for this, because I would hate to return it, I have a dish in mind."

"Yes, I am! But if it's practical magic, wouldn't it work no matter what the motivation?"

"Once you defile yourself, you forfeit the birthright. Such is the nature of the Alvan gifts: they are plentiful, but conditional."

At the checkout the groceries came to exactly twenty dollars, not a penny more, not a penny less.

"Would you like to listen to some music while you cook?" Anna asked.

"I will be honored if you play music for me."

"I don't play myself, but I listen to it, a lot. Seventies stuff mostly. My high school was heavily into liberal arts." With an awkward smirk, she set the phone into the speaker dock. "The music appreciation course was taught by a man who believed progressive rock was the pinnacle of modern sound. I suppose, I was one of the few students for whom it took."

"Does seventies stuff feature electric guitar?"

"It sure does."

She half-expected him to put on a show of a man trying to seduce a woman with his culinary prowess, with a bare chest under the apron and sloppy food tasting like in a TV ad for kitchen utensils, but he was beyond such conspicuous gestures. He moved with clinical precision and efficiency of someone not being watched. Still, the more she looked at him, the more something stirred inside her.

It wasn't how he wielded the knife while standing on one foot with the other propped against his knee, Ian Anderson-like; or how he tossed his head to get the hair away from his eyes; or how he licked his lips after trying the ingredients. It was the simple fact that he was doing all of this for her.

She'd never thought she could find a deep pleasure in watching a man engaged in something as banal as working in the kitchen. It was both comforting and exciting, as if by performing these simple little acts that make up everyday life, he made a promise she couldn't help but believe.

The meal consisted of vegetables and lamb stewed together in a creamy sauce with bunches of fresh parsley served on the side, as well as some bread—torn, not cut. The ugly tuberous vegetables gave the dish an appetizing yellow color and a subtle aroma.

"Aren't you going to eat?" she asked John, who served her a plate and now sat, staring at her with his cheek propped on his hand like Raphael's cherub.

"I ate as I cooked. I prefer raw."

She frowned. He laughed, misinterpreting her hesitation.

"Oh, you suspect poison, don't you? You, my dear, have all the markings of a true queen." He ripped a piece of bread, dipped it into the stew, and put it in his mouth with a bizarre mix of elegance, savagery, and sensuality.

She took a first mouthful and couldn't help but moan in delight. Food had never tasted this good. The sauce had a mild sweetness to it with a subtle bite.

"John, this is amazing! You could do this for a living."

"I'm good at fighting too. Doesn't mean I want to do it for a living."

"Is this typical Northumbrian fare?"

"I recall Northumbrian fare as rather unsavory. Salt was dear. Few spices were in use. This dish is my own, after Roman tradition." He shrugged in feigned modesty.

"Well, it's excellent. Thank you."

His blond hair was tousled, his cheeks and the pointy tip of his nose rosy from cooking, his gray eyes sparkling; a smile danced on the corners of his mouth; he looked so innocently pleased with himself that Anna felt laughter bubble up in her chest. Swallowing a giggle, she choked on her food a little and coughed. A warm palm tapped her lightly between her shoulder blades.

"Don't be greedy, precious," he purred through a grin. "I have plenty more for you."

His touch sent a vibration down her spine echoing the quiet cheer of his voice. The smell of food and spices made her salivate. The last time all her senses were tickled into such excitement must have been at least a couple years ago with Genie, and those experiences involved ingestible substances other than lamb stew.

I want him. The thought struck her, resounding like the peal of a bell in an empty hall. Anna needed a moment of privacy to contemplate it, so she quickly finished her food, excused herself, and went into the bathroom, the only secluded space of her small studio.

But why now? She knew better when he tried to manipulate her at the interview; she held her own when they touched inappropriately; even when he was waxing romantic on the top of the Empire State Building, she had managed to keep her cool. Why now, when he was slouching on the couch across from her, so artless, so homey, chewing his food and licking his fingers—why was she drawn to him now?

Okay. Okay. Could he have spiked the food with some aphrodisiac? No, it's impossible. I watched him cook. He had nothing on him but the hospital clothes earlier, and those are in the trash. The chemicals are of my own making. Oh, this is bad!

She stared at her reflection in the mirror. The freckled, hazel-eyed brunette who stared back looked more like a confused kid than a respectable young professional.

"So, you're drawn to him. It's not your fault," she whispered to her reflection. "It doesn't make you a bad person or a bad psychologist—as long as you don't act on those impulses. And it's not unreasonable, because he is hot."

"And he cooks," volunteered her reflection with a sheepish grin.

"Don't push it!" she hissed, pointing her finger at the mirror.

By the time Anna came back into the room, John had put away the dishes and cleared the coffee table. A neat stack of blank paper sat next to her notebook. He had lined up her smartphone and a pen, and was sitting on the futon with his hands on his lap, a picture of compliance.

"We could do more of your work now, if you like," he said. "Ask your questions."

She turned down the music as Fripp's guitar was about to go wild on "Starless", and sat in the armchair across from John. This was it, the chance she was waiting for to try her custom battery on him. But she was exhausted by her own mood swings, her head as empty as her belly was full, so she thought of nothing better to offer than the standard therapeutic question: "What would you like to talk about?"

His dark eyebrows arched. "You want me to tell you what to ask? Would you like me to digest your food for you as well?"

Anna leaned back in her armchair. "Let's play an association game. I'll say a word, and you reply with the first word that comes to mind. Don't think, just say it."

"Is it a riddle?"

"Sort of."

She pulled out a printout of the test—a standard list of words in a table, with empty cells to write down the patient's responses for further analysis.

"Head?"

"Heart," he replied without missing a beat.

"Green?"

"Hills."

"Water?"

"Snow."

The memory of the dream from the night before rushed over her, making her face throb with tiny pinpricks, as if she were running through a blizzard, and she blurted out the next word which popped into her head:

"Dead?"

"Born."

"Long?"

"Hair."

"Door?"

"Choice."

"Binding?"

"Broken."

"Wait, why did you say this?"

"Ah, but spelling out a riddle ruins all the fun! Which of them do you wish explained?"

"All of them, really . . ."

He recited, as if reading off the page: "Head descends to heart, giving birth to soul, which takes residence in the Green Hills. Water allows a passage, yet snow takes you further. Dead is what a skier is before he is born to run, and as long as he lives hair grows longer, until you choose to open the door, and the binding is broken."

"The last thing, what does it mean?"

"You tell me. It could refer to the snare of false perception or the device which fastens your shoe to your ski."

There was no way he could have known. From middle school and on, Nordic used to be her life, even though her parents never took the unpopular sport seriously. She was serious, totally committed.

It's not every day you find the one thing you're good at. But when you do, all your humiliating flaws—your ungainly height, your thunder-thighs, your wide chest—turn out to be your assets. You're no longer the awkward friendless kid, you're a member of an elite team, a top ranking skier of Olympic promise. Then, Dad dies, and in a few months Mom meets a guy in an online grief support group and marries him in a flash, and before you know it, you are stuck between your mother's new husband and your mother, already pregnant with the new husband's baby, in a moving van going east on I-80 to the city where high schools don't have Nordic ski teams. Your old life is gone, done for, over.

Quitting skiing wasn't Anna's choice, but when she quit, her quitting was as total as her commitment. She never touched the skis again, never watched winter sports on TV and never talked about it with anyone.

And now John was dropping words from that forgotten language, the same words spoken in a dream she remembered, the first in almost a decade.

A coincidence. *Must be*, decided Anna, trying to curb the fog of anxiety creeping up on her. Even if she wished to confront John, she didn't know where to start. She needed a moment to herself, to organize her thoughts and prepare a new line of questioning.

In the meantime, John curled up on the futon, hugging a pillow. Absentmindedly, Anna stared at his bare feet—he had kicked off the sneakers and socks as soon as they entered the apartment. His toes looked like they'd never seen the inside of an uncomfortable shoe, moreover, like they'd been pampered since his youth. She'd never seen a man with such nice hands and feet.

"Is your work done?" His question made her look up.

"Um . . . I'd like to go through my papers."

"May I browse your books while you do so?"

"Sure. What do you have in mind?"

John's choice of light reading was the Dictionary of Cultural Literacy she had from the time she was cramming for her GRE. For the rest of the evening they presented an oddly idyllic sight: her, clicking away on her laptop, earbuds in her ears, transcribing her recordings, and him, twirling a strand of hair between his fingers, leafing through the thick tome. Every once in a while she'd glance at him over the screen, and each time, he would lift his eyes from the page and meet hers, a hint of a smile on his lips.

I could live like this, she thought, and immediately hated herself for allowing it to enter her mind. She hoped that John hadn't sensed her discomfort, but she must have been staring at him, because he shut the book with a snap and let it slip to the floor.

"Have you finished the whole book?"

"Half of it. Do you want to test me on it?"

"No, but I would love to hear your impressions."

"All right. I found it curious that it begins with the Bible. The mythology and folklore section was amusing too, albeit somewhat inaccurate. Literature and philosophy—well, humanity had its share of insightful people. As well as many misguided ones. What else . . . World history up to the present day—yes, educational, but hardly surprising. I have yet to study the planetary maps, sciences, and technology." He yawned, rolling his head side to side. "The scholarly writing relies on Greek and Latin. It helps."

"It must be good for you to find modern English easily decipherable."

He gave her a quizzical look, as if weighing her sincerity.

"I've had centuries of practice in deciphering alien tongues."

"And what language did you speak as a child?"

"English, of course." He twitched his shoulder.

"Old English?"

"It was plain English to me."

On a whim, she picked her phone and put it to his face.

"Say something in your native tongue."

"Are you testing me again?"

"We have a deal, John."

"If you wish." There was a glint of mischief in his eyes when he leaned toward the microphone and began speaking. What poured forth from his lovely lips was nothing like English. At first she thought he was stretching his jaw like actors warming up—*nyam, mnya-mnya*—when he broke into a harsh, unfamiliar language with rolling *r*s and a variety of grating sounds originating somewhere in the back of his throat, as though his voice belonged to a larger, older, scarier man. The vowels he sang out with a dramatic inflection, a kind of taunting. His speech had a powerful rhythm to it, its severe melody utterly mesmerizing. It was as if Anna had cracked opened an ancient door and gotten a whiff of chilled air full of primeval vigor.

After he finished, he licked his lips and leaned back, grinning like someone who just made a clever joke.

"What did you say?"

"I said, firstly, I wish you called me by my true name. Secondly, I said—"

The ring of her cell phone cut him off.

"Hi, Ann," Ted's voice was tense. "Are you okay?"

With John turning her routine upside down, she had forgotten about her promise to get together with Ted, hadn't even called him all day.

"Oh, babe, I'm so sorry." She covered the receiver with her hand. "I was on a roll, doing some fieldwork, and I completely spaced out . . ."

"I figured that much," said Ted generously. "Frasier rerun is on. Want to watch together?"

"I can't talk right now, I'm with a client," she muttered into the phone. "I'm sorry . . ."

"At eleven at night? Isn't it a little late? Anyway, aren't you off today?"

"It's a long story. We'll talk tomorrow, okay?"

"Sure!" Ted dialed affirmation up a bit, like he always did when he didn't feel he was in a position to express disapproval.

Hearing his familiarly annoying intonation was just the kind of anchor she needed. Anna took a deep breath, appreciating the reality check.

"What was that?" John's wide-set, attentive eyes searched her face.

"*That* was Ted, my boyfriend."

"Your boyfriend?" he echoed with mock bewilderment.

"Fiancé, actually. We're engaged to be married." She couldn't avoid the subject any longer. It felt good, like pulling out a trump at the end of a losing game.

"How long have you been engaged?" John's voice became dull.

"About a week. Not that it's any of your concern. This is precisely the kind of inappropriate conversation we should avoid. Anyway, what was the other thing you said in Old English?"

"There's been enough speaking for a long day and a long night before it. I'd like to sleep now, if you don't mind." He gave the futon pillow a firm punch.

After contemplating whether she should let John crash on the couch, or treat him as a houseguest, flip out the futon, and make him a real bed, Anna decided on a compromise: the futon would stay closed, but she'd make him a proper bed with fresh linens.

The bathroom routine was unexpectedly easy: John washed his face and was done. Anna was tempted to make a joke about elves being above such prosaic matters as bowel movement, but held her tongue. John was still sulking. He nested into his bed, cocooning himself in the comforter so that only the tuft of his fair head showed, all of his being demonstrating that he had settled for the night.

In the bathroom, Anna changed into a pair of thin sweatpants and long-sleeved top; she hadn't worn this much clothing to bed since she was a kid. She took her time brushing teeth and combing hair, splashing water on her face again and again, trying to steady herself. To get to her bed from the bathroom she had to parade before John in her pajamas.

"Only one night," she muttered. "Tomorrow, back to normal."

Quietly, she poked out, and flipped the light switch. The room fell dark, but not before she registered John's clothes folded next to his feet with a kind of pathetic neatness: the ink-blue jeans and the purple NYU T-shirt. Those were all he had. The thought of him naked under the blanket gave Anna another jolt of discomfort, but it was also remarkably sobering.

The truth was, he was at her mercy, not the other way around. Indeed, it was her home, her couch, her school logo on his shirt. The food he cooked for her had been bought with her money. She has been the one asking questions. She decided if he stayed or went. She was the one with all the power. It wasn't the danger of being abused she should have worried about, but the danger of becoming the abuser.

She straightened her shoulders and marched across the room, saying as she passed the couch, "Sleep well."

"Likewise." From under the blanket his voice sounded childish, slightly cranky.

The swirling neon light of the downstairs barbershop stained the window with stripes of red and blue, illuminating her little alcove. She rolled to her stomach, pressing her breasts into the mattress, the fabric of her pajamas coarse against her nipples, and turned on her side with a pillow between her thighs. Red and blue lights danced in front of her eyes. Sleep wouldn't come. In silence, interrupted only by a rare car barreling down the street, she heard herself breathe. She wondered if John did, too.

"Anna?"

Her breath caught.

"Your body is too tense, and it's keeping me awake," complained John. "I could help you loosen up, if you'd let me."

She froze, biting her lip, horrified and thrilled at what might follow. The seconds fell hard, counted down by the pounding of her heart.

"Inhale through your nose, deeply," came his voice from the darkness. "Count two heartbeats, then exhale through your mouth, slowly."

She took a breath and held it, and pushed the air out through her tightened lips.

"Inhale and hold your breath for four heartbeats. Exhale. Now, eight. Do it again. Two, four, eight. And again. Good girl."

As the rhythm of her heart subsided, her heavy head sunk deeper into the pillow; she felt a pleasant tingle all over, pins and needles, her overwrought body becoming unbound; her eyes shut by themselves, and she was out at once.

Tuesday, December 2

She is back in the winter world, this time indoors, in a room where everything looks slightly off-kilter, haphazardly handmade, or as if it grew by itself. A fireplace, thoughtlessly carved into the corner. The doors along each wall, all different sizes, unevenly spaced. The candy-colored fur rugs on the floor, stitched together with no consideration of shade and shape. Not a single straight line. Everything is warped, yet strangely pleasant to the eye. She knows she doesn't belong here, but she isn't scared, rather annoyed. Yes, she is annoyed because the dream boy left her alone in this warped room, forgot all about her. No point waiting for him, even though she loves him so much. She loves the warped room too, but she can't stay.

She goes through the front door, but as she crosses the threshold she is back to the same room with the fireplace. She goes through the same door again, and there she is in the same room. She goes through the same door again, and there she is. She goes through the same door again and wakes up.

Anna sat upright in her bed, squinting at the unbearable brightness. The milky white light washed over the room, softened angles and blurred vision. She put on her glasses and couldn't believe her eyes: her window was snowed in, white fluff packed in the corners of the frame like cotton balls in a glass jar.

"It snowed all night," said a familiar voice.

She slid off her bed, wrapped herself in her throw, and came out from behind the bookcase. John, lounging with a book on his lap, lifted his bright face to her.

"How was your dream?" he inquired with the courteous concern of an attending physician.

"There were doors," she replied, surprising herself with her candor. "I kept going through the same door."

"Aha. Going where?"

"This is the funny part: nowhere." Immediately, she regretted that her need to share overpowered her reserve. "Never mind. Good morning to you, too. When did you wake up?"

"Right before the sun. No, I wasn't bored," he said, ahead of her next half-formed question. "I was busy cleaning your place."

Anna looked around. Her small studio looked the way she'd left it the night before: a crooked tower of books on the floor by the desk, papers strewn all over the coffee table, a pile of dirty dishes in the sink. Presiding over this vision of chaos, the shirtless and disheveled John sat cross-legged on the unmade futon, like a scraggly eaglet in a messy nest.

"Cleaning?" She all but flailed her arms, but checked herself for fear of dropping the throw wrapped around her body. "This is clean?"

"You haven't issued, um . . . direct instructions regarding housework, and I didn't presume to touch your things. In any case, superficial order is just that, superficial. What I did was arrange the space." He waved dramatically at the ceiling.

"Well, for the future, if you see a mess, you have my permission to clean it. Superficially is okay. And, John, could you please put on the shirt? Thank you," she grumbled, heading for the bathroom.

For the future? she thought as she stood under the hot shower. *What a dumb thing to say. There is no future. By this time tomorrow John Fairfax will be in his quarters at Saint Francis Residences, and I will be at my desk at Bellevue, filing his case. All by the book. Straight as an arrow.*

The warped room of her dream. It seemed her subconscious was signaling her to straighten up. The symbolism of a door became mockingly evident. Of course, the door meant entering another realm; after all, she was facing her subconscious. But the whole business of crossing the threshold only to find she hadn't gone anywhere—what was that all about? Perhaps she was stuck, not progressing fast enough. Were she talking to a client, she would have suggested that the dream reflected some real-life fear of change, like a lack of confidence in a career move or a hesitance to take a next step in an intimate relationship.

"Damn!" She cursed as her fingers involuntarily clenched and the bar of soap leaped out of her hand, bouncing of the sides of the tub. It was embarrassing. *Shoemaker's kid indeed.* How could she be so thick? Entertaining a paranormal explanation for her panic attack when it had been in plain sight all along: she had anxiety about failing at her dissertation and her engagement to Ted, the latter being the only reason she'd found herself drawn to John.

Finally, Anna managed to catch the evasive soap with her trembling fingers. As comically stupid as her situation was, it wasn't all bad. At least, being aware of her own weakness made it impossible for John to exploit it.

John. A sensual yet uniquely asexual object of an unrequited desire who insisted on taking her to strange places and leaving her on her own—sounded like the elusive boy from her dream. Except in the real world it was the other way around: her own neurotic reaction to the external stressors manifested in the dream image, which she transferred onto an unwitting patient. *Yeah, real professional,* she scolded herself, shame diluted by relief. In light of this new awareness, her visceral reaction to him no longer terrified her. Nothing special between them, certainly nothing supernatural.

Still in the shower, Anna considered washing her hair, but decided against it. *Not shaving my legs either, not for him.* Somehow, this small act of hygienic defiance left her empowered, reaffirming both her self-respect and her loyalty to Ted.

She planned the day ahead: she and John would eat (she'd cook this time), she'd call Ted and explain everything (maybe even ask for his professional advice), spend the rest of the day interviewing John. Tomorrow, she would finally sign up for personal therapy. She would address all the professional indiscretions of the last couple of days, as well as her insecurities about her work and her relationship with Ted. The thought of coming clean made her feel better.

Refreshed and reassured, with her hair in a loose ponytail, she came out to find the futon cleared, John's bed linens folded to the side, books put away, papers neatly stacked on the coffee table, and freshly washed dishes drying on the rack. The furniture was rearranged ever so slightly, but to a noticeable effect: everything looked cozier. Anna couldn't suppress a nervous laugh. It would have taken her at least an hour to tidy up this thoroughly. John had done it in mere minutes.

"This looks great." She meant it.

"Not as great as it truly is," John replied with a wink. He was wearing her purple T-shirt with the NYU logo. His hair was slicked back. With his chiseled features and enthusiastic expression, he looked like a model from a preppy catalog.

"I mean it, John, it truly is."

"Ah!" he waved his hand at her. "You can't see how it truly is."

"Why is that?"

"Because you do not possess true sight."

Right. The magic elf-sight.

Looking at John's sweet face, it was easy to forget that behind the facade of charm and cheer lurked mental illness making him no different from a miserable bag lady in an alley.

"You could try to look through a mystical lens," continued John in the same playful tone. He leaned forward like a dog who drops to his front paws in an invitation to a game of fetch. If he had a tail, he'd be wagging it right now. Anna knew she was expected to toss him the ball and ask *how*, and he would come back with some outrageous proposition, but it was too early in the morning for playing games.

Determined to stick to her plan, she offered John some cereal. He ate it with minimal theatrics. He tasted and rejected the coffee, opting for tea instead. Reveling in a moment of normalcy, Anna sat next to him on the futon and turned on the TV.

Evidently, while she was running through doors in the snow world of her subconscious, the real world had been dealing with the previous night's real snow.

"Unusually early, the winter snowstorm continues its march up the East Coast, and it's far from over," the local news channel anchor was saying. "The most impacted areas in and around New York City have reported between ten and sixteen inches of snowfall this morning, with up to fifteen inches in Central Park. The National Weather Service issued a winter weather advisory for the rest of the week. Alternate-side parking regulations have been suspended, and all public schools are closed for the day."

Ted! She needed to call Ted. She left John absorbed in the happenings on the television screen and stepped into her little alcove for a measure of privacy. Dialing Ted's cell number, she hoped he was in a session so she could just leave a message and be done with it. But he picked up at once.

"Ann! Everything's all right? Are you buried alive under all this snow?"

"No, no, I'm fine." She leaned against the windowpane with her back to the room, pressing her forehead against the glass.

"How did your late-night session go?"

"It went well . . . great, actually. I was up late, so I slept in. How is your day going?"

"Don't get me started on this snow, I have three canceled appointments because of it. On the bright side, I'll be done early. I have a client at eleven, so I can be at your place by one."

"Yeah, listen, I'm kind of in the middle of something . . ." Anna's finger drew thoughtless swirls on the foggy surface.

"Okay. See you later, around six, then?"

"I'm sorry . . . I need to work today. All day."

By Ted's silence she could tell he was confused. Tuesday was her Sunday, and they usually spent the night together at her place rather than his classy Upper East Side one-bedroom, which he preferred. Spending time at her place was Ted's concession to her, one she had negotiated and was eager to keep.

"Teddy, I'm on a roll here." She cupped the phone, burning her palm with the heat of her own breath. "I want to get some work done while I'm inspired." She glanced into the room, where her inspiration lay curled up on the couch, peering at the television screen. "Tomorrow I'm on call all day, but after the shift I'll come right over to your place. Hey, I'm doing you a favor, you don't want to hike across town in this weather."

"I suppose." Anna perceived a touch of relief in Ted's voice. Originally from Florida, Ted hated New York winters. "You stay warm, hon."

"Will do." As she hung up she realized she'd again forgotten to mention the male patient in her apartment.

"Ahn-nah!" shouted John. "Come now!"

"What happened?"

"Where is this place?" He was pointing at the television screen. The morning news reporter was standing next to a makeshift slope, talking to a group of kids with brightly colored plastic toboggans.

"I think it's Riverside Park." She adjusted her glasses. "Gee, I forgot how it looks under so much snow."

"We must go there!" exclaimed John. "Right now!"

"Why?"

"We must go there. Together. Please!"

Anna felt a rush of excitement. John Doe had been found in Riverside Park. Perhaps seeing it on television made him recover the truth behind his medieval fantasy, the real events that had resulted in his ending up bruised and naked in the park. Riverside Park was uptown, in the opposite direction of Saint Francis Residences, where they were expected by noon. But it could be the breakthrough she so hoped for.

"All right. Before I drop you off at Saint Francis, we'll swing by the park. But you'll have to wear this." She tossed him her NYU pullover hoodie. "And let me get you some warm socks."

"My Alvan sensibility makes me resistant to cold."

"I hope your Alvan sensibility makes you resistant to ridicule, too," she muttered, holding out the only clean pair of thick thermal socks she had: they happened to be hot pink with purple hearts.

She made sure he pulled on the hood, tightened the drawstring, and zipped up his leather jacket. Looking at him, she had to try not to giggle: puffy from all the layers and with his skinny legs ending in pink bobby socks, he looked adorably comical. She laced up her boots, threw on her jacket, and off they went, down the stairs and into the snowy street, like a couple of cartoon astronauts plummeting into outer space.

The bright blue sky had but a wisp of clouds here and there, and yet the snow kept blowing from nowhere, fine and crisp, filling the air with a sparkling mist. The sidewalk in front of her building was snowed-in with only a narrow trail of footprints leading from the door. The street, however, had been plowed and now was lined with high snowdrifts, burying parked cars up to the windows. A few men were out in front of their buildings, digging into the snow and throwing around salt the way sowers throw seed, like some fantastical snow-farmers. Anna's downstairs neighbor, the barber, was shoveling the sidewalk in front of his locked-up shop. He waved at her.

"My body craves motion," announced John, taking in a chestful of cold air. "I'm looking forward to a walk."

"It's forty blocks."

"What distance is that?"

"Well, twenty Manhattan blocks are approximately one mile, so it's about two miles."

"Two Roman miles?" John threw back his head with a hearty laugh. "Not much of a challenge. Even through the snow it will take us no more than an hour. These strong long legs of yours should carry you with grace."

His artless compliment made her self-conscious. Before Anna learned to harness the natural mechanics of her long-limbed body and fly over the frozen pond on her skis, she used to fall hard. One such crash had cost her a sprained ankle, only dumb luck saving her from a torn ligament. The ankle took forever to heal and flared up each time she overworked it, reminding Anna of its presence with a dull ache each winter. She found it hard to share John's enthusiasm about an hour-long trek through the snowy streets.

She considered the prospect of spending the next hour on the subway, waiting for a delayed train on a crowded platform, ankle-deep in the half-melted salty slush, rubbing elbows with fellow New Yorkers steaming in their down jacket, getting knocked on the shins by some kid's toboggan, all the while worrying she would bump into someone she knew . . .

"Might as well walk," she said.

Several blocks away from Bryant Park they turned left on Broadway, heading north. The usual morning crowd was much sparser today, but other than an occasional abandoned city bus, stuck in a snowdrift like a beached whale, there were few signs of devastation. On the contrary, the blinding brightness of snow-covered streets made the city pure and festive, like a veiled young bride.

"This road called Broadway is different from the other streets," noted John.

"It's the only avenue running diagonally. You might find it curious that Broadway started as a natural path formed in the terrain by the native people who lived here before this city was ever planned."

"Ah yes, I can tell, it has a different—" he waved his hand, "—flow."

As they walked through uncharacteristically quiet Times Square, he was intrigued by the giant billboards and electronic screens.

"Is it a form of art?"

"I suppose it is. Art in the service of trade."

"What do those people trade?" He pointed at a black-and-white photo of two mostly naked young people, locked in a staged embrace.

"They are selling clothes."

"But they are not wearing clothes."

Anna chuckled, remembering her social psychology class. "How should I put this . . . The image of models is supposed to make the viewers feel sensual, so that by buying other items from the same maker they can recapture this emotion—this is the basic idea behind advertising."

"Are these people the models you told me about?"

"Yes."

"This line of work is not about selling goods and services, but rather about mind control."

"You got it," said Anna, impressed.

They continued along Broadway. At Columbus Circle he insisted they stand in the middle of the roundabout. Anna thought he was curious about the rostral column with the statue of Columbus on top, but John just stood with his arms spread slightly, palms upward, slowly turning clockwise until he had made a full circle.

"Are most people these days left handed?" he asked.

"No, right handed. Why?"

"Then why are all the vehicles driving on the right side?"

"Because it's the traffic law in this country. Are you used to left-hand traffic?"

"It's only natural. Since most humans are right-handed, when you ride on the left your right arm is free to draw a weapon or to wave a greeting. Such was the rule in Britain, and in the Gaul, and in Rome. But, as I see, times have changed, and so have rules."

On they walked. Here and there he would slow down and point out this or that; each time it wasn't what Anna expected. After a while she realized that, instead of keeping track of John's eccentricities and trying to analyze what he'd meant, she was enjoying his company. Looking at the city through his eyes gave the familiar sights a sharper edge, a weirdly exaggerated high resolution.

At Seventy-Second Street they turned west. Right before entering Riverside Park, John asked her to stop "to rest his eyes on the water." He stood silently, taking in the view of the lead gray Hudson River and the snow-powdered New Jersey cliffs on the other side, breathing deeply, as if bracing himself for something.

John was leaning against the stone parapet, the ink-blue jeans tightly hugging his narrow hips. He had long shaken off the hood, and now the river wind was ruffling his hair, the blond strands moving like frosted grass in a wintry field. Each time she looked at him, Anna couldn't help a stupid grin. There was a gleam about him, even when he frowned and pouted like a petulant child. When he moved, he moved with grace; when he stood still, his stillness was complete. He was so hard, and yet so pliable at the same time; so subtle, yet so over the top it made her want to laugh with pure joy at being alive. Only Genie could make her feel this lightheaded, but Genie was an intimate friend who could be trusted with desires and whims. This man was no one to her. He had no right to make her happy.

Anna looked at her wristwatch and urged John to move on. As they entered the park, he kept shooting her quick glances: while she was observing him, he was observing her. *I better switch back into the interview mode*, she thought, *before he turns the tables on me again*.

"What's that?" John pointed at the fenced-off area where several dogs were cutting mad circles in the fresh snow.

"It's a dog run." Seeing his confusion, Anna explained. "Pet dogs are not allowed off leash in the city."

A small terrier was harassing a yellow lab, trying to steal its stick. The bigger dog wouldn't budge. Finally, the terrier gave up and began digging a hole in the snow. John observed this with a wide grin.

"Have you ever owned dogs, John?"

"I've owned many a living thing in my time," he replied. "Nothing was as rewarding as owning a dog."

"You don't say… What about cats?"

"One can never own a cat. Dogs, horses, cattle—those belong to you. Cats live with you." He turned to her. "Don't you agree?"

"I suppose. I never had a dog. Always wanted one growing up, though."

He nodded, puckering his lips thoughtfully. "Why didn't you get one?"

"My father promised to get a puppy but then he . . . it doesn't matter." He was doing it again, questioning her, making her disclose personal things instead of revealing more about himself. What's next? The therapist telling the patient about her father's death and childhood trauma?

"John, we didn't come here to talk about me," she said firmly. "You saw something on the television and demanded I take you here. What was it? What do you remember?"

"What do you remember?" he echoed in exactly the same tone, and it took all of Anna's composure not to smack him upside the head for mocking her.

"I remember you asking me for help. I am trying to, but you must work with me."

"I *am* working with you. Your feeling evokes a feeling in me. And this place evokes a feeling in you, I sense, more than one."

John knew the right button to push. This used to be her neighborhood. Twelve years ago, James brought Anna and her mother from Michigan to Manhattan, to an old brownstone on Riverside Drive overlooking the park, to his oddly-shaped, musty-smelling apartment that seemed like a set for a *Law and Order* episode. He kept joking that the unusually snowy winter was the city's housewarming gift for his new family, so they felt at home. Anna didn't want to feel at home. She imagined running away, but she didn't have any place to run away to, so she'd waste hours staring wistfully out of her bedroom window at the snow-covered park, longing for its promise of a fresh trail. But what serious skier runs in a city park? Besides, her new high school didn't even have a Nordic team. Her skis remained stuck in the back of the closet in her old bedroom, which now was her brother's room.

She'd never forgiven Riverside Park for betraying her with an empty promise, never felt tempted to explore its many corners and secret paths, in fact, never ventured away from the playground where she used to take Jack.

Anna shuddered. The last thing she needed right now was to run into her family. The building where her mother, stepfather, and now eleven-year-old Jack still lived, was a couple of blocks away from where she and John were walking right now. Her mother and Jack might be in the park because of the snow day.

I refuse to fall for this mind trick again, she told herself. *What are the odds? This is just my paranoia talking.* She won't be ashamed, because she had nothing to be ashamed of. Just transporting a client to a shelter, nothing more. A professional caretaker providing a personal touch.

"I'm hot," declared John, unzipping his jacket. Instinctively, Anna grabbed his lapels to zip it back up, the same way she would do for Jack. She caught herself only after she heard his chuckle.

"You were running a fever just yesterday." She snatched her hands away.

"This is my natural body temperature. The Alva . . ."

"Whatever it is, I don't want you to get sick."

"Endearing thoughtfulness." He tilted his head. "Your children will be blessed with a caring mother."

At least he didn't say, 'Thanks, Mom,' thought Anna, frowning. *Or, perhaps that was exactly what he had said.*

"Yeah, children," she said just to say something. "How about them."

"I want many children," stated John all of a sudden.

Their eyes met. Looking in his wide-set, clear eyes, she was struck by how little it took for him to sway her from a sense of complete control to a feeling of total chaos. She opened her mouth to make an annoyed retort, when out of nowhere came a gleeful scream:

"Annie!"

Swallowing a curse, Anna forced herself not to look. She was hearing things again.

"Yoo-hoo! Annie!" The call came again.

"Mom?" She spun around.

A few feet down along the path, her mother was waving energetically, and to make things worse, James was with her. Too late to run.

"Hi, I'm Nancy, Annie's mom!" her mother said to John as she approached.

"It is an honor to meet Anna's family," replied John politely. "I am—"

"Mom, James, this is John," Anna broke in. "He . . . he is helping me with my research."

"Oh, a fellow NYU student." Her mother smiled at the university logo on John's chest.

He mirrored her smile, neither confirming nor denying her assumption.

Perhaps the elven art of being evasive without lying is not so hard to master when everyone is so eager to offer their own half-truths, thought Anna, cringing inside.

Her worst fears had come true. She'd gotten caught, and by whom! By her own mother! She was ready to throw up.

Her unease, it seemed, rubbed off on her parents. Her mother appeared a little more animated than usual, as if she was trying to put on an extra layer of cheer. Usually composed James looked tense. But Anna was too absorbed in her own concerns to analyze others. Introducing a patient to the therapist's family was strictly against the rules, a toxic cherry on top of the horribly botched cake that was the case of John Fairfax. She cast a panicked glance at John, who brazenly stared her mother up and down, and now was giving the same attentive and appraising examination to James.

"I had to take the day off 'cause school's out," continued Mom, her youthful face aglow from the cold.

"Don't tell me that New York's finest take a snow day, too." Anna looked at James, who was shifting awkwardly next to her mother.

"Took a sick day," said James, exchanging a quick look with his wife, and added, "I mean, got to use those leftover hours before year's end, you know."

"Can you believe this snow?" Mom turned to John with a friendly expression. "What do you think, John?"

"I think it's faaabulous," sang out John. "Anna and I—"

"—are here on business," finished Anna. "We have to go."

"Wait, Jackie won't forgive you if he learns you didn't wait for him. He just went down the hill." And before Anna could say anything, her mother yelled for her brother. A little figure rose from the snowdrift at the bottom of the hill, waved madly, and ran up toward them. Before she knew it, a boy-shaped missile crushed into her, dusting her coat with snow.

"This is your sister's friend John, say hello."

"I'm John too." Jack's voice rang with preemptive defiance, the same guarded tone he always took with Ted.

"Well met, John Two," John said with a little bow.

The boy narrowed his eyes at the man. "Where are you from?"

"From beyond the known world."

"You mean New Jersey?"

"Annie." Mom got a hold of Anna's arm, lowering her voice. "I need to talk to you about something important, and not over the phone."

Anna rolled her eyes. She hadn't officially announced her engagement yet, and her mother must've been planning the wedding, choosing the dress and the caterers, probably had a whole list of ideas charted. The very thought was uncomfortable like a tight and itchy sweater.

"I'll come by on Friday," she muttered, freeing herself, and made a face at John, who seemed to have her little brother quite engaged. "Seriously, we have to go. Now!"

"I'll be seeing you, John," Jack promised gravely.

"Most certainly, John Two," replied John with an equally earnest intonation.

"It was a pleasure meeting one of Annie's colleagues," said Mom.

Mortified, Anna looked on as John stepped forward and took her mother's stretched out hand with a gallant bow.

"The pleasure is mine, Nancy." He bent his waist, leaning forward.

Please, dear Lord, don't let him kiss her hand! prayed Anna, and as he gently let go of her mother's hand, Anna breathed a sigh of relief.

"Bye, honey." Mom gave her a hug.

"See you Friday, princess. You've got to spend more time with your family." James's voice faltered.

"We just saw each other last week," murmured Anna, hugging him. It was unlike her stepfather to become maudlin in front of strangers, but as she hugged him, she noted the sallowness of his skin and a slight tremor of his hands. He hadn't been at the top of his game lately. *I better have that talk with him I've promised to Mom, about his smoking*, Anna thought absently.

"Nice meeting you," said James, offering John his hand.

John stepped toward James and clasped his hand. In a single powerful movement, he pulled the man in, flung his other arm around James's lower back, and pressed against his body, lingering in a close embrace for several nightmarish moments. As if in slow motion, Anna saw her stepfather's eyes widen and jaw drop, but before he could utter a sound of surprise or protest, John had already let go and was standing next to her, as if nothing had happened. With awkward smiles, her parents briskly departed, ushering away Jack, who seemed fascinated with the new acquaintance.

"That was not good, not good at all!" Anna began in a hot, angry whisper, taking off down the path. "I thought we were on the same page about this!"

"This what?" John kept up with her.

"Inappropriate behavior. You don't go around hugging strangers!" She was walking fast, her voice rising steadily.

"I certainly don't."

"What? You hugged my stepfather!" By now she was shouting.

"We were introduced, weren't we, so he was not a stranger. He . . ." John chewed his lip. "He will be fine."

That did it. She had allowed this charade to drag out too long.

Who the hell did John think he was? And who the hell was he in actuality? His disclosures were nothing but mind games. All she knew about him for sure was that he enjoyed musicals, was good at cooking, and hugged men without permission. Also, that he might have been damaged beyond repair. Perhaps it was time to admit: the exotic patient was not cutting it as the showcase study for her paper. Or was it that she didn't cut it, biting off more than she could chew with a patient well outside her professional scope? Did she even have a claim to any professional scope at all, after she'd been violating the rules of ethics over this man?

"Your mother and her husband," continued John thoughtfully, "have much love between them. They love you deeply, so does your brother. You belong to a good home, Anna."

There was genuine melancholy in his suddenly weary voice. It made her recall the imagery from his story: orphanhood, alienation, rejection, loneliness. Metaphors or not, he'd thirsted for belonging.

Anna understood it all too well. A good home . . . By the time she was old enough to notice, the relationship between Mom and Dad had gone pretty sour. The rare days when Dad was home from work were wasted on arguments or drowned in sullen silence. They didn't take their frustrations out on her, but sometimes she wished they did—at least it would have made her feel included. It was the ski team that offered the first taste of true belonging Anna consciously registered. The atmosphere fostered by the old-school Russian coach was cultlike; the kids on the team were initiated into a religion of body worship, where speed and endurance were the virtues; rituals were exhausting and demanding; and glory could be obtained only as a collective. It was intoxicating, so much so that having to quit the team seemed like more of a loss than her father's death. And, after tasting the team spirit, she was alone again—in a new family, in a new school, in a new city. Yes, she knew this thirst.

Her rage extinguished, and her angry swagger slowed to a shuffle, until she came to a halt.

"Please, just show me what we came for," she spoke in a conciliatory tone.

He stopped.

"We're here."

They stood on the narrow landing. Below them, a snow-covered staircase hugged the slope, at the foot of which sat the park rangers' shack, a small stone building with a faded sign on a metal door that looked like it'd been locked for the winter. This part of the park lay farther away from the main alley and the playground, and the fresh powder was undisturbed.

"Why did you bring me here?"

"The air is particularly clear in this spot. You can see through."

Anna took a deep breath. "The air seems perfectly normal."

"Things aren't what they seem, Anna." He waved at the shack. "Care to explore what's behind the door?"

"Care to read "Authorized Entry Only" sign? It means no entry for the likes of us. I imagine the gardening equipment it houses wouldn't be of any use to us anyway. I, for one, wouldn't know what to do with it."

"Are you saying a door is worth opening only if you know how to use whatever lies beyond?"

"That's one way to put it."

"If you opened a door and found something other than what you know, would it be worth your while, Anna?"

He's talking about himself, she thought. *Positively incapable of describing his inner motions without employing metaphoric speech. He's willing to open up to me, but fears that revealing the truth will scare me away, and he would lose the only connection he has.*

"As long as I can help you, it would be worth my while," she said with conviction.

John's lips quivered, a smile lit his face—a genuine, hopeful smile, so different from his sly smirk or his feral grin. He took a step toward her. Her glasses fogged up, and her vision blurred.

"And what if that which you thought unfamiliar, is not as unfamiliar as you thought?" His voice was a soft, low rumble.

"I don't know what you mean." Her breath caught.

"Do you wish to know?" They were eye to eye. She could count each eyelash.

"I do," she exhaled.

His hand found hers. She expected him to pull her in, close the space between them, but he stepped backwards, tugging her along.

"Come." He was leading her down the staircase. "Let's take a closer look at the door."

The door was nothing much to look at: peeling paint, rusted lock, faded sign. As soon as they neared it, John let go of her hand, and Anna felt foolish. How could she fall for this adolescent dare? He was like an immature teenage boy breaking into a neighbor's garage, and she, like an even less mature teenage girl, was eager to follow a crush into a risky escapade.

"It's only a door." Her voice was brittle with frustration.

"Will you open it?"

"This is ridiculous. I appreciate the symbolism here, but come on, John."

He was staring at her with wet, wide eyes, his lips parted. Obeying his silent compulsion, she all but grasped the rusted door handle, but at the last moment jerked her hand back. She was not going to let his puppy eyes manipulate her into more indiscretions. She had already done enough to undermine herself professionally.

Anna took a forceful step away from the door. Her overworked ankle gave in, and her foot slipped on the fresh snow. A momentary flush of adrenaline washed over her, and she scrambled to regain balance. But John was quicker—his arms held her up in a protective circle. Pressed against him, even though the down jacket she felt his heat, heard the even, tidal throbbing of his heart. With a misplaced surprise, Anna registered that they were perfectly aligned: being the same height, their bodies fell naturally into each other, hip to hip, chest to chest, eyes to eyes. Impossibly, it made their embrace chaste and simultaneously obscene, incestuous, like touching one's own twin.

Everything was hanging on invisible threads that threatened to snap at any moment. She wished it had never happened. She wished for it never to end.

With a rugged sigh, John lowered his eyelids. Anna blinked, except it took her forever, because time had slowed as the space shifted, flooded with

John's glow. In her mind's eye she saw his glow pulse and expand, about to engulf her into a shining cloud. Somewhere far beyond, back in the real world, she felt his hot breath on her lips, and, with the clarity usually possible only in dreams, realized that if they kissed, there would be no return.

But I have all these things I must do . . . return Mom's call. . . defend dissertation . . . marry Ted . . .

It was over in the blink of an eye. The arms around her unlocked. John stepped back. His face hardened, his gaze leaving Anna's face and narrowing on something behind her back.

"Mister!" She heard a hoarse voice call from behind. "A moment of your time, mister!"

She turned. A shapeless figure was approaching them in shaky, unsure steps: a man dressed in layers upon layers of mismatched clothing, a walking tent. His neck was bent, his ruddy face hardly visible between the knitted hat and the thick rag around his neck, but his intense eyes were fixed on them.

John made one imperceptible movement, and stood between her and the street man, shielding her with his body.

"It's okay." Anna muttered, talking to both men at once. "It's okay."

But the street man wasn't looking at her. He froze in a crooked curtsy before John, pressing his hands across his chest. His fingerless gloves revealed blackened fingertips with nails that hadn't seen a trim in months.

"Master," the man repeated, addressing John. "Forgive me, master."

"I do not know you," spoke John. His voice was calm, quiet, and so cold it gave her chills.

The man grunted incoherently, and spread his hands apart, palms up, in a gesture of complete submission.

"Speak," ordered John.

"I've trespassed. But not on my own accord. I . . . they commanded me, and I trespassed against you. I took something of yours."

"John, don't," warned Anna.

John didn't respond, standing straight and still.

"I've kept it, it's so, so beautiful. I wanted to sell it, but no, I couldn't sell it. I came here every day hoping you might show up, to return it. Just see, I'm returning it." He patted himself down, looking for something.

A weapon? thought Anna in panic, but the man dug into the folds of his many coats and pulled out what at first looked like a white scarf with long silk tassels, which he reverently offered to John. A gust of wind ripped into it, breaking it into strands, fine threads glimmered in the light: it was a bunch of human hair, about two feet long, tied with a rubber band at the top.

John caressed the back of his neck, and took the ponytail from the homeless man's unsteady hand.

"Confession accepted, forgiveness granted," he said in the same creepily serene voice. And he uttered something else, on the inhale, like a gasp of wind over a snowy ravine.

The homeless man's worried face slackened, as if years of trouble had washed off of it. He backed away, turned and took off in a fast-paced waddle, without looking back.

John combed his fingers through the ponytail and held it to the back of his head.

"Someone did cut your hair, like you've said!" Anna rubbed her temples. "You were telling the truth."

"I told you, I never lie."

"Then please tell me what just happened? How does that man know you? Why did you talk to him this way? And how did you end up naked, unconscious, with your hair cut, here, in this park?"

"I wanted this." John folded the ponytail into a neat knot and put it inside his leather jacket.

"Did you want these, too?" Desperately, she grabbed his arm and pushed up his sleeve. "These cigarette burns?"

For a moment they both stared at his narrow forearm with its trail of pale round scars running along his radial artery.

"These are not burns, Anna," said John, pulling his arm away and adjusting the sleeve almost prudishly. "These are ports for *Ylfête's* bracers."

"What does it even mean?"

"It means "she-swan." It is the name of my Alvan armor."

"No!" She thrust her hands forward, as if her splayed fingers could shield her from the torrent of his insanity. "I don't want to hear about the elves or other dimensions. I want to know what really happened. How did you get here? Why did that man cut your hair? John, if you don't tell me the truth, I can't help you."

"My precious girl, you have helped me more than you know."

Gently, he caught her hands and laid them against his chest.

"What does it matter, why one was compelled to cut another's hair? It's been cut, and it'll grow back. What does it matter, how I got here? I am here now, with you. You found me when I was lost, cared for me when I was ill, welcomed me under your roof, shared your food with me, gave me your attention. When the time comes, I will go into the world as myself, rather than a lost soul who is known by no one, wanted by no one. If humanity is redeemed, it is by you."

As the heat of his touch burned through the knitted fabric of her gloves, warming life back into her numbed fingers, Anna realized it was over. He was not going to tell her anything more than he already had. His fantasy had long subjugated his personality. He was damaged beyond what she could define, let alone fix.

John Fairfax was useless to her. What was worse, she was useless to him.

She had been arrogant to think she could tackle a case like his. She wasn't one of those soulful people who start out as everyone's confidants in middle school, serve as mediators to their own families, and become counselors right out of college. She was a studious researcher, better at keeping records than building instant rapport; her strength was data analysis, not counseling. She simply lacked the emotional insight and intuition to be a therapist.

Her personal integrity had been lacking as well. In her drive to score a curious case for her research, she had obtained consent from a sick man in no position to give it. To make things worse, she'd let her base emotions cloud her judgment, indulged his delusion, and nearly hurled herself at him, all but perpetuating the cycle of abuse he'd already suffered.

She had failed as a professional and a human being.

For a single last heartbeat, she allowed herself to enjoy his warmth.

"All right, Mr. Fairfax." She regained control of her hands and stepped away from him. "If you believe I've helped you, then my work here is done."

She took his file out of her handbag, pulled out the signed consent form, and tore it in two.

"Please consider yourself free from our contract."

John Fairfax was admitted to the Saint Francis Residences for the chronically mentally ill on Tuesday, December 2, at 12:15 p.m. As soon as they'd entered the facility, they were separated: John was led away, and Anna went to the office. Good thing the paperwork looked proper, if only on the surface—the only reason this exemplary facility considered a man with such an incomplete medical history was because of his origination from the Bellevue psychiatric emergency ward. Psychogenic amnesia with a high level of dissociation was entered as the diagnosis, with a recommendation for further therapeutic counseling.

"Do you have a counselor on this case?" asked the intake social worker.

"No," answered Anna. "Please assign whoever's available."

"Would you like to talk to the resident before you go?"

"No need."

It's for the best, she thought, as she walked home. *I've done as much as I could for this man. He is no longer my concern.*

Her studio felt smaller and plainer without John. Normal. The familiarity would have been comforting if not for his traces everywhere. The furniture he had rearranged ever so slightly to such a dramatic effect. The bed linens he had slept on. His voice on her recorder.

She picked up the neatly folded sheets and threw them into the hamper, followed by the towel he'd used. Touching the fabric that had touched his naked skin was unacceptably, unbearably intimate. She wiped her hands against her thighs, but even the sensation of her own touch was too much. More than the usual discomfort brought on by an overwhelming sensation of loss. *There's no reason to react this way,* she scolded herself. *Nothing happened between me and him.*

It was time for damage control. The official interview from his seventy-two-hour observation at Bellevue had been logged into her computer at work. Nothing damning there: just a routine case that wasn't a shining success. Her private notes and recordings from the last thirty-six hours, however, painted a different story—one of personal weakness and professional incompetence.

She roughly raked up all her scattered notes. Everything bearing his name had to be destroyed.

"Nothing happened," she repeated out loud. "Nothing happened."

She opened her laptop and methodically erased her notes on her interviews with John Fairfax. Instead of relief, though, it left a burning ache, as if the load she'd thrown off her shoulders had scraped a layer of skin. She felt a deep wound of professional failure, but also a sense of deeper injury, the same bitter taste under her tongue she always swallowed after another elusive dream fled her memory upon waking. She desperately needed to talk to someone about it.

If you were getting counseling the way you should, you could have discussed this with your therapist, nagged the voice of reason.

"I'll do better than counseling. It's about ten in London," Anna muttered, and opened a videochat window. The laptop screen lit up to the pixelated face of a bleach-blond girl, her bright red lipstick smudged by lag.

"Ánechka!" screamed the girl.

"Zhénechka," replied Anna in a matching tone, mangling her friend's Russian name as always.

"Good timing! I was halfway out the door, a party awaits."

"Communist Party, you nomenklatura apparatchik?"

"Fuck you too!" The blonde laughed. "A postproduction party, you capitalist swine."

Naturally, she was going to a party. There was always some party or other. Genie was a movable feast all by herself, a celestial giant in a petite girl's disguise, pulling everyone into her orbit. The only ones who didn't want to be with her were those who wanted to be her, whether men or women.

"I won't keep you, then," said Anna, her disappointment mixed with relief. What was she going to share anyway—nothing had happened.

"No, wait! You all right?"

"Yeah," she lied and quickly added a truth: "I missed you. I'll call sometime next week. Although, you know what? There is something. I have a favor to ask."

"Don't tell, let me guess . . . you are cheating on Ted and want me to cover for you?"

"I'm not . . . no! Ted and I are great. As a matter of fact, he has proposed, sort of."

"Sort of? How boring."

"Well, not everyone's life is a constant party, you know," Anna said more curtly than she would have liked. Now she regretted the call.

Genie stuck her tongue out at her. "You know, I'm happy if you're happy. I'm the maid of honor, yes?"

"Maid of dishonor is more like it," grumbled Anna. "Of course, you are, you freak."

"Is that even a medical term?"

"Aren't you late for a party? I have one simple request, and I'll let you go."

"Sure, love." A true chameleon, Genie now sounded like a Brit, which was particularly amusing, because during her years at NYU she had talked like a native Noo Yokah.

"Does Royal Holloway have an Anglo-Saxon studies program?"

Genie's animated face expressed righteous indignation.

"It's bloody England, every English department has Anglo-Saxon studies. Why?"

"I need a linguist to listen to a two-minute-long recording of something that's supposedly Old English. It could be gibberish, but I want to know either way."

"No worries, shoot it to me, I'll show it around."

"No, don't show it around. It has to be done discreetly."

"Ooh, secretive, aren't we? Is this for the bloke you're cheating on Ted with?"

"No. It's for a client . . . a former client."

"Cheating on your fiancé with a client, you slut?"

"Cut it out, Gen, I'm serious!"

"All right, all right! When did you get to be so dull . . . I'll say it's a fellow actor practicing an accent. How about that?"

"Girl, you're good." Against her will, Anna's lips stretched into a grin.

"I know." Genie rolled her heavily kohled eyes. "I must fly now, but we'll talk next week, right?"

"Enjoy your party, comrade!"

"Ta-ta!"

Still grinning, Anna attached John's voice recording to an e-mail and sent it: a shot longer than long, a farewell arrow into nowhere.

Her good cheer didn't last long. Talking to Genie made Anna miss her painfully; illuminated by the mood light of their festive past, her present and future with Ted seemed unbearably bland; her career—the only thing she found inspiring—had been tainted by her fresh failure. She had to resort to self-medication: watched some cute puppy videos online and ate some ice cream. But her mood remained lousy. So, she did what every woman knows to do to lift her spirits. She washed her hair.

Anna wrapped the heavy black mass in a towel and tried to collect her thoughts. Consciously, she avoided thinking about the white elephant named John Fairfax. She considered calling Ted, making nice to him and taking him up on his offer to share his client, but opted for a quick text message, letting him know she was exhausted and turning in early.

It was true. The hike up and down Broadway had aggravated her old ankle injury, which brought her back with a physical, not existential, pain. Anna sat on the futon with her foot up on the coffee table, a damp towel on her head, and a pack of frozen peas on her ankle. *I'll ice it for fifteen minutes*, she said to herself, put Procol Harum's "A Whiter Shade of Pale" on a loop and settled in the spot still soft with the memory of John's body.

A soothing numbness spread over her, and she drifted into the cool netherworld between sleep and waking. Her thoughts flowed glacier-like. Wintry images slowly faded in and out of her mind: a powder-dusted path, a ski trail in the fresh snow, a frosted door. The door that dared yet blocked her, a passage she longed yet dreaded to explore. All those times she ventured outside the mundane, be it with intellectual pursuits, or drugs and alcohol—ripping open all kinds of doors except the only one that led to the truth. Even sex, what was it if not a way for her to communicate without having to talk about the only truth that mattered?

She was tired of lying. She had been tired for so long . . .

Where did it begin? Did it have to be an inciting event? Any psychologist will tell you: traumatic experiences don't have to be specially induced; life is rife with them—everyday betrayals and disappointments, small wounds leaving shallow scars, the usual.

Every day a dozen events may occur that will change our life's flow dramatically, irrevocably; a dozen chances for the stream to take a turn or split. But is the water that flows past this turn the same as flowed before? Is it even the same river? If you rename the river after it changed its course, must you also name that rock which forced it to do so?

Where did it begin, that existence that she now knew as *her life*? The life of the person she was now rather than the one right before—before it began? *Where did her story begin?* Anna knew the answer, had always known it: it began with a dream.

She'd had a dream when she first came to New York. She dreamed she was skiing in Riverside Park, met another skier, a boy, and followed him into a magical Otherworld. People and beasts populated it, some cute, some gross. Everything was life or death, the way it always is for a teenager, and everything was about love. Love was a force, like gravity; a taut line reaching from one being to another. The monsters fed on love, greedily, endlessly leaching it out of the world. The young Skiers hunted and destroyed the monsters by using love as a weapon. The secretive Scouts used love to pass between dimensions. The alien race of Counselors used love to control everything. Because of her love for the boy, she became bound to that world. But the boy she loved didn't want her. Instead, someone else wanted her, a striking and eerie creature, all but a monster himself. But even his hard fingers around her throat weren't as scary as the realization that she was no different from a creature who craves love greedily, endlessly, monstrously. She didn't want to be a monster, so she fought: him, herself, the whole world. And she won. Won the right to go home, and a crystal chard from the Otherworld as her trophy.

She remembered how glad she had been to wake up back in her room. But the truth revealed in the dream haunted her waking hours. Once you love, you can't un-love. Once you know, you can't un-know. The plastic wrap of perception peeled away, exposing the silver threads stitching the universe together, revealing everything otherworldly that seeps through the tight weave. She returned to the real world, but now it was full of monsters.

Creatures of different shapes and sizes: rainbow-colored one-eyed rats in the subway, scaled horned ravens in the trees, six-legged spider monkeys running up telephone poles. Their blatant alienness was repulsive. They signaled reality gone horribly wrong, and it made her stomach turn with a dangerous, sucking fear. It was then when the fear began to twist into the spiral of anxiety, because just as she saw them, they saw her. They glared at her from under park benches and subway platforms, forcing her to pick up her step without looking back. They called her name.

Do you hear voices? Do you see things? Yes and yes.

She, too, had a name for them. *Wyssun*.

How could she tell anyone? It was crazy. With her mother's depression after her cesarean, there was enough crazy going around. She didn't want it to rub off on baby Jack. Also, she'd recently started at a new school, and didn't want to become known as a psycho.

So, Anna made the only sensible choice: pretended she saw nothing. And eventually, she saw nothing. At times, her heart pounded and her head spun, but those were only symptoms of anxiety, and what New York City teenager doesn't struggle with anxiety, right? When she decided her visions were no more than anxiety-induced hallucinations, she stopped wearing the crystal pendant. Or was it the other way around? In any case, she could no longer recall the disturbing dream, or any dreams at all. The world had dulled a bit, but losing a degree of awareness seemed like a fair exchange for gaining normalcy. She hadn't had an episode in years—that is, until the one with John Fairfax in the hospital three days before.

But none of it ever happened. It was nothing but a vivid nightmare. There was no door to the Otherworld, no boys on skis, no space elves, no monsters in the tunnels. I didn't have visions. I had panic attacks, triggered by . . . well, what triggered them? she asked herself and trembled. It was always the same thing: the nauseating lurch and palpitations always came right before she saw something that didn't belong in normal reality. Her skin prickled with goose bumps.

A weird noise came from the window. Not a typical city noise of screeching tires, the huffing of a bus's hydraulics, or a fading howl of a police siren. No, this noise was organic, like the clawing of a pigeon at the windowsill, except that even brazen New York pigeons don't fly after dark.

The sound shifted: now the noise was coming from the wall, a tapping of feet, a scratching of sharp claws in the walls and on the roof. Anna's heartbeat echoed in her clenched stomach. Another panic attack was coming. *Find your feet,* she ordered herself. *Now, inhale and open your eyes.*

Her skylight was an inverted pyramid of light in the darkness of her room. Across the glass of the skylight, a creature was staring back at her. It took her only one glance to know it was no normal animal, unless some mutation could turn raccoon's stripes into spikey horns, extend its muzzle into a beak, and arm its paws with long menacing talons. She knew exactly what the creature was. A wyssun. As physically real as an anxiety attack—a real monster.

> She is scared and confused, stuck in a weird room, surrounded by strangers who've nearly killed her a minute ago and now treat her as one of their own. One of them shows her his palm-sized pet. As she looks at the little one-eyed creature covered in iridescent neon-colored fur, she marvels at how something can be cute and ugly at once . . .
>
> She is scared and confused, trying to make a little talking beast who'd jumped out of the fire tell her how to get home, and getting only more confused by its riddles instead . . .
>
> She is scared and confused, in a fight for her life with a giant mutant rat-monster in an underground tunnel. The monster has just drained life out of the boy she loves who now lies breathless at her feet. She doesn't know how, but she is sure it's her fault . . .

And then, she knew she'd just screamed all the air out of her lungs. She gulped in another breath and jumped up, upsetting the coffee table, which crashed onto the floor. The booming thud shook through the old brownstone. She heard her neighbor fussing downstairs, probably disturbed by the loud noise.

"Anna?" called a voice at the door.

She cursed, searched for her glasses in vain, and limped to the door, preparing an apology for the angry neighbor. She opened the door and squinted nearsightedly at the bright light. A backlit figure took a step toward her, forcing her to back away into the apartment. Familiar heat enveloped her, hard fingers locked on her forearms.

"Hush," John exhaled into her ear.

"You . . ." she moaned, sinking down. "You shouldn't be here."

John held her upright at arm's length as she clawed at his leather sleeves. He was wearing the same biker jacket and ink-blue jeans he had on this morning, and she felt exposed in her tank top and a pair of clingy pajama pants. His concerned gaze seemed to scan right through the flimsy fabric.

"I don't need this." She made another weak attempt to shake him off.

"Oh, but you dooo," sang John, peering into the darkness of the room behind her back. The grip on her shoulders loosened, his hands brushed down her bare arms, his fingertips tickled her palms. Letting go, he slid past her into the apartment and flipped the light switch.

Her eyes darted to the skylight. As far as she could tell, the monster on the roof was gone. She looked around and couldn't help another moan. Her small space, so neat just several hours ago, was a mess: upset stacks of books, crumpled paper strewn everywhere. In the middle of the room, a helpless turtle of a coffee table lay legs up. The area rug was generously sprinkled with now defrosted peas, as if the turtle had puked before keeling over.

"You know, Alva believe that the state of one's dwelling directly reflects one's state of mind," declared John, surveying the space. He put the coffee table back in its place, picked up her glasses from the floor, and began to clean up the peas.

"How did you get into the building?" she mumbled, watching his confident ministrations in a stupor.

"Through the door. As usual."

"You shouldn't have come. You and I are done," she said dimly.

"Then, I suppose, you don't care to know how to protect your home from the wyssun?"

"What did you say?"

"The wyssun. You've been screaming like you've seen one. Nasty pests, aren't they?"

Her knees giving in, Anna propped herself against her desk.

"But don't you worry," said John brightly, as he cleaned up the last of her mess and rinsed his hands under the kitchen faucet. "As I told you this morning, I've *arranged* your space. You are safe here. All you need to do is *feel* it. Feel it!"

Anna let out a sob-like laugh. It seemed like such a simple solution: to make things happen by feeling them. Typical John. She wanted to be annoyed with him, but how can you be annoyed with a man who charges in in the middle of the night to chase away your monsters and tidy up your room?

"Look," she said. "I don't care how you know about wyssuns, but even if I were to accept for a moment—just for a moment!—that wyssuns exist, how do you propose I achieve this awareness?"

"Wear your amulet, and see with your own eyes."

The necklace had been in Anna's handbag since the incident at the hospital two days previously, when she had had to rip it off her neck. She dug into the purse and pulled it out by the cord.

"It's broken."

"May I?" He walked over to her, wiping his hands against the back of his jeans.

"Last time you touched it, you collapsed."

"I wasn't myself."

He twiddled with it; after a few seconds in his clever fingers, the clasp was as good as new. He held the necklace by the cord, offering it to Anna.

"So, what's special about it?" she asked cautiously.

"It's your amulet, you tell me."

She sucked air in through her nose sharply and exhaled. There was a small stirring in her mind, a quiet echo of some faraway music, like a promise made long ago and forgotten. Something tugged at her heart, pulling her somewhere.

"Well, I made it myself when I first moved to New York, and it's been with me through my teenage years. It makes me feel—" she paused, transfixed by the lights dancing in the facets, "—sentimental."

"Rightly so." He swung it in front of his face, tiny dots of light sprinkling his cheekbones with chromatic freckles. "Its crystalline perfection is reminiscent of a world beyond, while the crudeness of craftsmanship is quite poignant."

"Hey!" She tried to pull the necklace out of his hand. "I was a child when I made it."

"I know." Their eyes met, and John was the first to look away. "Wear it, Anna." He released his grip on the cord.

It seemed like a bad idea to follow any suggestion John made, but it couldn't have been any worse than seeing a green wyssun on the roof.

The clasp clicked, and the cold crystal lay on her chest. *Perhaps I was wrong. The crystal is not the trigger*, thought Anna, relieved. Her heart didn't pick up a beat, her breathing didn't hitch. And John, John too looked just the way he looked before: a skinny towheaded man standing in the middle of her room; a perfectly normal—well, perhaps above-average handsome man—ah, who was she kidding—a gorgeous man with shining eyes and a halo of hair floating about his head. The sublime creature offered his hand. She gladly took it.

His voice was like wind in the trees: "Behold with true sight."

He swayed his other hand, sending glowing traces through the space as if his motion had activated invisible strings that resonated as he struck them. Anna followed it with her eyes, seeing her whole room in its entirety, from above and within at once. An elaborate ornament ran around the room and over the walls and floor and ceiling, geometric runes and calligraphy in an unknown language. Each element glowed with its own light and rang with its own tone, together creating patterns and chords of complex harmony. The space was, indeed, arranged, woven through and through with silver threads. No evil could ever penetrate these defenses. Like he'd told her, he had protected her space with the most secure enchantment. All she had to do to be safe was to feel it.

It was a reality no less real, no!—more real than her normal reality, and now, superimposed on the mundane, overwhelming it. Everything he'd ever said inexplicably made sense. But it making sense made no sense at all.

I am hallucinating, she told herself. *The crystal did trigger a hallucination.*

She was about to remove the necklace, but a hot palm lay on her chest, promising relief. And relief came: the intensity of her vision began to subside, the glowing symbols on the walls faded and the ringing quieted, leaving only a trace in her mind, an echo of perception. She blinked. When she looked again, the world was the same except, perhaps, sharper and brighter, in higher definition. With this clarity came a profound awareness: she was safe.

She was standing in the middle of her room, her left hand pressed to her chest over her heart, holding the crystal, John's hand still covering hers. He stood within arm's reach, his hands' position mirroring hers, like frozen in a figure of a dance.

"What have you done to me?" She wanted to shout at him, but only a whisper came out.

He shook off doglike, his glassy gaze becoming focused again.

"I have done nothing to you. I have, however, put a protective enchantment on your home. Fine runework, isn't it?" He jerked up his chin with a proud smirk.

"I don't believe you. It cannot be." She snatched back her hands.

"You saw the silver threads of existence. Won't you believe your own eyes?"

"Not if my mind is playing a trick on me."

"No trick." He was still standing too close, so close she could see his teeth glisten. When did the curve of his lip become this familiar to her? She drew a breath, blood rushing to her cheeks. Slowly, he lifted both hands as if about to cradle her face in his palms. For a moment, it felt achingly recognizable, so much so that she wanted his hard fingers on her face to make sure. Instead, he carefully reached around and removed the necklace from her neck.

"This is a vessel." He placed it over the dry maple branch in the vase on Anna's desk, between the dreamcatcher and the Christmas ornament, the same spot where it'd been hanging all these years. "You've been using it for years unwittingly, and I can count each time you did, because even though we were worlds apart, I felt it each and every time—a thorn in my side, a twinge I couldn't escape. You used it to help me pry open my true self, and just now to engage your true sight. It's all but exhausted, but this crystal contained a small amount of a splendid power."

"Splendid power . . . what power?" Anna rubbed her temples. "Magic elf-power? Power to induce psychotic episodes? How is this even possible?"

"Do you remember nothing?"

"What are you trying to make me remember?"

"Anna, don't you see, I cannot make you do anything." His lips twitched, as if he wanted to add something. He frowned and shook his head.

"Why the puzzles? Why can't you tell me what you know?"

"You wouldn't believe me if I told you. People only believe what they wish to believe. The desire must come from you. You know—free will, mankind's greatest gift." He rolled his eyes.

Anna looked around again. Her room appeared normal. The thought of a green monster clawing its way through the skylight seemed absurd, as absurd as allowing John Fairfax back into her life.

"Look, it's late," She glanced at the wall clock. It was after ten. They had been apart for ten hours—ten hours she'd spent trying to forget she'd ever known him, ten hours rendered useless in the course of the last ten minutes. "You should return to Saint Francis before they lock down."

"You should know by now, I come and go as I please."

"Your coming here is against the rules."

"It stands to reason that since our contract is void, so are your rules." He smirked.

With a groan of frustration, Anna shook her head. The towel came undone, and a tangled black mass fell over her face. She grabbed her head. *The hair!* Instead of hallucinating elvish scripts on the walls, she should have been brushing her hair, which by now must have all but dried into one enormous free-form dreadlock on her head.

"You know," he sounded like he was grinning hugely, "The Alva also believe that one's state of mind is reflected in the condition of one's hair."

The bastard had forced himself into her home, caught her with her hair down, and now was mocking her. Shame and anger pumped adrenaline into her blood.

"You don't understand!" Anna pushed the hair away from her face and stumbled to the full-length mirror by the front door. She grabbed her brush and plunged it in like a knife.

"Oh, but I do," John said from right behind her. His quiet voice in her ears was deafening. She knew she was supposed to be afraid, try to escape this inappropriate intimacy, but she didn't move. *He can do anything to me, and I will let him*, she thought with an eerie detachment.

"I understand perfectly." John removed the brush from her hand, knotted his fingers through her hair and closed his fist, pulling ever so slightly, making her lift her chin. "You want me to make the choice for you."

He glided the brush down through her hair. With every inch of her back Anna could sense the even heat emanating from him. Her skin burned. In the corner of her eye she noticed that his hand holding her brush trembled. He was excited, as aroused as she was. Had he moved a step closer, their bodies would have melted into one another. But he didn't make a move, just drove his hand up and down in a controlled motion. His other hand caressed her tresses without touching her skin. She shut her eyes, afraid of seeing the reflection of them together.

"You are tired of carrying the burden that is mankind's gift. You want me to absolve you, to free you," he murmured, half-questioning, half-affirming, in time to his even strokes. His breath tickled the fine hairs on the nape of her neck. "Yes?"

"Y-yes," she exhaled.

"No."

He put down the brush and stepped aside, leaving Anna alone in front of the mirror. Her hair lay against her back like a freshly pressed satin sheet. She opened her eyes, facing the mirror. The woman before her looked pathetic, like a wretched child who'd had candy ripped from her sweaty little clutch. Anna whirled around, pointing an accusing forefinger at John's chest.

"You can't do this! You can't barge into my life, behave as if you are attracted to me—"

"I am not attracted to you," he cut her off flatly.

"Huh?" Her arms dropped.

"I am not attracted to you," he repeated with a deepening scowl. "After I've revealed myself to you so fully, how can you know me so little?"

"I thought—" she mumbled, her eyes treacherously welling up.

"You thought wrongly!" he cried in exasperation, his face shadowed with nothing short of rage. "This is no attraction. Between two skis there's attraction. Between a hunter and a wyssun there's attraction. What I have for you is true love!"

She watched his chest rise and fall, as if he were about to burst into sobs, and with a shock, realized that what she took for rage was desire. She had never felt this much passion focused on her person. It was intoxicating.

"I want you more than anything. I'm bound to you with the same silver strings that stitch together the fabric of creation." His voice faltered. "From the moment we met, I've acted in your benefit. I treasure your welfare above my own. Your wish is my command."

Anna could barely hear what he was saying, because her ears felt clogged, like she'd been launched high in the air. All she could discern was that John had just declared his love for her. This man—this outrageous, fantastic, enticing man—loved her, wanted her. Wasn't it what she'd hoped to hear? The longing she felt for him despite herself, wasn't it the same as in her dreams? The sunlit boy of her forgotten fantasy, could it have been him all along?

"Who are you?" Her voice came out hoarse. "Where do you come from?"

"I am Yaret, son of Ælfled Fairfax, a human of Earth, and Yarbonél Dé Fal, an alva of Alvaheim. I entered this world from the realm human legends call the Otherworld."

"What do you want from me?"

"I shall let you guess the answer . . ." He took a step toward her.

"No tricks, no puzzles! Answer the question. What is your ultimate purpose?"

He froze.

"Anna, you don't know what you're asking."

"So, this is what your word is worth? All this talk of being incapable of lying, all this "your wish is my command". If you have any consideration for me and respect for the relationship we've developed, you will tell me the whole truth, in terms I can comprehend."

He winced.

"The whole truth is," he said after a heavy pause, "that the Alva are the universe's firstborn children, the custodians of the cosmic garden. Some seed worlds, nourish species, cultivate civilizations; others prune and cull. I am . . . *was* one of the latter, an awesome Alvan Voidwalker."

Anna's jaw began to ache. Fear, hope, lust—all the excitement was rapidly melting in the puddle of disappointment. What was she thinking, allowing herself to see him as anything but a sick man? The grandeur of his narcissistic delusion was matched only by her willingness to ignore the obvious.

He went on: "On the wings of *Ylfête,* my living armor, I traversed the void, alien planets' soil, and planes of existence that cannot be described in human tongue. For a thousand years I tended the garden with an unfaltering hand. I knew a day would come for my childhood homeworld to be subject to Alvan worldbuilding, as it had been many times in the past. I didn't care, for my own humanity had long been lost to me. Then you ripped through my dark skies like a shooting star, and never left my heart and mind."

We met five days ago, and he's already developed an intimate obsession, incorporating me into his fantasy, Anna thought wistfully. *I am stuck in a room with a psychotic erotomaniac who is fixated on me, and, instead of plotting escape, I am trying to assign him a role in my own fantasies. I must be as mad as he is.*

She cast a glance at the door.

"It was for your sake that I requested to establish a Haven on Earth, to exempt this world from destruction. I made it my purpose to become a Lord of Haven. A Lord of Haven must be of the local bloodline. There had been several bids in the past, all by purebred humans. None succeeded. But never before has a being of shared earthly and otherworldly lineage claimed this position. Odds are in my favor. For as long as my children and their children walk the Earth, it will be safe."

"What does it have to do with me?" She knew the answer, but his reply still made her skin crawl.

"There is no one in this world I desire to bear my seed but you. To prove my faith in our shared destiny, I crossed the threshold naked, stripped of my armor, powers, and memory, on a hope you would accept me by the seventh dawn."

"And if I don't?" She blurted out and immediately regretted it, because John wrapped his fingers around his right wrist, and writhed his hand in an eerily familiar, terrifying gesture.

"Then it is the beginning of the end." He sounded deadly serious, perhaps with a tinge of remorse. "So, my beloved Anna, now you know. The truth I hoped to spare you is that Earth is up for a culling."

"Bad news for Earth, I'm sure," she muttered, inching toward the door while he looked away. He was dangerous. She needed to be careful not to antagonize him.

"On the contrary. Good news for Earth, bad news for mankind."

"Well, isn't that something." She took another step toward the door.

All of a sudden, he sank to one knee and froze with arms opened wide and low, head down—a graceful pose disturbingly mirroring the awkward bow of the madman in the park. There was something unnatural, distinctly alien about it. Anna's stomach clenched and she froze half-step.

When he spoke again, his voice was a quiet rumble. "The one who comes to end life has come to beget it. The world will be redeemed by our sacred marriage. Be mine, as I am yours."

The tightness in her stomach gave way to the queasiness of falling, of failure. She had been wrong about him, yet again. She had presumed that pretending to be a time-traveling alien was too overtly fantastical to be a successful con game, so it had to be mental illness. What if all this time he was both, a mentally ill conman? Greedy for an exciting case, she had chosen to think him delusional, while she was the delusional one. A willing mark, eager to help him get a new identity, providing a temporary shelter to lie low. He'd used her successfully up to now. Why not take the mark for the whole score and get her into bed as well?

"Please help me understand this," Anna strained to keep her voice even. "Are you saying, that if I don't . . . ugh . . . *marry* you, it will be the end of the world?"

He dropped his head even lower.

"John?"

He didn't respond, fair hair hanging over his face, concealing his expression. Without taking her eyes off him, she made another cautious step toward the door.

"Um . . . Yaret." As she spoke his name, he looked up. His eyes flashed, lips parted. Yearning and, in quick succession, hope lit his face.

"You said my wish is your command?"

"By true love, I swear." Desire radiated from him, blinding her. In any other world, he was beautiful. In the real world it was a dreadful sight. How far was he willing to go to claim what he desired?

Quickly, she backed into the door and flung it open. The cold iron frame cut into her spine, grounding her with a welcome anchor to reality.

"Yaret, I command you to leave."

He rose to his feet unsteadily, staring at her with darkened eyes, all of a sudden looking small and frail, almost transparent.

"Ahn-nah!" Her name fell off his lips like a moan. "By true love!"

"By true love, leave!" she shouted from the doorway. "Get out of my house! Go away!"

"Hey! You okay?" her downstairs neighbor called through his half-open door. "Want me to call the cops?"

"I'm fine!" Anna yelled. "Sorry!" Turning back, she said firmly, "Leave, Yaret."

She listened to the sound of his steps fade as he descended the stairs. The building front door slammed, and everything was quiet. Anna returned to the apartment, locked the door, and fell on top of her bed without turning off the light. Her skin was crawling. Her ears were ringing. Her vision was blurred.

She couldn't stay in this place. She had to leave at once.

She jumped up, threw on some street clothes, and ran outside. Before exiting her building, she looked around. John Fairfax was gone. She stumbled toward Fifth Avenue. A lone yellow cab was trudging through the snowy street. She hailed it and gave the driver Ted's address. All through the car ride she fought nausea.

She opened the door with her key. Ted was in his living room, predictably, watching the local news.

"Ann?" An apprehensive smile creased his face. "I thought you said you were turning in early."

Without a word, she dropped her purse on the floor, kicked of her boots, shrugged out of her coat, and climbed onto the couch next to him, cuddling up to his soft, pajama-clad side.

"Couldn't stay away from me, huh?"

She whimpered into his shoulder.

"Well, it's unexpected, but . . . romantic. Wait, hon, you're burning up. Are you all right? Let me get you some aspirin. You need to lie down."

She whined, shaking her heavy head.

"Do you want me to carry you to bed?" His playful threat brought on another surge of nausea. This was all wrong. But she stretched her lips in a grateful grin, and dragged her feet to the bedroom.

Wednesday, December 3

She doesn't want to fight with her mom, but it happens again, and it is her fault, so she grabs her skis and runs to the park across the street. She has just moved to New York, and she has also just found out her mother is having a baby with her new husband. She feels unloved and alone, but she doesn't mean to run away for real, only to clear her head. She is about to go back when her busted right ankle gives in and she falls. A boy with braided hair helps her up. She follows him, although she knows she shouldn't. He is so special to her, this boy with braided hair. There is a connection between them. It must be love.

Suddenly, she is no longer in the park, but in the Otherworld, the world that lives on love, sings of love, rings with love. But love is not what she thinks it is. Love isn't about being nice. It is a force to give life, or to take life. It is everything and more. The Otherworld is run by elves with long ears and long hair. They use love to nourish each other, and to destroy monsters. She is not sure if she is to be nourished or to be destroyed.

She sees the silver strings stitching the universe, hears their pulse. She is terrified, for she is no more than a tiny speck of dust caught in the infinite glowing web. It is overwhelmingly powerful, and she has no idea how to handle it.

Hot tears scorch her eyes and she wakes up.

Anna sat upright, clutching her blanket. It took her a couple of panicked breaths to realize she was at Ted's place. The imagery of her dream was still vivid, scorched against her closed eyelids. It went beyond the images.

She vividly recalled the smell of snow, the ache of her ankle, the thrill of an intense attraction, and the horror of being lost—not a recollection of a dream, but a clear and distinct memory. So, here she was, after not having recalled a dream for a decade, suddenly dreaming up suppressed memories.

She squinted at the alarm clock: quarter to seven, alarm was about to go off. Before it woke Ted, she slid out of the bed and padded to the bathroom.

To take her mind off the dream-memory, she let the hot shower stream massage her numb neck and thought of the night before. She rarely initiated intimacy with Ted, not while sober anyway, but last night she'd needed more from him than his kind concern about her health. She pushed herself on top of him, digging her nails into his thick shoulders, squeezing his hips with her thighs, pulling his chest hair until he yelped. She pressed into him with a feverish desperation, in time to Led Zeppelin's "Whole Lotta Love" screeching madly inside her head. But neither her mind nor her body had been in the right place. She'd rolled off him tired and bitter, her only measure of satisfaction the sensation of control over the man beneath her.

"Good morning, sexy." Ted's muffled voice brought her back. He was brushing his teeth, bent over the sink. "How're you doing today?"

"I'm fine, thanks, Teddy." She turned off the water and stepped out of the tub. "Listen, if I was weird last night . . ."

He looked back and smiled with a foamy mouth, his cupped hands overflowing with water. As it sometimes happens with large people, Ted's movements had a delicate unease to them, a kind of awareness of all the fragile things surrounding him. This was how he held his hands under the tap, carefully. This was how he touched her, too. But she wasn't fragile, she was tough, she fought and defeated monsters . . . she *was* a monster.

"I mean, I . . ."

"Ann, it's okay." Ted reached for a towel. "I love you, babe, in weirdness and in health." He wiped his face and wrapped the towel around her wet back. "Well, your fever seems to be gone. See, Doctor Ted will take good care of you."

Their parting kiss was tender, minty, and left her miserable.

One advantage of spending the night at Ted's was the morning commute: an easy subway ride down to the Twenty Third Street stop a few blocks from Bellevue. Anna's own building was awkwardly away from all the nearest train stops, so her usual commute was a hassle, but a familiar one. Since she'd landed on the western shores of Manhattan over a decade ago, Anna had never stopped being a westsider. James' building was near Riverside park; her high school was a block away from Lincoln Center; her NYU classes all took place at the West Side campus, walking distance from the West Village apartment she'd shared with Genie. Even the uptown Armory Track, where she attended the running meets in high school and as undergrad, was west of Broadway.

Now, standing at the packed platform of the East 77th street station, she attributed her flare of anxiety to what Ted called her "West Side prejudice". She felt her feet and breathed deeply, as the anti-anxiety self-help protocol required. One impatient man next to her on the platform craned his neck in the direction of the expected train, and several others followed suit, all freezing in the same awkwardly bent pose, like a gang of meerkats. Hit with a rush of claustrophobia, Anna stared in the opposite direction.

She wished she hadn't. She saw a movement near the dark mouth of the tunnel at the end of the tracks. A figure appeared out of the darkness, shifted out of sight, reappeared on the other side of the track, shifted and reappeared again back where it had been, standing upright. It glowed neon yellow, then neon pink, then violet. Short arms ended with beastly claws and a ratlike muzzle, disturbingly, with a naked trunk. She stifled a gasp. As if it heard, the wyssun turned toward her, sniffing, and stepped back into the darkness of the tunnel. It all took less than a second.

She whirled around, hoping to catch the eye of a fellow passenger who'd seen what she had, but everyone seemed absorbed in their phones or looking in the opposite direction.

I know I saw what I saw, but in reality it was just a tunnel worker standing under a colored lantern, she was saying to herself as she squeezed against her fellow riders on the downtown train. *Nothing but a play of the light and dark distorted by the glare on my glasses.*

In the lobby of the hospital Anna, distracted, nearly bumped into Gloria, the chief ER nurse who had woken her up on Sunday morning with the news of the rape attempted on John Doe. For a moment Anna feared that Gloria would bring it up. *Stop it. Stop fixating on him.*

"How're you doing," she mumbled, unbuttoning her coat and pulling off her hat.

"Fine," replied Gloria, giving her an appraising look, "Your hair looks nice. Did you go to a salon?"

"Uh. . . no?" Anna twirled a strand between her fingers. Even after the restless night, the humidity of the shower, and the abuse of the morning commute, brushed by an otherworldly hand hair was wondrously smooth and silky.

"You're in the ER today, right? I'll see you there." Gloria smiled with approval, and Anna realized that in the nine months they'd worked side by side, this was the first time they had an exchange beyond the necessary. In the microcosm of the ward, psychology grad student Anna Reilly was inconsequential to veteran psychiatric nurse Gloria Salazar, who, unlike the doctors, had neither the obligation nor the luxury of time to nurture each annual crop of interns.

Relishing the feeling of camaraderie, Anna walked under the arch of the metal detector and across the wide red line painted on the floor to indicate the border between the mundane world and the world of madness. Today, she felt more normal here than on the outside.

She squared her shoulders and stepped across the line. Several patients at the lounge were staring at a television, its screen protected by Plexiglas. Farther down the corridor she saw a man handcuffed to a wheelchair, his face covered with a respirator-like mask. *A spitter,* thought Anna, picking up the pace, *or a biter.* She noticed the bandaged hand of a cop talking to the intake nurse. Definitely a biter. A woman strapped to a gurney was howling in a low, sorrowful voice, "You don't know me! You don't know me! Don't talk to me like you know me!" The sharp smell of disinfectant couldn't cover the distinct body odor permeating the air.

Anna imagined how out of place John must have felt when he was brought to the ER six days ago. Could it have been only six days ago? It seemed like an eternity.

She was doing it again! She needed to stop thinking about it. About him. Wipe the slate clean, start from scratch, begin anew—any optimistic cliché applicable.

But she had to do damage control first. The nine o'clock appointment with Dr. Stevens was looming. She braced herself and entered her supervisor's office.

"Good morning. How was your vacation?"

"Oh, it wasn't much of a vacation, just took the boys to visit with GramMa," Dr. Stevens replied casually, waving Anna in. She looked rested, her brown skin refreshed by the touch of the tropical sun. Her manicured hand was resting on top of a folder, which Anna recognized as the John Doe folder she herself had filed.

"So, Anna, have you given more thought to the events at the ER last week?"

Anna nodded, relieved that Dr. Stevens hadn't opened with the dreaded case. She felt like a kid who'd been studying his father's Playboy instead of the class assignment, having to muddle through an improvised show and tell with random objects found in the bottom of his school bag—which was still preferable to telling the truth.

"How do you feel?"

"I feel fine. Absolutely fine."

"Observed any unusual, out-of-place sensations afterwards?"

"After it was over, I kept smelling the scissors, I mean, the metallic smell of the blades on my hands. I washed my hands repeatedly, but the sensation persisted. It was . . . It is as if I can still smell it."

Anna listened to her own dispassionate voice, focusing her eyes on the framed diplomas above her supervisor's head. A loud peal of bells made her jump; she patted herself to find her cell phone. With an apology, she turned it off. She'd never left her phone on during a supervision session before, how could she forget . . .

"Anna," said Dr. Stevens warmly, "Could you please name the symptoms of post-traumatic stress disorder to me?"

"Intrusive reliving of the experience including flashbacks; hypervigilance, exaggerated startle response, impaired concentration and attention . . ." Anna heard herself recite in monotone.

Dr. Stevens arched her eyebrows, her face encouraging.

"Flat affect," finished Anna with a defeated sigh. "I get it, Janice."

"Good. And what is the most effective course of treatment?"

"Cognitive behavioral therapy in combination with SSRI antidepressants."

"Excellent. So, you understand how to proceed. I'll be happy to consult with your personal therapist on the treatment. Now, why don't we talk about the amnesiac case."

"He is no longer an amnesiac."

"Has he recovered his memory?"

"He claims he did," replied Anna carefully.

It was the correct answer. Dr. Stevens paused, waiting for her to elaborate. Giving Anna a case custom tailored for her dissertation had been a favor, and Anna owed her more than a formal report.

"There was no reason to keep him any longer, so he was discharged to a shelter."

"I trust all the paperwork is in order?"

"As far as I can tell." Being evasive without lying outright wasn't difficult after all—the elven art of truth-telling worked.

"I don't have to remind you that we are a municipal hospital."

She didn't. Anna knew what it meant: each step taken at the hospital was regulated by the city and state agencies plus an independent commission, and all records were kept in the event of a potential lawsuit.

"Especially if you are planning to use this case for your dissertation," added Dr. Stevens.

"That won't be happening," said Anna quickly. "He is no longer my case. I had to terminate before I could start."

"May I ask why?"

"He wasn't responding." Anna looked down. "I couldn't create rapport."

Dr. Stevens waited, giving her charge a chance to elaborate.

"Actually, I might have . . . taken it more personally than I should have. It would be unethical not to acknowledge that I might have experienced some countertransference."

Dr. Stevens' face remained impassive, but Anna felt the air in the room compress.

"Do you have reason to believe boundaries were crossed?"

Anna remembered the momentary sensation of John's flesh hardening against her palm and the overwhelming desire to smell her hand afterward.

How his lips scorched the thin skin of her wrist, and how his heat filled her with drunken giddiness. How he pulled her hair when he brushed it, and how he let go and stepped back, leaving her lost outside of his orbit, longing for more. How the two of them had shared a roof, food, clothes, and a dream.

But none of it had happened to Anna Reilly, the psychologist, and John Doe, the mental patient, because by then those people were no more. Whether she was willing to admit it or not, that relationship ended as soon as he kissed the crystal shard and from the amnesiac John Doe turned into the otherworldly Yaret Fairfax. Oh, it was a shared reality all right, but not a one of this world.

"I believe I've crossed an internal boundary," Anna spoke with sincere contrition, and felt safer at once, as if by surrendering a small understated truth she managed to protect the grand lie.

"Nothing inappropriate happened during the initial interview, you can see for yourself from the transcript. The patient was playful but not flirtatious. In fact, I've got the impression he may be homosexual. He kept going in circles, provoking me, like my little brother when he wants to be contrary, and I noticed I was slipping into a familiar pattern with him. I felt a sense of duty toward him, even fondness, but . . . there was a lot of anger on my part. I was in no position to continue. I secured a bed at the shelter for him and terminated the relationship."

Dr. Stevens' full lips formed a small smile.

"When you brought up countertransference, I thought you meant the sexual kind," she said. "It's more common than one might think. Most therapists, male and female, have experienced erotic attraction to their clients at some point. It's normal. Of course, acting on such impulses would be catastrophic. But any kind of transference, positive or negative, can be a confusing and challenging experience for both the client and the therapist. Bringing up your feelings toward your brother demonstrates an excellent degree of awareness. Another issue you should address with your personal therapist."

"I don't have one," exhaled Anna, suddenly out of breath.

Without missing a beat, Dr. Stevens picked up her notebook, leafed through it, wrote on a piece of paper, and handed it to Anna. "Please, call all three of these therapists, choose one, and make an appointment a.s.a.p. This is not a suggestion, Anna."

Anna felt a little guilty using Jack as a decoy, but what was this new small shame compared to her failure in handling a promising case, abandoning a severely disabled patient midway, lusting after a man other than her fiancé, and, to top it all off, lying to her mentor? Another drop in an industrial-sized vat of toxic waste. Her supervisor was right. She needed to start sorting out this mess: dreams that felt like memories, memories that seemed like hallucinations, hallucinations that looked material. This had gotten far beyond anxiety attacks. She'd been in denial for far too long.

Anna walked back to her office, fully intending to follow Dr. Stevens' direct order and make an appointment for personal therapy. But when she sat in front of her computer, there it was, a note from Genie.

Subject:translation
From:GenieS<E.Sokolova@rhul.ac.uk>
To: Anna Reilly<anna.reilly@nyu.edu>

Anny-bunny,

I've sent your file to dr. Ward at our dept. of english/medieval, here is his reply. He is a bit of a prick about it, no? cute though.

Love, G.

P. S. Im going to Morocco for a shoot till mid-january, an assistant director opportunity came up. Call you when I get back!

Subject:RE: a reading in old english
From:Alfred Ward <A.Ward@rhul.ac.uk>
To:GenieS <E.Sokolova@rhul.ac.uk>

Dear Ms. Sokolova,

Apropos your request for transcription and translation of the recording you sent, below is my brief commentary. Although somewhat idiosyncratic, the reader's pronunciation was overall consistent with the phonetic rules of Old English insofar as we know it from reconstruction.

The first phrase is clearly "*Ic willaþ ge sæge mec mid min trēowe nama*," which is translated literally as "I wish for you to call me by my true name."

The second sound bite I transcribed as the following:

Lēof
Syle mé héafod mid feaxe
langum fægrum feaxe
scírum and scínendum
flówendum gyldenum unáwæscenum.
Syle mec feax þe þider niþer fealleþ,
Sculdor lengðe oþþe lengra
hēr bearn, ðǽr módor
gehwǽr fæder fæder
Feax feax feax
flōwaþ hit íewaþ hit
swā lang swā god mæg hit āweaxan lǽtan
Min feax.

Below is the literal translation:

Beloved
Give me a head with hair
Long fair hair
Shining glowing
Flowing flaxen unwashed (?)
Give me hair down to there
Shoulder length or longer
Here child there mother
Everywhere father father
Hair hair hair
Flow show
Long as god may grow
My hair.

As far as origins of the text, I'm afraid I must disappoint you. While grammatically correct, the text does not appear authentic. Although it is semantically consistent with pre-Christian tradition, perhaps a pagan battle blessing referring to an enemy's head as trophy (early Anglo-Saxons were known to be headhunters), the reference to the singular yet unnamed god in this context indicates a Christian influence. Most Anglo-Saxon texts have survived by being preserved in monasteries. I find it extremely unlikely for a pagan text of such a nature to have survived, which draws me to the conclusion that this is an exercise by an Old English enthusiast.

The usage of "*mec*" rather than "*me*" is indicative of the Northumbrian dialect, which makes me suspect the individual who composed this text had studied his Old English from *Cædmon's Hymn* and *The Lindisfarne Gospels*.

To sum up, while I commend your fellow-actor on his effort, I would suggest he use an authentic historic Old English source for his exercises rather than a creative substitute.

Regards,
Alfred Ward

Anna rubbed her eyes and reread the translation. As she scanned the lines, she felt a wave of hysterical mirth rising in her chest. She quickly googled *Hair song musical*. The first video clip to pop up was the scene from the movie in which an uptight psychiatrist interviews a blond rebel who breaks into song and turns the whole jailhouse upside down. It was so ridiculously obvious, and it so obviously smacked of John's mischief.

"Here baby, there mama, everywhere daddy, daddy, haaair!" Anna mouthed soundlessly to the music and burst into laughter. When she was done shaking, she leaned back in her chair, weak from laughing, and tried to think straight.

So, John had translated a song from a movie he'd just seen into Old English on the fly. He was telling the truth about speaking the ancient language. *Well, all it proves is that he speaks it*, Anna said to herself. *Nothing more*. But there was more. It also meant that—unlike her—he was telling the truth. She had asked him to present a display of his powers, and he had revived a dead plant. She had asked him to prove he spoke Old English, and he had. She had asked him to leave, and he had left.

Anna typed a quick e-mail thanking her friend for her help. Genie had come through for her as always, no questions asked. The latter likely owed more to her self-absorption rather than thoughtfulness, but Anna felt genuinely grateful. She signed the note with her usual "Love, A.," and rested her hands on the keyboard.

In the four years they lived together, she'd shared much with Genie: joints, bed, boys. But never her nightmare of the Otherworld, never her visions of monsters. Never the truth. Of course, Genie knew about Anna's anxiety attacks, but she had treated them with her typical offhandedness.

"Big deal! Heart palpitations accompanied by a sense of doom? In Russia we call it Tuesday," she used to say. "When you have palpitations, you clench your sphincter, pick up that log you're carrying, and carry on."

Genie's severity resonated with Anna's own harsh sense of discipline. But for hedonistic Genie this theatrical callousness was the key to a deeper enjoyment of life, the opposite of Anna's self-denial. Back then, Anna had decided not to let her wounds fester and scar into an impairment. She was going to use pain as a source of strength, transfigure it like the Jungian *wounded healer*. And she had been doing so well, perhaps not as a clinician, but as an intuitive and insightful researcher. She had it together.

Why did this man have to come into her life, why did he have to remind her how thin the film of reality was, how uncanny the lining.

"Ready?" Michael Campbell's shiny shaven head poked in.

"For what?" Anna rubbed her forehead.

"It's Wednesday. Brisket at the cafeteria."

"Right. Do you mind if I invite Ramon? I owe him a lunch."

"Ramon from Radiology? Sure."

They had to wait for another ten minutes for Ramon, who was finishing a procedure, so Anna suggested they swing by the inpatient unit to check on Mr. Willis. Since the encounter the week before, Anna hadn't had a chance to talk to him. He'd been put on suicide watch when admitted, but his attending psychiatrist conceded it was only a precaution. As soon as the antipsychotics kicked in, Mr. Willis became perfectly reasonable.

They found him in the common room playing a game of cards with another patient. He looked up at Anna with a friendly, distracted expression.

"I was in the ER when you came to us," she said carefully, not registering any recognition in his eyes. "Just wanted to see how you're doing."

"Doing good," he replied. His voice sounded different without the wheezing.

"And your asthma?"

"Better, much better. The doctor gave me a new inhaler, powder. It's much better."

"How about your hearing?"

"I don't have a problem with hearing. Never had. Always had a sharp ear. I still do."

"Come on, man," said his game partner.

"We won't keep you any longer," said Anna.

"I still do," repeated Mr. Willis. "Hear them in the walls. But they don't scare me no more. The medication makes me not scared. I'm doing good."

"Who doesn't scare you?" asked Michael, leaning in.

"The devils."

Michael and Anna exchanged quick glances.

"What kind of devils?"

"The kind like in the Bible, the hairy ones of many colors."

"Are you playing or what?" nudged his game partner impatiently.

"Thanks for your time," said Anna.

"I should mention this to his attending," she muttered as they rode the elevator to the cafeteria. "The meds are not working."

"The meds are working," disagreed Michael. "He's no longer paranoid."

"Right, now he accepts the existence of the devils as but a mild nuisance."

"Would you prefer he didn't believe in devils but was scared of something more plausible?"

He was talking about Linda, his recent case. A fifty-year-old woman with a history of chronic paranoid schizophrenia, she had been an inpatient at Bellevue a few times over the years. She believed she was "being zapped by the CIA." In interviews she would jump out of her chair and twirl around before settling back in, "to throw off the radiation." For the most part, she was well managed with medication; she lived in a group home in the Bronx and had a part-time job. Ironically, what had made her spin into a downward circle this time was a real-life event: the Mayor was coming to the Bronx to launch a new nonprofit, and the secret service was obligated to interview her because of the many letters—some threatening—she'd sent to the Gracie Mansion over the years.

"I'd prefer if there were no devils," said Anna wearily. "Real or imaginary."

They met Ramon in the cafeteria and he joined the conversation with the easy grace of a good relay runner.

"I remember something in Leviticus about devils—the word is directly translated as *the hairy ones*," he said between bites. "Maybe that's what the patient meant."

"Impressive!" Michael dropped his fork to clap his hands.

"Six years of Catholic school, bro."

"Ouch. I've done my time in Sunday school too, but I'm not familiar with this bit. You're some Bible scholar."

"Nah," mumbled Ramon, chewing. "Just got a memory for random facts."

"Anything about devils of many colors?" asked Anna.

Ramon looked at the ceiling, thinking.

"Joseph had a coat of many colors . . . other than that, I don't think so."

"See, biblical imagery again. It can be argued that Mr. Willis' delusion is based in reality."

"This is not the point." Anna felt queasy. "Of course, the delusion is based on something, be it religious beliefs or individual experience. The mind doesn't form imagery in isolation. The question is whether it's acceptable to allow a patient . . . a person to remain in his or her delusion-driven world if the person is comfortable in it."

Michael triumphantly lifted his forefinger. "Which, my friends, raises the question: what is real?"

"Come on, we're not going to define the nature of reality here, at this table." Anna pushed her plate away. The lingering hollowness at the pit of her stomach was killing her appetite.

"This table is real," chimed in Ramon.

"Yes, it feels solid to the touch," Michael stroked the tabletop with his palms. "But it's made of molecules, which are made of atoms, and on a subatomic level it's only space between particles, some of which, like quarks, only exist when observed. Not real outside of perception."

"Aw, don't give me that undergrad philosophy bullshit," spat Anna. "Our goal is to help people adjust to the commonly shared experience, not to the unique reality of their own making."

"But sometimes it's the best we can do," replied Michael, looking Anna in the eyes with a soft, soothing smile, and she couldn't help but smile back. Michael was a natural.

"Just like my brother-in-law says, *reality is perception,* " said Ramon peaceably.

"Is your brother-in-law a philosopher?"

"A car salesman."

Both men laughed. Anna joined in, almost sincerely.

The rest of Anna's day was spent leading the outpatient substance abuse group and attending a discharge planning seminar with the rest of the interns. She was back at her desk right before it was time to go home.

As soon as she sat down, her cell phone vibrated: her mother, calling again after a missed call. With a sigh of resignation, Anna picked up.

"Hi, honey. You have a minute?"

"Yeah, sure. But if you want to talk about the wedding—"

"Annie, something happened."

Anna's heart froze.

"Jack?"

"No, Jack is fine. It's James." Mom's voice was apologetic, almost ingratiating.

The light dimmed and the air thickened. Anna's heart slammed against her ribcage. With the same soft, apologetic voice she'd been called out of her seventh- grade social studies class and told about Dad. *Hard attack*, she'd heard. Dad worked hard and had a hard attack. Her hardworking contractor father died from a heart attack, and her cop stepfather—in the line of duty, although with his smoking a heart attack was a possibility; now that would be ironic . . .

"How?"

"What? No! Annie, he's fine, everything is fine."

"Mom, hold on a sec, okay?" She put the phone down and let out a silent scream, nearly dislocating her jaw, then picked the phone up again. "Go on," she said evenly, if a little hoarsely.

Apparently, in early November James had undergone his annual physical. He'd been having some abdominal pain, also, he'd been tired a lot, but who isn't? James wasn't the kind of guy to complain, but since his wife had been on his case about the stomach ulcer, he reluctantly consented to some abdominal scans. The day after Thanksgiving he received a call from his physician, who in no uncertain terms informed him of some troubling news. After James's blood test indicated high levels of enzymes consistent with jaundice, the general practitioner ordered another comprehensive test to exclude the possibility of hepatitis. It came back positive for a protein commonly associated with pancreatic cancer.

"When were you going to tell me?" shouted Anna, regaining control of her voice. She didn't need to be a medical doctor to know: pancreatic cancer had the worst prognosis, impossible to catch before it was too late. If he'd been diagnosed at all, it meant James had about two months to live.

She needed to get herself together. Her family needed her to be strong. Again. It was happening again. Her shoulder sunk under the weight.

"I'm sorry, honey," said Mom. "James didn't want to tell anyone, not until he saw the oncologist."

"And?"

"And he saw the oncologist yesterday. Actually, he was on his way to the hospital when we bumped into you in the park. The doctors did a TC scan—"

"CT," Anna corrected mechanically.

"—and more blood work for specific tumor markers. Annie, he is cleared! It was all some kind of a mistake, the first test must have been wrong, he never had cancer. He's fine!"

Her mother continued chirping about how "you can't trust doctors, they always exaggerate everything just to scare you, good thing the NYPD insurance covers the tests," and all Anna could think of was John's blood-drained face, his pale lips moving as he said, "He will be fine," after he held James in his arms.

He said he had healing powers. He said he could revive a dead man. He said he always told the truth.

After she hung up, Anna took a moment and sat at her desk rubbing her face.

The voice of reason told her it was impossible. There must have been a mistake with the original diagnosis. No way John Fairfax—or Yaret, or whoever he was—could have cured cancer with a touch. And yet, she knew with every fiber of her being: that was precisely what had happened. It was no longer a case of her playing along with his reality, not even a case of her witnessing it. This they shared.

Every time he'd complained about the overwhelming unhealthiness of the people around him, he must have felt a physical assault on his senses. If he truly had a compulsion to heal, it must have been a painful urge he had to resist constantly for fear of exhausting himself. Facing the sickness inside James forced him to do what he was capable of all along.

What else was he capable of? What could he do to her?

"Fulfill my dreams," she answered out loud, and bit her lip so hard it hurt.

She wasn't a dreamer. She had never been the one to waste her desires on the unattainable. *You can't always get what you want*, she'd told herself again and again. And it had worked before.

But she wanted him.

He'd been off limits from the start. Touching him would have tainted her: a woman cheating on her fiancé, a counselor molesting a client. No recovering from this kind of disgrace; a misstep like this would surely lead to a complete fall.

And yet, she wanted him.

The desire was overwhelming, a visceral need. Every inch of her skin itched from the inside, the impossibility of sating the urge made it ever more unbearable. She twitched her shoulders, trying to shake it off, but her muscles spasmed; with a moan, she dropped her head into her hands, and the black waterfall of her hair poured between her fingers onto her face.

I want him. With me. Around me. Inside me. I want him back. I want him in my life. Forbidden thoughts scorched her mind. *What have I done?* And then, *What am I going to do?*

The magic of the snow day had worn off. In the aftermath of the untimely blizzard the city was sullen, sitting under the low gray sky with an air of defeat, like a hungover bride in a sullied veil waking up the morning after the party, alone. By midday the melted snow had filled the gutters and potholes, turning intersections into perilous swim holes. Mounds of hardened snow forced pedestrians to navigate around them, luring them into pools of salty slush that lurked under greasy ice camouflaged as asphalt by the deceptive reflections of the city lights.

Anna had always prided herself on her sense of snow. No matter how distracted she was, her feet could always find solid ground in the murky sludge splashing by the curb. She'd negotiate drifts and puddles with confidence and grace. But not today. Just over the few blocks from the subway station to her street she had misstepped twice, once so deeply her midcalf boots took in water. She didn't even register the cold wetness spreading between her toes.

Let's be logical, she reasoned. *There are two scenarios.*

First: John Doe is as sane as a man—or elf—can be, he is telling the truth, the Otherworld exists, monsters are real, your dreams are your memories. It means you are not crazy, in which case, everything you thought you knew about the world is wrong. Then . . . who knows what then.

Second: John Doe is mentally ill and/or he is not telling the truth, the Otherworld doesn't exist, monsters are not real. Your worldview is safe. In which case you are losing your grip, you are delusional and hallucinating.

What you have is a classic double bind, a lose lose. To make things worse, you're achingly drawn to a man other than your fiancé who may be a con artist at best, a psychopath at worst, or—at the absolute worst—an alien. A lose lose lose.

Anna felt so sorry for herself, she could cry. She had never indulged in self-pity. Anger, jealousy, fear, self-righteousness—she had the courage to acknowledge the shadows within. But never had she felt sorry for herself, until now. And it wasn't because she was in the present and real danger of ruining her life or losing her mind. It was because she wanted something she couldn't have. She was pitiful indeed. Pathetic.

The cold wind slashed at her damp eyes, and she turned her face down, walking blindly, so she almost bumped into a large black dog blocking the entrance to her building. The dog's huge pink maw was wide open, issuing puffs of fog with each rapid pant.

Anna braked, giving the animal wide birth. The massive pit bull terrier wore a hellish spiked collar. The collar was attached to a metal chain. The chain was wrapped around a man's bare fist, black metal links cutting into the pale skin. Anna shuddered.

"Hel-low, Ahn-nah!" sang a lilting voice. John tugged the chain, reining in the dog, lifted his denim-clad behind from the fire hydrant he was leaning on, and stood in front of her in all his absurd extravagance: leather jacket, ink-blue skinny jeans, and white canvas sneakers with pink bobby socks. Apparently, his newest accessory was a canine.

"You're back," Anna stated, dumbfounded.

"I have come to tell you that I forgive you," said John with a gracious bow.

"You forgive me?"

"Yes, for being a poor host. In turn, I ask your forgiveness for being a poor guest. I've said things that could have been misconstrued, I should have been more considerate of your . . . ah, cultural prejudice. You see, for Alva, host and guest are sacred roles. When I first arrived to Alvaheim . . ."

"John!" She flailed her arms in exasperation. "Stop! Just stop it with the space elves. What is this?" She waved at the dog, who fixed its beady eyes at her, intentions unclear.

"Oh, a peace offering, so to speak." He slackened the chain and the dog waddled toward Anna, laying back its cropped ears and wagging its thick tail. "What do you think? Isn't he a beauty?"

The dog opened and closed its steamy jaws, and Anna opened and closed her mouth in bewilderment. But as she lifted her eyes from the dog to John's smiling face, she felt a hot surge of happiness strike through the core of her being. He was a beauty, indeed, beaming joy at her, dissolving her doubts in his warm radiance. He had come back. He had returned to her.

"Yeah," was all she could muster. Instinctively, she extended her hand to the dog and was treated to a vigorous licking.

"I named him Black Shuck, as in the hell hound. Hilarious, don't you think?"

"Where did you get it?"

"I needed to collect my thoughts after you . . . after we parted," John continued, choosing his words tactfully. "I craved to be by the water, so I walked east till I reached the river. Several young men loitered there, and, it would seem the socks you gave me drew their attention. One of them tried to sic his dog on me for sport. He was abusing the poor beast. I compelled him to surrender the dog to me, because, clearly, he wasn't fit to master a living creature."

"You compelled him, and he complied?"

"Indeed. This dog is a gentle beast, not meant for blood sport, are you, puppykin?" He patted the pit bull's scruff. "This is why his name is so amusing, see, *scucca* means demon."

"In what language?"

"In English, of course."

"Of course. And the other men let you take the dog?"

"Ah, they ran off after I—never mind. Well, shall we go upstairs? Black Shuck needs a wash if he is to live with you."

"Live with me . . . what are you talking about?"

"I got him for you," said John with a delighted smile. "You mentioned you've always wanted a dog. I promised to repay you for your expenses. I reckon a good dog is surely dearer than what you have spent on me so far. Besides, he will ward the wyssuns away."

"John, no! I can't—"

"Don't be shy. It's my pleasure to give you something you desire."

"No, I mean I can't accept a dog, especially a dog you took from some boy."

"He wasn't a boy but a man of age. He had warrior's ink all over his throat and was armed with a blade. A small blade." John spread his palms a good eight inches apart.

"Oh, no, don't tell me you've expropriated some gangbanger's pit bull! What if he comes back for it?"

"He won't." John's grin grew feral for a split second, and turned sweet again. "Black Shuck is mine, and I am gifting him to you. Come, Anna, let's go inside." He pushed the front door and held it for her.

Why is the front door unlocked? Anna thought vaguely and then remembered that Lord Yaret didn't require keys to open doors.

"Up, Shuck!" he commanded, and the dog ran up the stairs, making a racket with the heavy chain dragging behind him. As if in a dream, Anna followed. Climbing the stairs to her apartment, she registered that, despite the complete absurdity of the situation, she was excited to have the dog, even for a short time. She'd always wanted a dog, perhaps a nice yellow lab rather than a scary black pit bull, but a dog was a dog, she couldn't in her right mind leave it on the street, just as she couldn't leave John—John, not Yaret!—on the street. Of course, she was going to bring the pit bull to the animal shelter, just as she was going to send John back to the homeless shelter.

Upstairs, John kicked off his shoes as usual, led the dog into the bathroom, and closed the door behind him. Without taking off her coat Anna sat on edge of the futon, listening to the noises from behind the bathroom door. There were sounds of struggle and running water, the dog's whining and John's laughter. After a while, barefoot and bare-chested John emerged, his skin glistening, his jeans stained with moisture.

"As clean as a newborn pup." He beamed. "Behold!"

The pit bull ran out of the bathroom with an expression of extreme relief on his broad mug, took a wide stance in the middle of the room and gave himself a full-body shake. It began at his nose, propelling his flapping jowls first, spreading to his massive shoulders and back all the way to his thick tail. As if in slow motion, Anna watched droplets of water fly off his shiny black coat, forming multiple sine waves, drenching her whole apartment. She opened her mouth to scream when John threw himself in front of her, shielding her from the spray. She was still screaming with wet, slippery John on top of her, laughing like a maniac, when the dog joined in on the fun by trying to wiggle in between them and reach their faces with his tongue. For a moment all three struggled in a wet twister, and Anna couldn't tell if it was John's naked skin under her hand or the dog's slick coat. Finally, she managed to push the laughing John and the wiggling dog off of her and realized she too had been laughing. John slid to the floor next to the couch, holding off the dog, who kept trying to climb back onto Anna's lap.

The play-fight left her equally exhausted and excited, because in the few messy moments of their struggle for one split second they were in each other arms absolutely still, in perfect union, as open to each other as two people could ever be.

She'd never felt this way with a man. One time, when she was still skiing, she and this other girl on the team got what their coach called "a bad case of the giggles." She didn't remember who threw snow first, but in a blink they were both on the ground, shoving snow in each other's faces and laughing madly. Winded from the laughter and roughhousing, for a split second they froze and stared at each other. The intimacy was overwhelming. They both stood up, shook off the snow, and it was like it had never happened, except that they couldn't look each other in the eyes. She wasn't even friends with that girl, neither before nor after.

"Ahn-nah," John's voice was hoarse from laughing. "I've wet myself." And he burst into laughter again, encouraging a new wave of enthusiastic slobbering from the dog.

"Very mature." Anna finally stood up. "I can't believe this is happening."

"Aw, it's but waaater," drawled John.

"Get dressed." Anna tossed him his T-shirt, aiming to hit him in the head. He caught it in the air and got back to his feet, still grinning.

"And please clean my bathroom after your dog!"

While John cleaned the bathroom, she ran to the deli downstairs, returning with a bag of kibble for the dog, a sack of Macintosh apples for John, and a reuben sandwich for herself. The pit bull ate and stretched peacefully on the rug, while John curled in his corner of the couch, chomping down on his apples.

Seeing him so subdued gave her a sense of relief; her feet had finally touched solid ground. Her appetite restored, Anna wolfed down her sandwich, and it tasted just right.

Before the feeling of control dissipated, she began talking about the responsibility of dog ownership in the city and the reasons she couldn't take it upon herself. She expected John to argue, but he didn't. He didn't even look offended.

They talked some more—Anna, mostly. She pointed out the importance of proper identification papers and promised to arrange an appointment for him at the Social Security office, given that he stuck with Saint Francis'. Anna realized she sounded officious, even condescending, but something had changed between them. She was still in a position to help him, but John Fairfax was back in her life not as a client or a patient, but rather as an eccentric acquaintance and perhaps—someday—a friend.

Both kept their voices low, as if afraid to wake the dog snoring at John's feet, and it struck Anna how fake their reasonable exchange felt in comparison to the sincerity of the foolish abandon earlier. The strained conversation rolled to a halt. For a while they sat in silence, John absentmindedly stroking the dog with his bare foot, and Anna staring at his tight, elegant toes.

"Well, I've heard enough." He stood up. "Let's go, Black Shuck."

He picked up the chain with the spiked collar from the floor. The dog sat upright and cast a panicked glance back at Anna. For a large, powerful dog, he certainly knew how to make puppy eyes at people.

"Hold on. Animal shelters are already closed, and they won't let animals into Saint Francis Residences. How do you expect to bring a dog in?"

"The usual way, through a door," he said wearily. "I use doors, Anna."

"If you sneak in a dog, you will both be expelled and end up in the street."

John shrugged, and his fatalistic dismissiveness made Anna bristle. "What kind of person do you think I am? I wouldn't kick a living creature out into the night in the middle of winter."

"You wouldn't, would you?" He chuckled.

"That was different." She blushed. "The dog will stay the night, I'll take it to a shelter tomorrow before work."

"Lucky dog. I, however, am on my way. Thank you for the apples."

He walked towards the door. The dog followed him with his eyes and made a noise that could have been interpreted as either threatening, or sorrowful, or both. The teeth in his wide mouth were half the length of Anna's pinky. Slowly, she rose.

"Um, John?"

She heard him sigh.

"Yaret?"

He turned around.

"I don't want to be left alone with . . . him."

He leaned against the door frame, arms folded across his chest. The light from the table lamp hit his hair just so, painting it gold, softening his stark features, making him look younger, like the golden-haired boy of her dream. Her heart fluttered in her chest.

"Tell me what you want me to do, Anna." How did he manage to sound so submissive and lordly at the same time?

"I love dogs, but I've never owned one," she explained, looking away. "I'm . . . I would be more comfortable if you stayed over tonight, to watch him." If he as much as smirked right now, she would have hated him, and herself for being so manipulable. But he met her eyes with an earnest expression and bowed his head.

"If you wish." He padded across the room and dropped his body back on the futon. Reassured, the dog returned his heavy head to his paws.

"Let's be clear," Anna kept talking as she dug through the hamper for the linens she'd so resolutely discarded a few hours before. "I'm still taking him to the shelter tomorrow, and you—I mean, this is the last time you will sleep on this couch, you do realize that, don't you?"

"I do." He stifled a yawn. "Do you?"

"And no more talk of doom and marriage, understood?"

He made himself busy with the dog and didn't respond.

Anna made his bed on the futon, falling into the motions of the routine. Changing into long-sleeved pajamas seemed hypocritical since he'd seen her in a flimsy tank top the night before. They'd been dancing this awkward dance for several nights, and it was becoming second nature—in fact, nothing seemed more natural than having this man in her home. And now, she also had a dog—a strange but not unnatural presence. *A temporary presence!* chimed in the voice of reason, but it was drowned by the dog's contented snoring.

Finally, both settled into their own places. Anna's heartbeat, the harbinger of a panic attack, had subsided. Despite all the absurd and disturbing events of the day, she felt good.

The boy she loves lies dead by her feet. He died because of her, and she is being judged. One of her judges is an elf clad in a living armor; he taunts her, wants her to admit she is a monster, incapable of love. She is told to choose between herself and her boy. She chooses the boy to prove she is not a monster, even though it means she can never go home, which, in turn, means she will end up turning into a monster anyway, because that's what this world does to people. She chooses love.

But this armored elf doesn't believe her. *Your choice is made out of lack, not from abundance,* he says. He locks his fingers around her jaw; the surges of light from his armor blind her. She claws at his gem-incrusted gauntlet. It's hot to the touch. He turns her face side to side, sliding his mouth over her cheeks without touching her skin. His long hair floats up as if underwater, surrounding them both. She is not sure if he's about to strike her or kiss her; she doesn't know which she is more afraid of. Her own hair lifts, too, like from a static charge. She is imprisoned in his power field, unable to move, melting from inside.

To give away love you have to have it first, he says. The gloved hand lifted above his head begins to glow, pulsing with electric flashes, about to strike.

She knows he wants her to say some magic words to make him stop: he wants to be proven wrong.

But all she says is, *no, it's the other way around,* and somehow it is enough. He lets go of her throat and catches her almost tenderly by the back of her neck. His face comes close, and this is when she gets to truly see him. She knows this angular face with black-rimmed pale eyes under the drawn eyebrows, the curve of this mouth. She knows his name . . .

"Yaret!"

Before the name had left her lips, hot palms cradled her face, and the soft voice filled her ears: "Hush, hush. Be easy, darling, everything's fine, everything's good."

"I had an awful dream . . . Why does this keep happening . . . Someone I loved died, and it felt like it happened because I didn't love them enough . . . like it was my fault . . ."

"But it wasn't, was it?"

"And this man, he was going to hurt me . . ."

"But he didn't, did he?"

"No."

"See? You are safe. Go back to your dream."

"I don't want to."

"Don't you want to know how it ends?"

"I do."

"You must see your dream through, precious girl. Dreams must be fulfilled." He stroked her face with a light, sure touch. It was comforting. So warm, so pleasant, so safe. "Go back to your dream. Sleep."

"I'm afraid to sleep."

"I'll sleep with you."

He made it sound so innocent. Normally, she would have been amused by this semantic incongruity, but she was too exhausted to appreciate the humor. Without a word, she rolled to her side, making room for him. Also without a word, he lay on top of the blanket, his body contouring hers from behind. She felt his hand slide around her waist, and she slapped it lightly. He hissed with a feigned affront, but the hand withdrew.

Lying next to another body with a blanket between them was exciting and relaxing at the same time, like the sleepovers she'd had as a little girl. She yawned.

As if on command, Black Shuck jumped on the bed and cuddled next to her. He did it with a sneaky haste, as if he was afraid to be punished but was determined to take his chances. Lilac perfume tickled Anna's nostrils—John must have used up all her good shampoo on the damn dog. She chuckled.

The dog whimpered and curled tighter, nestling his bulk into the curve of her belly. His velvety sides rose and fell, and with her stomach Anna felt the inhumanly fast beat of his heart. So soft without his armor, the elf wrapped her from behind, his breast against her back. His heartbeat was much slower than hers. His breathing, too, was deep and slow, and with each exhale his body relaxed as if deflated, pressing against her with a gentle weight.

As she lay there, squeezed between the two beings, each competing to impose his rhythm on her, her heart found its own measure, began to expand, grow, until her aching chest could contain both the black dog and the fair man, the whole room, the whole building, the whole city with its five boroughs, the whole world.

Then something came over her, a feeling she thought she knew but had never truly known, yet recognized at once. It was that impossibly rare instant when the world is in order and everything belongs where it should—the perfect moment.

Thursday, December 4

She is inside a huge cave the size of a concert hall. Gigantic pointed crystals protrude from the floor and the walls, creating a labyrinth of cross-beams. The walls are studded with sharp rocks and sparkle like snow in the moonlight, the floor covered with crushed crystals. She picks up a pinky-sized, perfectly pointed clear crystal rod. The fourteen-year-old Anna is scared, but the adult Anna knows she is doing the right thing.

She knows some of the people there. Her golden boy is alive. Somehow, the adult Anna recognizes the green-eyed homeless man. The armored space elf who tried to kill her before is present as well, he wants something from her, no, he wants all of her, and he wants her to want him. But she doesn't want him, she wants to go home. *All it takes is a kiss*, he says. No way she will ever want to kiss him! *Ways change*, he says. And her real self knows he is right, but it's not for her dream self to know.

Then it begins, the grand event that brought her there, the transformation. Color and light dance, and everything is decided by a simple kiss. When it's her turn to choose, she chooses herself to be her own savior, her own source of love. Her dream self seals a kiss in the facets of the crystal shard. She is burning all over, so when she steps into the fire, it doesn't hurt. She emerges on the other side, and her real self feels the cold burn on her lips.

Anna was curled up on her side, just as when she'd fallen asleep. As soon as she opened her eyes, she saw a man's hand inches away from her face, so close that if she shifted her head a bit forward, she could take the thumb into her mouth. It was a lovely hand. The faint blue veins created an oddly regular organic ornament under the pale skin. The hand was relaxed yet composed, fingers folded into a tranquil half-open flower bud. She recalled the sensation of these hard, hot fingers around her jaw, and the thrill of terror echoed with another kind of shudder, making her face flush and her thighs tighten. At that moment she realized Yaret's body was wrapping hers from the back, with her head rested on his arm and her behind firmly planted on his lap.

Even through the fabric of the blanket between them she felt his chest pressing against her spine. His slow, soundless exhales tickled the nape of her neck. The extreme intimacy of their position was only made more outrageous by the fact that, aside from threading his forearm under her head, he had not laid a hand on her.

As soon as she stirred, the arm under her pillow moved. With a little sleepy purr Yaret shifted away from her. Anna pulled away too, bumping the dog, who hopped off the bed, waddled to his bowl in the corner of the kitchenette, and began lapping water. Judging by the noises, he was making a mess in the process.

Still digesting this new reality, Anna glanced at the man lying next to her. With a prick of disappointment, she noted that he didn't appear aroused. In fact, he couldn't have looked more relaxed. He had obliged her by throwing on her sweatpants before getting into her bed last night, but his torso and arms were devastatingly bare. Illuminated by the blue light of the early winter morning, his milky-white skin seemed to emit an inhuman radiance.

Gingerly, Anna reached over him to the night table and turned on the lamp. In the warm electric light, he looked like a man again. The thought was comforting.

He was stretched languidly on his back, a slack hand over his eyes, his chest rising and falling slowly as if he were still asleep, but the corners of his lips quivered—he was awake and aware of her.

"In my dream," spoke Anna, her voice coarse from the sleep, "you were taller."

"Only because you were shorter." He uncovered his eyes, shot her a look of mock indignation, and broke into a childishly-delighted smile.

"I know it cannot be, but . . . I remember you," said Anna.

He kept staring at her, still smiling. She rose on her elbows.

"The last time we spoke, I said to you . . . What was it I said to you?"

"Well, as I recall, you declared in no uncertain terms that there was no way you would ever want to kiss me."

"And you—"

"—and I said, "ways change"." He rolled to the side and faced her. "Have they?"

"Yes." The word escaped her mouth, and she leaned forward following its sound. His eyes grew huge as she brought her face closer; his mouth fell open in a gasp. She shut her eyes. The next thing she felt was his fingers grasping her by the forearms, holding her off.

"Almost," his whisper was barely audible. "But not yet."

"Seriously? You were so obsessed with stealing a kiss from me, and now—" She shook off his hands and dropped back on her side of the bed, feeling like a fool. "What happened to "a kiss has great power"? What else did you say . . . "a kiss will seal the world". . . "

"A freely bestowed first kiss of true love may seal or unseal the world." He quoted his own words precisely. "This is neither the time, nor the place. Believe me, darling girl, nothing I desire more," his thumb brushed her lower lip, "but not yet, not while prone on this profane bed."

Anna reeled.

"Profane bed! What's that supposed to mean?"

His clear gaze met her glare. "It means, this sacred rite may not be performed while being prone. It's essential to be standing straight for proper alignment."

Anna bit the inside of her cheek, bothered by her own flare- up. She was too quick to take offence, to hear an accusation of promiscuity in his words, as if she were anything but proud of her own sexual history, her experience. *An absurd proposition*, she thought, considering she hadn't shared this particular bed with anyone but Ted. Yet, defensiveness was a textbook sign of insecurity.

This sudden glimpse of insight took her aback. Self-analysis should have been the last thing on her mind with this beautiful and bizarre half-naked man lying next to her, this self-proclaimed virgin with pickup lines straight out of a cheesy Renfair script. This man—this creature—was like liquid silver: everyone who looked at him faced only their own reflection.

His finger drew a circle over her bare shoulder. She shifted away, his hand followed. He seemed absorbed in examining her freckles, arranging his fingertips into a pattern, and walking his fingers over her skin to tap out another pattern. Her skin tingled.

"What do you see when you look at me?"

"Heavenly constellations. Each freckle is a mark of a star making love to you. How many wonders does the universe of your body hold, my star-kissed lady?"

"Sun-kissed," she corrected automatically.

"Sun is a star."

"So, sun will kiss me, but you won't."

"You sound disappointed." The tip of his forefinger traced her clavicle, traveled up her neck and tickled her earlobe.

"More like surprised."

"Why? Did I ever give you a reason to think I am incapable of restraint? Restraint, my darling, is another expression of desire. I've waited for a thousand years, now it's your turn," he murmured, edging closer. "But so that you know, your, um . . . brazenness makes my regard for you ever greater and thrills me beyond words."

All he did was lightly touch her, and it was electrifying. Denied a baser caress, her senses heightened. Suddenly, she was glad he refused to kiss her.

"So, what do we do now?" she spoke after a pause.

"What do you want to do?"

"I no longer know what I want." Speaking the truth felt good.

"In the Alvan language," he said mildly, "the word for *want, must*, and *can* is one and the same. If you don't know what you want, do what you must, or at least what you can."

For a while they lay next to each other in silence, his hand on her forearm, his thumb mindlessly caressing the inside of her elbow, where the skin is most tender. She almost drifted back to sleep, when her phone alarm went off. Swallowing a curse, she leaned over Yaret again, much less gracefully this time. Her nipples brushed his chest, and the tranquil mood dissipated at once.

"I must go," she muttered, fighting dizziness.

"Must you?"

Anna listened to herself. Going back to the hospital meant leaving the enchanted sanctuary of no boundaries, where dreams were real, and magic was not only possible, but welcome. The whole world had resolved to this room where she didn't have to lie, pretend to be reasonable, fake sanity.

"I can take a day off." It came out with amazing ease. Still light-headed, she plopped back on the bed and checked her phone. There were three voice messages from the day before, two from Ted and one from her mother; she would deal with them later. She typed up a brief message to her supervisor, stating that she was taking a personal day.

"See, my day just freed up."

He stretched, flashing a hairless armpit, and propped his head with his hand; a fine vein pulsed along his white arm; the tip of his long ear poked through some strands of hair. His face was calm, but the gaze from under half-closed lids was keen, like that of a resting animal.

She shoved her phone under the pillow and mirrored his pose: for the first time since they had met six days ago, she was truly looking at him, looking to see. He appeared lean and fragile, but every time he shifted, hard muscles moved under the smooth skin. His breath was cool, but his touch burned. The man was not what he seemed, neither on the outside nor on the inside—in fact, he was barely a man at all. In her dream world he had been a supernatural villain who'd tormented her and threatened her with execution. In her present he declared his love and obedience. Yet, in the Otherworld, a promise to kill turned out to be an act of mercy to stop her from losing herself and becoming a monster. Were his submission and devotion also concealing their opposite?

"Do you fear me?" His question interrupted her thoughts. He sounded a little offended.

"Are you reading my mind?"

"Not mind. Heart. I can't help knowing what you feel."

"Yeah, and that's not scary at all."

He sighed. "For what it's worth, I am apprehensive myself. I have never given myself to another completely. But the desire to give myself to you is stronger than the fear of your possessing me." A slight blush touched his cheeks, spreading to his long ears.

Anna felt her face burning, too. His story from three nights before flashed in her mind. It seemed so long ago, in another lifetime, when Anna Reilly, the cognitive psychologist, was interviewing John Fairfax, the research subject. But how could she forget? His past lovers—the witch, the monk, and the slave—were all unfulfilled promises, unconsummated affairs. Perhaps a kiss was significant not because of some supernatural sanctity, but simply because he hadn't had much practice. Before he was the awesome Lord Yaret of the Otherworld, an alien-human hybrid of peculiar physiology, he was a hypersensitive and lonely young man. So, he wasn't an ordinary man with trauma, he was an extraordinary creature with trauma.

Her chest ached as if it wanted to break open and empty out, which embarrassed her more than any emotion she'd felt so far.

"Inexperience is nothing to be ashamed of," she said carefully.

The dark eyebrows over the gray eyes arched, he threw his head back on the pillow and laughed—the same chilling silver peal that had made her skin crawl in her dream. It stopped as abruptly as it had begun.

"My precious girl, as a savage from a backwards planet spirited away to the most advanced world in the universe, I've had ample opportunities to face my inexperience. In fact, I moved beyond shame a thousand years ago."

Anna shifted away.

"Just as I think I get you, you say or do something so . . ."

"I understand your misgivings." His hand found hers. Still grinning, he nudged closer, reducing the space between them. "You hoped for someone not so unlike yourself. Believe me, I do understand. You see, since I was a boy I had dreams of a mate able to appreciate me by the virtue of similitude. But years came and went, and I remained alone. When I learned that yet another human had crossed the veil, I harbored no hope. So many times before had I felt the pain of deceived expectations."

He wasn't simply pulling her closer to him, he was pulling her into the story. Her story. The ties connecting her to the mundane strained, ready to snap at any moment.

"I trapped her in a bad way to get a closer look, to see how fast she'd turn into a monster, like all the others. She was but an ignorant and arrogant child, with neither faith nor powers, with little imagination." He chuckled, shaking his head a little. "With my true sight I saw she was my opposite yet my match, the way a reflection in a looking glass is the opposite from you, but also is you. I was horrified, for at that moment I belonged with her, against my judgment and will. A boy's love is out of need, a man's—out of abundance. What I didn't know was that I no longer wanted to be appreciated, but to share myself with one special being."

"What made her special?"

"The right place, the right time." He lifted her hand to his lips and brushed his mouth over her knuckles.

"So, it could have been anyone—another woman, or another man for all you cared?"

"Umm." His lips lingered over her skin, and he continued without looking at her: "Could have been anyone, yet it was he. But she didn't care for me. I needed time to let her see me, but time was one thing she was short on. And I couldn't overtake her with my powers."

"Why?"

"Forcing people is not the Alvan way," he recited the rule, and Anna sensed a tinge of mockery in his tone. "This time, however . . . I won't say I wasn't tempted. But I wanted her to want me. Had I unleashed my magic upon her, she would have submitted to me despite herself."

"You must have quite a high opinion of your magic."

"You should well know its effects." He squeezed her hand lightly.

Suddenly, as if a projector had been turned on by a push of a button, an image popped before Anna's mental eye. She saw a large hall reminiscent of an underground train station, light pouring from multileveled lanterns high above, rows of tall pillars framing the hall with lacy shadows. A crowd of light figures moving on the lustrous marble floor without touching each other, like a fantastic chess set. Anna knew this hall. It was the place she had seen in her dream memories, except never before with such clarity. Now she had no doubt she'd been there before. The vision sped up, jumbling the images and Anna's emotions: a face was in front of her, a striking and fearsome face of a man with mirror eyes. She didn't want to want him; his coal-hot fingers gripped her face and his ice-cold breath was on her cheeks, and she was terrified. And all of a sudden, she was wrapped in his power field, and both of them were floating, and she was melting from inside, and his desires were her desires, because at that moment his love was her love.

And then the vision was over. It wasn't a dream. It was a distinct memory.

Her fingers hurt: she had clenched his hand so tightly his knuckles turned white.

"Awful," she muttered, splaying her fingers. Yaret loosened his grip but didn't let go.

"Awful or awesome, Alvan magic is love."

"How is this love?"

"What we call love is an actual force that holds the universe together, binds particle to particle, creature to creature. Alvan magic is application of this force to affect the world, using the force of love as a tool."

"Or as a weapon."

A mirthless chuckle. "Or that."

"That is . . . monstrous."

"Each of us is capable of the monstrous. You were capable of turning into a monster, but you didn't, and that's what matters. You know it in your heart. The heart doesn't lie."

He laid Anna's palm against his chest. Through the lean breast muscle, the beating of his pulse felt almost obscene, as if her hand held a naked organ.

"You and I are not so different, Anna. We are bound together."

"By the crystal I brought from the Otherworld?"

"By an infinite number of ways. The crystal is only a token for you to be reminded that eyes may lie, and for me that the heart will not."

"So, each time I wore the necklace and saw a monster in the shadows, or experienced the space shift around me, you felt it too? What did you feel?"

"The ache of a heart overwhelmed with unanswered love . . ." he hesitated, "it is like flying, falling and failing to grasp a hold. It is a mighty heartache, its bitterness equal to its sweetness. I felt it each time you touched the crystal, through your years of childhood and youth, and my bond to you grew stronger, for the pain I couldn't escape became a pleasure I sought to relive. As you see, my darling, you've been inflicting delightful torments on me since you were a child."

The thrill of flying and the fright of falling, the vertigo of glimpsing beyond the veil—she knew it well. Also, the heady high of power over a being possessing an even greater power over you.

"I am sorry," she murmured, her head swimming.

"I am not. Alva view pain as an instrument of spiritual growth."

"Pain, not pleasure?"

"Pleasure too. But pain doesn't have to be cultivated, only transformed."

"And pleasure does?"

"It does indeed. In fact, cultivation of pleasure is paramount in Alvan culture. You see, Anna, since sexual congress is sacred rather than recreational, sensual rather than sexual enjoyment of each other's bodies attains greater importance. Alva excel in cultivating sensual pleasure."

He drew his hand along her forearm, and her skin tingled in the wake of his touch. With a flick of his thumb, he dropped the thin strap of her tank top and cupped her bare shoulder. His hot palm slid to her chest, lingered over the swell of her breast, little finger making a quick excursion under the loosened fabric, sending an electric charge through her nipple. But instead of taking hold of her breast, his hand moved up her throat to her chin and held her face, thumb caressing her jaw. Her skin surged with a myriad of tiny delightful fireworks.

She too reached out and glided her fingers down his cheek. The velvety smoothness of his skin felt unnatural, and unnaturally pleasant. She felt him tremble. He closed his eyes and leaned into her touch.

"Oh, yes, Anna, how you know me," he purred, slipping his arm under her neck, pressing her head to his shoulder. "True, true, it's all true . . ."

His knee parted her thighs, pushing her leg over his hip. As their stomachs touched, Anna's arousal was overwhelmed by a deep sense of comfort, a kind of coherence she never thought possible between two bodies.

"I had to come for you. I had to try. This world may no longer be my home, but you are. Together, we will build a haven, make it safe . . ."

Even as he was pressing against her, draping his limbs all over and rubbing his face against her hair, he continued to speak in his melodic, measured voice, uttering words of love like lines in a poem. The detached intonation of his speech was at odds with the sensation of his warm, enveloping embrace. He was mesmerizing and confusing at once. The extreme strangeness of the situation hit her.

Anna had never been this intimate with anyone, man or woman. The girls she'd made out with in high school weren't even friends. In college, her brief sexual encounters with boys had always been, well, brief; at least, it was easy with boys, no room for misinterpretation, everything was in the open. She'd always preferred the efficiency of male sex, even when her heart was set on a girl. And her best girl . . . Casual sensuality came naturally to Genie, but to Anna it had always been tempered by her need for more, painfully unattainable. As for Ted, the language of their relationship translated to a coupon exchange. Whatever she had with Ted was no longer relevant. None of her experiences were.

Being with Yaret was like getting high on an unfamiliar drug, not knowing when the peak will hit, or how hard the comedown will get. Whenever she had endeavored such experiments in the past, she had resolved not to let fear ruin the trip. She had to do the same now.

If she were not insane but had indeed been to the Otherworld and back, then the rest is true too. Magic exists in some parallel worlds. The wyssuns are not a hallucination, they truly are everywhere. The legendary elves truly are a space-faring humanoid race with a penchant for genetic experimentation, and Yaret Fairfax truly is a half-elf born in the Dark Ages. *And when he says he loves me, it is true.*

"All true," she echoed her own thoughts.

He answered by hiding his face deeper in her hair.

"You are mine as I am yours," she heard him whisper.

The simple intensity of his words made her shudder. He flexed his arm and leg, reeling her in even tighter, locking her in a tender but total captivity; she didn't want to struggle. She buried her nose in the hollow above his clavicle, drinking in his scent—a barely perceivable metallic freshness like air after a lightning storm.

It felt good to take a spatial account of their bodies: her head on his shoulder, their fingers locked, chests pressed together, legs interwoven, her feet resting on his insteps. Snugly tucked in, she must have drifted off for a moment, King Crimson's "Moonchild" playing in her head.

Far away, on the other end of the universe, she heard a key turning in the lock, and Black Shuck's alarmed bark. She felt Yaret's body tense and pull away, leaving her cold outside of his embrace. Still disoriented, she rolled off the bed and stumbled from her alcove into the room to see Yaret holding the snarling pit bull by the scruff. The dog's beady eyes were fixed on a tall man in a winter coat lingering in the entrance doorway.

"What the hell is going on here?"

Ted's eyes darted from the rumpled bed to the half-naked man, then to the dog, then to the disheveled woman in her pajamas, and back to the bed. His broad face quivered, but instantly assumed his usual professional expression meant to convey thoughtful confidence.

"I called you at work yesterday, they told me you'd left early. I called your cell, you didn't pick up." Ted's voice was dull with strain. "I called your mother, she couldn't reach you. I called the hospital this morning, and they tell me you've taken a day off. I come here and this is what I find." His hand, still holding his key to Anna's apartment, waved in the direction of the bed.

"It's not what it looks like, Ted," mumbled Anna, fully aware of how idiotic she sounded.

"Ah, so this is Ted," said Yaret with satisfaction. He looked genuinely amused. The dog made another desperate attempt to break free, clearly aiming for Ted's throat.

"Get the dog out of here, now!" hissed Anna.

With a huff, Yaret shoved the struggling dog into the bathroom and strode across the room back to Anna's side, while the bathroom door shook under the weight of the massive body crashing against it.

"Are you okay?" Safe from the dog's reach, Ted regained his usual air of authority.

"I'm all right."

"Who is this man in your apartment?" Ted inquired, without so as much as casting a glance at Yaret.

Anna filled her lungs. "He is not a man, strictly speaking."

Nothing moved in Ted's face.

"His gender identity is not in question here," he said evenly. "But your professional integrity is. This is the client you told me about, isn't it? The one you were interviewing so late at night?"

"He is no longer my client."

"What is he doing in your apartment? Did he spend the night?"

"I asked him to stay. I needed his help with the dog."

"Which begs another question: why is that vicious animal here?"

"It was a gift." She and Yaret exchanged a quick look like two conspiring kids, and Anna couldn't suppress a stupid grin.

"Let me understand this: you allowed a patient to get you a dog as a gift, and you invited him to stay at your home? Ann, are you on drugs?"

"Drugs?"

"You weren't well the last time I saw you. You were feverish; perhaps you've had an adverse reaction to something. I'm trying to find a rational explanation for the gross impairment of your judgment."

"Well, no, it's not like that at all. See, he and I are not strangers. We have a connection. He knows things about me, things no one knows, even you."

Ted nodded thoughtfully, his professional mask now firmly on.

"Delusional patients can be quite manipulative. What is his current diagnosis?"

"Since he's recovered from his amnesia, I can't find anything wrong with him. I mean, he is a colorful character, but medically . . ."

"Borderline personality disorder manifests impulsivity, excessive emotionality, fractured identity, intense fixation on others, don't forget manipulativeness. Colorful enough?"

"A curious man, your boyfriend," said Yaret, tilting his head. "Such insight into the souls of others, yet oblivious to his own. He would talk about anything except ask the only question which burns him."

"What?" she turned to him.

"All he wants to know is whether you and I . . ."

"Have you slept with him?" interrupted Ted.

"No!" cried Anna. From the corner of her eye, she saw Yaret open his mouth. "I mean, yes! We slept together, but nothing happened, seriously."

Yaret threw back his head and burst into his wild laughter. The scene was so absurd, Anna felt like laughing too.

"Grossly inappropriate behavior," commented Ted, still talking only to her. "Could be schizotypal personality disorder with comorbid delusional thinking."

Anna felt offended for Yaret, but also for herself. She wished Ted would get off his high horse and show some base emotions for a change, would fight for her as a lover would instead of dispensing professional judgments.

"Whatever the diagnosis, he can't remain here. And since it's your case, it's up to you to dismiss him."

Anna looked at Ted, then at Yaret. For a moment, it grew very quiet. Even the dog stopped fussing behind the bathroom door.

"I will not do that."

"Do you even realize how improper this is? He needs to go."

"Yooou need to go," drawled Yaret. Anna felt his palm run down her spine with a sure, possessive caress; it left a trace of electric sparks, and she clearly remembered flashes of silver light pulsating in the charged-up crystals of his unearthly armor, ready to shoot a deadly lightning from the palm of his hand.

Ted's face turned crimson, and his big body shifted forward. Yaret mirrored his motion with loose, arrogant grace.

"Don't you hurt him!" Anna exhaled.

Both men looked at her.

"I take issue with the suggestion that I'd descend to physical violence," declared Ted indignantly.

Yaret said nothing, but his grin turned feral. Anna was right to be horrified: poor, oblivious Ted didn't stand a chance against Lord Yaret. Even while still afflicted by amnesia, this ethereal blond had brutalized a wannabe rapist, reducing a heavyweight ex-con to a pile of bloody flesh. After he'd regained his memory and skills, he playfully sent a knife-wielding gang running. A Dark Ages Anglo-Saxon warrior who for millennia hopped around the galaxy exterminating whole planets, he had no problem descending to physical violence. Anna shuddered.

"Don't," she mouthed silently. Yaret met her pleading stare and put both hands behind his back.

High on the absurdity of the situation, Anna stepped toward Ted. Finding herself between two men who seemed ready to fight over her was an unexpected sensation. It washed over her, making her alive with a visceral thrill; like a drop of blood in a shot of vodka, shame mixed in.

At that moment, Yaret moved to insert himself between her and Ted.

Next to Ted—over six feet tall, heavyset, made even larger by his puffy winter coat—barefoot and bare-chested Yaret looked particularly fragile. Yet, his presence was overwhelming, like a pillar of fire: touch it, and be incinerated.

"If you wish to speak with me, you may address me directly," he offered in a creepily calm, low voice, looking down his nose at the taller man.

Anna wanted to object to being referred to in such possessive terms, but her mouth fell dry.

"I will not dignify this," Ted spoke to her over the other man's head. "Ann, we need to talk in private. You owe me an explanation."

"I can't explain this, Ted," she managed with effort. "There's nothing I can say. . ."

"Nothing to say," echoed Yaret. "Except farewell, Master Ted."

"It's Dr. Newman." Ted finally acknowledged him with a steady glare. "And I will not take commands from a patient."

"Oh, I have been patient thus far," replied Yaret, his hands still loosely clasped behind his back. "But it is ill-advised to test my patience, for I am not one of your helpless charges whose wings you so enjoy clipping."

"What are you . . . Ann, what is he talking about?"

"I know what you are doing to that dragon hatchling." Yaret spoke in a soft growl, so low Anna could hardly hear him. "You won't tame her, she will fly out of your reach. And if you keep poisoning her, she may fly off a roof."

For a moment Ted's wide, open face remained slack, like he was trying to comprehend Yaret's cryptic speech. He looked at Anna with an expression of angry and righteous hurt.

"This does it, Ann. I am very, very disappointed in you. I can understand that you've allowed some perverted empathy to overpower your professional judgment. Playing house with a male client is reckless and unethical. Still, I can understand, even forgive. I am mature enough to rise above petty jealousy. But discussing my patient with yours? A suicidal minor? This is beyond unethical!"

He almost ripped the door off the hinges as he flung it open.

"Not to mention personally disloyal." Ted lingered in the doorway. "I don't think I'll be needing these anymore." He dropped the spare keys by the door and walked out.

As his heavy steps thundered down the stairs, Yaret let out a weary sigh, and said, "How sad."

It was as though the curtain had fallen on a Theater of the Absurd play, but instead of applause all Anna heard was the ringing in her skull, like from a hard smack.

"What the fuck?" she grabbed her head, pulling her hair. The pain was sobering. "Why did you say that about the dragon? Dammit . . . now Ted thinks I've told you about his case! But I've never . . . have I? No! How did you know?"

He opened his arms, palms up, another one of his little gestures, so odd and so recognizable.

"I didn't know. I guessed. Unfortunately for that girl, I guessed right. A young female dragon smell is all over this boyfriend of yours—who, by the way, is neither a boy nor a friend—and, since he isn't one himself, I deduced it must have been his patient. That girl is in danger, Anna."

"You can't know that!"

"I can and I do! Anna, wake up!" he exclaimed in exasperation. "If only you trusted yourself, you would see it. If only you trusted me . . . Let me show you!"

This is the first time he has raised his voice with me, noted Anna with detachment. Without fear she took his hand, letting him pull her tight against his chest; her temple pressed against his cheek; the beating of his pulse pounded in her head. His fingers squeezed her shoulder, hard. He embraced her not as a lover, but as a solider supporting a comrade in arms.

And right in time, because her legs gave in, her body weakening as her senses dialed up. Distance between objects, outlines of shapes—everything became more prominent and filled with meaning. She was falling into a bottomless well of meaning, desperately grasping for notions, and it took all her strength to be able to sort out what meant the most. Then, a flash of images. The glowing, spinning runes flowed inside the walls of the room. The whole space turned inside out in an impossible projection, the view of each angle at once. With it, a rush of scents. She sensed the smell she knew well but never had been aware of, unmistakably Ted's: coffee breath, Listerine, the dry cleaner's starch. Intermingling were distinct animalistic odors, the dog of course, but also something else. A smell of fresh water and electrically charged air, the smell of magic. The smell became a sound: slithering of scales and grinding of fangs, and a desolate cry of a marvelous beast suffering an exquisite pain.

She tried imagining what kind of creature could smell and sound like that, but you don't need to imagine what you know in your heart.

"The girl who thinks she is a dragon . . . really is a dragon, isn't she?"

It was impossible, yet she knew it with certainty: there was a teenage human girl living in New York City who was a dragon. A huge, scaled, reptilian creature. Moreover, she realized what she was, and the knowledge was killing her.

Anna freed herself and scrambled to the futon. Her heart was racing, and she writhed her hands to quell their violent shaking. She watched Yaret release the dog from its confinement. For a minute Black Shuck frantically inspected the room for traces of the intruder, and settled by the door.

"If elves are ancient extraterrestrials, what are dragons?"

"Intelligent animals, also ancient, who used to live in this world long ago."

"Right. Elves and dragons are real. Who else? Grays? Hobbits? Vampires?"

"Not sure what you mean by gray hot bits, but vampires of human legends are not real."

"That's a relief." She grimaced. "But how can this human child also be something nonhuman?"

"Rarely, but it does happen." Yaret sat next to her and cradled her trembling hands. "The veil is thinner than most think. A random mixing of souls between different creatures from different planes of existence occurs at times. Some human beings in this world are blissfully unaware of their true nonhuman selves. An echo of an unfamiliar call in the wind, a fleeting memory of something that couldn't have been, a gentle ache of unfulfilled fantasy is all they know. Or, perhaps, resentment for anything otherworldly, anything alien. Perhaps, some of those poor souls end up in hospitals like yours, not knowing what they are, everyone thinking them mad. This one, however, knows what she is because not only does she have a dragon's soul, she also is blessed—or cursed—with true sight. When she looks in the mirror, she sees her essence."

"What do you see when you look in the mirror?"

He sighed.

"When I look with plain sight, I see an ordinary man. With my true sight, I see a shape of light, swirling with life force. An Alvan double cocoon that looks like radiant wings. I've always seen this way. It was one of my first painful life lessons to learn that others don't."

"But I don't possess true sight. How could I see without the crystal?"

His fingers stroked her cheek, lingering to gently squeeze her chin; thumb tapped her lower lip.

"The more you are with me, the more you shall perceive. Join me, and you shall have true sight. Bear my seed, and you shall penetrate the mysteries of the universe."

Outside, a police siren faded in and out of the traffic hum. Clicking his claws against the parquet floor, the dog waddled up to Anna, ran to the door, then back to her and back to the door again.

"This dog needs to go out," she said, grateful for a distraction.

"Go out, Shuck!" Yaret walked to the door and flung it open. The dog wagged his tail apologetically, not sure how to interpret such a command, glancing at Anna for support.

"You can't let the dog out by himself! You . . . we need take him out, on his leash. Dogs are only allowed off leash in dog runs, remeber?"

"What about the park we passed on our way the other day? It's nearby."

"Bryant Park? No, there's a skating rink open all through winter, no place for a dog to run." She consulted her laptop while Yaret watched over her shoulder with polite curiosity. "The nearest dog run is about ten blocks south, at Madison Square Park. Each block is about two minutes walking, so twenty minutes?"

They threw on their street clothes, fastened the chain to the dog's collar, and went outside. Black Shuck pulled in to the nearest fire hydrant and lifted his leg. Anna grinned. Dog ownership was turning out to be pretty predictable and not too taxing, especially when Yaret took the lead. He did look impressive in his leather jacket with a black pit bull on a chain, the pink socks adding an ironic twist to his cliché cool.

Her enthusiasm faded as they walked south down Sixth Avenue, and the dog began meticulously marking each fire hydrant they passed by. The park was about three blocks away when the dog stopped in his tracks. With a sorrowful expression on his mug, he arched his back and took the biggest dump Anna had seen, right on the sidewalk.

"Dammit."

"What?"

She pointed at the "Clean After Your Dog, It's the Law" sign above their heads, with a picture of the disciplined stick-figure citizen dropping a neat baggie into the trash bin.

Yaret considered the sign for a second and passed the lead to Anna. He scooped some snow from the nearby car with his bare hands, and, using the snow as lining, picked up Black Shuck's pile and dropped it into the nearest trash bin.

"There." He dusted off the snow from his hands. "Why are you looking at me this way?"

"Nothing. It's. . . I'm surprised to see you being so, um, not squeamish."

"You are forgetting, I apprenticed under a village healer. Before I was fifteen, I delivered a dozen babes and countless cattle. Much messier than one small turd, I assure you."

Anna laughed.

"What's so amusing?"

"Nothing, it's just, to hear you say that word . . ."

"Turd is a commonplace Anglian word, like shit and f . . ."

"Okay, I get it," she waved her hands at him. "It's commonplace. You're ordinary. Everything is normal."

The park was quiet on a Thursday morning. They were alone on the path, and Anna began to relax.

"Is he friendly?" somebody yelled from across the lawn.

A young man with two small dogs on a double leash was walking toward them. She squinted above the rim of her glasses: the dirty-blond dreads hanging from under the guy's beanie hat and his ripped jeans were in stark contrast to the two prudish pugs in Burberry coats ambling at his side. *Dog walker*, she guessed.

"Is he friendly?" repeated the guy, pointing at Black Shuck.

Anna looked at Yaret. "Is he?"

He rolled his eyes and made a short hissing sound at Black Shuck. The dog lay down on the snow, his whole pose showing eager submission.

The guy approached, his fat little pugs treading carefully over the snow-covered ground.

"I hesitated because I wasn't sure," Anna muttered. "I've . . . We only got him yesterday."

"A new rescue? Hey, big guy." The young man beamed at the pit bull, who smiled back by laying his ear-stumps in a doggy grin. The two pugs exchanged a glance, and their round faces expressed disapproval; clearly, they considered fraternizing with rabble beneath them. "Getting a forever home, aren't you a lucky dog." He lowered his voice. "Being, you know, black."

"What does that have to do with anything?" Anna frowned.

"Okay, so there have been these studies that show black dogs are less likely to be adopted," explained the dog walker. "And you know which kind of dog is *the least* likely to be adopted? A black male pit bull. The average life of a dog like this in a city shelter is seventy-two hours. So, good on you, you know, for adopting him and all. Well, you take it easy, okay? Come on, ladies." And he walked off with his pugs.

There was only one other dog in the fenced-off lot of the dog run, and as soon as Yaret let Black Shuck in, the owner called his pet and left. Yaret walked to a circular bench around one of the tall trees growing right in the middle of the lot, brushed off the snow from the seat, and plopped down his narrow behind. Anna sat next to him.

The patio umbrellas, folded for the winter and now topped with snow, stood behind them like guards with conical helmets. The powder dusted the patchy bark of the mighty trees, cotton rolls of snow lined thick boughs, the fading veins of finer branches dissolved into the gray clouds. Outside the perimeter of the park, traffic was rushing up and down Fifth Avenue, but here snow ruled.

"What are those trees?" Anna wondered out loud.

"Elms," answered Yaret without hesitation. He lifted his face, squinting at the sky, a dreamy smile playing on his lips. "I love elms."

"You love many things, don't you," said Anna, almost without any sarcasm.

"But I must. Alvan magic works on love. You see, to manipulate an object you have to be deeply in love with it, commune with it on the most basic level, give yourself to it, and take it in as lovers do. Do you love snow, Anna? I do."

Yaret grabbed a handful of snow from the bench seat. The white lump in his pink palm shrunk at the edges at once, melted by his body heat.

"Absolute focus and complete trust harness the power of true love. It's the rule of reciprocity: one must submit to possess. After that, it comes down to the economy of how much life force any single object contains and therefore how much love force it requires."

Transfixed, Anna observed as the handful of snow became water in his cupped palm, the puddle gathered into a globe, lifted and hung suspended a good two inches above his open hand. The transparent globe began to solidify, expand, became opaque, and suddenly Yaret's hand plucked a perfectly round snowball out of the air. He tossed it up, and Anna jerked up her chin to see the snowball fly above their heads and silently come apart in a tiny explosion of snowfall.

"A magic trick!" she exhaled in awe, and this time truly meant it.

"No trick, I am most sincere in my love. Were you seeing with true sight, you would have known that I took as much as I gave." Yaret wiped some snowflakes off her cheek. His hand was warm and dry, as if he hadn't played with snow a minute ago.

"This is the source of Alvan powers. To compel a bird to carry his message, an adult Alva needs only a small loving wish. To make a tree bloom takes more effort and focus, and more giving of yourself. To pilot a dimensional vessel, one gives himself all but completely. To command the power of a star, many immortal beings have come together in a fiery climax."

"And in the end," said Anna, unable to resist, "The love you take is equal to the love you make, isn't it?"

Yaret nodded, serious.

"The way you refer to love is as if it's a force of nature, like gravity."

"The silver strings you've seen with your true sight, the threads that stitch the fabric of creation together—that is love. It is a force of nature, and as such, it can be . . . applied. Several species have this capacity, none as skilled as the Alva. Weaving the silver threads is an Alvan innate gift. But only one race in the whole known universe is capable of creating it, and it is not the Alva."

"Don't tell me, humans are the only ones who can make love."

"About one in twelve humans, to be exact, is able to generate out of nothing the force that holds the world together." He rolled his eyes as if marveling at this odd bit of cosmic luck.

"How?"

"Prayerful contemplation is the proper method to generate pure love, but it's arduous. The easiest way to make love is with sexual intercourse."

"You don't say!" She grinned.

"Trouble is," Yaret went on without returning her smile, "Humans misuse and abuse their gifts. Profane sexuality serves only to wear out the silver strings. One of the reasons why there's so little magic left in this world."

Anna's amusement evaporated at once. Was she one in twelve? According to her quick calculation, it made about eight percent. Not great odds, especially considering her history. Talk about profane sexuality.

"So, considering the Alva cannot make love, and you are half-Alva, can you? I mean, your human half, does it share the gift?"

He didn't answer, and she was glad, because, in truth, her question was not about him.

The air darkened as the snow began to come down again. It seemed they were alone in the whole park by now, alone in the whole city.

As much as Anna had spent time in the snow as a little girl, playing outside during long Michigan winters and later, skiing with her school Nordic team, she had never sat aimlessly under the falling snow. She felt an unexpected sense of luxury in this simple act of being quiet, allowing winter to slow things down. Everything seemed insignificant against the snow's silence. She wasn't even that cold, which she ascribed to Yaret's closeness.

For a while Yaret kept making snowballs and tossing them to Black Shuck, who hurled his powerful body high in the air, catching them with impressive agility. He seemed so genuinely disappointed when his prize dissolved in his mouth, so that Yaret had to make another ball for him to catch, and then another, and another.

"Enough, Shuck. Go seek!" He threw the last snowball into a snowdrift. The dog obediently went digging. Anna chuckled at the pit bull's gullibility.

"Every time you do it I am reassured," said Yaret, who'd been watching her. His eyes sparkled with joy.

"Do what?" She stood up and dug into her pocket for the tissue to wipe her glasses.

"Laugh." Yaret rose too. Without her glasses, what she saw was an alien mask: dark-rimmed white eyes, a dark slit of a mouth in the white face haloed by white hair.

"Reassured of what?" She felt a tinge of queasiness, a coming wave of anxiety.

"That I'm right about you. When I first saw you, I watched the little things you do—how your nose wrinkles when you hide mirth, how your eyes widen in anger, how your breath gets shallow in excitement. It amused and aroused me as nothing had in a long, long time. I saw how you yearn for passion and yet restrict yourself, how you succumb to guilt and fight it, and how you pull yourself up after you bring yourself down. I imagined how I would delight in exploring the fine threads that weave the tapestry of your character, lacing in my colors between yours, how we could make the cloth of our life together, and how sweet it could be—"

She bit back the urge to ask, *and?*

"—and it came to be wonderful beyond my imagining."

Snow was falling on their heads. Anna didn't bother to put her glasses back on, and, as her unfocused gaze took in the marvelous vision, her anxiety gave way to a thrill. The snowflakes in the air slowed down, stopped moving and now floated suspended as if inside a snow globe. By the way the air glittered, she knew the space and time had shifted. The figure of the man in front of her took on a shape of light, softly pulsating and radiating toward her, filaments wrapping her body, surrounding both of them. The light caressed her, and an overwhelming sense of relief washed over her, as if she had finally come home and all was well and good.

She wasn't sure if she was seeing the real world with true sight, or if the world she was seeing was a different world altogether, but she wished to seal it, make it last, for this was the world where each moment was perfect.

She reached her free hand for him, and he met her halfway; their fingers locked; his face momentarily came into focus and blurred again.

She expected his kiss to be slow, skillful. Instead, his spare hand gripped her head as he pressed into her with aching urgency, their lips colliding hard. It was artless and childish and devastating. She shut her eyes, opened her mouth and drank him in. He tasted . . . He tasted like the first gulp of hot tea after an endurance ski race, bittersweet and strong. It scorched her tongue, made her dizzy with a sugar rush. She drank and drank greedily, until she was out of breath.

Was she unsealing the mundane world to let the magic in, or sealing the newborn world of her own creation—she didn't know or care. He had something, she didn't know what, but she wanted it without the need for definitions. Something huge and hot was growing inside of her, breaking out of her body like the unfolding wings of a butterfly. Her shut eyes burned as she sensed the iridescent veil of light engulf them both, and she surrendered to it. As they stood still locked in an embrace, she felt seconds become years, *and the long years were measured by the wheeling stars above them*—she couldn't recall where those words came from, but that's how it was.

Anna came to from the cold seizing her feet, and pulled away. She stood ankle-deep in the snow, snow piled on her head and shoulders. Her hand was still in his grip, fingers of his other hand knotted in her hair. They must have been standing still for some time. She put on her glasses and focused on the man in front of her. Yaret opened his eyes and blinked, then his face lit up with such sincere bliss that they both laughed.

She heard the dog's whimper: the poor guy had had his fill of playing in the snow and wanted to go home.

On the way home, Yaret wouldn't let go of her hand, holding on to her like a child. He didn't speak and didn't try to kiss her mouth again, just kept lifting her hand and touching his lips to her wrist. Each time their eyes met, he laughed with joy.

She laughed too, in disbelief.

Back at the apartment, Yaret kicked off his shoes before unleashing the dog. Anna shuffled to the couch and plopped down, only now registering the old ache in her ankle. Walking in the snow had been a bad idea. She moaned, shaking her head. Yaret knelt in front of her.

"Allow me."

"I can take my own boots off, thank you." She huffed, pulling off her boot before he had time to tend to her. Like his haughtiness, his servility manifested itself seemingly at random.

Yaret tossed his head in mild exasperation.

"Your ankle needs healing," he explained. "It won't get any better by itself. Let me help."

A scene flashed in Anna's mind: her stepfather's shocked face as Yaret held him in an unwelcome embrace.

"Is this what you did to James?"

"Oh." Yaret's eyes opened wide, making him look like a boy caught in the middle of some shenanigans. "I didn't realize you'd seen me at the time. Unlike yours, his ailment was a fresh one, although much more malignant. Not to worry, it's been repaired in time." He stood up, his face assuming a dismissive expression. Was that embarrassment?

So eager to brag about the little things, yet so shy when it comes to something important, thought Anna with a rush of tenderness.

"All right, and how do you intend to cure my decade-old injury?"

"Well, full body contact is not required." With a sly grin he plopped next to her on the couch.

She flushed.

"Ah, now give me your hoof, you silly little heifer."

Nobody had ever called her a stupid cow to her face before, and nobody had ever said something so outrageous in such a charming manner. Playful and familiar, this Yaret was so different from the fantastical being who'd poured his otherworldly love over her a little while ago. She couldn't tell which of the two was more irresistible.

She placed her foot on his lap. As soon as he hiked the bottom of her pant up to her knee and pulled off her sock, she was hit with acute shame for the chipped blue paint on her toenails, for her rough soles, for the stubble on her shin, belatedly horrified that her feet might smell, and then, that all of the above could be a sordid fetish for this unpredictable man.

"Easy, now," he murmured, as she imagined one would speak to a skittish calf. He cradled her foot with such unassuming tenderness and brushed her sole so gently that her toes curled up.

He started at the back of her heel, lightly probing, pulling, pushing the muscles around the hurt tendon, as though rearranging the tissue. Instead of moving down to the foot, his fingers walked up her calf, applying spot pressure here and there, seemingly at random. But Anna, who'd received her share of physical therapy for her sports injuries, saw he was guided by precise knowledge of anatomy: he went right for the spots where the muscles attach and connect. Her reflex was to expect pain, but his touch seemed to have analgesic power. She leaned back, letting him have his way. She thought she saw a little smug smirk as he returned his attention to her foot.

His fingers wrapped around her ankle, thumb caressed the skin in probing circles. A warm touch grew hotter as he pressed his palm. Her skin prickled. It no longer felt like a delightful and skilled massage. He was working his magic for real.

"I want to see you do it," she said. "With true sight."

"Open yourself."

"How?"

Looking her in the eyes, he took a deep breath. She mirrored him. They exhaled together, and she felt the air shift from their mixed breath. Gradually, the world around her came into focus. All the objects resolved to flowing streams of light. The man in front of her was woven with glowing threads and so was she, except they were different somehow. She was a shape inside a cocoon of swirling light. He, however, existed in the overlap between two spheres, their curves creating a likeness of huge flaming wings unfolded over and around him. She heard the harmonious resonance of the flame, felt its heat. It was alive and breathing, pulsing with the beating of his heart.

His awesome wings enveloped her; at that moment his being became open to her; as if she were watching through his eyes, she saw the glowing filaments comprising her flesh melt under the light pouring from his palm, scarred tissues and sinews reshaped and restructured, until they vibrated to the perfect pitch set by the harmony of his flame.

She didn't know how much time passed. When her vision faded, he was still cradling her foot. The ache was gone, replaced by the sweet fatigue of a worked-out muscle.

"Thank you," she added, "Yaret."

"Ah, my name on your lips is the best reward, darling."

He lowered his face down to her leg and rubbed his cheek against the stubble on her shin. His hot breath made her hairs rise. Before Anna had a chance to be mortified, he placed a quick kiss on her knee, adjusted her pant leg, and fell back on the pillows, grinning like a man with a job well done.

"Your body will be repairing itself as your blood replenishes. I presume you bleed with the moon?"

She opened her mouth, unable to produce any sound besides a mortified mewl.

"Don't strain your leg until the new moon," he said, rolling his head and stretching. "And drink a lot of water. Aren't you thirsty? I know I am."

Anna licked her parched lips, unsure if it were thirst or some other visceral sensation. The sensuality of his touch and his words was raw beyond anything she had ever known, yet so innocent in its earnestness.

"I think I have some juice in the fridge." She began to rise.

Gently, he set her back in her seat. "You need to rest."

"There are some apples, too, if you'd like," she called after him.

He unceremoniously dug through the meager contents of her fridge.

"Is this what I think it is?" He dove deep into the fridge and pulled out a bottle of Killian's Red. She'd been so intoxicated by his presence that she'd forgotten she had an almost-six-pack in the fridge.

"Do you drink beer?"

"I do, indeed! That's all we had to drink back in the Old Wall country. I've never developed a taste for wine, you know, not even after years in Rome. And on Alvaheim . . . anyway, how do you open this?"

"I don't know what is more unbelievable, that you were born in Dark Age England or that you flew through space in an alien ship."

"It's not so much in space as between dimensions." He bit on his apple and washed it down with beer, making Anna shudder. "And not in a ship. A Voidarmor. An armor, vehicle and weapon, all in one."

"Spacesuit." She grabbed the encyclopedia from the pile of books by the couch. An article on space exploration had a photo of an American astronaut on the Moon. "Like this?"

"No. Voidarmor is the masterpiece of alvan craftsmanship. It fits like a second skin, in fact, reaches under the skin." He slid his fingertips over his forearm dotted with pale round scars like holes on a flute.

An image of lean limbs encased in a spikey skin-tight catsuit flashed in her memory.

"I was clad in my *Ylféte* when you saw me at the Council. Wasn't she splendid?" Yaret continued wistfully, his eyes clouding. "Voidarmor a living thing, uniquely cultivated for each Voidwalker."

"Cultivated from what?"

"From the same matter that makes the Alva themselves, more specifically, alvan females. One of their many priceless gifts to their race. Just like all the living weapons and vessels, all armor is female. You see, the Alva may be ancient and ageless, but the race doesn't stand still. Alvan women advance to the higher planes of existence—what you may call evolve— faster; women are rare and are worshipped. Being clad in a Voidarmor is the closest most alvan men would know to being inside a woman, a major incentive to becoming a Voidwalker." The tips of his ears turned rosy, and Anna felt a pang of jealousy.

"Well, I've known of human males becoming intimately attached to their cars, but this takes love of a vehicle to a whole new level." Immediately ashamed of her tone, she added, "I'm sorry you had to part with something so dear."

He didn't seem to take offence. "We're never fully apart. I left *Ylféte* suspended in slumber so I can still reach her in my dreams. You will, too, should you choose to share my dreams." He edged closer.

"So, *Ylféte* is a weaponized living spacesuit you can commune with in your sleep."

"Simply put, yes."

"How does this work?"

"How does this work?" He picked up her smartphone.

"There is a computer inside. It receives signals and data and processes them into meaningful information."

"But how does it work?"

Anna huffed. Her knowledge of computer science was basic. *How would I explain it to Jack?* she asked herself, and thought that the eleven-year-old Jack probably could have explained a thing or two to her.

"Well, the metals and plastic components are all interconnected on the circuit board to an energy source. When the electric current passes through, it's switched on and off, and since we use binary code, I guess, everything gets coded and decoded in the sequences of zeros and ones. Sorry, it must make no sense to you . . ."

"It makes perfect sense to me, darling. I may not be an intellectual, but it doesn't take one to understand your sciences. The principle of your computer technology is an electron energy transmitted as binary code through a physical medium, isn't that right? Now, instead of electrons, imagine some other particles, instead of binary system, say, duodecimal, and instead of physical media . . . well, something based on a living energy."

Yaret lifted his hand and drew a complex figure in the air. The air shifted, and an image unfolded around his pointed finger like a flower: a celestial sphere full of swirling constellations, all unfamiliar. A pulsing dot in the center of the three-dimensional moving image was aligned with the tip of Yaret's finger. After a few seconds, his fingers fluttered, dispersing the image.

"Relational locator map, a basic spell," he explained before Anna could utter a word. "No different from the map on your phone: sequences of commands and responses written in light. You see, all magic is technology, and all technology is magic. Any process where a creature affects the creation can be called by either name."

"What's the energy source?"

"I am."

Anna took a deep breath. In all honesty, the astounding things he'd shown her by now surprised her less than the ease with which her mind had been accepting it all. No matter how incredible, everything kind of made sense, each new display of magic like a missing piece of the puzzle she'd been subconsciously assembling since her brush with the Otherworld.

"I suppose to our ancestors Alvan tech appeared magic," she said after a pause. "Even our contemporary technology would have. One must have an open mind."

"I thought I did," Yaret replied wryly. "My mind had been made open by the practice of witchcraft, but some revelations are too much to comprehend, even to an open mind."

She remembered Yaret's account of his life, trying to imagine a Dark Age Anglo-Saxon warrior taken aboard an interdimensional space vessel by an alien race. A worldview overthrown by things that cannot be possible, knowledge that cannot be processed . . . The shock of your world crumbling around you.

She stroked his cheek with the back of her hand. He caught her hand and kissed her knuckles.

"You and I both know the pain of the same wound." He looked her in the eyes. "Our scars are a testament to our survival."

What a fool I am, Anna thought. She presumed he appreciated her compassion, while all this time he was tending her own wounds with utmost tact and kindness.

Entrapped in her therapeutic pattern of trying to see the other, she neglected to see herself in his story. A rational modern girl who had the supernatural shoved in her face, too shocked to process the inexplicable reality—how was she different from a Dark Age savage who'd just been shown Earth from space?

"Perhaps you were better equipped to deal with the unknown than I was," she said. "At least you knew that there exists a world outside of your immediate senses. Your mind was ready. It's not such a great leap from believing in magical elves to believing in space-faring aliens—"

"I've told you before," he said mildly, "The basic principle for the Alvan technology is love. What matters isn't a mind's capacity to grasp. It's a heart's capacity to feel."

She listened to her heart. It felt raw, as if it had been beating too hard for too long against a cage too tight.

"You must have been exceptional." She took a swig of her beer to wash down the lump in her throat.

He shook his head. "Exceptionally lacking, to be exact. Nothing but an ignorant brute. But in the Alvan culture, the least receives the best. I was mentored by the finest masters of every art, and each of my gifts has been developed to its fullest. I am the best I can be. I must be, for you."

He was looking up at her, his expression submissive, yielding—a contrast to the lofty extravagance of his words. How could he be so irresistible to her in all the right ways?

"All this hard work just to make a human girl fall for you." She managed a crooked grin.

"I don't want you to fall for me. I want you to soar with me. We can have it all."

She groaned and rubbed her face with her palms. The incongruity of her situation made her skin crawl. A lovely man was saying lovely words. From anyone else these words would have sounded like irony at best or an idiotic cliché at worst, but from him they came filled with pure, unadulterated meaning. Each word meant only what it meant. She believed that he was truthful. But she couldn't believe him.

I am willing to accept the existence of magic and parallel dimensions, but not a declaration of love. What the hell is wrong with me? She wanted to cry.

His thumb and forefinger touched her chin, gently lifting her face.

"You are drifting away into shadows, precious. Have my words offended you?"

"No, no. It's difficult for me to hear them. Trust issues, I suppose, loss of a father at a young age, all that." She choked on a chuckle. "The usual stuff."

"My mother died by my seventh morn, but I felt her love. Was your father a loving man?"

"He was . . . an ordinary man." As she spoke these words, Anna felt her eyes well up. The predicament of mankind revealed itself to her in its stark squalor: not all people were capable of love, and no amount of wishful thinking or social optimism was going to change that.

She swallowed hard. This beer was turning her into an emotional wreck.

Yaret tilted his head to the side, doglike, looking at her intensely, as if trying to memorize each of her freckles, until she turned away. He clasped her wrists and gently pulled her to his chest.

"You cannot bring back my mother. Neither can I be a father to you, my darling," his melodic voice was soft and low. "All we can do is be that to our children."

She did cry a little, but Yaret said something ridiculously affected that made her chuckle, and his reaction to her comment was so eccentric that she couldn't help but laugh out loud.

A week ago, they were worlds apart. He had been a figment of her imagination, a dark shadow in a forgotten dream, an impression of hard hot fingers around her throat. Today, he was cuddling up to her side on her couch, the same hand playing with her hair, stroking her shoulder, and caressing her back as gently and easily as it petted the dog stretched at their feet.

More than once his lips found hers, as if he had forgotten her taste and was curious to recall, but each time it was as innocent as a kiss on the temple. More than once she wished to return his kiss with a greater passion, but each time she was too overtaken with tenderness to upset this precious tranquility.

They each had two beers and split the fifth, drinking from the same bottle, which was silly and childish and delightfully sensual. The two and a half beers could by no means account for the languid trance she was in. Perhaps the stress of the early morning confrontation with Ted and the long walk in the snowy park were finally taking their toll. Besides, as much as the simmer of desire had become a permanent feature of the last few days, keeping it in check had exhausted her.

The conversation flowed, lazy and light, like his touches.

"So, what was behind that door of the park rangers' hut?"

"If you opened that door yesterday, all you'd have seen would have been gardening tools. If you open it today, now that you remember the wyssun world, you would see a portal."

"To the wyssun world?"

"Wyssun world is only a hedge-world, an Alvan outpost on Earth. But from it one can open a door to the Green Hills, which is a fundamental focus. From the Green Hills one can get anywhere in the Otherworld."

"Even Alvaheim?"

"Even Alvaheim."

"Can you say something in Alvan?"

"Beware of what you ask. Alvan is a true language, each word is a word of power. A command in Alvan will be obeyed." He tugged at her hair lightly.

"I doubt you would be able to make me do something I don't want to do. Especially after such a warning."

"Let me make it clear: you want to make me make you do something you don't want to do?" A mischievous smirk danced in the corners of his mouth. "What does your psychological science say about this?"

"I am merely conducting a scientific experiment."

"I thought we were beyond that." He tried to pull her against his chest again.

"Are you refusing?" She evaded his arms.

"May it be writ into the Book of Life!" he proclaimed with mock solemnity, and sat straight, regarding her with narrowed eyes. "Anna, do you wish to dance?"

"What, right now? Ah, I see. No, I do not wish to dance."

"Dance for me!" He snapped his fingers.

"No." She got up to her feet and crossed her arms. Defiance rose inside of her, inflamed by his leer and his annoying finger-snapping.

"Are you sure?"

"Quite sure."

He hung his head and sighed as if in pain, snapped his fingers again, and tapped his bare foot lightly. He went on snapping and tapping, creating a complex rhythm with these little noises, while drawing ragged breaths and exhaling in time, as if containing sobs.

When he lifted his pale face, his lips and eyes glistened, and for a moment she worried he had been indeed weeping. But he looked her straight in the eyes, and in his inhale she heard, "dance," and in his exhale, "maiden." Those were not the words in any true sense, yet she was sure he spoke to her, sang to her like the wind sings in high trees.

"Dance, maiden," she heard the whisper-song. "Dance for me."

It was music, subtle and sensual, the kind of rhythm that makes you want to sway your shoulders, your hips; your legs begin to tremble, and you must spread your arms and dance, dance slowly to the silver song of love.

"What are you doing?" Yaret's voice, now cool and distant, took her out of her daze.

"Huh?"

She froze in midmotion. From his spot on the floor the dog gave her a side glance without lifting his big head from his paws. She was standing on the middle of the room with her hands in the air, unable to recall how she had gotten there.

She had been dancing. He commanded, and she obeyed before she knew it, like a peasant girl in a folk tale, dancing herself to death, unable to resist fairy music.

She'd known him for seven days now, the last three of which they had spent under the same roof. They had slept in the same bed. Had he revealed the full scale of his hypnotic power earlier, she would never have let him in as far as the threshold.

He could have made her do anything he wanted, all this time.

It was a scary thought. Scarier yet, it thrilled her. She'd never known herself to get a kick out of submission—if anything, she'd always enjoyed taking the lead, sexually and otherwise. And yet, each fiber of her soul was singing in harmony. It wasn't the act of compliance that felt so liberating, not dropping the reins that brought bliss. It was her attunement to the singer, the magic created between them, both of them submitting to it together.

"Had I wished to simply bed you, all I had to do was tell you to give yourself to me." Yaret spoke, echoing her thoughts. "My girl, I can make you come with a single word. But I desire to give myself to you as wholly as I desire to possess you. This is how my kind loves. It is all or nothing. It has always been."

He sighed and leaned back, his hands folded loosely across his chest, his very pose indicating quiet resignation. He was going to neither force her, nor trick her, nor beg.

"I'll be right back, okay?" said Anna and made a beeline for the bathroom.

She'd used to do that, escape to the bathroom to collect herself before emerging as a lover, or a friend, or a stranger, depending on her mood and the attractiveness of the partner, the latter usually based on the former, and both often dictated by the quantities of intoxicants consumed. It was a ritual, something she developed when she lived with Genie, something that gave her a sustaining illusion of control amid the happy chaos of those years. Before each of those unforgettable nights with Genie she stood in front of the bathroom mirror, too, asking herself: *do you want this?* and the answer has always been: *yes!* The true reason why she stopped doing this with Ted wasn't because their comfortable routine left no need for self-reflecting inquiry, but because sometimes she didn't want to hear the answer.

As she splashed cold water on her face, Anna silently mouthed to her reflection in the mirror: "You are about to cheat on your fiancé with a homeless mental patient. Will you be able to live with yourself if you do it?"

"Let's rephrase," answered her reflection. "You are about to make love to a man—literally—out of your dreams, who is gorgeous, makes you feel sublime, and who just might be your soulmate. Will you be able to live with yourself if you don't do it?"

"Touché." Anna winked at the mirror. She had her answer.

She took off her glasses and placed them on the edge of the sink. She wasn't going to need them. She twisted her arms behind her back, unhooked her bra, and pulled it off through the sleeve, leaving her T-shirt on. The worn-in cotton fabric clung to her freed breasts, alluring and demure in equal measure. *He will love that*, she said to herself, and then, *I know how he is*. The thought sent a shiver of delight down her spine.

There was an open box of condoms in the mirror cabinet, and Anna pocketed two. She thought a little, and took the rest. Whether she was a one in twelve or not, she was going to make love tonight.

He was sitting where she had left him, cross-armed. She climbed next to him, letting her breasts rub against his arm, and kissed the corner of his mouth.

He turned to face her. His hand slowly, almost distractedly rose to her face, fingertips tracing her temple, her cheek, her jaw, as if he was giving her time to reconsider. But the time was up—fingers slid behind her neck, thumb locking her chin. With a sharp push he lifted her face upward. His open mouth traveled from her clavicle up her neck, searing her skin with his breath without kissing. Oh, how she longed for a kiss. His face was before her, eyes wide open, staring, unbearably close.

"I want you," he exhaled. "Do you want me?"

"I want you."

With a moan of relief, he threw himself against her, pinning her down. His body was light but hard, she noted with satisfaction. Without breaking his stare, he ran his hand over her shoulder to her chest, cupped and weighed her breast, flicked the nipple, counted her ribs, squeezed her hip. His touch was both possessive and worshipful, a warrior-priest venerating his sacred treasure. Her head swam. His hands traveled down, and her body responded to each touch with tiny warm waves about to become one, high and hot.

"My lady, my queen, my magnificent mistress, it has always been you, only you. I've seen it in my heart, our life together." His breath tickled her ear. "A tall house on a hill amidst blossoming apple trees . . . and six, oh, wait—" his hand grasped her crotch, "—seven perfect children . . ."

"That's a hell of a lot of children," Anna broke his feverish whisper. It was unpleasantly sobering to hear him wax domestic after oozing seduction a moment before. The talk of children and a house in the country jarred her with its prosaic plainness. Her arms, wrapped around his back, let go.

Above her, he froze and tightened his embrace. If he held her any tighter, it would've hurt. It was uncanny how he could be so subtle one moment and so severe the next. In a flash of panic, Anna wriggled under him, and he sat upright, jerking her up with him, so that they faced each other, their arms and legs intertwined.

"You told me you want me." His gray eyes were like lead.

"I mean it."

"So you consent to our marriage."

"Marriage?" She twitched, making him ease his lock. "Who said anything about marriage?"

"You have declared your utmost intent," he spoke gravely. "You said you want me. Me, as I am, body and soul, past and future, in a sacred betrothal."

His hands dropped, and the space between their heaving chests became a chasm, so deep it made her sick; it was lonely outside of his arms, cold and wrong; the separation was unbearable.

"Oh, enough with the Renfair talk already!" She straddled him, grabbed his head with both hands and bit into his mouth, stifling his groan. She saw his eyes darken. They crashed back on the futon and kissed for what seemed an eternity, their tongues battling for dominance.

In the back of her mind she hoped for the invisible wings to unfold and envelope her again. It didn't happen. Something was different, missing, but it didn't matter. The pounding of her heart drowned all thought.

She pulled his T-shirt up and over his head, lingering long enough to see him squirm, faceless, under her. Looking down at his naked torso she laughed with joy: he was built so neatly, not a single plane out of place, lean muscles rolling under the taut silky skin. She'd never touched a body so fine yet potent at the same time, so full of promise—no! guarantee—of intense pleasure. To have something this exquisite in her hands was empowering. He made a growling noise. Relenting, she freed him; mad eyes stared at her, pupils wide and dark, and she knew he loved her roughness in this primal struggle, craved yielding as much as conquering.

Anna laughed again, drunk with desire. She heard him exhale her name as she kicked off her jeans and straddled him again, squeezing his narrow body between her bare thighs. Through the damp fabric of her panties she felt the tautness of his stomach. Her grinding left a slick trail on his skin.

He buckled under her. She heard him groan, "No!" but his hands on her breasts said otherwise. Vengefully, she exhaled, "Yes!" and dug her nails into his shoulders, forcing him to moan through his clenched teeth.

The more she pressed, the more he melted into her grasp; she too was melting, inside and out. She fell on him again, devouring the eager, responsive mouth. When she tore herself away for a breath, she saw his glowing face in the halo of fair hair; he was so delicious that she wished she could swallow him whole. She'd never wanted anyone like this. She'd never known she could.

She brought her face down to his belly, inhaling his scent—clean, metallic, dangerous smell of electrically charged air, the air of magic. The thought of tasting him made her mouth water. She cupped his crotch, expecting the same tantalizing, terrifying fullness that had filled her palm once before.

His jeans were new and stiff, and her fingers slipped as she fought with the button and zipper. Her hand came empty. He was not hard.

She had seen him produce an instant erection on cue only three days earlier. They were all over each other, and it felt so deep, so real. She was turned on so much it hurt. Why wasn't he? Was she not attractive, not seductive enough? Had she put him off? Had she come on too strong?

"Forgive me." His eyes were shut, face frozen. "I cannot be one with you. You cannot love me."

All of Anna's self-doubt and disappointment at once were swept away by excruciating sympathy. She'd been too self-conscious to notice the obvious:

he had exhausted himself with his own expectations, couldn't perform under their pressure. A master of the universe, a slave to his self-imposed imperative of all or nothing.

"I can try." She lowered herself on top of him and took his face in her hands, smoothing his furrowed eyebrows with her thumbs. "It's okay. Come on, look at me. It's all right."

"No, it's not all right, and it is my fault. I am a fool, a feeble, impatient fool." He shook his head remorsefully, still avoiding her eyes. "I shouldn't have—"

"Shouldn't have what?"

"Revealed that your consent would save your homeworld."

Anna laughed. "You don't think I've believed it, do you?"

His eyes snapped open and he sat up, grabbing her by the shoulders.

"Then why do I sense a compulsion in you? Compulsion, not love."

Before she could say anything, he pressed her against his chest, filling her ear with a frantic whisper.

"I beg you, my precious darling, forget all I said to you on that dreaded night. Wrecked by desire, I wasn't . . . entirely truthful. Indeed, mankind is safe for as long as the Alvan blood flows in this world." He seized her hand and pressed her fingers against his throat. She felt the mad beating of his pulse. "Feel it? Alvan blood flows in my veins. As long as I'm alive, it flows in this world. You don't have to—"

"No, I don't have to, but I want to." She put her fingers on his lips. "It's not all or nothing. Take me to bed. Make me come."

He looked up. There was a flicker of hope; he shut his eyes again, and so did she, because when their lips touched she no longer needed eyes to see.

She could barely register him lifting her off the couch, carrying her to the alcove, and laying her on the bed. She was bathing in his glow. His fingers fluttered along the flute of her spine; each touch awakened waves of resounding light, which collided and refracted in spectacular patterns. The light was pleasure, the pleasure was light. What she felt, she saw: he was not simply caressing her, he was reaching within her, seeking something to ignite, something to vibrate in time to his frequency. He was not finding what he sought.

She was on the verge of understanding what it was when he held her tightly and exhaled a word into her ear. An explosive wave of heat rushed from her core to her limbs, ecstasy coursed through her body, too agonizing to sustain, impossible to escape. A spasm shook her and she collapsed in his arms.

She felt him cradling her, his lips pressing against her temple; she heard him pull in air sharply through his nose, sniffing her hair, and she chuckled lazily. She was far from done with him, hadn't even started, she was going to show him . . . She drifted off, holding on to that thought. She was still floating on the warm waves of pleasure when she realized he'd been gone for some time, so she slid off the bed and stepped back into the room.

It was a small studio apartment. It took Anna less than a minute to discover that Yaret was not in the bathroom or behind the futon. Agitated by her frantic movements, Black Shuck sat up, blinking his beady eyes.

"You're here, dog, so where is he?" Anna's purple NYU T-shirt she'd just peeled off of him was draped listlessly off the side of the futon. Her hands shaking, Anna ripped open the closet doors. The biker jacket was gone. So were the tennis shoes. He'd walked out into the New York winter night wearing only a short leather jacket and a pair of skinny jeans. Anna opened the heavy entrance door and stood in the doorway, staring down the empty staircase. The cold copper of the threshold burned the soles of her bare feet. She felt exposed in her T-shirt and panties, so she retreated back into the apartment, picked her jeans and sweater up from the floor and pulled them on.

Outside, dusk was congealing into winter darkness, heavy as the snow that covered all the tracks. The man out of her dream was gone. He'd given her a glimpse of another world and left her in-between, cold and ashamed.

The line binding her to reality had snapped, but instead of soaring, she floated in a void. What she had always considered real turned out to be no more than a thin film of illusion over the infinite and intimidating true reality. His presence had illuminated this fathomless expanse, but now he was gone, and without him she was lost. She looked at her hands and didn't recognize them. She tried to recall the names and faces of her family and friends, and couldn't. Her body felt foreign, unwieldy mind refused to interpret the signals of her blunted senses.

An animal's growl. A knock. It took her an eternity to comprehend what that sound was. She stumbled on deadened legs; crossing the room seemed an impossible feat, but a name and a face lit up like a beacon—Yaret. It gave her strength to make it the rest of the way and open the door. The lock unlatched, but the door wouldn't budge, held from outside.

"Is that dog still here?" said a man's voice through the crack.

Instinctively, Anna grabbed Black Shuck by the collar and shoved him in the bathroom. In the back of her mind, she noted the initial resistance of the animal's powerful body and how obediently it eased as soon as she laid her hand on it. Exactly how she liked it. How she needed it.

"May I come in?" Ted's big body filled the doorway.

"I didn't expect you to return."

"I had to take some time to clear my head. Regardless of my personal feelings, I couldn't in my right mind leave you alone with that man. Where is he?"

"Gone."

She stepped aside, letting Ted in. For a moment they performed an awkward shuffle in the entryway, he, not sure if he was going to take off his coat; she, not sure if she wanted to take it. Finally, the coat was off Ted's wide shoulders and on the hook by the door. They stood still for a moment, then both walked to the couch and sat down next to each other. Thick silence hung between them.

"Annie, what happened to you?"

She looked into his kind face, contorted with genuine pain, and turned away. She wanted to explain herself to this sympathetic stranger. She wanted to say, *After years of wandering in the lonely wilderness, as I stepped on the threshold of my one true home, it came crashing down around me, and I am alone in the cold again.*

"I don't know," was what she said instead.

"What exactly was the relationship between you and that man?"

"I'm not sure."

"Did you fuck him?"

"No."

Ted nodded, his broad face involuntarily reflecting relief with a touch of superiority, an expression that fit him poorly, like a pair of skinny jeans two sizes too small. Now, Yaret—he rocked superiority.

"This is what we're going to do. We're going to work through this like two adults and two professionals." The tone of his voice was even, too even.

Poor man, thought Anna in a flash of cold clarity, *Scrambling to stay on the high road. I should feel compassion for his valiant attempts at saving his shattered world and the shattered me in it.* Under all the calluses he's worked up over the years of training and practice, beneath the armor of procedure he was just another boy afraid to be passed by, afraid to lose the girl. She'd never seen him so closely before, so exposed. She would have felt compassion, but her feeling organ was broken.

"It would be a shame to throw away your future over a momentary lapse of judgment. You are capable of getting over it. Well, I love and support you, and I believe myself capable of getting over it too. You made a mistake, you're only human. At least you didn't cross the ultimate line."

She stared at him blankly. She strained to figure out if he was talking about the boundaries of professional ethics she'd so gleefully violated, or the bonds of their relationship she'd betrayed with little hesitation. Or was he talking about the line binding her to reality, which tore as she came flying? Her thinking organ, too, was out of order.

"Of course," continued Ted, "it would be absurd to presume a woman like yourself . . . that you would . . . want to . . ."

Anna felt her numb knees unbending, as if pulled by invisible strings. Her body jerked up. She rose, towering over Ted.

"Oh, I wanted to." Her voice was rough. "He was Peter Pan, Heathcliff, and Lady Galadriel rolled in one hot enchilada, topped with a dollop of puppy love. No, I didn't fuck him, and guess what, the loss is mine."

"Ann!" Ted stood up. There was a warning in his voice, but Anna couldn't stop herself.

"Wanna know why I didn't do it? 'Cause I blinked, and he was gone, like that, poof! in the cloud of pixie dust. Oh, I should've fucked him, I should've had his babies, all seven of them!" She broke down in hysterical laughter.

"Now, Ann, you are out of line. I can see . . ."

"Line? Is that all you can see, the line? Don't you get it, there is no one line, it's all one scary mess of lines. I know because he's shown me. He was brighter than the sun, and his light made me see the truth. And the truth was scary and beautiful . . . like him, because that's what he was, beautiful at everything he did, even the scary things. And he was hilarious. Beautiful and scary and hilarious, like . . . like a wild animal. He made me laugh. He made me high. He gave me back my dreams. He healed me. He made me whole! You can see? You see nothing! I saw the silver strings with my own eyes. I smelled a dragon. I can prove it. Look!"

She leaped to the window, grabbed the potted plant from the windowsill, and shoved it in Ted's face.

"It's fucking green! Do you understand what that means? It means I'm not crazy! I've never been crazy. I no longer have to lie 'cause it's been true all along. It was real . . . the monsters were real . . . the magic was real . . . it was real and so was he, and you with your understanding—you are not even close to real, you, all of you, your whole reality's a joke!"

Anna was choking on laughter. In the distance the dog barked. It was so funny, he was barking as if he was trying to talk to her. What could he tell her she didn't already know? Stupid dog. It was so silly she could no longer hold in the laughter. She was shaking so hard, her hands opened; the pot fell to the floor, soil spilled on the rug. Why wasn't Ted laughing? The tear stealing down his cheek looked so out of place . . . He should have seen his own face, it was comical. She couldn't breathe, but laughter flooded her till it hurt behind her ears, till her stomach spasmed; the dirty floor rushed to meet her face and she was on all fours, vomiting into the spilled soil. Through the hum of blood pumping in her ears, and the mad barking of the dog, Anna heard Ted make a phone call and speak in a faltering voice. She made out the words "acute psychotic episode" and "discreet."

The medication worked right away. The ache wasn't gone, but shut down, quieted, the way a heavy dark blanket over the cage quiets the frantic bird. They took away her phone with her music, but Pink Floyd's "Comfortably Numb" had been playing in her head on the loop each time she laid it on the cool, firm pillow of the hospital bed.

Are you suicidal? Are you homicidal? Do you hear voices? See things? She had nothing to tell them, so she refused to be interviewed on the intake. The only time she spoke was to her mother, who rushed to the clinic to see her.

"Where's the dog?"

"God, Annie, that dog . . . Animal control took it away, I guess, it's at a shelter."

"Which?"

"Oh, I don't know, Ted said someplace up in Harlem?"

Seventy-two hours. That's how long a black male pit bull, the dog least likely to be adopted, had before being euthanized. Ironically, seventy-two hours was also the time a patient is kept under initial observation, so she would be lucky if she had a couple of hours after her release before Black Shuck's execution.

Anna knew the drill: they wouldn't let her out until she told them what they wanted to hear. She was at the disadvantage because they knew she knew. Pretending wouldn't do. She wasn't much of an actress anyway. The only way out was to tell the truth and nothing but the truth, elven-style.

So, after contemplating the situation in drug-induced quietude for two days, on the third Anna requested a meeting with the psychiatrist and issued the following statement:

"It took me some time, but I now understand what has happened to me. After losing my father as a teenager, I never had time to process my grief, instead having to deal with my mother's remarriage and the consequent birth of my brother, whom I had to parent for the first few years. Recently, the increased pressure of the engagement commitment, a challenging case at work, and the workload at school put me into a vulnerable emotional state. The man, initially a client, triggered me, enabling my reverting to an emotionally immature behavioral pattern. His amnesia and his sexual ambiguity mirrored my own internal conflict. As much as I was aware of the ethical breach, still I became influenced by a mentally unstable person. His abrupt departure brought back the abandonment issues, leading to a breakdown. But now that I see everything clearly, it's over."

She assured the psychiatrist that she would be starting regular therapy right away, and she was released. Her mother picked her up in the family car. She specifically asked for her mother. She couldn't be alone with Ted, although he'd checked on her every day.

Half an hour after, she was filling paperwork at the animal shelter in East Harlem. The way the huge black pit bull danced when he saw her erased all the doubts about her ownership. Riding in the car with her mother, Anna marveled at the clean, dry, sunlit New York outside the car windows. Only three days ago, the city had been hidden behind a veil of snow, ghostly in its monochromatic splendor, a dreamscape of a million aspects where everything was possible. The intense sunshine of the new day rendered the city flat, impenetrable in its blatancy, forbidding.

Shivering, Black Shuck kept trying to climb on her lap, his claws painfully pressing into her thighs. It was the first physical sensation she had registered in three days. She ended up wrapping her arm around his muscular shoulder, letting him snuggle up to her side. He smelled like medical disinfectant, and she gave him a perfume-scented bath as soon as they got home. That night he slept in her bed, curled up against her belly. And so, ended the third day.

On the fourth day, Dr. Stevens summoned her to inform her about the lawsuit the ex-con who'd been brutalized by John Doe was filing against the hospital. They were hoping to resolve the issue without a scandal, but since she was named in the suit as the employee who had deemed John Doe not dangerous to self and others, they had no choice but to terminate her internship. Also, Dr. Stevens said she was going to personally call each of the colleagues she'd recommended and make sure Anna had enrolled in personal therapy.

On the sixth day, Anna sent a formal request to her PhD program to postpone her dissertation defense for health reasons.

On the seventh day, Anna had her first session with her new therapist.

"Please tell me why you are here today," was the standard opening line.

"I don't know what's real anymore," Anna said honestly.

The therapist kept the inquisitive silence, and Anna obligingly recited the story of her uneventful all-American childhood, complete with a promising athletic career so rudely interrupted at the age of fourteen when her father died from a heart attack and her mother remarried and moved her to New York City.

At the second session, the therapist suggested they talk about her mother. Anna explained that her mother had always been *good enough*, except that year when her father died, and the year after when they moved to New York, oh, and the next year after Jack was born, which hadn't been her mother's fault since postpartum depression can be extremely impairing.

During their next session, her therapist asked her to talk about her father. There wasn't much to tell, because her father had been an ordinary guy: a little overworked, a little unhappy in his marriage. He hadn't been abusive or particularly neglectful; they just hadn't had much in common. Had she picked a more popular sport, like softball or soccer, perhaps he could have come to her games, could have been proud of her trophies. But she'd joined the ski team, and all her important events required driving to the lake outside of town where they had groomed tracks. It meant standing for hours in the freezing wind just to get a glimpse of some kids breezing by—not a spectator sport in the least. He never made it to her big races. Perhaps in his mind he had nothing to offer her, that's what she was telling herself later when she decided that, perhaps, she had nothing to offer him. And then, before she could even begin to try, he was gone.

Her stepfather—now, there she'd lucked out. With James they were partners, in a pact to keep her mother happy, to take care of Jack. James called her "princess," which she'd hated at first but later began to find endearing. A New York cop, he'd seen his share of juvenile delinquents, so he was bent on doing right by the teenage girl who was now part of his instant family. Like her father, James also worked long hours, but somehow he was always within reach when needed. He was a guy's guy, embarrassed if he found her girly things in the bathroom, shy when it came to physical contact, perhaps due to his PC training. But by the way he chuckled at her jokes, bragged about her track trophies, and always got her exactly what she wanted for Christmas, she knew he cared. A few years after Jack was born, he offered to formally adopt her, but she was almost seventeen by then, so it didn't make much sense.

Three weeks into the therapy Anna brought up that dream she had, about being lost in the Otherworld, after which the world never seemed the same.

"It sounds like an important watershed. Why don't you write this dream down," suggested the therapist.

"But I'm not a literary type. I've never even kept a diary. I wouldn't know where to start."

"Where do you start an academic paper? Title, subtitle, chapter one, and so on. Just write."

That same afternoon, after she walked the dog, Anna sat down at her glass desk, turned on her laptop, opened a new document. As she hesitated with her fingers floating over the keys, she felt the numbness give way to a nearly forgotten anticipation—the glowing, vibrant white space was a virgin snow field, waiting to be trailed. She braced herself, like before pushing downhill, and typed:

PRINT IN THE SNOW: Anna's Adventure in the Wyssun World
Chapter I, in which Anna finds herself in a really dark predicament.

HOMECOMING

Winter

"It would make a very special pendant," said Anna. "See?" She stapled the tiny plastic mistletoe charm to the paper garland and handed it to Larry. "

"Give us a kiss." With a gappy grin, the old man lifted the garland over his head and nudged Anna.

"No, Larry, there won't be any kissing." She smiled back.

"When if not on New Year's Eve? Aw, you're no fun."

Larry was one of the more or less permanent residents at the New Hope homeless shelter during the colder months. Like many at the shelter, he had for years stayed "one paycheck away from being homeless," until something happened that he couldn't recover from: for Larry, an accident at a job left him with a thrown back, addicted to painkillers, and on the streets. He was a nice guy, always volunteering to help out, like now, helping Anna set up for the party in the lounge.

She had been working at the shelter since Christmas. After she lost her Bellevue internship, her mother and James had begged her to take some time off, stay with them, even offered to take her in with the dog she was adamant about keeping. But she began searching for a new job, any job. With her degree in cognitive psychology and an impressive clinical record, Anna Reilly looked good on paper. Too good, perhaps. The single place that responded to her application was the New Hope day shelter.

"You do realize you're overqualified for the case associate position," said the woman who called Anna. She introduced herself as the program director. "The minimum requirement is a high school diploma or GED. It's basically a housekeeping job."

"I can lift heavy things, I'm available for night shifts, and I'm good at record keeping," replied Anna. "I want this job."

She could tell, the woman was dying to ask *why* while at the same time trying like hell not to look a gift horse in the mouth. Anna got the job. Her salary, modest by Manhattan standards, was just enough more than her internship stipend to allow her to budget for Black Shuck's kibble.

She took the graveyard and holiday shifts, and didn't shy from hard labor, which earned her instant points with the staff, who at first treated her with the distrust of battle-tested grunts forced to welcome a demoted officer to their unit.

After the New Year party wound down, day staff left, and the residents settled for the night. Anna finished cleaning the lounge and sat in the corner under the unkillable money plant, and read—another new habit in her life. It began with her picking up Mrs. Dalloway during one of her quieter nights, the same old paperback she had read as an undergrad. It struck her how different the same words seemed now, like a new and improved translation. She swallowed the little novel in a couple of nights and moved on to Orlando, which she had to put down a couple of times, so personal it felt. It didn't help keep her mind off Yaret, but it gave her thoughts a more philosophical flow, and it was a welcome relief from the incessant undertow of physical longing.

The first night of the new year was blissfully uneventful. Only once did a resident try to sneak out for a forbidden smoke. Anna made her a cup of tea and spent half an hour in the lounge, distracting her from the craving with conversation.

She greeted the day shift worker at quarter to seven in the morning and went home. The shelter, like most of the similarly unglamorous properties in Midtown Manhattan, stood on the periphery of the island, between Second and Third Avenues on the East Side. Not bothering to wait for the cross-town bus, Anna plugged in her earbuds, pulled her beanie hat over her ears, and headed west along Forty-Second Street, toward where the sky was the darkest.

The City That Never Sleeps wasn't about to change its habits on account of the new calendar year. The predawn street was still full of revelers in different states of drunkenness, coming from nightclubs and parties: survivors of the ball dropping, exhausted tourists in their sensible shoes, and locals—including the stalwart Bridge and Tunnel contingent—dressed with wacky ostentation and much too lightly for the weather.

Infected with the spirit of the celebration, Anna decided to walk through Times Square and halted, mesmerized by the sight. Bright shapes hovered on the twilight mist above ground. Their movements seemed random, and she strained her eyes out of nearsighted habit to perceive a meaning behind the image.

In the now empty square, sanitation workers were removing last night's festive trash. It was a little after seven in the morning, minutes before sunrise. The cleaning crews must have begun working as soon as the ball dropped at midnight, because most of the sidewalks had been cleared. Some workers were taking apart the metal crowd-control fences, others were sweeping the mounds of colorful garbage from underneath. Barely visible in the dim morning light except for their fluorescent vests, they seemed to be participating in some kind of witchcraft, stirring the vibrant brew with their long poles, their glowing garments as bright as the loose bits of paper confetti they trampled upon.

Anna crossed the square slowly, enjoying the acute sense of her own uselessness amid all this purposeful activity. It felt good not to belong, to walk unseen, free to notice every little thing without being noticed.

A flash of gold sparkled in a pile of trash: a shred of metallic confetti hit by the first ray of the morning sun, just as the mellotron kicked in with a heavenly organ chord at the end of the third movement of Yes's "Close to the Edge," flooding her heart with warmth and gratitude, as if the universe had given her a friendly little nod, promising that bad times were left behind and good times surely awaited ahead.

A ray of light tapped her on the shoulder, made her turn around; it lifted her face by the chin and kissed her forehead. She looked up. In the narrow spaces between the tall buildings, the sky was lighting up like a switch had been flipped, putting to sleep the neon signs and waking up the billboards. She squinted against the sunlight at a gigantic poster above and laughed: appropriately, it read SWITCH in capital letters next to a minimalist bottle and a man's face—probably a perfume ad. Anna looked closer, and laughter died in her throat.

Looking down at her from a billboard above Times Square was the chiseled face of Yaret Fairfax.

Anna had been seeing her therapist three times a week for over a month now. She knew better than trying to repair the fabric of her life all at once; instead, she was knotting one loose thread at a time.

Each time she sat down on the couch in the neat, well-lit office, she resigned herself to being truthful, if not with her therapist, then at least with herself. But she could only talk about the wyssun world through the metaphor of dream. Anna wouldn't insult her memory by calling it a dream outright, but kept her language vague enough to leave room for interpretation. It worked. They discussed the imagery of the dream and the archetypal symbolism of its characters, and the clarity obtained by these ambiguous means felt soothing, the same way a medicine brings relief whether it's obtained by prescription or stolen.

Her therapist was aware of the chain of events that had landed Anna in treatment: a violent altercation resulting in possible PTSD, leading to a botched case and the subsequent psychotic break with reality. As far as the outside world knew, Anna Reilly's error in handling John Doe's case was an unfortunate misjudgment of a stressed-out, inexperienced trainee—neither unthinkable, nor inexcusable.

Inside, she was dying to talk about him. How he licked his fingers after devouring an apple whole—core, pips, and all—teasing with the wooden stem between his teeth. How he pursed his lips and lowered his eyes when he encountered something unfamiliar. How he looked down his nose at men twice his size, and how he could stare anyone down. How he stared right at her, seriously, with those bright, dark-rimmed eyes. How he glanced at her sidewise, those same eyes sparkling with laughter, before breaking into a wide, feral grin. How he uttered the most profound and most idiotic statements in the same breath. How he made exciting mundane things, like buying groceries or making the dog fetch. How he laughed and wept and played the fool, how easily he bent others to his will, how eagerly he submitted himself to her.

After she saw Yaret's face staring at her from the billboard in Time

Square, she requested an emergency session and a favor.

"Is there a reason you didn't follow up with the shelter yourself?" asked her therapist.

"Right after we terminated, everything was chaotic," answered Anna honestly. "And after I was released from the clinic, I was no longer in a position to inquire about residents."

"Since I deem it pertinent to your wellbeing, I've made inquiries on your request. Mr. Fairfax left Saint Francis Residencies on December 4 and never returned. As of now, his whereabouts are unknown."

"Dammit!" Anna groaned. "I know it's textbook paranoia, but I think I saw him in Times Square."

"Is it possible he's stalking you after developing romantic delusions about your relationship?"

"Our relationship was nominal."

"That never stopped erotomaniacal stalkers."

"No, I don't feel stalked. In fact, I feel like a stalker myself."

"How so?"

"I think I'm hoping to see him, so I see him everywhere."

"The time you saw him in Times Square, did he see you?"

"What? no, it wasn't him in person. It was his face on a billboard. A Times Square billboard advertising some designer perfume, of all things." A nervous chuckle.

"Was it him or someone who looked like him?"

"I can't tell. I didn't stay and look. It's disconcerting. It's not the first time I've seen reminders of him."

"It's possible that a former patient is stalking you. It's also possible for you to have unresolved feelings regarding his case, which make you perceive neutral things as being related to him. But is it possible that this man, who was homeless and unemployed last time you checked, not to mention struggling with a multitude of mental issues, was recently hired to advertise a designer perfume—which, I presume, is a hard gig to get?"

"With his face it's not impossible—" Realizing how defensive she sounded, Anna added, "—but extremely unlikely. To the point where odds are against its being real."

Her therapist kept the encouraging pause.

"So, I must've imagined his face on the billboard," Anna conceded.

And the wind calling my name in his voice, and his messages in the shapes of light and shadow, and all those times the dog ran to the door for no reason and I was sure it was him . . .

"It is my brain interpreting random events in accordance with my neurosis," she finished out loud. "It's all in my head."

The last time Anna had heard from Genie was on Christmas Day. She sent a holiday greeting, a selfie with a camel, and her love. They were filming in the Moroccan desert till mid-January, cell connection was unreliable, and she didn't expect an answer until her return. At the time, Anna registered a vague sense of relief. But by the end of the year her body adjusted to the medication, and therapy had desensitized her to talking about the things she didn't want to talk about. When Genie called from London to wish her a Happy Old New Year on January 14, Anna told her about the breakdown. Despite her weak protestations, Genie was on the next flight to New York.

It was Genie's first time in Anna's Garment District studio. It felt weird. Their existence in the same space belonged to another time. But Genie had been known to create her own time and space continuum.

She brought with her a Moroccan tan, a wacky British accent, and a pile of seemingly random and, upon closer inspection, very thoughtful gifts. Among them was an ivory-olive tie-dye Stella McCartney scarf that ignited the flecks of green in Anna's hazel eyes, and for the dog, a tooled leather collar with—ironically—Anglo-Saxon interlace. Genie and Black Shuck loved each other at first sight; Genie seemed much more comfortable roughhousing with the dog than Anna ever had been.

Genie refused to drink out of solidarity since Anna was on her meds. They spent the first night talking over pizza and Pepsi (Genie had a categorical preference for Pepsi over Coke for some or another Russian reason she'd once explained and Anna had forgotten). It always struck Anna that her extroverted friend, who'd always been good at reflecting her environment and who'd lived abroad for almost as long as she'd lived in the old country, possessed an almost obsessive habit of playing up her exotic origins. For the first time, Anna saw it for what it was: armor.

"Spill it," Genie demanded right away. "And no holding back like you always do."

Anna wanted to protest: of all the people, Genie would have been the one to witness her at full abandon, unrestrained. But the pain of accusation confirmed its fairness, so she began speaking, not bothering with qualifiers and understatements, describing everything the way she remembered: from the moment in Riverside Park twelve years ago, when she met a boy on skis and followed him to the wyssun world, to the moment when an elven lord seduced and deserted her.

Anna talked for a long time, pausing only to take bites of her pizza, cardboard-like by now. After she finished her story, she sucked down the rest of her soda and leaned back, too exhausted to search her friend's face for traced of indulgence reserved for the mad.

"The crystal necklace, is it the same hippie bling you've always had hanging around your desk?" said Genie after a pause. "You still have it?"

Anna took it from the dry branch on her desk and handed it over, and Genie bravely threaded her head through the leather cord. She sat there for a minute, blinking.

"Nothing. It must be all used up." She offered it to Anna, but Anna recoiled, and Genie returned the necklace to its place on the branch. "Or maybe it's not meant to work for anyone but you."

"You, too, must think I'm nuts," muttered Anna, "I wouldn't believe myself either."

"Have I ever told you where I grew up?"

"I thought you grew up in Moscow."

"Before things picked up and daddy dearest got in on big business, he was a regular gas engineer at a plant fifteen hundred miles northeast of Moscow."

"Siberia?"

"Yamal-Nenets Autonomous Region, a little territory in the West Siberian Plain, twice the size of France, covered by arctic tundra, half of it in the Arctic Circle. In the summer the sun doesn't set, but the sky is dark with mosquito swarms, and winter is, like, nine months out of the year. I was born in Nadym. Don't bother pronouncing it. It's a town built around a natural gas deposit, wooden barracks and all. I lived there till I was seven."

Her voice lost the tone of ironic self-deprecation and now rang heartfelt.

She leaned forward, hunching her back, and rested clasped hands on her parted knees, a pose so unlike her glamorous self yet utterly natural, and Anna saw the unassuming little girl from a wooden barrack lost in the snows of Siberia. At the same time, she couldn't shake the feeling that the tough little Siberian was yet another stage costume from Genie's wardrobe, like a brash New Yorker or a posh Londoner.

"The native people are deer herders and hunters, nomads; as much as the Soviets kept forcing civilization on them, they remain unspoiled; they're animists. But even shamans have to send their kids to the state school, so, some of my mates lived in deerskin tents. When you grow up in a place like this, you see things, and I don't mean the Northern Lights." Genie looked Anna in the eyes, and finished earnestly: "Strange things happen in the snow. Creatures appear. People follow an enticing longhaired White Maiden into tundra never to return. It happens. A lot. What I'm saying is, I don't think you're nuts. I believe what happened to you is real."

She wasn't acting. Anna threw her arms around her, settling into her friend's embrace.

"I'm sorry for not telling you earlier," she muttered, swallowing a sob.

"Thank God you lived to tell." As Anna buried her face in Genie's neck, she felt the tremble of Genie's throat against her mouth. "And this man, John-Yaret, he knew all about it?" Genie shifted away, trying to look Anna in the eyes.

"He knew me better than I knew myself."

"Was the sex good?" Genie inquired with a sly smirk.

Anna winced. "Kind of one-sided. He did go down on me . . . I think. Or maybe I dreamed it. Anyway, I didn't get a chance to reciprocate. But yeah, it was good. Skies-open-above-and-you-die-a-thousand-deaths kind of good."

"So, you fell in love with a dream, and it turned out to be a nightmare."

Her words, in all their clichéd dramatic ostentation, struck Anna with a simple truth. This was the first time she had framed what happened in these terms. Infatuation, obsession, psychotic break . . . no, she had fallen in love with an unavailable man who broke her heart. The answer was right under her nose, mocking her with its triviality, and it took a visitor from the other side of the Atlantic to point it out to her.

"Did he ever say I love you?"

Anna thought for a moment. "No. Not in those words."

"It may not feel like it right now," said Genie after a pause, "but this can be a good thing."

"Me falling for him, or him leaving me?"

"Both."

"Please don't give me that "suffering ennobles" Russian bullshit. There is no silver lining to this disgrace. I'm an embarrassment to myself. I fucked up everything there was to fuck up: lost a prestigious internship, fell off the doctorate course, ruined it with my fiancé. My professional integrity is in shreds, so is my self-esteem. I've been institutionalized, I'm medicated, and, guess what, I'm still seeing things! Do you realize I see his face everywhere? Just the other day, I look up and see him in a billboard ad in Times Square—"

"An ad?" Genie's expression of pensive compassion morphed into businesslike concentration. "An ad for what?"

"Does it matter? Some cologne, Swap, something or other. Whatever, it's not him, he's gone forever, back to the other dimensions. Back to my imagination."

Genie dug into her bag and produced a copy of Vogue with her airplane ticket sticking out. As she frantically flipped the glossy pages, they released a whiff of perfume samples and fresh ink, the unmistakable scent of glamour condensed to print. Finding what she was looking for, she broke the thick spine at a full spread and shoved the magazine into Anna's face.

It was an ad for Switch, a unisex fragrance. On the left page of the spread was a black-and-white photograph of a young man wearing jackboots and a half-buttoned military uniform. With one hand he was undoing the belt of his breeches, and with another holding a long switch, pointed right at the viewer. His dark-rimmed pale eyes were maniacal, like a rabid wolf's. The opposite page had a contrasted white figure against black background: a nude man with his back to the viewer, reclining against the confines of the page. His hands were clasped behind his back as if cuffed, and he was glancing over his shoulder with a raw mix of curiosity and desire. The deliberately uncomfortable pose was poignant, but he was graceful in his submission, just as the image on the opposite side was gracious in its teasing. Both photographs were tongue-in-cheek and over-the-top sensual, saved from crossing into vulgarity only by the artistic skill of the photographer. The juxtaposition of the two images was especially provocative because, as the name of the perfume implied, the model in both photographs was the same person.

Anna knew each line of this lithe, sinewy body, each plane of this angular face. She knew the smirk, the pout, the shadows the eyelashes cast on the cheekbones. It was, without a doubt, the same being whom she'd met in the wyssun world, whom she'd interviewed at Bellevue, brought into her home and into her bed.

With a groan, she pushed away the magazine. "It's him. I don't know how, but it is."

"I must say, the bloke is fit." Genie licked her lips. "The photographer is Mario Solari. *The* Mario Solari," she added meaningfully, making Anna roll her eyes. "The model's name isn't on the page, though. Let's do some sleuthing; it must show up somewhere. An ass like this won't go unnoticed."

Her pragmatic reaction was anchoring. For as long as they'd known each other, Genie never worried about tomorrow. Having no qualms about making use of her estranged father's bank account for her and her friends' entertainment, she could afford to be frivolous, take chances, live in the moment. Despite her frivolousness—or perhaps thanks to it—this confirmed bohemian was incredibly good at practical logistics, and it dawned on Anna that Genie would indeed make an excellent director someday.

Genie went online, and Anna went to put on the kettle: even before becoming a Londoner, her friend wouldn't consider a day complete without a cup of tea.

"You ought to sit down for this," Genie said when Anna returned with two steaming cups. Anna obliged.

"I searched for *Switch ad male model*," Genie spoke in the clinical yet kindly tone of a PI explaining her procedure to a newly cuckolded spouse. "The first thing that popped up is this: *Following his breakthrough appearance in the controversial Switch fragrance ad campaign photographed by the illustrious Mario Solari, up-and-comer John Y (pronounced, ever so cleverly, as Why) ends a buzzworthy fashion week with a feature in the January issue of Vogue Paris, photographed by Noel and Neve. Appearing alongside Marishka Tenkovska and Gudrun Lärk in a futuristic set styled by Charlie Blau, androgynous John steals the show.*"

"Sorry, I don't speak glam. Translation, please?"

"It means the name of the man in those ads is John Y and he is a professional model."

"I don't believe it."

"Look for yourself." Genie twirled her iPad toward Anna.

The entries were few: a couple of articles on the new campaign in fashion industry publications, a mention on some style maven's blog. Most articles were reposts of the Anti-Defamation League denouncing Nazi-themed imagery in a fashion ad and encouraging consumers to boycott both the designer and the photographer. No mention of the model other than a reference to his being new to the fashion scene.

"I still don't understand."

"You sure it's him? The John Doe you know as Yaret Fairfax? Not his better adjusted twin?"

"It's him. His face, his body, the way he clasps his hands . . . here, the same scars along his spine! And the name, John Y—Y must stand for Yaret. Naturally, he won't deign to use his real name. But how could he be in a magazine when a month ago he was in this very apartment, with me, without a social security number or a driver's license, with only Bellevue psych ward release papers for an ID?"

"A lot can happen in a month. Maybe he was scouted in the street. Many models are."

Anna slapped the tabletop, making Black Shuck jump up. "On the first day out of the hospital he was approached by a woman who said she was a scout. She gave him her card . . . Son of a bitch!"

John was nothing if not opportunistic. With his supernatural empathic ability, he could easily exploit anyone he met, making them accommodate him and help him achieve his goals. He had needed her to escape the hospital, find a temporary shelter. But what else could she give him? Not the life he desired, apparently, not even the sex.

"He used me," she finished with a crooked grin. "Took what he wanted, discarded what he didn't, and moved on to the next target."

"It's what they do." The blue eyes over the rim of the tea mug were glistening, and Anna couldn't tell if her friend was speaking playfully, figuratively, or from experience. "Can't trust them. They should teach it to children: don't run with scissors, don't get in cars with strangers, and don't ever trust the fair folk."

"Trust . . ." Anna let out a bitter laugh. "I trusted my eyes and ended up distrusting objective reality. I trusted my feelings and ended up with my heart broken."

"As far as objective reality, *there are more things in heaven and earth, Horatio, than are dreamt of in your philosophy*." Genie set down her mug and wrapped her arm around Anna's shoulders. "As far as him breaking your heart, it doesn't diminish the truth of your experience, but confirms it. Perhaps Lord Yaret of the Otherworld has always been the villain in this fairy tale."

They walked the dog together, and jet-lagged Genie fell asleep on the futon. Anna kept tossing and turning in her bed. She wished she could blame the dog's snoring for keeping her up, but that wasn't it. Quietly, so as not to wake Genie, she crept to the futon and picked up the copy of Vogue from where she'd tossed it. She tiptoed to the bathroom, locked the door behind her, turned on the light, sat on the edge of the toilet, and opened the magazine to the Switch ad.

Yaret stared back at her from the white page, his eyes inhumanly bright under the peak of his military cap. His smile was the smile of a villain, but it was his smile. In the opposite photograph his blond hair was shorter, tousled by the skilled hand of a stylist—the only feature that looked different to Anna. Her fingertip dragged over the slick page, following the lines of his body: lean arms, muscular back, sharp hip bone, perfect ass. The clever play of light and shadow elevated the sensuality of his nudity to an abstract, sculptural quality; still, it insulted her that numberless others were seeing his body this way, the way she should have and never got to.

The hurt burned her eyes, scalded her heart, pooled at the bottom of her belly with a throbbing heat, and she slid her hand under the elastic band of her pajama pants and between her thighs, the other hand pressing to her lap the heavy, cool magazine, fragrant with a multitude of perfumes.

Genie's flight to London wasn't until midnight, so they had the whole day to themselves until Anna's night shift. They went to Joe, their old hangout on Waverly and Gay, for a nostalgic breakfast of coffee and doughnuts, and afterward sat on a bench in Washington Square Park, watching NYU students pass by.

The day was sunny and still with the deceptive mid-January balminess that tricks you into taking off your hat and gloves. The lawns, now free of snow, were so green you'd think it was spring, if not for the deep chill creeping from the blue shadows of trees that cut through the bright green. There was little reminder of the recent blizzard; it hadn't snowed since. Overcome by salt and sun, the mighty snowdrifts had slowly receded, leaving nothing but greasy slicks on the asphalt, like chthonic slugs dragging their tails back to the chaos from which they had come.

Anna took off her glasses and turned her face up to the winter sun.

"I always envied your sable brows," said Genie, looking at her with a kind of wistful fondness. "They're beautiful."

More amused than flattered, Anna ran her thumbs over her wide, unruly eyebrows. She had long suspected her friend's concept of beauty to be as abstract as theatrical makeup: the world stage was populated with performers who either failed or succeeded in matching the roles Genie cast in her head, and the latter she admired, no matter how crooked the nose, pitted the skin, or misshapen the body. Herself blessed with a pretty face and a petite, well-proportioned figure, she had no time for conventional beauty in others. That's why Anna used to take her most flattering compliments with a grain of salt, like when Genie obsessed over her feet. Anna was a tall woman with the generous feet of a runner. Genie called them statuesque.

"They belong in gladiator sandals," she'd say, trying to pinch Anna's long second toe.

"So, I've got Morton's toe, big deal," Anna would grumble. "It's bad enough I have to go up a half size in my running shoe, now I'm subjected to your pervy notions!"

"Shut up," Genie always replied. "It's beautiful."

Anna smiled. She thought of the night before, of Genie sleeping under the same roof with her for the first time in two years. She had anticipated the unease of misplaced lust, but all she had felt was gratitude and warmth. Her jealous desire for Genie, fermented by admiration, had made a full circle and matured into a loving acceptance without the need to possess. As for her lust, it had become focused elsewhere.

"Zhénechka, why didn't we become a couple?"

Genie sighed with the relief of someone who's been fearing a difficult question for too long.

"We did one better. We became friends. Now it can last forever."

"We were good together."

"We still are. But I've never wanted a family life. You always have."

"When did I ever say that?"

"It's the way you didn't say it. You love kids, all that fuss. Each time we passed a playground, you'd get all googly-eyed, while I . . ." she pretended to retch. "The whole idea of commitment is a bit of a turn off . . . look, both my parents are on their third marriages, you know?"

"You're not bound to their behavioral pattern."

"Ah, don't bother, love." Genie laughed softly. "I'm not struggling with my nature, I'm celebrating it. I love the little old me."

"So do I. It wouldn't matter if you were a girl or a boy or a tentacled monster."

Genie blinked and looked up, suddenly quite interested in the wispy clouds smearing the pale winter sky.

"Speaking of tentacled monsters," she said after a pause. "When was the last time you saw one of these . . . wyssun?"

"Haven't seen one up close since the night it tried to break through the skylight."

"The night Yaret dumped his big revelation on you, and you dumped him?"

"I did dump him," admitted Anna with unexpected satisfaction. "Twice, actually. Shit, why did you have to bring him up? And we were doing so well, almost passed the Bechdel test."

"But daaarling," drawled Genie, fanning herself. "We are in a love story."

"I wouldn't know. Never read one, I guess."

"You have, just didn't realize it. What do you think *Анна Каренина* is? *Un amour de Swann*? *The End of the Affair*?" With the obliviousness of an aristocrat taking her cultural wealth for granted, Genie assumed everyone had read everything she had.

"Don't they all end badly?" Anna ventured, mentally adding titles to her reading list.

"A story doesn't have to have a happy end to be a love story. The best love stories tell of how love hurts."

They returned to the apartment, walked the dog, ordered in, and watched some ridiculously pretentious art film by a friend of Genie's. Anna hadn't felt this normal in a long time.

Before she climbed into the cab to go to the airport, Genie embraced Anna tightly and kissed her on the lips. Then she folded three fingers together and cast a quick sign of the cross over Anna, as if darning a hole in her friend's aura.

Genie's visit hadn't exorcised Yaret, but her presence was now superimposed on the memory of him, dulling its intensity. Most days, Anna felt okay, if a bit fragmented. Some days, she was absolutely sure about seeing the things she'd seen, the supernatural being nothing but another layer of the natural. Other days, she thought of the Otherworld as an internal journey, a spiritual experience outside of the physical. And on yet other days, she was sure the neurons of her brain were misfiring, making her mind re-create an elaborate hallucination.

When she returned to Bellevue to pick up her books and notes, she made a point to avoid seeing any of the people she knew, except Dr. Stevens, who was glad to hear that Anna was in treatment. Dr. Stevens also let her know that the lawsuit against the hospital filed by the ex-con's lawyer had been found without merit.

A few times Anna had coffee with Michael Campbell, who eagerly shared the latest gossip. Her resignation had officially been presented as health related. Contrary to her fears, nobody bad-mouthed her behind her back after she left the program so abruptly.

Worse than being dismissed as a quitter, she had been terrified that her crossing the line into the patient category would make her a pariah in the eyes of her former colleagues, but according to Michael, the effect was diametrically opposite. Her presumed diagnosis of PTSD had an air of nobility, like a battle scar received on the front line. Even Thomas, her constant rival, had expressed regret that she'd left. There was almost a sense of professional envy, as if by experiencing a mental breakdown Anna had empirically gained an exclusive, privileged knowledge most of her colleagues gathered from books.

"You're officially *the wounded healer*," Michael told her as they sat in a coffee shop near Gramercy Park. "Being able to relate to a patient on a deeply personal level is a priceless gift for a therapist."

"I never aspired to becoming a therapist. I'm not like you, Michael, not a natural."

"I don't think there is such a thing. It's natural for any human being to seek and create bonds. All a therapist does is offer a safe space to exercise this need."

"Intellectually, I understand." Anna told him. "But lately, I find myself uncertain about my own inner workings, let alone the emotional landscape of another soul."

"I think what's important is not so much having certainty, but the ability to cope with uncertainty. If not knowing generates anxiety, then accepting a degree of unknowability alleviates it."

"But if I am an unsure counselor, how can I facilitate change in a patient? How does one help another person change?"

Michael glanced at her sidewise, as if tempted to share a secret and contemplating the risk. Anna looked away. She knew this hesitation. She herself had always chosen silence, and now its weight made her shoulders ache.

"You know, I used to be into conspiracy theories during my goth years—"

"You, goth?" Despite herself, Anna burst into laughter.

"Hey, I wasn't with the in-crowd in high school. For me it was either the goth kids or the skaters, and I can't skate to save my life." Michael rolled his eyes. "Anyway, I came across this little book online, called *KUBARK Interrogation Manual*. It's a CIA guide to torture from the Cold War times. That book is what shaped me."

Anna stopped laughing and stared in disbelief. While it was comically weird to imagine Michael Campbell, a mild-mannered young man from a middle-class Black family, as a goth kid, it was inconceivable that a torture manual could have been the bedtime reading of a man as dedicated to social justice as he was.

"This book convinced me not only of the blatant inhumanity but the total impracticality of torture." Michael lowered his voice. "Think about it: one says just about anything to avoid pain, while the other dies before he reveals anything; in either case, the intel you get is unreliable. Anyway, what struck me the most is how spectacularly plastic the human mind is. It can't be broken, but it can be bent. See, it's possible to get around the subject's strongest moral prohibitions. For instance, if you order someone to kill his beloved mother, he'd die before he did it. However, if you convince him it's not his mother but an impostor, an alien, a demon who took her form, and by killing it he'll be freeing his real mother . . . see what I'm getting at?"

"I understand. Data disagreeing with deeply rooted concepts doesn't become informative, it remains white noise. To become information, it has to interact within a context, so the notions must be adjusted to accommodate the contradictory command."

"When I was a kid," said Michael, "I often felt unfree. Pressed by parents, by teachers. By bullies. This book helped me realize the thing that made me want to become a counselor, and it was profoundly liberating on a personal level." He paused for dramatic effect.

"Which is?" obliged Anna.

"No one can make a human soul do anything."

They sat in silence for a while, he enjoying the impression his story made, she digesting his words.

"But if no one can make a human soul do anything," she said slowly, "How can you make a soul let go of its demons?"

"You can't. The soul will still have its demons. But you can try to make it so that the demons no longer have that soul."

"No way you're dragging it home. Give me that!"

The pit bull's wide maw obediently sprang open, flashing a fleshy pink tongue and two rows of glistening teeth, eerily white in the dimming light. The stick, or rather, the massive log he'd been carrying around, thumped on the frozen ground in front of Anna's boots. The dog looked up at her expectantly, ready to play fetch. Overcoming her squeamishness, Anna picked up the saliva-smeared gnarly branch, made a wide swing, and pretended to throw. As the dog shot in the direction of the throw all the way across the dog run, Anna quietly shoved the piece of wood into the trash bin by the bench. She watched the dog search in vain, his powerful black body almost invisible in the descending dusk; he returned to her wagging his tail and laying back his cropped ears with an apologetic expression on his mug. She registered a sharp pang of guilt for deceiving the simple-minded creature who trusted her so explicitly.

"What, didn't find it? It's okay, I forgive you." Anna patted his scruff with the tips of her fingers. "You're such a sucker, you know that?"

After three months of living with a dog, she was still ambivalent about the whole arrangement. The dog owners' guides she'd studied were marginally helpful: she had developed a healthy routine of feedings and workouts, but in her heart she never knew what was right for him, was afraid to touch him most of the time. Her anxiety dissipated only at night, when Black Shuck curled up by her side in bed, and they snuggled into each other like two animals yearning for comfort.

Out of the corner of her eye, Anna saw a young woman stop and lean over the fence. For a moment Anna worried she was some neighborhood busybody compelled to express her distrust of the breed, but when she looked closer she saw the woman smile.

"Aren't pitties great," said the woman in a conspiratorial tone, as if extending a secret handshake from one pit bull lover to another. Anna grinned back.

"What's his name?"

"Shuck."

The woman giggled. "As in "all shook up"?"

"As in Black Shuck."

"Is it from a movie?"

"It's some mythological reference, I'm not sure. It's not my dog." Anna pulled the dog closer, fastening the leash to his collar. "Take care," she said to the woman as she led the dog out of the gate.

"You, too," replied the woman and took off running, like she heard a starter pistol.

Apparently, the fellow pit bull enthusiast was a jogger, a part of a quiet but never-ending stream of people in the park's paths, some bolting, some shuffling away from something and toward something else. As the woman's tight behind disappeared in the distance, Anna realized she never looked the woman in the eyes as they exchanged pleasantries. Not that she, once a cross-country runner herself, had anything against casual joggers, although as she walked the large scary-looking dog, she often got glares from them.

She knew firsthand about runner's high, and since she had begun working with drug addicts daily at the shelter, she had often considered the sad irony: those who chase after the perfect moment never stand still enough to enjoy it. Always on the move to escape something, to catch up with something, whatever their want or need. Never present.

And no different from them was she, either reliving a sensation of being alive or anticipating another chance to feel it. The only times she'd been present in the moment were with Yaret.

The dog coughed. She hadn't noticed her arm had jerked the leash.

"Well, what do you want," she grumbled, loosening the grip. "It's his fault you're stuck with me. He brought you in. You're his dog. Don't like how I treat you? Go live with him, wherever that is."

Black Shuck blinked his beady eyes and laid back his ear stumps. There was no point taking it out on him, he was a sweet stupid dog, as submissive as he was scary looking. Nothing is what it seems.

"But if nothing is what it seems, then neither is it whatever it doesn't seem," she recited in time to her steps and chuckled to herself, so sagaciously-idiotic did this idea sound, like something Yaret would utter.

Suddenly light-headed, she sat down on the nearest park bench. The dog put his heavy head on her lap, staring her in the eyes. His eyes were like small amber drops against the black velvet of his face. He sighed.

"I know, Shuckie, I know. You're still waiting for him."

In the meantime, someone was waiting for her. After he had Anna hospitalized for an acute psychotic break, Ted behaved as if they were still together. He checked on her every day at the hospital even though she refused visitors. He called; she didn't pick up, so he showed up at her apartment. Their first post-breakdown conversation had left things mercifully uncertain. As weeks went by, Anna's time became consumed by therapy and her new job. They'd eaten out a few times, but hadn't touched each other beyond an awkward hug. Ted was nothing but tactful, yet Anna couldn't help but wondering if his generous patience with her was self-serving, a ritual performed for a long-dead god by an obsolete cleric clinging to a false sense of purpose.

A week after Genie returned to London, Anna, who had been dodging Ted's calls, decided it was time. It would have been in bad taste postponing the inevitable conversation till too close to Valentine's Day. She asked to see him at his place.

As she waited for the local uptown train on the subway platform, she braced herself for a wyssun in the shadows. A downtown express train barreled by the opposite platform, its windows shining a discrete frame-by-frame reflection in which she recognized her own broken silhouette. With unfocused eyes, she observed the optical illusion of her ghostly presencc among the people on the platform across the tracks, and for a moment it felt as if she were seeing with true sight.

"Why don't you take off your coat," Ted spoke calmly, but his voice was brittle.

"Sure." She took off her coat and sat on the couch, keeping the coat on her lap like a security blanket.

She watched Ted move around his living room as if he didn't know what to do with himself.

"How's the new job?"

"It's good."

"I'm not asking you how you're feeling."

"I appreciate it." She smiled. "But I'm all right. Therapy three times a week plus twenty mil of Paxil daily does the trick."

Hearing her speak his language made it easier for him to look her in the eyes.

"Any side effects?" His businesslike tone couldn't conceal genuine care.

"Not that I can tell."

"No weight gain then. I mean, you look good."

"Thanks."

"It's good to see you back here." He stood next to the couch, towering over her. She'd forgotten how large he was, even with his shoulders hunched.

"I don't think we can continue seeing each other, Teddy." She took his keys out of her purse and laid them on the coffee table, trying not to make them jingle.

"Is this why you wanted to come over? Wanted to give me a home turf advantage?"

"Your stuff at my place, I've packed it," she continued, looking up at him. "I'll leave the box with your doorman."

"Why are you doing this, Ann?'

She looked down. "Because we can't go on like this. I am sorry for causing you pain, and I don't want to cause any more. But my life's unraveled, and to patch it together, I need to trim the loose ends."

"Is this what I am to you? A loose end?"

Anna sighed. Trying to avoid clichés, she'd swayed into rudeness. "I'm sorry, I'm not the most eloquent. By loose end I mean myself, not you."

"Ah, the usual "it's me not you" routine."

"But it is me. It's always been me."

"It's a bit presumptuous, don't you think?" he broke out bitterly.

"It is what it is, Teddy. I'm sorry."

"Are you seeing anyone new?"

She shook her head.

"How about that man?"

"Ted, if you mean the former client you saw with me, that was the last time I saw him as well. He is gone." She hoped testiness in her voice would mask guilt. "That was never real."

"Do you still have feelings for him?"

"If you mean feelings of frustration—yes, I do." That she meant.

Ted nodded. His shoulders relaxed. "Would you like a drink? I mean, nonalcoholic." He took a heavy step toward the kitchen. "I've got Pepsi. I got it for you."

"Ted," she called after him. "Stop. Look at me. I'm not the same anymore."

He came over and sat down. For a moment they sat next to each other, both staring at the house keys on the coffee table in front of them. Anna turned her face to him and waited.

"What happened—happened," he said finally. "We all go through changes. We can start again."

"We can." She put her hand on his arm. "I can't."

"You will get better."

"But it will still be me."

"I'll give you as much time as you need. As much space as you need. We can still work it out together. You know we can. We're both good people—"

"Yes, we are both good people. You'll love me because it's unconscionable to fall out of love with an injured partner, and I'll love you for that. You'll make a point never to remind me about your sacrifice, and I'll make a point to stay injured out of gratitude. Our mutually perpetuated martyrdom will become the essence of our lives, it will grow, and eventually this cross will bury us both under its weight. I don't want that. We both deserve better."

His eyes welled up. He reached out to her, and she came into his embrace, resting her head on his wide chest. She had always felt small in his arms. Now it was too tight, like clothes she'd outgrown. Perhaps, she'd never been meant to feel small.

"It's good," he whispered in her ear. "Isn't it?"

"It is." She gently freed herself. "But I must go."

"I love you, Ann."

She stood up. The words *I love you too* quivered in the back of her throat, ready to slip off her tongue. Speaking them would have made everything so much easier, she wouldn't even have had to lie. But words themselves were the untruth. The truth was beyond words.

"I'm not sure I know what it means, Teddy. To love. I'm not sure I know how."

Spring

Three months passed before Anna told her therapist—who, she was sure, had long seen through her awkward understatements—that she was still harboring feelings for her last client. She stayed within a reasonable frame of reference. She described her initial high hopes, her ambitious plans to use the amnesiac's case for her dissertation, the intellectual fascination he presented from the start; how the fascination became more personal, and how his insight into her own subconscious mind resonated with her. She confessed to violating the rules by bringing him into her apartment, her struggle to keep the relationship professional, and how, one after another, her concessions to him turned their dynamic on its head.

Short of describing the otherworldly magic Yaret had revealed to her, Anna truthfully recapped the events, including the final horribly humiliating detail.

"In retrospect, I am grateful it didn't end with sex. It would have made the whole experience disastrous. I should be thanking him for walking out on me. I should count my blessings and go on with my life. But I can't. I guess, if I understood his motivation, if I could make sense of it, I could move on. What did I do to make him react this way?"

"You seem to assume both responsibility and blame for his inability, or reluctance, to consummate your relationship sexually. Why is that?"

She thought of Ted. "Because I'm presumptuous like that."

"You are, of course, familiar with attachment theory," said her therapist in a tone of tactful affirmation. "It primarily deals with the dynamics of infant-caregiver relationships. It is common for a child who'd been abandoned by a caregiver to assume responsibility for the adult's leaving.

In the context of a dysfunctional romantic relationships, being terrified of both intimacy and abandonment, evading commitment for fear of vulnerability, leaving first to avoid being left—all are the markers of an avoidant type. Makes sense?"

"Of course! Yar—John left me because he was afraid I'd leave him, is this what you mean?"

"No, this not what I mean," replied her therapist patiently. "It would be unethical and, frankly, impractical for me to claim to understand a third party's motivations. The only understanding that'll help heal your wound is the understanding of yourself."

So, this was not about Yaret, but about her. Anna cringed. She hated being pinned like an insect, labeled and boxed in one of the myriad boxes in the endless storage unit of academic cases. She was well acquainted with both the storage and the box—hell, she'd studied the same insect collection. The specimen wasn't at all exotic, a dime a dozen: an awkward girl-child who'd never gotten enough love from Daddy and learned to earn love only to reject it, because being loved for a reason is as worthless as not being loved at all.

"I know a loss of a parent is a red flag for abandonment issues, but I don't see how this is applicable here. Yes, I've experienced trauma in my youth. But I've recovered. I have a stable, loving relationship with my family. I have a deep connection with a female best friend. I may not have been that keen on commitment in the past, but I do. . . did have a solid relationship with my fiancé, at least until recently. . . I am not a victim." She heard hysterical notes creeping into her voice as she spoke; she paused before she finished: "I was the responsible one in the relationship with my client, and if I accept the responsibility, I must accept the blame."

"Refusing the role of a victim doesn't mean assuming the role of a villain."

"It's hopeless no matter how I look at it. Either I took advantage of a sick man, or a sick man took advantage of me."

"Isn't double bind a bitch."

"But I didn't ask him to leave, I mean, not then," Anna continued hotly. "He was about to get what he wanted when he walked out."

"How can you be sure of what he wanted?"

"Sex, what else. But then he says he wants to marry me and have children with me." She rolled her eyes. "Quite a turn-off that was."

"It's not unreasonable to be turned off by an idea of marrying a homeless and unemployed man, no matter how physically attractive."

Anna bristled. Social inequality was the least of the obstacles between them. She wanted to explain how little lack of domicile and gainful employment mattered to a magical creature adroit at playing the silver strings of creation, but it wasn't the language she spoke in therapy.

"It's not that," she mumbled, wringing her hands.

"What about children? Is that something unacceptable to you, a deal breaker?"

"It's not that! I'm good with kids, I practically raised my brother. But his idea of a happy family is seven children. Seven! I mean, I wasn't even sure I wanted to keep his dog."

"Do you regret keeping his dog?"

Anna thought of Shuck, his big powerful body curled up against the hollow of her belly, taking so little space. When he laid his heavy head on her lap, his amber eyes looked into hers with complete trust, leaving her no choice but to offer him the same trust. The privilege of knowing he could easily snap her wrist with his mighty jaws, and yet never would, blew her away every time.

"It's not that. I've always wanted a dog."

They sat in silence for a bit, her therapist holding the pause.

"I suppose he didn't offer me anything I didn't want." Anna stared at her hands.

"Let's talk about what it is you want."

"What I want is impossible."

"What is it?" asked the therapist with the smile of someone who'd heard everything.

"I want to love and be loved in return, to be needed out of free choice, not weakness. I want bonds, but also freedom. I want to parent without losing myself in my children. I want a fine home without turning into a slave to possessions, and a work that gives me a sense of accomplishment without draining my soul. I want to know the secrets of the universe without being embittered by my knowledge. Plus, mind-blowing sex. I know one can have some of it, not all of it, but I want it all," she caught her breath, "and I want it guilt-free."

The smile grew wider.

"Well, the last part is something we can work on."

About four months into her treatment, Anna's sessions were reduced from three times to once a week. According to her therapist, the diagnosis of PTSD wasn't applicable to her any longer, if ever at all. Her tendency to self-incriminate was a different story.

Every once in a while, Anna still tried to turn their conversation to Yaret, although she'd never called him by his true name, referring to him as John Fairfax when she brought up her botched case, and John Y when she talked about the fashion model.

Her therapist gave her space but didn't indulge. They had talked at length about her fear of abandonment and tendency to self-blame. Intellectually, Anna was fully aware of her issues, could recite all the instances where she had either reenacted or worked through them. By now the very thought of Yaret had become a marker for many other thoughts, and sometimes she was unsure if his name had a meaning or had become an abstract signifier for a more abstract idea. Still, every session wound down to the same subject.

"I know when I ask myself why he had to leave, I'm only a little girl asking why Daddy had to die. I guess the impossibility of getting an answer makes it impossible to get any sort of closure."

"Are you familiar with gestalt techniques?"

"You mean the empty chair improv?" Anna didn't mean to sound dismissive. Although gestalt therapy wasn't highly regarded by her clinical psychology professors, Ted had mentioned successfully using the techniques with his adolescent patients, and some of Genie's actor friends raved about it.

"Why don't you visualize the person in question over in the opposite corner of the sofa, and communicate your questions. Then, assume the seat and respond, reversing the role."

Her therapist encouraged her to take her time and think it over, limiting her first try to three question and three answers. Anna twirled a strand of her hair, and turned to the empty space.

"Here goes nothing." She imagined Yaret curled up in the corner with his feet up, hugging his knees, tipping his head like a curious dog, training his attentive eyes on her. She took a breath, and spoke:

"Who are you? Why did you lie to me? Why did you leave?"

She took the place of the imaginary Yaret. The upholstery felt cool, like everything must have felt to him, who was always hot as if running a fever. She heard herself say:

"I told you who I am, you chose not to accept it. I never lied to you, you refused to believe me. I left because you didn't love me."

She put her hand over her mouth, but the words had already escaped. Catching her panicked glance, her therapist motioned for her to resume her original place.

"How do you feel?"

"It's true," exhaled Anna. "I wanted him, but I didn't love him. I wouldn't know how. I've never loved a man. I don't know if I ever loved my own father enough to learn how."

She was aware that the Yaret she'd talked to was a mere reflection of the real Yaret in the depth of her own pupil, a facet of her own self. A few months ago, glimpsing this reflection of herself would have left her consumed with guilt, and then anger, and then more guilt. Now, she welcomed the insight, not as the triumph of solving an intellectual puzzle, but as a simple relief from pain.

"So, how does it make you feel?"

"Like it's time to let go."

It was then that her therapist suggested Anna could begin tapering out of her meds.

Since Anna decided she'd never loved Yaret, the thought that he'd never loved her no longer hurt as badly. It's fair, she kept telling herself, we're even. She was sobering up from both the high of his presence and the hangover of his absence.

The writing project she'd undertaken at her therapist's suggestion had an unexpected effect. As she tried to faithfully retell her journey into the Otherworld and back, Anna observed that she was reliving not only the experience, but also her memories of the experience, and the memories of experiencing the memories. With the melancholic detachment of a scientist, she noted each instance of self-referential semantics and the archetypal Jungian imagery behind each character.

There was teenaged Anna the Child, as selfish as she was lovelorn. There was Anna the Self, struggling to do the right thing. There was Anna the clumsy arrogant tomboy, the way the Skiers saw her—the Persona. There was the sunny boy she was in love with, young Anna's Animus. There were the adult Alvan males, benevolent or threatening, as incomprehensibly alien as men are to a young girl. There were the monsters of many faces—the wyssun—who could be anywhere, even inside of her. There was the Scout, able to travel between worlds disguised as a homeless drifter she was pretty sure she'd passed by in the street—the wise teacher, her Helper both in the wyssun world and in the real New York. And of course, more real than real, there was Lord Yaret—the Trickster, the Shadow, but also her silver mirror who insisted on showing her the reflection of her true self no matter how much she turned away.

Rereading the written account of her adventure, she was surprised by how much it sounded like a children's story, something she'd have read to Jack. She shared it with Genie, who immediately proposed to turn it into a script for a stage play.

"Zombies are all the rage now," she said with her characteristic flippancy. "Isn't that what your Skiers are, like, hot undead teenage boys from different cultures and eras?"

"They are not undead!" cried Anna, rightly appalled. "Skiers are brought into the Otherworld at the moment of their death, yes, but they are not zombies. They are perfectly normal boys. Immortal boys. Who don't retain any conscious memories and don't know any motivation but hunting the wyssun—but no, they are not zombies!"

"But the Alva are really elves, aren't they?"

"Oh, I don't know, Gen! They do have long ears and they do have technology that looks like magic—Clarke's Third Law and all that—but they are aliens. Extraterrestrials. Extradimentionals."

"Whatever, as long as they are hot. I can totally see this: a young heroine accidentally falls into a parallel world where she has to face monsters, both real and her own. It's the Alice in the Wonder-fucking-land for the 21st century, complete with zombies and aliens!"

Curiously, Anna's therapist never asked to read her story, and for that Anna was grateful.

She never had any more of the vivid dream-memories Yaret's closeness had brought. The dreams she could recall were now mundane, easily traced to the sensory impressions of the previous day. In her waking hours, though, she kept seeing things, and not just the usual monsters in the dark. Every so often, an elm leaf, mottled like an inscribed parchment, would blow in from nowhere and lie at her feet in the middle of a busy intersection; a shadow made by a torn wire fence of a construction site would create a geometric, almost runic pattern in the dust; a seagull, too far away from the shore, would leave lines of wet scribble-like tracks on the polished granite cornice of the hotel down the street. In moments like those, it seemed to Anna all she needed was to see with true sight, and she could read the messages the universe was sending her. Anna rationalized that is was no more than her human brain utilizing its natural acumen at pattern-discernment, yet, sometimes, she would take off her glasses, and the cityscape, reflected in her nearsighted eyes as a painting in broad careless strokes, was rich with meaning so profound it didn't require interpretation.

Meanwhile, as Yaret dispelled into an abstract, John Y was coalescing into something concrete. Once, she was delivering some paperwork to the Housing offices down at Federal Plaza and saw a familiar Switch billboard with a huge chunk of paper ripped out of the middle, as if it had been fired upon by a cannon—likely vandalized by someone miffed by the pseudo-Nazi uniform. Looking at the tear, she thought of the hole Yaret had left in her heart, how he'd ripped through the fabric of her life, leaving it frayed at the edges, and kept shooting into space like a comet.

I'm not even holding on to the comet's tail, she noted with a new sense of wonderment, I am holding on to the edges of the hole.

A couple of times, she furtively leafed through scented fashion magazines at bookstores, looking for his angular face. The notorious Switch ads showed up once or twice in different versions, all featuring John Y as both the aggressor and the prey. Once, on a whim, she picked up a European art photography magazine and found a series of tightly cropped close-ups of John Y with a stunning ebony-skinned female model, their limbs entwined in complex and coolly asexual positions, juxtaposing the contrast of their skin. It was so beauteous she couldn't even feel jealous. Another time, she indulged in an online search—something she promised herself to avoid—and found a Facebook page of some Midwestern boy trying to make it as a model in Los Angeles, who was "giving mad props to his man John Y" for "being awesome" during a grueling job in Rome, which was the boy's first trip abroad. In some of the group selfies, she recognized a familiar face.

So, a man without a Social Security card now had a passport. Ahead of her, again. Anna tried to appreciate the irony: the only exotic destination she'd visited, not counting the Otherworld, was Saint Croix on spring break, specifically because it didn't require a passport. John Y, the fashion model, was even farther away from her than Yaret, the lord of the Otherworld.

At work, she still hauled laundry and trash bags in between processing intake, managing paperwork, and performing "other duties as assigned." But week after week, the "other duties" included more and more of actual case work. At first, it was making phone calls and writing letters, hacking through the government red tape on behalf of the shelter residents. Soon, one after another, the residents began to seek her out for a piece of advice or a conversation. It started casually, like sitting with Serena through the wee hours of the night to help her curb her nicotine cravings till morning, or like finding a clever resolution to the long-standing feud between Jamison and Don. Then the word got out about her helping Mike through his crack relapse, which, if discovered, would have gotten him kicked out of the shelter. Soon, the program director suggested that Anna's "other duties" should also cover a substance abuse counseling group.

"Your training is sufficient," she said. "Until you get the formal certification, you could do the work under the facility's mentorship program."

Anna was going to explain that she wasn't a clinician and didn't have a therapist's talent, but self-deprecation was a luxury she could no longer afford. Three months into her job, she was leading two groups and worked several individual cases in the official capacity of a shelter's trainee counselor.

"Our sessions are becoming less like personal therapy and more like professional supervision," noted her therapist at one point, and Anna realized she hadn't talked about Yaret in a while.

Her mind's eye had been turned inward for so long that spring in the city caught her unawares. One morning in early March, while walking the dog, she noticed an arrogant daffodil shoot breaking through the tarp of mulch. Still-naked trees had their limbs swollen with buds, and from afar the crowns looked as if they were veiled with shimmering golden-green organza. The winter was over.

Except for regular visits with her parents and an occasional coffee with Michael, Anna didn't go out at all. She hadn't seen Ted since she'd returned his keys. The box with his stuff had been left with his doorman. When she found two DVDs belonging to him, instead of going to his home again, she decided to drop them off at his office in a building off Lexington Avenue. It was one of those typical old New York prewar high-rises, boxy and multitiered in the way of a Babylonian ziggurat; fittingly, Ted's office space was built like a labyrinth in consideration of his clients' need for privacy, so that the arriving and departing patients never ran into each other. She hoped to leave the small package with his receptionist without having to talk to him.

The elevator doors opened. Anna, who hadn't been expecting to see anyone, narrowly avoided bumping into a young Asian girl who was getting on. At the last second, the girl swayed aside, giving her a wide berth, much wider than necessary. There was something irregular about it, and Anna, despite herself, stepped back into the elevator.

The girl was about fifteen or sixteen, stocky, ordinary looking except for an out-of-place resolute and grim expression on her round, still childlike face. Somehow, her compact body filled the space, making Anna back into the wall. Without glancing at her, the girl pushed the T-button for Terrace. With a soft tug, the elevator went up.

The top of the girl's head barely reached Anna's chest. Her hair was shiny, the same bluish black as the patent leather of her loafers, and Anna fought the impulse to lean in and sniff the girl's head. She was sure it smelled like water. Water and lightning. Anna closed her eyes and inhaled, but instead of the smell she distinctly heard a soft grating of scales. And pain. The creature was in pain. It was exhausted by doubt and despair. It wanted the pain to stop.

The lurch of the stopping elevator returned her to reality. She opened her eyes: the girl had already exited; the doors were closing. Anna slammed her body in between the sliding doors and leaped out. The corridor was empty. Panicked, she looked left and right. The girl was gone. Anna pulled in air sharply through her nose in a mad hope to pick up her scent. Instead, she heard a door bang, and she ran to the roof exit. Vaguely, she thought of Ted mentioning something about terrace access in his office building, how uncomfortable he'd felt with the low parapet on a terrace twenty stories above street level.

Her heart pounding, Anna pushed the door and was at once blinded. It took her a few seconds to see a small dark figure against the unbearably bright spring sky. The girl was standing on the ledge, only a low metal railing separating her from the clouds floating in the indifferent windows of neighboring skyscrapers.

Anna took a careful step. Gravel crunched under her foot, the girl's shoulders twitched. Realizing she'd been discovered, Anna froze.

"It's not what you think." The girl's voice was thin and raspy.

"You don't know what I think."

"You think I want to jump," the girl said with contempt.

"You think you can fly."

The girl's plump mouth twisted in a disdainful wince, like she'd already heard anything Anna could say and wasn't about to dignify it. She swung her legs over the metal railing and stood on its outer side, holding on with awkwardly twisted hands.

"You are not going to fly," continued Anna, making an inhuman effort to stay in her place. "You are not that kind of dragon."

The girl blinked and cast a sidewise glance at her. For a split second, distrust and hope battled in her eyes. Distrust won. She frowned.

"Are you a psychiatrist?"

"A psychologist."

"So, you've overheard my session with Dr. Newman. Guess it's not as confidential as he promises."

"I smelled a dragon on the elevator." The girl looked at her again, and Anna allowed herself to smile. "Also, the sound your scales make. You're pretty noticeable . . . what's your name?"

"Emily," replied the girl, bewildered.

"You're pretty noticeable, Emily," repeated Anna. "I'm no expert, but, as far as I can tell, you are a water dragon. You don't even have wings."

Emily's mouth fell open, she blinked and frowned, struggling.

"Come down." Anna motioned with her head, making sure her hands stayed submissively still. She heard the familiar metallic buzz of anxiety in her ears—a knot at the pit of her stomach was tightening. Half-consciously, half by instinct, Anna unfolded the line and threw it to the girl on the ledge, a desperate protective tendril.

"Who are you?"

"My name is Anna Reilly."

"Can you . . . see me?"

"Come down, Emily."

Emily glared. Her little hands were clasping the railing so hard her knuckles were white.

"I will come down," she said firmly, "if you tell me my colors, exactly."

Anna shook her head. "It's not like that. I don't have true sight . . . exactly."

Emily frowned again and leaned forward on her outstretched arms. A gust of wind ripped through her hair, throwing it over her face. An impossibly bright color flashed, igniting the silver string stretched taught between her and Anna.

"Blue!" Anna shouted. "The scales are blue, and the belly is . . . what do you call it, turquoise?"

Emily made a gasping sound and fell backwards, like jerked with a rope. In one giant leap, Anna covered the space between them and caught the small body in her arms. The girl was surprisingly heavy.

"I was not going to jump," she moaned into Anna's shoulder in between sobs. "I was here because . . . I don't know why! Please don't leave me! I don't want to be alone."

For the next hour, Anna sat across from Emily in a corner Starbucks, her coffee long cold, listening to the girl's breathless speech.

Emily Xiǎo Coleman, who had recently turned sixteen, had been adopted from a Guangzhou orphanage as a baby by a mature, educated Caucasian couple who adored her and did their best to avoid the usual pitfalls of transracial adoption, neither parading her as an exotic pet nor whitewashing her in a misguided attempt at colorblindness. According to Emily, they encouraged the conversation about race and were attentive to any sign of racism their daughter encountered. Ironically, the most negativity Emily had experienced was from Asian American kids of first-generation immigrants, who saw her as a privileged White. As far as Anna could tell, Emily was, precisely as Ted had described, well-adjusted. Until her, as she put it, "awakening" began.

"I always felt taller than I am and bigger, like I take up more space. I didn't mind, only I always felt not accurately represented, you know? One day, about a year ago, I looked at my reflection in the water, and saw my real self. I wasn't even scared, it all started to make sense."

Despite her bravado, Emily's first impulse was to look up psychiatric diagnoses online. Soon—but not before a scarring experience with some bizarre fetish porn sites—she stumbled upon the dragonkin community.

"Dragonkin?" repeated Anna, not believing her ears. "Isn't it a video game character?"

"No, that's dragonborn," Emily waved her hand dismissively. "This has nothing to do with roleplaying. Dragonkin are people who are dragons on the inside."

Her research made her comfortable enough to tell her parents, who predictably made an appointment with a psychiatrist. Since she hadn't acted out in any disruptive way, she didn't check out for any other disorder except persistent delusion, that's what Dr. Newman told them. At the mention of Ted, Anna's jaw began to ache.

"Emily, I might have to inform Ted, I mean Dr. Newman, about your suicide attempt. God, this is complicated . . ."

"But it wasn't! If you tell him it was, he'll have me locked up in a hospital on suicide watch. Do you know what it's like, being a patient in a mental hospital?"

"As a matter of fact, I do."

Emily's pudgy hands rolled into fists. "If you saw me, you'd know I wasn't going to jump."

"I don't know what I saw," said Anna honestly. "I am as confused as you are. Besides, I am not your therapist; he is."

"I thought you were different." Emily's eyes welled up, and Anna noted with amazement that even in her despair, this young girl was a powerful presence. Her tears were not of weakness, but of righteous indignation. "I thought you could help."

"Dr. Newman is better equipped—"

"He's put me on Risperidone." Emily sneered. "It doesn't do anything, except make me gain weight. My parents worry I'm developing body dysmorphia when I say I'm big. But I don't mind. My true form is big."

Anna wanted to tell the girl there was nothing wrong with her weight, but the way Emily said it was full of such dignity that Anna's well-intended assurance would have been out of place. Emily didn't want encouragement of her self-acceptance. She needed acknowledgment of her self-perception.

"He's, like, "your ideas are not reality-based"," continued Emily. "It's not fair! You know, a person can say they're a boy in a girl's body because, guess what, there is such a thing as transgender people, and it's not okay to be a bigot to them. But if I say I'm a water dragon in a human body, it's okay to call me delusional. How am I delusional, if it's my reality?"

Anna took off her glasses and rubbed the bridge of her nose. She thought of Yaret telling her about the random mixing of essences from different realms, causing alien souls to be born within human shape, tormented by their existence in a wrong body. This kind of body dysmorphia was different from anything she'd studied. She was out of her depth.

"I don't think it's appropriate to compare a transgender person to a—"

"Otherkin. We're called otherkin, as in kinship to the other than human."

"Fine, otherkin. What does it mean to be an otherkin?"

"Different things for different kin, although similar in some ways. For me, it means looking in the mirror and seeing a double image: a human girl and a reptilian creature. It means being drawn to mythology as if it were personal history. It means to experience phantom limbs, except it's the whole phantom body that sometimes itches, sometimes hurts, and sometimes is full of power beyond the strength of a normal girl. It means experiencing the world incomparably more clearly than anyone around me, feeling deeper, feeling differently."

Anna shuddered. Emily's words echoed Yaret's, almost precisely: "Perceive the world incomparably more clearly . . . feeling incomparably deeper . . ." The words he used to explain his Alvan senses to her on their first morning together, when she put her hands on him for the first time. She felt lightheaded.

"I'm tired of fighting with my parents about it," said Emily, oblivious to Anna's struggle. "I'm tired of their either treating it as a mental illness, or being all culturally sensitive about it, like it's some kind of metaphor for being Asian."

"How is it between you and your parents?"

"It's fine. At least it used to be, until, you know, I told them. But they're great, really. They don't deserve this either." Emily swallowed. "You're a psychologist. Can you be mine?"

"What are you talking about?"

"Can you take me on as your patient?"

"No, I can't. I am not a certified therapist, I can't take private clients. Emily, there is nothing more I want than to help you, but I am not in the position to do so."

Emily was quiet for a minute, staring at her hands, then looked up at Anna and said seriously, "You've already helped. You saw the real me. Blue and turquoise."

Anna wanted to tell the girl that she'd lied, that blue and turquoise was nothing but a lucky guess. She wasn't wearing the crystal necklace; the vision of a dragon wasn't as apparent as the otherworldly sights Yaret used to manifest before her eyes. She couldn't be sure where her glimpse of Emily as a dragon had come from, whether its source was the same affliction that made her discern wyssuns in the shadows, or whether it was a product of something even less tangible—therapeutic intuition telling her that, instead of looking for the dragon inside a little girl, she should have been looking for a little girl inside of the dragon.

A raspy voice sang about the lizard shedding its tail, making Anna listen in. Apparently, Starbucks's music selection now included old Genesis. Peter Gabriel recited his parting council for the ancient children, and Anna felt inspired.

"Why is it so important to be acknowledged as a dragon?"

Emily frowned. "I have the right to my truth. It makes me miserable to lie about something that's a big part of me."

"What would make you happy, Emily? How would you want your parents to acknowledge your truth? Do you want them to run screaming from a monster? Do you want them to worship you as a god? Do you want them to study you as an exotic animal?"

"No! I just want to be understood."

"It's a tall order. Human beings barely understand themselves, let alone others, especially when it comes to the matters of the soul. I don't know if it's even possible to fully understand others. But it is possible to accept each other without the condition of understanding."

"Like, unconditional love?"

"Yes. Look, you and your parents have different genes biologically, but it doesn't stop you from loving each other. Does it matter if you belong to different species in spirit?"

Emily gave her a long look. "It doesn't," she said after a pause. "I didn't think about it like that."

Anna looked at her watch.

"So, this is it for today," Emily's voice was comically heartfelt. Anna guessed she was aping Ted. "Thanks for the Frappuccino. And the talk. You're good at this, you know. And don't worry about me. I know flying is not my thing. My thing is swimming. Last year I ranked top twenty in the Manhattan Island Marathon Swim, the youngest female swimmer to circle the island."

Anna didn't fool herself. What she'd achieved with Emily was no therapeutic breakthrough. She was no trained therapist, no master of *the talking cure.* All she did was clumsily patch up a dreadful tear much above her level of craftsmanship. She kept replaying her conversation with Emily in her head, hoping she hadn't made things worse by indulging the girl's experiential anomaly. By encouraging the young girl to focus away from the core of her drama, had she steered her toward better adjustment or conformity?

The research on the otherkin phenomenon Anna conducted over the next few days left her ambivalent. Otherkin was an umbrella term for people who self-identified as nonhuman. The most common kintypes seemed to be animals, real (naturally, wolves but also big cats) and legendary (unicorns and dragons). Predictably, only the cool beasts made the list: nobody identified with the naked mole rat or the blobfish. Also, miscellaneous mythological humanoids appeared often, particularly—here Anna burst into nervous laughter—elves.

The subculture had a virtual community of sorts, spread over several social media platforms and pre-social media forums. There, mileage varied.

The more flamboyant folks fashioned themselves into a perfect target for internet trolls by inventing new kintypes after pretty much anything, from random anime characters to food stuffs. Others were serious, achingly sincere, and deeply closeted. Those were likely to propose rational explanations for their experience of otherness, from defining a type of body dysmorphic disorder ("species dysphoria"), to suggesting a specific genetic combination or brain morphology, to interpreting the whole thing as a spiritual experience.

Anna was the last person to diagnose an anonymous online poster, but most of those people seemed to her like textbook maladjusted adolescents with problems ranging from mild psychological to severe psychiatric. It would have been easy to attribute the otherkin phenomenon to existential loneliness and social alienation, or even maladaptive daydreaming disorder. But if she were to accept the reality of multiple dimensions and reincarnation, she had to accept the possibility of nonhuman souls existing in human form. She could dismiss it altogether, laugh at it, or try to come up with a fitting diagnosis, but there was no denying it: even after sifting out impressionable wannabees, what remained was a tribe of misfits united by a shared experience, and she would have lied to herself if she ignored its chilling similarity of their altered perception to her own true sight revelations. Who was she to insist on one definition of reality when she herself lived between worlds?

The otherkin beliefs, odd as they were, were no more far-fetched than the dogma of any established religion. *At least these guys don't start holy wars,* Anna said to herself, and then, with less surety: *Not that we know of.*

By the end of the week, her head was swelling with the new data. Something intimate, which she could only define in terms of her internal life, was turning out to be a public phenomenon with a social fringe attracting the oddest types. She chose not to share her discovery with her therapist until she knew what to make of it.

Anna didn't need a therapy session to realize that the encounter with Emily had offered unexpected enlightenment but also added another layer of confusion. She was grateful to fate for placing her on the roof of Ted's office building and putting the right words in her mouth to change a young girl's mood from despair to hope. But taking credit for saving Emily would have meant admitting not only that she was capable of true sight on her own, but also that having it was a good thing. This, Anna wasn't ready for.

On April 1, April Fools' Day, Anna had her first day shift at the New Hope shelter. Everybody had been joking about her promotion all day; it was repetitive, but she laughed sincerely. The air smelled like spring. She decided to treat herself to a long walk home through Central Park.

She entered the park at East Seventy-Ninth. It was about half past seven, and there were plenty of joggers on the paths, the midtowners from both east and west sides on their after-work runs. Anna hadn't run in a while, and seeing them sent a shiver of excitement through her body, like the shivers of an old circus horse when the band plays the familiar march. She promised herself to return soon, with Shuck.

She turned off the wider path toward the Ramble, a patch of wilderness in the middle of the park, right above the lake—the most secluded spot in the park, peacefully shared between birdwatchers and discreet gay men. James used to tell stories about New York when he was a young cop right out of the academy: back then, the Ramble was notorious both for wild cruising and gay-bashing gangs, and a dangerous spot for a female hiker as well.

But on this clear spring evening, in the light of the Golden Hour, the park was transparent, like see-through lace. Only the tall Japanese cherries, smothered in pink blooms, stood among the still leafless undergrowth. A clear falsetto in Anna's ears sang a hymn to the beauty of nature, Uriah Heep weaving the sublime melody of "The Park's" first movement.

A hand-holding couple, obvious and oblivious newlyweds on a New York honeymoon, nearly bumped into her on the narrow path.

"Excuse me, miss," said the young man, and she pulled out her earbuds. "Which way is to the Bridle Path?" The girl giggled with bashful glee. Did they think the word was Bridal?

Anna smiled. The first time she had gone for a run around the reservoir, she too had thought the Bridle Path was poetically named after some mysterious bride. She showed them the way, and off they walked.

Squinting against the slanted rays of the setting sun, she stood under the canopy of blossoming cherry trees, the ground beneath her feet carpeted with pure pink, suddenly connected to the world as never before, as if vibrating silver beams of light had reached from her heart and illuminated the world, making her aware of everything to the last glowing dust speck: the old song, the young couple, the reek of mulch, the rough naked elms, the ostentatious cherries, with herself at the center of it all. She felt fully in love. This love had little to do with the emotional rewards of being nice to fellow men, or being moved by the splendor of nature—or, rather, it had as much to do with those things as a glare spot reflected on the water has to do with the celestial body earthlings call the Sun. It wasn't a feeling at all. It was being fully present.

"Ahn-nah!"

Anna took off her glasses and put them back on. In front of her on the petal-lined path, backlit by the golden halo of the spring sunrays, stood Yaret Fairfax.

He was the same yet different—more precise, as if the time apart had honed his already fine edges. His hair, which she remembered coming down to his shoulders, with strands hanging across his cheek, now was smartly cut with short sides and a slicked-back top. The new haircut didn't hide his inhuman ears, but they didn't look all that remarkable. He wore a simple navy blazer over a white T-shirt, and a pair of gray jeans, but a huge Louis Vuitton scarf flamboyantly draped around his neck negated any pretense at inconspicuousness. His face was radiant.

"I'd say I don't believe my eyes," spoke Anna, her voice coarse, "but those words have long lost their meaning."

"I came as soon as I felt you felt it."

"Felt what?"

He blinked, a shadow passing over his brow, then beamed again ever brighter.

"Your heart overflowing with true love."

He opened his arms. Anna stepped back, raising her palms as if she were about to push his hands away.

"I don't know what you're talking about, and I don't care. What do you want from me?"

"That which I always wanted. Nothing has changed."

"Everything has changed!" cried Anna. "What do you expect me to say? Welcome back? You left. I didn't know why or where you went. What was I to think?"

His luminous face broke apart as if she'd thrown a rock at a stained glass window; its sharp angles reassembled into an alarmed expression.

"I've sent you signs and omens." He dropped his arms. "I know you've received my messages."

"What messages?"

"But you must have . . ." His voice trembled. "I felt your heart resonating. Anna, I sent you a message the night I left, and continued doing so every other day."

"He sent me messages!" She flailed her arms, looking around for witnesses for this in, but they were alone under the blooming trees. "Was it before or after Fashion Week in Paris?"

"Before. And after."

He looked so innocently puzzled by her anger, so defeated by her disavowal, that for a moment she felt like laughing.

"You seem surprised. What did you expect me to do, greet you with open arms? While you were climbing the social ladder, I was losing my mind, doubting myself, questioning everything . . ."

"After all your eyes have seen, do you still question whether I am who I say I am?"

"Oh, no, Lord Yaret." She gave him a mocking bow. "No questions there. You are a fairy all right. A sociopathic fairy who doesn't think twice about playing with human hearts, charming his way in to get what he wants."

"Do you doubt my love for you?"

"Love? You dumped me! In bed! Took what you needed—which, apparently, didn't include sex—and left. What was it? I didn't show enough enthusiasm for the prospect of becoming your breeding mare? Or I wasn't established enough for your world domination schemes, so you moved on to more powerful women? Or is it men?"

"Is that why you think I left?"

"Why, I have an alternate theory, which is even more humiliating. You dumped me in bed because I wasn't one of the chosen few who can make love . . ." She choked on a spasm of wild guffaw.

"It's true."

She swallowed her laughter.

"You are not one of the few. You are the only one," he spoke with desperate intensity. "I have always been a slave to your desire, even when your yearning for me was tainted with fear and contempt. A moment longer, and I would have succumbed to it. Blinded by my want, I nearly forgot that for two beings to come together in true love they must meet halfway, or such union will only breed iniquity. I was eager to go down, but you were not ready to meet me. And then I knew: it is not to you, but to my own humanity I must descend. So, I left in a hurry. I went into the world. I took a job I thought most demeaning only to find it superbly edifying. I traveled without the comfort of portals only to find it soothing. I made friends among humans only to find how many of them were filled with their own magic. I did all those things for you. I even tried my hand at the stock market, as you advised."

When did I advise that? she thought distractedly.

But the meaning of his impassioned speech was seeping through like venom. The answer to the riddle of his disappearance was as simple as it was insulting: he thought her beneath him.

A wave of bitter hurt rose from her heart to her throat, her skin suddenly sticky with cold, numbing sweat.

"It was wise counsel," he continued enthusiastically. "Unbearable as it was, in the crucible of our separation a true bond has been forged. Now, when you've embraced mystery as I have embraced the mundane, you and I can build our haven. We shall have a tall house on a hill amidst apple trees, like these." He waved at the blossoming trees.

"These are cherries."

"Join with me, my darling. Be mine, as I've always been yours. Tell me you love me, tell me you'll never leave me . . ."

"Fuck you," said Anna wearily. "Fuck you and your apples. Go away, Yaret."

He jerked his head, as if he'd been slapped in the face, and genuine pain distorted his handsome features.

"I beg you, do not dismiss me! Not for the third time!" Tears slicked his long dark eyelashes. "If you do, I won't be able to return."

"Good. Get out of my life, and don't come back, neither in the flesh, nor in my dreams."

She pushed by him on the narrow path, roughly brushing his shoulder like she'd swat away a stray branch. He spun on the spot, making no move to follow her. She didn't look back, but by the way the fine hairs raised at the nape of her neck, she could tell: he stood where she had left him, following her with his mad eyes.

Anna was still incensed when she exited the park, so instead of getting on the train, she walked into the nearest bar on Columbus Avenue and had two shots of vodka, straight, chilled to viscosity, the way Genie taught her to drink vodka. It stabilized her shaking, and by the time she got home, she felt pleasantly unfocused.

Black Shuck greeted her with crazy jumps.

"Easy, you fool, what is wrong with you," she grumbled, struggling to fasten his new leather collar around his thick neck. "Yeah, yeah, walkies! Settle down."

But he wouldn't. Usually obedient, even timid on the street, Black Shuck was going nuts. He kept sniffing the ground, tracking invisible trails, pulling like a possessed locomotive.

"I have no energy to take you to the park tonight," she told him. "Tomorrow, okay? I'm off tomorrow. We'll go to the park, promise."

But the dog kept pulling her up the street, in the opposite direction from Bryant Park or the Madison Square dog run. With growing aggravation Anna realized, he was dragging her north.

"You want to go to him, you fool?" She stopped, trying to rein him in. "Don't you get it? He doesn't want you! You are a big scary monster. The best you can hope for is that someone puts up with you, but no! you're expecting that someone will come, full of light and laughter and infinite patience, and they will adore and desire you, not because of how you are or how you are not, but just because. . . for no reason at all. But it's a fantasy. It doesn't happen in real life!"

She yelled at the dog and yanked the leash, ignoring the passersby's disapproving frowns. Black Shuck tugged back and spun in one spot with his tail between his legs, finally ripping the leash out of Anna's fist. For a split second the dog hesitated, not believing his own luck, then he bolted up the street. Anna screamed his name and ran after him, maneuvering between people, but she was no match to the four-legged creature. Within seconds she lost sight of him, his dark coat making him dissolve in the shadows. Blinded by the flickering lights, Anna strained her eyes. Everything was a blur. She didn't know where to run.

Honking and screeching of tires.

Anna sprinted to the intersection. Several people on the sidewalk were frantically fingering their cell phones. She elbowed her way through. Black Shuck was lying next to the curb, motionless. She kneeled next to him. There was no blood. She pressed her palm to his silky black side. No breathing either, no beating of a pulse. Carefully, she lifted his heavy head. The amber eyes were dull, unmoving.

She pulled off her jacket and covered Black Shuck.

A police cruiser pulled up, and two cops, male and female, got out.

"Whose dog is this?"

"Mine," said Anna thickly. "He's my dog."

"What happened, ma'am?"

"A car hit him." She stood up.

"Was he off the leash?" asked the male cop, articulating with purpose.

"He broke free. I ran after him. Then I heard the sound."

"Did you see the vehicle?"

Anna shook her head.

The cops exchanged glances, and the male cop stepped aside to have a quick exchange with some people on the sidewalk.

"The witnesses all confirm she was chasing after her dog," He told his partner. "And no one came forward about the vehicle."

The female cop seemed relieved. "You're lucky it's a hit and run," she told Anna. "You could have been liable for the damage to the car."

"What do I do now?" Anna didn't recognize her own voice.

"Check with dispatch," the female cop told her younger partner. "I'll stay with her."

"Deceased animals' bodies are taken to the animal care centers for proper disposal," he said after a short conversation over the radio. "There's an ACC up in East Harlem."

Anna rubbed her face. It felt numb, like when she had had too much to drink. She wanted to thank the cops, but suddenly worried about alcohol on her breath, and just nodded.

The male cop chewed his lip. He and his partner exchanged glances again, as if they had a telepathic connection.

"Ah, come on," said the female cop. "Get in the car," she added, answering Anna's dumb stare. "We'll drive you."

"The dogs I've autopsied in cases like this, it was all a sudden death due to internal bleeding," said the ACC veterinarian who came out to receive the body for cremation. "If he was hit in the belly, it could have been a ruptured spleen, meaning instant death. If in the chest—a ruptured heart vessel. Also, instant death. I mean, he didn't even have a chance to feel fear or pain, if it's any comfort."

Anna didn't get home until midnight, barely able to drag her exhausted body up the stairs. She shut the door behind her and leaned against it, too winded to make another step.

She'd been preparing herself for the emptiness of her home, but she didn't expect it to hit this hard. His bowl on the floor, the sleeping pad he never used, his mangled chew toys under the coffee table—it physically hurt to look at them.

She thought she knew how guilt felt: the weight on her shoulders, the hollowness in the pit of her stomach. It had been there for a long time, that vortex filled with coils of what was once love and now loss. That spring had been always wound tight, but never this tight.

She stumbled toward her desk, pressed her palms over its cool glass surface. Her fingers trembled. And then, the spring uncoiled, she grabbed her chair by the back, ripped it off the floor in a furious explosion of power, and hurled it down. The glass tabletop shattered with a thundering bang, tempered glass shards spraying like water. Down came the shelves with books and files, her laptop, the vase with all her stupid tchotchkes dangling off the gnarled dry bough.

Anna hovered above the pile of debris, holding the chair by its back, until she felt its weight and let it slip out of her grip. It landed with another loud thump. A wheel popped off and rolled under the couch.

It would be hell to clean tomorrow, she thought, grabbing her phone.

"Mommy?"

"Annie? You okay?"

"No," she mewled. "Can I sleep over tonight?"

"Aw, Annie, do you want James to pick you up?"

"No, I'll grab a cab."

She opened the door to her parents' apartment with her own key, took off her shoes, and quietly padded along the corridor, trying not to wake up Jack. The kitchen light was on, her mother and James sitting in the nook. When Anna appeared in the doorway, they turned to her, and she was flushed with a déjà vu: she was fourteen, she had just come back from the wyssun world, her mom and stepdad sitting around the Formica table, and she'd never been happier to see them.

"Oh, baby." Her mother rushed to give her a hug. She didn't ask what had happened. After Anna's breakdown, both she and James tiptoed around her as if she were made of glass.

"Black Shuck has been killed by a car."

"Oh, baby!" Mom covered her mouth.

"I didn't see it happen," Anna hurried to say. "It was quick."

A drink would have been perfect right about now, but there hadn't been any alcohol in the house since Jack's birth. Steeping hot lemon tea with honey, she told them about the pit bull's last moments. They nodded in unison, their faces lined with the same concern and compassion, as if over the decade of marriage her delicate mother and her hardboiled stepfather had developed an elusive but obvious resemblance to each other. A spasm of tenderness crushed Anna's heart.

"I'm sorry about the poor mutt, but it could have been worse," said James. "He could have caused a major traffic accident, people could have been injured, and you could've been held responsible."

"It can always be worse."

"I'm going to make your bed, Annie," said her mom.

"Listen, princess," said James when his wife left. "You've been having a tough year. That year your mother and I met, you know, that was a tough year for me. My own mother passed away, and my partner was shot. I was drinking back then, too. It didn't seem like it was going to get any better, only worse. But the same fall I met your mom, and . . . well, you know the rest. Sometimes I think, if it hadn't happened the way it did, I would've never ended up meeting you two, and Jack . . ." He swallowed hard. "There would've been no Jack."

On any other day Anna would have told James such thinking was a logical fallacy, assignment of a redeeming quality to suffering in an attempt to make sense of a senseless tragedy—a therapeutic technique not necessarily harmful, but ultimately futile.

"I'm not saying I paid for this with that," he continued, as if answering her thoughts. "It's just . . . the pain broke my heart open enough to let love in, know what I mean?"

"James," said Anna, no longer able to contain the warble in her throat, "My heart's been broken for a long time. I thought if I could figure out why, I could fix it. I tried so hard . . . and I failed. So, no, James, I don't know what you mean. All I know is that I've fucked up."

"It's good," said James softly, "that you're humble like that. Love comes right after humility, princess."

Anna looked at him through the tears. "Twelve steps?"

"They work."

"I made your bed in the living room, Annie," her mother called quietly from the doorway.

"I'm sorry about Black Shuck," she whispered, tucking in the blanket. Did she actually remember his name? "I know you always wanted a doggie." Mom signed. "I'm sorry I couldn't always give you what you wanted, honey, and you were always so good, so smart. So strong. . . But it's okay not to be strong sometimes, you know?" She kissed Anna's hair and left.

The sheets were cool. Anna curled up around the unfamiliar pillow, squeezing it into the hollow of her belly where Black Shuck would have been, and was out at once.

She woke up when it was still dark outside, folded her linens, and left as quietly as she had come. The train car was empty enough for her to get a window seat, and she dozed off with her temple against the glass. In her half-awake state, she registered a wyssun scampering along the tunnel wall around Fifty-Ninth Street.

She dragged her feet up the stairs, mentally preparing herself, and flipped the switch; the light bulb in the entryway lamp flickered with an ominous buzz and went out. Everything that could have gone wrong, had. She didn't have any energy left, not even for exasperation.

It was a bit after six on a bright April morning, the sun was about to flood her apartment any minute. She dropped her body down on the futon and waited for the first sunray to pierce through the skylight and illuminate the scope of devastation.

The metal frame of her desk stood bare and bizarre, a leviathan's carcass in a pool of broken glass. Floating on its surface were other objects that had the misfortune of being caught in the storm of her impotent rage. Papers and textbooks, pens and pencils, broken pieces of the vase and everything in it: cracked bough, smashed ornaments, a blue jay feather she'd picked in the park, some twigs, dry leaves, and other natural junk she'd been compulsively collecting over the winter—all crushed.

And that was when she saw it, reflecting a ray of light with the tiniest rainbow: her crystal necklace.

She reached out for it and jerked her hand back with a pained yelp. A shard of broken glass pricked her finger; a red drop was blooming on the tip. Without thinking, she sucked on her finger, and this small gesture reminded her of Yaret, of their first day together in this place, his reviving her dead plant with a drop of his otherworldly blood—and further into the past, their meeting in the Otherworld. She glanced at the plant on the windowsill. After successfully surviving a rough encounter with the floor the night she'd been committed, the plant was thriving. She put the necklace on.

It hit her like a windstorm. The space dilated, walls shimmered, protective runes flashed and rushed along the walls and across the ceiling. Anna grabbed the desk frame for support, but kept her eyes open wide as hologram-like images flowed and orbited each other in elaborate patterns, bright as a laser show at the Hayden Planetarium. After five months, Yaret's runework held.

The other reality was superimposed on the mundane. With the true sight she was perceiving the solid walls as intricately fretted fractals, birthing and consuming each other like Escher's impossible objects multiplied by infinity, strikingly similar to LSD-enhanced colors and patterns of psychedelic geometry.

Before, when she had experienced this shift with Yaret, she'd been too scared and overwhelmed to find her bearings. Now, she was on her own. Too exhausted to fight it, she allowed the event to live itself out. The intensity subsided, the mundane floating to the surface of her awareness. But the profound sense of the other reality didn't fade away.

She closed her eyes. In an instant flash that lasted for eons, she felt simultaneously taken apart and restacked as she faced the entirety of existence, vibrating to the music of the silver strings. There was no place for grief in this harmony, no place for guilt. There was no loss, because everyone and everything was forever present. She could still register the pain, but it no longer had a hold on her, because pain was no different from any other sensation, and they were all in harmony. When she opened her eyes, she looked at the world anew.

Her apartment was still a mess, but in the way of a rough surface of freshly gessoed canvas. Upon it an exquisite image was painted with strokes or light. Besides the elaborate runework along the walls, the room was dotted with sparks like midsummer woods with fireflies. The glow was the brightest around the broken glass of her desk. She knelt next to it, acutely aware of each sharp facet, noting a degree of bodily control she'd never known before.

She forgot when and where she had picked up the blue jay feather, but she remembered bringing it home to add to her collection. The crash ruffled it, but didn't break its striking blue pattern, which was now emitting a strong neon glow.

With a sure hand, Anna plucked it out the pile. As she drew the feather through the air, it left spectral tracers. She took off her glasses to get a clear close-up, and gasped: the feather contained text—not literally scribbled with readable signs, but filled with meaning, impossible to misinterpret. It said: "Beloved, you are all over me."

After searching her apartment, Anna discovered over two dozen objects enchanted with Yaret's missives. Roughly placing together their time line, she knew there were more she'd missed.

A small oak branch with a leaf and a juvenile acorn still attached; Black Shuck had picked it up on their awkward first walk together the same day Anna got out of the mental clinic and retrieved the pit bull from the kill shelter. The way he pushed the slobber-smeared twig into her hands made her heart shudder with fear and tenderness, so she kept it. It must have been the first message Yaret had sent her, because its style was distinctly archaic.

Now she knew what it said:

> You and I are so apart.
> In the same city under the same sky you are far from me. Anna my Anna. I draw these dark words from a deep well of wild grief dredged from my regretful heart.
> A warrior must always be stern, full of belief, enduring his heart cares. He must look cheerful in a tumult of grief. My desire for you has made me heartsick. But I fasten my heart not to let grief escape for my grief is also the source of my strength. Into the cold world I go to gain my right of return.
> You and I are so apart.

A rusted skeleton key with an ornate bow and a thick stem, old enough to be useless but not enough to be an antique, fell out of the garbage bag Anna was dumping after the New Year's Eve party at the shelter. She didn't know why she'd pocketed it. Its message was:

> Now, when memory of the Otherworld is alive in your mind, do you think of me as I was? I do think of you as you were. Although you were at my mercy, it was I who kneeled before you, a mere child, and as I gazed up at you, my heart's desire was only to remain at your feet. I confess, in a moment of weakness during the years after your departure from the Otherworld, as I shared your heartaches and anxieties, I regretted not keeping you in the Green Hills for eternity, living a multitude of lives in a blink of an eye, free of pain and decay, which is the price of human life. But seeing you as you are now, a woman maturing in beauty and accomplishment, I would rather be deprived of your company than deprive you of your own path.

The amber bead was a gift from Jack. He'd found it in the park and given it to Anna, insisting it was special. He couldn't say why. The bead contained the following message:

I have an Internet now. Did you know there is þā Engliscan Wikipǣdie? I find it extremely entertaining to read about your space exploration in my mother tongue. I consider contributing an article or two. L.O.L!

There was a seashell—a small white cowrie shell she'd found on the windowsill in an empty coffee shop on Christmas Eve. As she showed it to the barista, she registered its blatantly sensuous shape with a momentary embarrassment. "It's for you," replied the young man. "Merry Christmas." At the time, she presumed he was flirting. The shell said:

It would amuse you to learn that I now live with five boys who also work at modeling. It has been long since I shared quarters with young human males and it took all my composure not to hit them during the first few days. But I am committed to avoiding unnecessary violence. Also, men will follow almost any commands for the promise of a cooked meal.

My boys often talk about what excites them in women. It appears most young men find a display of weakness attractive. What entices me in you is strength. My precious Anna, from the top of your hair to the tip of your toe there is not a thing in you feeble or indistinct. Your grace is as mighty as your rage. Oh, how I long to touch you again, to delight in your power.

You have asked if I possess the ability to make love. I do. The thought of you and me making love together is what sustains me through our separation.

There was a small marble made of cheap green glass with a little air bubble off center. She had found it on the sidewalk near her apartment building after she put Genie in the cab. It tickled when she held it. It said:

Do you love Leonard Cohen? I wish I could sing some of his songs to you, but my singing voice is vile according to my dear Féargas. Do you remember Féargas Dé Egore of the flaming hair? He remembers you. He was quite popular at the club last night, irresistible world hopper he is. He sends his regards and

> wishes he could assist me in my quest to establish myself in this world, but the rules of engagement prohibit it. They do not prohibit him from coming to Los Angeles dressed like an eighties pimp and dancing to Erasure whom Féargas adores, apparently. Féargas can be awfully tacky. But to an Alvan ear Erasure's voice is most pleasing, unlike Leonard Cohen's.
>
> I found a small glass orb on the floor at the club. I hope when you hold it in your palm it tickles like champagne bubbles. Also, I am sure this bit of knowledge will tickle your scholarly curiosity: cocaine has no effect on me. I would love to share a bottle of champagne with you on the top of the Empire State tower, or is that too tacky?

A copper coin she'd picked up while trying to pass the Saint Patrick's parade crowd in Midtown; she bent over to tie her shoe, and there it was, with an unfamiliar profile on one side and a three-mast sailboat on the other, a British penny minted in 1947, likely dropped by a drunk tourist. It said:

> Unlike your scholarly mind, mine is superficial as a water strider on the face of a pond, yet one of its innate Alvan gifts is an ability to count odds. Last week in France I was introduced to the game of poker, an easy way to get the coin needed for my first foray into the stock market, which I found no different from games of chance if even more predictable. I am glad to report that my first experiment was a success, although modest so far. I shall continue to educate myself on this matter, since my current earnings are sorely insufficient for my goals. In fact, the singular reason I am still engaged in this droll line of work, is the opportunity it affords for me to observe this world's customs while remaining virtually invisible, for no man is better concealed than the one in the spotlight.

The most recent one was on a broad, leathery sycamore leaf, still green but delicately rusted at the edges, which fell to her feet the next day after she talked Emily off the roof. It read:

The silver strings sing to me that it is time.
Caireann taught me how to make them resonate in harmony, how to weave my own threads into the divine ornament, gave me my first triumph and first loss.
Valerian pulled me up from my despair by reaching out a hand in friendship, sharing more than I ever hoped for or deserved.
Martha, who had nothing to share, allowed me a chance to give.
I took and shared and gave. I was a child to Caireann, a sibling to Valerian, a parent to Martha. To you I can be all that and beyond, an equal in love and life. I want to be all to you, and I want all from you, no more and no less.
I am coming for you, Anna, my true love.

There were more signs and omens she remembered seeing with her then unseeing eyes. Yaret had been speaking to her in the play of light and shadow, professing his love in the birdsong; his desire had been echoing in her own spells of vertigo and spells of lust.

Among the enchanted objects Anna had discovered in her apartments was a thick, two-foot long braid of platinum-blond hair. It gleamed with the light of the Otherworld, but bore no messages.

She was sitting with Yaret's braid on her lap when Genie called on videochat. Anna showed her the hair and told her about the letters.

"What are you going to do?"

Anna buried her face in Yaret's hair. It smelled like a thunderstorm.

"I must find him."

"You know, there is this type of fairy tale in every Norse culture," said Genie. "A girl loses her bridegroom and must reclaim him. In the Russian version, she has to wear out three pairs of iron shoes and blunt three steel staffs on her journey. She talks to elements, like the Sun, the Moon, and the Wind, all totally archetypal, I'm sure. She finds him, but she is too late; he's engaged to a wicked witch, so our heroine has to steal him away from the false bride."

"Sounds like a cultural narrative meant to legitimize male dominance," said Anna, only half-joking.

"For fuck's sake, woman! The only meaning is of your own making. What do you want?"

"I want him."

"Then go get him."

"I don't know where to begin."

"For a smart girl you're quite dumb sometimes. Your stepdad is a police detective. I bet he can find a guy."

"No!" The thought made Anna shudder. "Not if I can help it."

"Fine, then take the scenic route. You may start by looking up the modeling agency that represents John Y. It can't be that hard to find."

Anna wanted to reach across the computer screen and give her friend a hug.

"That's exactly what I'll do. You called at the perfect time."

"Oh yeah, the reason I called. I hope you don't get pissed off at me, but I showed your story to an acquaintance who runs a weird fiction magazine, and she wants to publish it online. I mean, you won't get paid, but . . ."

"It's fine, do what you want with it. Just don't put my real name on it."

"Okay, I'll come up with some exotic nom de plume that won't trace back to you. How about something Russian?"

"Make sure to add some grammatical mistakes to the text."

"Fuck you too!" Genie blew her a kiss.

Summer

It was easier than she expected, making her wonder what had stopped her earlier. A half-a-dozen clicks, and Anna had the name of John Y's agency. Next to his photo on their website were his stats: Hair: Blond; Eyes: Gray; Height: 5' 11" (180cm); Weight: 155 lb. (70 kg); Shoe: 10. It was peculiar to see him, who had become larger than life to her, reduced to bare numbers.

His runway experience was limited. During his single season of modeling, John Y had walked in only two fashion shows, but has opened and closed both. Anna, who'd been quickly picking up on the lingo, presumed this was a prestigious position for a runway model. His list of editorial features, however, was so long she had to scroll down. The photographs were sublime, the names of publications exotic: some foreign, others too exclusive to be known outside the fashion industry circuit. When she saw the now familiar art photo set of Yaret with an African model, she felt a tickle of happy recognition. The Switch spread was there, as well as a few other breathtaking images by the same photographer, Mario Solari.

Solari. The Sun! She had to talk to him first.

She tried to secure an audience with the celebrity photographer, and wouldn't even be allowed to talk directly to his assistant—until she referred to John Y as John Fairfax. His real name worked like a password, and she got her fifteen minutes.

As she walked into his studio, Mario Solari was checking his intimidating-looking camera. He didn't as much as glance at her.

"I'm Anna Reilly." The photographer gave her a sharp look from under his heavy eyelids. "I'm searching for John and would appreciate any help."

"And why should I help you, Anna Reilly?"

"There was magic between you and him. It was the same between him and me."

"Don't tell me: you had him and you lost him." He glared.

"Yes," replied Anna, holding his stare.

"Well, so did I. You understand?"

"I do."

"You are prettier than I imagined," he said in a tone that excluded the possibility of a compliment. "In a chinny, Waterhouse-maiden way."

Anna didn't reply. All she could feel was empathy for the aging man, the artist without his muse. The unrestrained compassion in her eyes must have thrown him off. He was the first to turn away, fussing with the camera on his lap.

"I create a photograph in a way of a painting," he spoke after a pause. "I paint with bodies. I design the image so the viewer looks past the image, past the body in the image. John, he could be anything, understand? The ultimate instrument. But beyond that, he saw into my vision before I could define it for myself. He is a muse. He could have been my muse."

"Could have been? You have created striking art with him as your model."

"He did a few sessions with me, and then he was gone."

"Can't you request him from his agency?"

"Ha! He has negotiated a unique contract, the clever devil. He is quite . . . um, convincing when it comes to negotiating. Do you know that his rate is the same as a top female? Nobody has a deal like that. He does what he wants, and right now he doesn't want to be photographed. Apparently, he doesn't want money. Instead, he wants to help some idiotic linguist with some idiotic riddles, for free. He speaks three dead languages, do you know?"

"Latin, Classical Greek, and Old English," she said. "I know."

The photographer chewed his lower lip, staring past her with narrowed eyes. "But of course you do. I'm aware of where you met."

Anna shuddered. Could the celebrity photographer be another agent of the Otherworld, like the homeless man in the park?

"You were his shrink."

"I wasn't," she protested, relieved. "I—"

He didn't let her finish. "The kind of power you wield over him, it's out of this world. It doesn't make me want to help you, understand, but here is his cell number. I still harbor a hope that he might change his mind and return to working with me. I won't call him, I have my pride. But when you talk to him, tell him . . . ah, don't tell him anything."

As soon as she walked outside, she punched in the number with a trembling hand. It had been disconnected.

Although Anna felt much more at home navigating academia than the fashion world, it still took her several days to figure out the name of the scholar the photographer mentioned, and over a week to make an appointment with the linguistics professor from the department of English and comparative literature at Columbia, who was also a member of the Anglo-Saxon Studies Colloquium and specialized in early English poetry and riddles.

Professor River Silverstein turned out to be woman in her sixties who looked like she'd pinched her outfit from the clothesline between two gypsy caravans; the flowing garment, woven of some organic Mother Earth-approved fiber, looked spectacular on her. Her large body appeared so gloriously feminine that Anna wished she could someday get away with such flamboyancy.

"Last time I chatted with John was in late May, yes, the summer term had just begun." Professor Silverstein's voice was as rich and flowing as her garment, and Anna thought her lectures must be a treat. "I don't expect him to contact me until after the annual meeting of the Linguistic Society of America in December, where I will be presenting my research. I'm sure he'd be curious about the reception it gets, after all, it was our discussions that inspired my breakthrough."

"If I may ask, what was the nature of his academic involvement?"

"When you think of early English literature, what is the first work that comes to your mind?"

"*Beowulf*?" Anna blinked, sensing a trick question.

"Precisely! *Beowulf* is a part of the school curriculum. They make movies based on it. Everyone who loves the history of the English language loves *Beowulf*. John caused a stir when he declared he was "not all that keen on Geatish heroes." He spoke of the source texts the way a modern boy speaks of comic books: "I'm not into Superman, I'm into Batman," except he posted in Old English. See, most language enthusiasts are compelled to translate Old English texts into modern English, not the other way around. His forum posts were all in the original language, witty and modern yet impressively authentic. Also, he and I shared the interest in a literary genre slightly more subtle than epic poetry. Are you familiar with *The Exeter Book*?"

Anna shook her head, making another mental addition to her ever-expanding reading list.

"*The Exeter Book*, or *The Codex Exoniensis*, is a tenth-century manuscript containing most of the surviving Anglo-Saxon poetry: lyrical poems, such as elegies; religious, such as the Lord's Prayer; and riddles. Now the latter. . . Some are more straightforward than others, but not one is as notoriously obscure as *Wulf and Eadwacer.* Battles are waged by linguists from different schools of thought about its meaning." Her eyes sparkled with the mad twinkle of true obsession.

"And Yar . . . John had something to contribute to the debate?"

"He suggested an exquisitely original interpretation, putting together pieces of the puzzle with an insight nothing short of magic. Of course, I had to establish a proper academic foundation to make the argumentation work. I can't reveal much before my research is published, but it may revolutionize the field."

"How was he when you talked to him?" asked Anna, trying not to allow desperation to seep into her voice. "Was he happy? Did he give you any idea about his plans for the future?"

"Oh, but I've have never met John in person. We interacted in an online linguistic forum. It wasn't in the nature of our relationship to be intrusive, so I wouldn't know much about his personal life. To be honest, I'd hoped you could shed some light on his background. I gather, John is an exceptionally intuitive linguist in complete absence of formal training. Do you mind telling me where he studied Old English?"

"He spoke it at home," answered Anna honestly. "He had an unconventional upbringing."

"Ah! Now it makes sense."

"What does?"

"Well, I found him . . . how should I put it . . . sheltered for a man of his intelligence."

"How so?"

"He didn't seem to have a grasp on some basic realities of life. For example, once I mentioned difficulty of acquiring research grants for the department, and the next day he sends me—with a courier, no less—the business card of his stock picker."

"His what?"

"His financial adviser."

"You wouldn't still have that card, would you?"

"You may have it. I have no use for it, not with my academic salary."

Professor Silverstein shuffled through her old-fashioned Rolodex, then shifted her large body, leaning over her desk to hand Anna the card. The collar of her embroidered top opened, revealing monumental mounds of flesh. Anna politely averted her eyes, but not before seeing a heavy pendant dislodge from between the woman's breasts. Framed in elaborate metalwork was a large opalescent moonstone.

Yaret's financial adviser turned out to be a Wall Street CEO. His secretary informed Anna that he wasn't available until mid-August. She expected it to be a dead end, and was surprised when precisely two weeks later she received a call back with an invitation to an informal meeting.

It was violently windy in downtown Manhattan, which at this point made her laugh. The glass skyscrapers of the Financial District looked spectral against the stormy sky, like blue crystal clusters on the rock matrix of the prewar brownstones. She touched her own little crystal on the cord around her neck, energy of all kinds swirling all around her. For better or worse, this was a place of power.

When the banker said informal, he meant it. He met her in the little park behind the windswept marina of the Staten Island Ferry, an inconspicuous middle-aged gentleman in a fine suit, his face deeply suntanned; when he offered his right hand to Anna for a handshake, she noticed it was paler than his left. He looked her up and down with polite curiosity, and she felt hopeful, but he only chuckled at her request for John Fairfax's contact information.

"I'd hate to waste your time," he said without hostility. "Therefore, I must refuse right away. All the communications between a financial adviser and his client is privileged, which applies to the client's personal information. Surely you can appreciate."

"Why did you agree to meet me then?"

"Ms. Reilly, markets are about faith and perceptions, not unlike magic," he said with a wan smile. "Mr. Fairfax is one of the few people who understands this. I find him an impressive man. I was curious to meet the woman he finds impressive."

"If you talk to him, will you tell him I am looking for him?"

"Good day, Ms. Reilly." The banker bowed his head. "And best of luck."

"Burnt by the sun, mooned by the moon, blown off by the wind," she told Genie later that day. "I'm a fool on a fool's errand. A perfect fairytale character."

"Perhaps it's time to ask for your stepfather's help," suggested Genie reasonably. "Like my priest says, sometimes a combination of prayer, communion, and haloperidol is more effective than just prayer and communion."

In the weeks after her true sight's awakening, Anna often questioned her own sanity. But she kept reminding herself that mental illness is defined as a behavioral anomaly that impairs everyday functioning, and her new awareness was anything but impairing. She'd never felt more at peace. Once she understood her anxiety attacks as a transition before a reality shift, they no longer affected her. Quite simply, she existed in an augmented reality.

Initially, she tried to approach her own altered state as a scientist. She experimented with times of day and locations. She used true sight with and without her medication. The results strengthened her in a single important realization: she hadn't become a psychic, neither had she developed an ability to see the world's underpinnings, Matrix-like. Although she wore the crystal necklace around her neck at all times now, she had no more life-changing revelations like the morning after Black Shuck's death.

Her new ability to sense the supernatural seemed to be on a need-to-know basis. She could clearly visualize the protective runework inside her apartment. She could sense a wyssun before it made itself visible so that they no longer startled her—more often than not she found the little monsters amusing. Every once in a while, she would see a faint trace of the otherworldly glow, like a whiff of smoke curling around an ordinary-looking person or an object, but that was the extent of it.

Anna tried to systematize her observations, keeping notes of different images her true sight allowed her, but after a while, she came to admit that the power of perception meant little without the ability of interpretation, like simply being able to distinguish a foreign language doesn't make your truly appreciate the richness of its poetry.

Fall

Anna had always loved fall more than spring, perhaps, because the story's ending is always more interesting than its beginning.

The rain that lasted all through the last week of September wasn't coming down hard enough to knock the still green leaves off the trees, so when the weather service issued hurricane warnings, the jaded New Yorkers just sneered. But by the second day, it became clear that the main drama was unfolding away from the city limits, over the Caribbean, where a tropical storm strengthened into a hurricane, made landfall over the islands, killed fifty people, and continued toward the continent. By the third day, most of the Eastern Seaboard had declared states of emergency, preparing for devastation.

The talking heads on television were discussing the erratic weather patterns brought on by climate change. Folks at Anna's shelter were talking End of Days. As she worked to prepare the facility for the emergency, Anna remembered the previous year's early blizzard, the one that brought—or was brought by—Lord Yaret of the Otherworld. Could this natural disaster have been a preview of the culling he spoke about?

The hardest wind and rain came down on the fourth day, and immediately after the storm surge hit, flooding the subway tunnels. The train system had been shut down by then, so now whole city blocks were cut off. Anna spent that night at the shelter, comforting the residents. A few dozen people slept in the corridors and in the lounge. The shelter had been filled beyond capacity, but at that point anyone who made it in was welcome to stay. There were a few moments when even these street-hardened New Yorkers were genuinely scared.

The storm left dozens dead, thousands homeless, and millions without water and power. Most of downtown Manhattan lost electricity and water for two days. Many of those still with power had friends or relatives from the damaged areas stay with them. Busy as she was at the shelter, Anna found time to check on Ted. He was all right, volunteering as a trauma counselor at an emergency center. It was good to have the excuse to talk to him.

In the wake of the destruction, things were better than expected. People were stepping up to help each other. Hard crime was down. James, who spent the first few nights at the precinct, was exhausted but in good spirits.

"Funny creatures, humans," he said to Anna, who came over to check on her family; their Upper West side building wasn't affected. "We always need some tragedy or another to get our shit together." He spoke to her like to a comrade.

Only when she was back at work next day did Anna realize that she'd forgotten to ask for her stepfather's assistance with her search.

In the weeks after the hurricane, she found herself in the best place possible: in a position to help. The city emergency services were overwhelmed with people affected by the devastation, and all service was welcome, so Anna volunteered as a grief counselor. Her clients were ordinary people who thought nothing like this could happen to them. Most had lost precious possessions. Some, all. But whether a family album or a family home, none was as demoralizing as the loss of that sense of invulnerability.

Anna never thought herself special, neither in accomplishment nor in loss. For years, she told herself that her own loss was no big deal. After all, she hadn't been a daddy's girl, hadn't lost him to a dramatic act of violence. Her life hadn't been irrevocably ruined after he died. If anything, it had improved. It was cynical to admit, but it was the truth. What counsel and consolation could she, with a shallow and well-healed scar, offer to those with a fresh, gaping wound? All she could do was listen, spreading over the other person the protective canopy of love woven with the silver strings that hold creation.

The few words she spoke to others were the words she herself wanted to hear: stay present, count your blessings, don't dwell on the past, look for strength in loved ones, look for meaning within, forgive yourself. Simple as it was, it worked. And then the strangest, most predictable thing happened:

as she asked others to forgive themselves, she began to forgive herself. By the time she was ready to forgive Yaret, she had nothing to forgive.

Now she understood why his rejection had devastated her beyond the rage of a woman scorned. She, who never saw herself as desirable, needed constant proof of being wanted; when she was refused love, she was in world of hurt; but when she received love, she doubted she was wanted for the right reason—a vicious circle, a double bind, a perpetual war with the world. Like a silver mirror, Yaret only showed her herself, and since she had begun to look at herself with kindness, the reflection no longer hurt.

There was another unexpected development. A few weeks after the hurricane, Anna was working at a disaster relief center downtown. She was bent over a desk, filling some forms, when she felt a scent of water and lightning; then a small but heavy hand tapped her on the shoulder.

"Hi," said Emily. "Remember me?"

Before Anna knew it, she was looking with true sight. It was as if the girl stood inside a glowing turquoise and blue hologram of a dragon coiled around her small figure. It was the first time since her revelation that Anna witnessed an otherworldly presence this closely and clearly. Anna's eyes followed the magnificent curves of Emily's dragon body around and above her human form, and as Emily followed her gaze, the girl grinned with satisfaction.

"You do see me, don't you?"

"You're . . . you look amazing," said Anna breathlessly. "What are you doing here?"

"Helping with my Y's youth volunteer group."

"How've you been?"

"Awesome. Off Risperidone for one. Met someone. Not dating," she giggled. "Just a friend. Another dragon. Except, he's not awakened yet. Want to meet him? Jason! Can you come over for a sec? Meet my friend Anna."

Anna, who was still looking with true sight, backed away, nearly upsetting the table. A creature was coming right at her who looked like a compact T-Rex with flaming wings.

"He's on fire!" She blinked back to normal sight and saw an average-looking young man in his twenties.

"You bet he is. He's a fire dragon. Jason, show her." Emily nudged him with her elbow. "It's cool, she's an expert."

"Are you a tattoo artist?" asked Jason.

"Me? No, why?"

"He has a dragon tattoo on his arm that looks just like his true self," said Emily proudly.

"Oh, no, not with this otherkin thing again," moaned Jason. "Listen, nice to meet you . . . er . . ."

"Anna."

"Yeah, nice to meet you, Anna, but I've got to go. Ems, you got to stop telling people my personal stuff," he said in an annoyed whisper.

Looking at his back as he walked away, Emily frowned. "I think I pissed him off."

"You can't force awakening." Anna felt strangely giddy.

"I better go apologize." Emily signed. "I know you don't want to be my therapist, but do you think we could just, like, get together and talk sometimes? Some things I can't discuss with my mom, you know. And I don't see Dr. Newman anymore."

They met the next week, and the week after. Emily talked about school, Jason, swimming, her parents, being a dragon. It was pretty basic stuff; after all, she was, indeed, a well-adjusted kid. Anna only listened, and it seemed enough.

Between her regular work, the disaster relief, her family, and Emily, Anna had been too busy to search for Yaret. Although she hardly thought of him anymore, she never felt apart from him either, as if by departing from her mind, he had taken up permanent residence in her heart.

She had long since covered the naked carcass of her broken glass desk with a sheet of plywood and replaced her bookshelf and file holders. After she threw away the broken vase and the crushed mementos, she never redecorated her desk with another display. The enchanted objects, including the coiled braid of Yaret's hair, she locked away in her desk drawer.

When Genie asked her how the search was going, Anna replied that she was no longer looking.

"Have you given up?" asked Genie.

"No," said Anna. "I have let go."

She might have stopped searching, but she couldn't help feeling a stir each time she glimpsed a trace of the otherworldly. It was as subtle as the shift of air on the platform right before a train comes out of a tunnel, and became as ordinary. She hardly registered it when she felt a familiar presence while taking a shortcut across the hall of the Grand Central Station. And then, she saw him, meandering though the busy day-after-Thanksgiving crowd.

"Change, somebody, anybody . . . change!"

She shouted his name, his otherworldly name she had known all these years.

The Scout stopped and turned around. The eyes on his weather-beaten face were the color of young grass. "Why hello, kiddo."

The afternoon commuters streamed around them, casting curious and confused glances at a tall young woman sobbing against the shoulder of a homeless man in a tarp parka.

"There, there, easy now."

"I missed you."

"And I you, kiddo."

"I'm sorry I didn't recognize you a year ago. I was . . ."

"Ah, but you've changed since."

"So much has happened. Yaret and I . . . but you know, don't you?"

"A little bird told me, one year and one day ago he made a hard bargain with the Alva to return to this world to be with you. We Scouts were forbidden to help him."

"A Scout cut off his hair."

"No, that poor sod wasn't one of ours. He saw through the veil but could never cross. A torturous existence. Thankfully, Lord Yaret has put him out of his misery."

"Is he dead?"

"He lives. But he no longer remembers. I'd first be dead, but to each his own. Talking about remembering, look at you, kiddo, you're a new woman! It looks like Lord Yaret's high gamble paid off: the Earth still turns, New York City still stands, and you've accepted him."

"I have not, Semille, and I've lost him. I could reconcile with the existence of magic, aliens, and other dimensions, but couldn't believe that a man's love for me was true."

"Believe then."

"That won't change reality."

"Reality . . ." He sighed, and spoke softly, like to a child. "Reality may be that you never came home from that ski run in the park, all they've found after the snow melted was your fourteen-year-old body, and this is your afterlife. Or that you didn't die but fell through the veil and got trapped in a dimension without time, living out one of the infinite simulations staged for your sake by a benevolent alien. Or that none of that happened at all, and you are lying in the psychiatric hospital bed pumped with drugs, hallucinating, me being a figment of your deteriorating mind. Or, you could be standing in the middle of Grand Central, wasting precious time on idle chatter with some old tramp, while your train is about to leave."

"What train?"

"The one departing . . ." he lifted his finger, "right now."

The Scout was pointing at the Departures display. The northbound Hudson line train was leaving at 3:30 p.m., on time. Anna looked at her watch: it was 3:27.

"Well? Don't dawdle, run along now." Semille flipped his hand, waving at her, and a silver bell-charm tinkled on thin chain around his wrist.

"Is this how I find him? Where should I go?" cried Anna. "Where do I get off?"

"Aw, don't be so dramatic, kiddo. Here's a hint: what's the magic number?"

"I don't know . . . three, seven, twelve? Semille, for Christ's sake, tell me!"

"Well, if you ask for His sake . . . Yes, it is one of those. Now, run like a good runner."

And Anna ran, like the good runner she was.

She barely made it in before the train doors shut, and dropped onto a pleather-covered seat, steadying her breath with deep inhales. A conductor came down the aisle, his ticket punch clicking like a medieval torture instrument, and Anna asked for a one-way ticket to the last stop.

The conductor stuffed his old-fashioned punch in his belt, whipped out a smartphone, and sold her an electronic ticket to Poughkeepsie.

As the train chugged out of Grand Central, she vaguely considered how ironic it would be to find magic in a prosaic small town, and how laughable she was for getting on this train to nowhere.

As soon as the train caught up with the river, Anna found herself transfixed by the view outside her window. The celebrated fall foliage along the banks of the Hudson had peaked, but even after being pruned by the recent storm, the woods were still dazzling. Against the colorless overcast November sky, the ambers and coppers and crimsons burned with vehement opulence, and it seemed the sky's and the river's only purpose was to serve as a looking glass for the trees' vanity.

Anna had a moment of panic when the conductor announced that the train was going express, but then she took a deep breath, put her playlist on shuffle, and waited for signs. "Kozmic Blues" was playing as the train pulled into the seventh stop.

"I ain't never gonna love you any better, baby, I'm never gonna love you right," belted out Janis Joplin, "So you better take it now, right now!" and Anna realized this was her cue.

She leaped from the train's steps onto the damp platform of Cold Spring, just as the streetlights were turning on. She expected to see a typical suburban development, but found herself in a small town with an actual Main Street that crawled away from the river all the way up the wooded ridge. Pastel-colored houses with ivy-covered porches and red-brick buildings with porthole windows lined it, interspersed with flaming autumnal trees. The village of Cold Spring looked absurdly adorable, like the imaginary European towns from Japanese anime she used to watch with Jack.

She focused her true sight but saw no otherworldly traces anywhere; in fact, the whole place felt incredibly neutral, clean, and quiet—perhaps, because the streets were empty. Aimlessly, she walked along Main Street. She couldn't help but like this town, although it did seem a bit staged, a place New Yorkers would call "quaint" when they mean to say "overpriced."

"Love your necklace!" a woman's voice rang with practiced cheer.

"I do—," Anna fingered the crystal on her chest. "—I mean, thank you."

"Looking for something special?" Even without looking at the name of the business over the doorway, it was apparent this well-kept woman of indeterminate age was a real estate broker.

"A tall house on the hill amidst apple trees," she said half-jokingly.

"That property has been sold," replied the woman without missing a beat. "A historic Italianate stone mansion on twelve acres of traditional apple orchard overlooking the Hudson, both in need of a little TLC, but marvelous, a rare find. A gentleman asked for it in those same exact words, I showed it to him, and he bought it outright. I wish every deal was that smooth."

Anna felt her cheeks heat and the rest of her body chill.

"John Fairfax," she exhaled.

"Yes, Mr. Fairfax. But of course, you must be one of his guests! He was getting groceries for a picnic the other day," the agent added in a conspiratorial tone. "You better hurry before dusk falls."

"I'm lost," said Anna, taking ahold of her voice. "Would you mind giving me directions to his home?"

"Are you driving?"

"I came by train."

"I'll call you a taxi. Lynton Orchards is right outside the village, but it's uphill all the way. You'll see the house from the road. Tell Mr. Fairfax Melanie sends her regards!"

Anna was prepared for dusk to fall by the time the car reached the property, but when it turned onto the dirt road to the farm, the overcast sky brightened, the late sun gilding the soft gray clouds with its slanted rays. Sure enough, high on the hill above the road, floating over the sea of treetops was a three-storied house, indeed reminiscent of an ancient rustic villa with its rows of tall narrow windows, a bay to the side of a broad portico, and a tower over a low-pitched roof. No lights were on.

She told the driver to stop, paid with her last remaining singles, and stepped on the ground, pebbles crunching under her city-shod feet. Never in her life had she done anything this final, taking a step beyond the point of no return. Now, there was nowhere to go but forward.

Anna walked off the path and into the mist under the trees. The orchard looked as if it had been neglected for several seasons. The grass between the rows of thick apple trees was overgrown. Some of the trees' gnarled boughs were still heavy with red and green fruit amid bright yellow leaves, but most of the abandoned harvest was littering the ground beneath, apples broken and bruised, filling the air with a musty, heady scent. Suddenly, Anna felt dizzy with hunger. A heavy, low-hanging apple nearly caught her in the forehead; she picked it off the branch and devoured it whole, the tangy sweetness of its flesh mixing with the bitterness of its seeds. The last rays of the evening sun lit the transparent leaves like the cracked stained glass of an abandoned church, and she was overwhelmed with gratitude.

Silently she thanked the old trees, and they must have understood, because the seemingly endless grove receded, trunks parting to show her a clearing ahead. There were people in the meadow, men and women. They were folding blankets and packing away food baskets, their picnic over. She recognized his silhouette at once. At first, she thought his light illuminated others the way sunlight lights up the moon, but her true sight told her: most people on the lawn glowed with their own life force. The whole place overflowed with the otherworldly.

Yaret Fairfax was surrounded by creatures with magic in their blood, and not all of it human. Revealed in the true sight, one man looked uncannily wolf-like; two others had alien double cocoons of energy fields hovering over them like angelic wings. From where she stood, Anna could see him talk to one of his friends, then the other, as if each were the only person in the world, and at that moment she desperately wished to stand in his light once again.

A young, very pregnant woman said something; he laughed, bent down and laid a kiss on her protruding stomach. A soft glow responded from inside. The woman was carrying a magical baby. Judging by the size of her belly, this woman must have conceived no later than eight months ago, right about the time Anna told Yaret to get lost and never come back.

She was too late.

I rejected him, but someone else did accept, thought Anna, her heart shuttering. In the fairy tale, the heroine steals her beloved from the false bride, the wicked witch. But what if the other woman wasn't a wicked witch, but a young woman like Anna, but less inhibited, less hung up on her own anxieties, with an open mind and heart? Someone capable of making love.

No, Anna couldn't knowingly destroy that other woman's happiness, even if it meant walking away from love. But she couldn't walk away either. Denying love would destroy the only meaning she had carved out of the relentless chaos of the mundane. It was the wyssun world double bind all over again: she'd be a monster whether she fought for love or rejected it. Nothing she did mattered.

And then it hit her: what mattered was up to her. This was her dream, and she had to see it through, whether she was at its beginning or end. Dreams must be fulfilled, she told herself, and took a step forward. He looked up and saw her. The rest of the world faded away.

They met halfway and stood in silence for a while. His pale face was ghostly in the dusk.

"I have come for you," she said flatly.

"Why?" His voice sounded far away.

"I followed my desire. I had to, even though I can see I'm too late. You have the life you wanted, a tall house on a hill amidst apple trees, a magical child on the way . . ."

"So, you possess true sight now."

"Enough to know the truth."

"What do you know?"

"I know that all is not what it seems. There's more to the universe than the eye—the human eye, clouded by guilt, fear and regret—can see. There is more out there than a mind can comprehend, and none of it in itself may have any meaning. The only way to create meaning is to tell a story. Whether I am capable of making love or not, I can make a story. So, everything that happened to me before I knew you, and when you were with me, what will happen to me—I love it all. My story is richer for it, and for that I thank you. Nothing more for me to say." The words fell on the dusky air, and Anna felt unburdened. "You don't have to say anything either, go to your friends and your lover, to the home you've built. I want for you to have all that your heart desires."

She saw his hands rise, and felt his palms cradle her face, burning hot against her skin.

"All my heart desires is you." She could barely hear his words for the pounding of her pulse in her temples. "You are my home. It's always been you."

"But the pregnant woman . . . in the fairy tale . . . the witch . . ."

"She is a witch indeed, a friend, wife to a friend; her child is her mate's."

"I am so wrong about so much." Every muscle in her body grew taut with a desperate, dangerous hope.

"It's only human," he said earnestly, and before she even thought of swatting at him, he pulled her in, locking his chin over her shoulder, and talked to her in a language that sounded like wind in the high trees. She understood. He was rejoicing at the sight of her, thanking her for her persistence, and begging her forgiveness, all in one breath.

She threw her arms around him. Laughed. Cried.

"Black Shuck has died. You could have saved him."

He shuddered and held her tighter. "If only I could have kept watching over you."

"Why couldn't you?"

"Your wish is my command. Thrice you wished me away, thrice I came back. I ran out of returns, and there was nothing I could say to change your heart."

"Sorry would have worked."

"I have much to learn about human psychology."

"I can teach you."

"That I know."

"Did you know I'd come for you?"

"No," he exhaled, his body relaxing, and at that moment she understood his fear and loneliness. "But I hoped. It is also human."

She kissed him then, a rough and sloppy human kiss.

"You taste like apples from my garden." He whispered into her mouth. "Do you know what must happen to those who taste fairy food?"

"I know. They can't leave. But what would they want to do in the magical world?"

"What indeed? Well, they can set up shop, since a village full of magical creatures could use a human counselor. They can make a home, get a dog."

He pulled away to look her in the eyes. "They can marry their fairy lover, bear a child, write a story. They can have it all. You see, it's not that they can't leave. They wouldn't want to. In the fairy tale the word for want, must, and can are one and the same."

"Well, I must stay then."

"And if you don't want to bear my children, you and I will still have a long life, longer than—"

"I want to bear your children."

They walked back to the meadow hand in hand.

"This is Anna, dears. She came for me," announced Yaret, smiling and frowning at once.

His friends, human and not entirely, surrounded her with the gleeful curiosity of puppies looking at a butterfly. There were exclamations of surprise and joy, laughter. Anna was blinded like a rock star on stage, electrified and horrified in equal measure, but, strangely enough, not uncomfortable. Hands gently brushed her shoulders and squeezed her wrists; words of greeting and welcome were whispered to her. The pregnant woman came over and gave Anna a clumsy and delightful hug over her big belly.

The greetings immediately turned to farewells. Even the least considerate souls would recognize impatience in their host to remain alone with this dark haired tall woman who had walked out of the apple garden, and Yaret's friends were nothing if not sensitive. One by one, they said their good-byes. Eventually, they all got in their cars and drove off. Watching the taillights of the final car fade in the twilight like the last buoy at sea, Anna felt herself carried away by a mighty tide, further and further away from the shore of the mundane, but this time she was the tide. There was no room for fear.

Now they were alone under the starry sky. Everything was falling together—madly, magically—the impossible was happening, the dream was reality.

"Are you ready to do it, my love?" Yaret whispered in her ear.

"To do what?"

"To make your story happen you must say the right words."

"Words. . . You mean, vows?"

He nodded and took her hands in his.

"Now?"

"Now is all there is."

"You're not much for ceremony."

He laughed. "Oh, we will have a proper human wedding later, with any and all the ceremony you dream up. Now we do it the Alvan way."

"What do I do?" She felt intense joy bubble up inside her.

"Say what you feel."

"Is that all?"

"All that matters."

She looked into his eyes, and said, "I love you, Yaret Fairfax."

She felt him press her fingers when he said, "I love you, Anna Reilly," and this subtle caress nearly stopped her heart.

"May our union last for as long as our love lives," he pronounced solemnly, and then exhaled, as if he'd been holding his breath for centuries. "And so, it is done!"

Anna exhaled and looked around. It had grown dark, the only illumination coming from myriads of fireflies filling the still November air—by far, the least impossible occurrence. To her sharpened senses everything around her was as bright and clear as the prickly stars in the deep sky.

The world was rich with poignant beauty, and she knew it all, and she was deeply in love with it. She could feel the tingle of the starlight above her head. She could sense the bitterness of silver wormwood and silkiness of the little wild asters in the meadow; hear the rustle of downy goldenrods along the road and the thump of a fruit hitting the ground on the far side of the orchard. She felt juices flowing wearily in the trunks of the old apple trees and the cooling of the air above the hills. The night breeze from the ridge stirred each hair on her head with a separate, gentle caress. Along the river a commuter train sped by filled with beings, each of them uniquely alive and precious, and she was connected to every one of them with the silver threads that hold the universe together.

Anna looked back at Yaret, expecting a mystical transformation, but he remained as he was: a slender, fair man with an angular face, his dark-rimmed gray eyes fixed on her. She had never beheld anything brighter. She reached to hold him, but he gently held her off by the shoulders.

"Now I offer you my wedding gift. It is sacred above all and above all secret."

"But I have no gift for you. . ."

"It is customary for the Alvan male to manifest his devotion by making a special offering to honor his mistress. Her acceptance of it is her gift to him."

Yet again, Anna couldn't tell if his tone was that of sincere deference or of playful derision.

"As the starry sky is our witness, this I offer to you, my wife: from this day on, I shall sleep with no one but you." Breathlessly, he searched her face for reaction.

"Isn't that expected in a marriage?" She tried not to sound disappointed.

"Unconditional love comes with harsh conditions, precious. I have placed a geis upon myself. A sacred bond. Empowerment by interdiction. Our union is blessed beyond human imagination, but if separated from you for any long time, I am cursed to die from the lack of sleep. My gift to you is my life. Do you accept?" he finished with an oddly inappropriate cheer.

Will I ever be able to understand him? a question passed through her mind.

Acceptance surpasseth understanding, her heart answered.

"I do," said Anna, and, as the breath left her lips, he caught it with a kiss; she felt a shift in the air, and knew that this was it: the perfect moment.

True love can only be borne from true commitment, for such great bond may come into existence only out of great freedom. Like all absolute truths, this one was a paradox.

"I will be worthy of your gift, Yaret." This was the first time she called him by his name in earnest.

"As I of your acceptance, Anna." His hand over hers was warm and firm. "Now let's go home and make love."

They looked at each other and laughed with joy; at the sound of their laughter the fireflies around them became snowflakes; snow began falling on their heads and the ground under their feet; upon the first snow they walked home.

Spring, five years later

She wakes up with a start and reaches for him, but her hand brushes against the cool, firm pillow. She is alone in the big bed. She must have been floating in and out of a dream: his arms locked around her; his gentle relentlessness; his voice in her ear whispering, again and again, the same silly syllables which stopped making any sense a long time ago: I love you I will never leave you. Some dreams you don't get used to.

A sunbeam parts the moving curtain, touches the pillow, caresses her cheek. The sound of the morning bird chorus grows louder, and the perfume of lilacs and rain soaks the room; it takes her a moment to remember that the birds are real, as are the lilacs, wet from the last night's thunderstorm. Jubilant chords of Supertramp's "Dreamer" sing in her head as she rolls out of bed, throws on a robe, and pads across the cool wooden floor to the tall window. Windows are wide open all night, every night. Right outside, the madly blooming lilac bushes with glistening heart-shaped leaves. Farther, the rain-washed apple orchard. Farther downhill, the river with the Hudson Highlands on the horizon. On a clear day, she can see as far as the green hills.

A massive bobcat stalks across the lawn with something hanging from its fangs, acknowledges her with intelligent golden eyes. The gardener moves between the trees like a gray shadow; she knows he can smell her across the lawn, behind the curtain, under the robe, but he politely turns away. Where does her husband find them? How do they find him? Not like there is a billboard on the Interstate 87 saying, "Nonhumans Welcome Here."

He told her from the start that theirs would be an open house, but he is nothing if not pragmatic. A stray bobcat? Of course we keep it, the house could use a mouser. A homeless werewolf who happens to be vegan? Of course he can stay, the farm could use a guard/gardener. An undocumented alien—literally? Of course we sponsor her, the town could use another tech startup. A few more nonhuman and mixed families recently bought houses in the village, and there's always someone staying in the cottages across the orchard. It's a vast estate. Pets and cattle, tenants and workers, because—the magic Rule of Reciprocity!—everyone must have a purpose. Also, the never-ending stream of guests. Doors and windows never shut. On the other hand, she hasn't cooked a meal in years, hasn't even made her own bed—helpful, considering that her private practice and academic research keep her hands full. When little things are taken care of, it's easier to see the big picture; after all, her most curious case is at home.

She closes the robe over her slightly sore breasts, walks down the corridor into the adjacent room. He is sitting beside the crib, arms and chin resting on the railing, eyes half-closed, lips moving. She lets him complete the spell, then comes over and kisses him on the top of his fair head, arranging the long ponytail between the sharp shoulder blades. How his hair has grown. . . His ageless beauty still stuns her, every time. Still brighter than the sun, only the eyebrows draw tighter when he frowns, and the dimples crease more deeply when he smiles. He promised her they would grow old together, but it will take a very, very long time. He never lies.

He turns to her, flings his arms around her hips, parting the robe with his face, blows a raspberry into her belly button.

"Two down, five to go, right?" She nods at the sleeping twins, still unable to believe these two living breathing beings came out of her hardly over a year ago. Conceived under the apple trees, happily carried, easily born. Magical. If she turns her eyes just so, she can see their glow. Their serene faces are doll-like, thick golden fuzz around their heads like halos, elongated ears stick out, little bellies calmly rise and fall in time to each other. Elf babies don't cry and don't get sick; collect all seven—increased cup size comes as a bonus. She thought she could never love anyone as she loves their father, and she was right: motherhood has unlocked a new chamber inside her heart, which keeps expanding with each beat.

"Four," he murmurs, nuzzling her belly.

"Oh. You're sure?"

"I'm sure." He looks up with his queer little grin. "A boy."

She stands in silence for a moment, then speaks to hide the excitement: "Aren't you bored, knowing everything?"

"I don't know everything." He chooses to ignore to her sarcasm. "Today's negotiation, for example. I have no foresight about it whatsoever."

"Nervous?" She squeezes his shoulders.

"The House of Fire can be obstinate when it comes to obliging the House of Winter."

"Is it the issue of . . ."

He growls quietly. She knows better. Secrecy is the pledge, fairness is the key. The Fairfax conditions.

The growl fades into a little whimper. She tickles his ear.

"You'll do fine. You are in a strong resonance with both Houses."

He whimpers again. For an exacting ruler of an interdimensional refuge, he can be quite needy, if only with his wife. She smiles. She is the resident mental health care provider, after all. So, she holds his head firmly, turns his face upward and stares into his eyes.

"You are the Lord of Haven, the sacred neutral ground at the heart of the Creation. This is your purpose. The great Houses of the Otherworld seek your mediation because they trust your magic and they recognize your humanity, and that is the reason they love you."

"Why do you?"

"For no reason."

He lets out a sigh of contentment, pulls her down onto his lap, falls quiet with his cheek against her breast. She never knows if he truly craves her reassurance, or if he plays along to satisfy her desire. Doesn't matter. Desire makes reality, for the sake of the gods who still believe in us.

ACKNOWLEDGMENTS

There are many people who have directly and indirectly helped me develop and fulfill my vision, but here are those who I must thank personally:

Jacob Miller, whose generous guidance and mentorship over the years allowed me to develop into the writer I am today.

Everyone at Ananke Press who followed the characters of the Wyssun World into the real world.

Special thanks to Alex Fidelibus, the typographer extraordinaire, for his unique touch that took the cover to the next level, and to Alex AG, whose inspired photography perfectlly illustrates the spirit of the New York City magic.

All the dear friends who read the many iterations of this story over the years with kindness and patience, and who helped correct this Russian girl's hopelessly confused definite and indefinite articles—you know who you are.

My beautiful husband Nigel for putting up with my wyssun obsession and never losing his sense of humor.

My parents for being ever-encouraging.

All the dogs I've ever known for opening my heart to the magic of true love.

And lastly, to the incomparable David Bowie for being my True North in every creative pursuit.

DISCUSSION QUESTIONS

1. What do you think of the book's title? What do the Green Hills represent? What other title would you choose?

2. What do you think the author's purpose was in writing this book? What ideas was she trying to get across?

3. If you could hear this same story from another characters's point of view, whom would you choose?

4. Yaret speaks of love as a force of nature akin to gravity. What do you think of this concept? What is your concept of love?

5. Do you think it is more important, to love or to be loved? Why?

6. Anna made many missteps as a psychologist. Are her mistakes forgivable? Was her punishment sufficient?

7. Do you think Yaret will find professional success as a fashion model? In your opinion, what occupation would suit him the best?

8. Do you expect Yaret and Genie to get along if they met?

9. Do you think Anna's true sight would have awakened of not for the tragedy?

10. What kind of dog-owner do you think Anna will be in the future?

11. Of all the types of otherkin, which reflects your personality the most? Why?

12. If you are otherkin, was your awakening similar to Emily's? How was it different for you?

13. What reaction should a person identifying as otherkin expect from their loved ones in an ideal world?

14. During their reunion at the Grand Central Station, Semille suggested several interpretations of Anna's reality. Which do you think is the real one? Which would you choose?

15. If you were making a movie of this book, whom would you cast?

16. After reading this book, which places in New York City would you most like to visit?

17. Share a favorite quote from the book. Why did it stand out to you?

18. What new things did you learn?

19. What questions remain unanswered?

ABOUT THE AUTHOR

E. V. Svetova is a life-long New Yorker, who studied psychology as an undergrad and later received her Master's in humanities from NYU. Her creative nonfiction was published in *Anamesa* and *Ancient Paths*; her young adult book, the first in *The Green Hills* trilogy, is a gold medalist of the Independent Publisher Book Awards. E. V. Svetova lives at the edge of the last natural forest on the island of Manhattan with her husband, a digital artist, sharing their old apartment with an ever-expanding library and a spoiled English bulldog.

www.ingramcontent.com/pod-product-compliance
Lightning Source LLC
Chambersburg PA
CBHW070836020826
48982CB00020B/1370/J
* 9 7 8 0 9 8 4 9 0 4 0 8 2 *